About the Author

This is the fifth book by Brian Clewly Johnson. He has worked in television, advertising and marketing, and has lived in China, South Africa, England, Europe and the United States. Today, the author divides his time between London and Cape Town.

Other books by Brian Clewly Johnson
DEEP MEMORY
A CAPE TOWN BOY
A ROLLER COASTER MAN
LETTERS FOR JOSIE

all available on Amazon

Everything Goes

Brian Clewly Johnson

Everything Goes

Olympia Publishers
London

www.olympiapublishers.com
OLYMPIA PAPERBACK EDITION

Copyright © Brian Clewly Johnson 2023

The right of Brian Clewly Johnson to be identified as author of
this work has been asserted in accordance with sections 77 and 78 of the
Copyright, Designs and Patents Act 1988.

All Rights Reserved

No reproduction, copy or transmission of this publication
may be made without written permission.
No paragraph of this publication may be reproduced,
copied or transmitted save with the written permission of the publisher, or in
accordance with the provisions
of the Copyright Act 1956 (as amended).

Any person who commits any unauthorised act in relation to
this publication may be liable to criminal
prosecution and civil claims for damage.

A CIP catalogue record for this title is

available from the British Library.

ISBN: 978-1-80074-605-3

This is a work of fiction.
Names, characters, places and incidents originate from the writer's imagination.
Any resemblance to actual persons, living or dead, is purely coincidental.

First Published in 2023

**Olympia Publishers
Tallis House
2 Tallis Street
London
EC4Y 0AB**

Printed in Great Britain

Dedication

This book is for the real Peggy Steele who, like most mothers, was an exceptional woman.

Acknowledgements

THANKS! Maryann Canio, Candice Dowding, Kat Gordon, Susan Grossman, Michael Hu, Eve Karlin, Susan Kramer, Chowee Leow, Nikki Mansergh, Barry McCallion. Rene Reay, Charlotte Resnekov, Stella Sinclair, Pamela Thurber, Jeff Upshaw, and, most notably, my 'fresh pair of eyes', Peter Wallach.

Also, members of the Amagansett Writer's Group, NY, and the Ashwagh Hall Writer's Group, NY.

'Mobility is the true purpose of the human spirit. One who remains immobile, who speaks but remains supine, is he any better than a rock or a log of wood?'
Inscription on a samurai sword, c1660.

PROLOGUE

Brooklyn Heights, New York
1987

The city was a heat blanket, the subway barbecue-hot; Saturday afternoon and the train half-empty.

The man got off the 2 Train at Clark Street and stepped onto the baking sidewalk. For luck, he dropped a five-dollar note into the lap of a woman sitting by an ATM. She scratched her neck; nodded, grunted. The smell of frying bacon wafted across from the Clark Street Diner.

The man was aged forty-seven: brown-eyed, lean, of medium height, with dark hair. He wore khaki shorts and a pale blue shirt, sleeves turned up to the elbows.

He looked left, his glance taking in the sapless, leaf-curled trees next to the Blockbuster video store. He turned right and began to walk, his left arm held crooked across his flat stomach. One hundred paces brought him to the junction with Hicks. He turned left and walked another hundred paces through air like wool. A minute later he faced a small apartment building, looked for the number: one sixty-seven. He crossed the street to the lobby, looked at the wooden post boxes, relics of a time before vagrants broke them open. Two of the ten boxes had no doors and three others hung by hinges.

He studied the name tags that still clung to some of the boxes: Tait, A; Bratton, S; Broderick, J; Soria, A; Zoltan A. His eyes went back to the last name.

Shallow breaths. He pressed a buzzer. Up top, a door opened. A woman's voice, 'Ja?'

He couldn't find spit. Dry-mouthed, he managed: 'Sorry to trouble you, ma'am, but did you know Stanley Parker?' A beat. Then the voice, suspicious, asked, 'Who wants to know?'

Again, hesitation. 'I knew him.'

'Well, come up, then. I got a bat.'

The man climbed two flights of stairs, his shorts clingy in the heat. He turned at the top to face an open door, blocked by the bulk of a grey-haired woman holding a baseball bat. She stared at him, pop-eyed, then whispered, loud enough for him to hear, 'Stanley!'

SHANGHAI, CHINA
1942

Someone was pounding at the door. By the time Peggy Parker reached the hallway, Wu, her houseboy, was standing in the entrance. Facing him was a Japanese soldier carrying a briefcase. Her breathing shifted when she saw two armed guards, bayonets fixed, behind him.

The British Consulate had called with a warning a week before; Rollo Vigne, his young voice urgent, had said, 'The Japanese are clearing the Settlement, Peggy. I fear they'll be at your door. We can't help you.'

He went on, his voice breathless with – Peggy wondered if it was panic. 'Best pack as much as you can, my dear. But no more than one cabin trunk. Take clothing suitable for hot and cold weather. The Japanese have in mind some type of internment. Since Pearl, they've been organizing various facilities around Shanghai. Is Stan available?'

'No, Rollo, he's at sea. There's no way of reaching him.'

'Ah yes, of course. He's –'

'I don't know, and if you people don't know, who does? Tom Trencher might.'

'Oh, right, right; of course. That means it's just you and…'

'My son, Jonny.'

'Ah, yes, Jonny. How is the little chap?'

She didn't respond; she recognised insincerity. Another pause, then Rollo again.

'Well, best of British luck, Peggy. Allegra and I are as bewildered as anyone. We'll close the Consulate by the end of the week, pending further orders from London.'

'Or Tokyo, surely.'

'Indeed, or Tokyo.' He paused. She closed the call for him.

'Well, goodbye, Rollo. Take care of Allegra.'

'Of course, of cour–' Peggy put down the phone.

***

Now Peggy assessed the hard face of the soldier at the door. The guards had taken up a position behind him, facing each other. She caught the odour of the three men: a blend of maleness, garlic, and boot polish – a conflation of smells so strong it seemed to discolour the air. And yet, within the smells, almost ridiculously, was the impression of an anxiety that wasn't Peggy's; an aura of hesitation flickered in the eyes of the man in front of her: a small Asian charged with removing a European woman from her home.

She nodded the houseboy away. She turned to the Japanese officer, 'Yes?'

Even at her slight height, the three men were a few inches shorter than Peggy. The man in front had a scar running from the edge of his right eye to his chin. His pink ears – sticking out of his field cap with its single star – seemed pasted on to his skull. He displayed a colourful swatch of medals on his uniform. He seemed to be pushing out his chest to advertise his battle credentials.

The soldier stared at her for a few seconds. She noticed how his right eyelid drooped. Then he dipped his head, bowing so casually it seemed like an insult.

'*Ni ha!* Missy Parker. I am Colonel Tomoyuki, Imperial Nipponese Army.' His words came like bullets. Speech had banished his apprehension.

She could have returned his greeting in Japanese, but since the Occupation, the time for social niceties had passed.

'Congratulations,' she paused, 'and?' Peggy looked down at him while the officer, unblinking, surveyed her slim figure in navy slacks and grey silk blouse, her hazel eyes and tumbling auburn hair.

The Japanese seemed not to have registered her coolness. Or her sarcasm had been lost in translation.

When he spoke again, his voice was softer, his English better than she expected.

'In nineteen thirty-seven Japan conquer Chinese in the glorious Battle of Shanghai and take capital, Nanjing. After second glorious victory in nineteen forty-one by Imperial Japanese Air Force at Pearl Harbour, all Japanese forces enter world war. All nations and people who oppose forces of Japan and its allies' become enemies.' He cocked his head at her. 'Here in International Settlement, you stay protected all this time. But now things change; now you enemy. Now you go.' He arced an arm, 'Everything goes.'

He continued, his voice gathering speed and menace. 'Now all people in International Settlement – British, French, American, Canadian, Russian – all become prisoners of Japan.' He bowed elaborately; his voice hard. 'Now you pack. Furniture stays. You? You go.'

He shrugged and raised his hands as if to say, 'that's it.' In the moments it took Peggy to absorb *Tomoyuki*'s announcement, the colonel looked pointedly around the hallway as if he were a prospective buyer. Such arrogance – how dare he inspect her home this way, this ominous little stranger? If Stan were here, he'd give the man short shrift. But Stan was not here; her throat tightened, but she managed a shallow breath, trying to quell the fear.

She continued to watch the Japanese nod appreciatively at Natasha's charcoal drawings of *Shanghai's* streets; his gaze strayed to the gleaming rosewood library table with its scattering of mail deliveries and magazines. His eyes, now less friendly, returned to her.

'You leave all things in house.' He frowned. 'Things belong your husband's boss, yes? Husband's company, yes?' He didn't wait for her reply. 'Furniture not belong you, things not belong you, house not belong you. Now all this –' again, he waved his arm – 'all this belong Nipponese people. You go!'

He cocked his head, dark eyes narrowing in his pallid face. 'Gracious Emperor keeps all western people safe in China till war over. Then we take you different place.'

She saw a rictus twitch of his cheeks. Seeing her still unresponsive, her stare steady, he looked down at his boots, mucky from the December slush. Then he jerked his head up and blurted, 'We sor-ree for trouble.'

She didn't respond to his effort at *kimochi*, friendliness. She considered his words then, shaking her head, said, 'Why sorry, Colonel? I don't think you are sorry. You are moving into our home, the only home we have – you and your men. And you are sending us – where?'

His face became as blank, she thought, as only his race could make it.

Peggy gave him what she hoped was a piercing look. 'To a concentration camp?'

'Japanese not call this place concentration camp.' His nostrils flattened. 'Britishers make concentration camps first time when you fight colonial wars in Africa, long time past, yes?' He stopped then blurted, 'Japanese say Civilian Assembly Centre.'

He raised a finger. 'Now, you take clothes – pack. Two small suitcase or one big suitcase. You mark suitcase with label, you put name on label – Family Parker.' He stretched his arm. 'You go away long time. Then Japan, Germany, Italy win war. Then we see.'

He drew a large envelope from his jacket pocket, lowering his head as he passed it to her. Surprisingly, after such a show of *braggadocio*, the Nipponese now seemed embarrassed.

'This for you, Missy Parker.'

She took the envelope as he continued to speak.

'Inside envelope you find three new passports. You give old British passports for you and son to next officer.'

'My son is only two years old, colonel.'

'Ah, so.' He grinned, eyes flickering, a flash of bad teeth. 'Then you must take good care of son and passports, yes?'

She saw another nervous tic or attempt at civility – she didn't know which – cross his face.

She opened the envelope while he waited.

She glanced at the documents. She saw that what he called passports were thick cards, each showing a poorly coloured depiction of the Japanese flag and, underneath, the legend **'Family Parker 5312.'** On the reverse of each card were the names and birth dates of the members of **'Family Parker: Stanley Parker, Peggy Parker, Jonny Parker.'** There were sepia photographs of each of them, the one of Jonny indistinguishable from any other new-born.

How did they get the photos, the dates of birth? She was appalled as the thought hit her: Had the Consulate opened its files to the invaders?

'Now sign.' He handed her a pen.

She signed the sheet of paper confirming receipt of the cards. As she did so, she noticed that *Tomoyuki* was trying to see behind her.

'And your husband, Parker-san?' He flipped his notes. 'He is good friend of Admiral Ohta Tang, yes?'

Ignoring his question, Peggy looked past him at the lawn, patchily white from the night's light snow. She knew the colonel would be annoyed by her silence. But what business of his was it? It burned her to think that this little man knew of Stan's relationship with *Ohta Tang*; he probably knew more of Stan's movements than she did.

The Japanese shook his head, turned around and said something in Japanese to his companions. The three men laughed together – their voices high, girlish.

When he turned back, his face straight, the colonel again asked, 'Where your husband? He not on shore?'

'No, he not on shore.'

The Japanese grimaced. 'And you not know where he go?'

She shook her head.

Tomoyuki looked past her, squinting at her Chinese staff who, moving soundlessly, had gathered behind her – her own praetorian guard.

Peggy turned around to look at her servants, reduced to five since *Han* had fled. The Chinese stood with their shoulders slumped, looking at the floor: *Wu* the houseboy, *Wang Fang* the cook, and the two garden boys, *Lin Wei* and *Lin Na*. Her son's *amah*, *Zhang*, was sobbing quietly, a handkerchief pressed to her face. Peggy was vexed to see that the hankie was one of her own that had been missing for some months.

Sensing their anxiety, Peggy patted her hand in the air. 'Okay, okay,' she said.

The colonel gave a sharp command in Chinese. With a hiss of slippers, her staff disappeared into the house.

Peggy faced him again. *Tomoyuki* cocked his head, 'Missy?'

She stared at him, her lips tight: 'As you say, we go.'

'*Otsukare sama*,' he said, thanking her but, at the same time, using two words that, she knew, acknowledged that they had co-operated on a difficult negotiation. He saluted her, bowed, and left the hallway. His guards clicked heels. He said a few words to them. 'Hai!' they chorused, then saluted. They remained at the door as *Tomoyuki* marched down the garden path.

Peggy slammed the door and uttered a low groan. She turned towards the stairs. But she could not move. Her body began to shake, her legs pulsing uncontrollably, incapable of forward movement. The helplessness of her situation surged through her, a wash of fear – icy, then burning. She brought her mind back from the abyss, whispering, 'Calm, Pegs, calm.'

Never had she felt more alone as she mounted the stairs, coming to terms with her new situation. Being prepared for the evacuation was not the same as confronting it. Her country had failed her and her husband – he'd only left a few days ago – God, where was Stan? How could she and Jonny survive? What had happened to her little family?

'Jesus, save us!' she mumbled inwardly, the mantra of her Catholic childhood arriving unbidden.

PACKING
Shanghai 1942

She was in the bedroom a minute later. Her son, Jonny, was still sleeping in his cot, where she had left him to answer the door. She added more clothes to the drawers of a large cabin trunk. She had started to pack two days ago, then re-packed as she separated what she liked from what she needed.

She heard the thump of boots in the downstairs hall. The sound travelled upwards. A soldier, younger than *Tomoyuki*, entered her bedroom. He saw Jonny immediately and nodded towards the boy. Her body fizzed.

'I also have a son – Aki. How old this boy?'

She looked down, folding clothes, ignoring his question.

He seemed unfazed by her attitude. 'I am Lieutenant Nomura.' Again, he looked around the room, sucking his teeth, his head moving side to side, assessing everything.

Nomura crossed to the dressing table, stepping over the strewn clothing and picked up the silver-framed photograph of her and Stan on their wedding day.

'This your husband? He not here?'

Were they all this haughty? she thought, does it come with conquest? Well, two could play at that game. Exaggeratedly wide-eyed, she looked around the room and raised her hands, palms empty. 'Apparently not,' she said, biting the inside of her lip, frightened by her own mock heroics.

Nomura looked at her through half-closed eyes, seemingly unaffected by her response.

'I hear your husband is good friend of Admiral Ohta Tang, officer commanding glorious Imperial Navy here in Shanghai.'

She went on with her packing.

She had noticed that the lieutenant was taller than the average Japanese; She'd spotted that a lock of hair had escaped – or deliberately had been set loose – from his Army cap. She thought the effect was of manufactured nonchalance, a rare pose among the *Bushido*-disciplined

Nipponese military.

Peggy roamed the room, selecting items to pack. She became aware of *Nomura's* eyes on her. The wash of fear had now become a storm. She thought of her friend Natasha, raped by Russian soldiers after Stalin's invasion of Belarus. She didn't look up; she would not show any weakness.

Books – she needed books – not only because they had helped her to understand this strange land but also because, since childhood, a book was where she could make a different world. Perhaps there would be books where she was going. Where was she going?

Her fingers ran along the small bookcase near her bed. She rejected the JB Priestley but picked out Galsworthy's 'The Forsyte Saga', and the final novel in the Pearl Buck trilogy, 'A house divided– it wouldn't be a trial to read the book again; she had loved it so much. She also took 'Safety pins' by Christopher Morley – a present from Aunt Gertie that she had never read – and a book of poems by Keats.

Nomura spoke: 'You?' He was offering her the photograph.

She nodded, holding out her hand for the silver-framed picture.

The Japanese shook his head, raising a hand before opening the back of the frame. He removed the print and handed it to her. He pocketed the silver frame, giving her a small smile as he did so.

He nodded towards Jonny, who had woken from his nap. The toddler blinked at them both and started to make train noises as he pushed a wooden engine along the frame of the cot.

'How old this boy?' *Nomura* asked again.

The child looked up at the intruder and, perhaps sensing strangeness, elevated the sound of the train. Peggy suspected an outburst was forming in his little head.

'Twenty months, he's nearly two.'

The soldier put his fingers on his mouth to create a 'woo-woo' siren effect. Jonny giggled, delighted.

She'd been told that the Japanese loved children. Then she remembered reports that when the Japs were at war, no little girl older than eleven was safe from their uniformed rapists.

Jonny had been born a few months before the start of the Battle of Britain. Her son was named after an RAF squadron leader, Jonny Irving, who had been Stan's best friend at boarding school. Peggy had never met Irving, but Stan had promised her that she would. But Stan had made a lot of promises that now were unlikely to be fulfilled – the most basic being that he would see her again; would Jonny ever see his father again – let alone meet the young pilot for whom he was named?

Nomura's soft movements brought her thoughts back to the room; the man seemed to lurk around her. He sucked his teeth. His garlic breath made her gag.

'Big trunk – good. You finish pack now. And for boy. Now!'

As soon as *Nomura* raised his voice, Jonny began to whine softly. 'No, No, Daddy, Daddy.' He dropped the little wooden train and picked up a soft toy monkey from the bedclothes. They had named the monkey 'Jacko' after Stan had brought it back from one of his regular trips to *Tsingtao*. Peggy often wondered if holding the toy gave the boy some connection to his absent father. When Stan was away, Jonny seemed to play with 'Jacko' all the time.

Jonny's *amah* bustled into the room. *Zhang* paid no attention to the lieutenant – nor did she give any sign of the distress she'd shown at the front door.

'Lunchee. Lunchee,' *Zhang* said as she scooped Jonny into her arms. 'Who love Jonny? Who love Jonny?' she sang.

The boy giggled. 'Zhang love Jonny, Zhang love Jonny.' This was their game.

'Be quick with his lunch, Zhang,' Peggy said. 'Then dress him warmly.' The *amah* left, taking Jonny with her.

Peggy wrestled the two sides of the large, vertical cabin trunk and manoeuvred them until she heard them click shut. *Nomura* watched but made no offer to help. She found two plain luggage labels, took a pen and marked them with the number on her new 'passport', **5312**. She drew in her breath as the soldier moved towards her – she was trying not to inhale the garlic smell that hung about him.

Nomura took the pen from her and added an extra line of capital letters to the label. He pointed at what he had written. 'You go Fu-xing camp,' he said, pronouncing it 'Fu-shing.'

'Fu-shing? Oh God, fucking camp,' she mumbled to herself. She hardly ever swore, but if there was ever a time to swear, it was now.

Nomura must have heard her because he snorted and cackled, 'Fu-shing, fucking' and again, 'Fu-shing, fucking!' He placed his hands akimbo, continuing to repeat the words, grinning then laughing at her as he realised the English word association. She smiled faintly; glad Jonny had left the room.

Taking advantage of the lack of tension, she asked, 'How will we get to this camp?'

His face hardened. 'Colonel give you Japanese passport?'

She nodded. 'Identity cards.'

'Give me British Passport!' he said.

She handed over the small blue book, 'A receipt?'

He ignored her. He glanced at the passport, which showed a picture of her and one of Jonny. Grunting, he tore the little book in half. 'You go. Take boy, *amah*, go!'

'My servants, my house staff – what will happen to them?'

He raised his hands, palms upward. 'Chinese no important.'

'No one is not important.' She raised her voice.

'Chinese no important!' *Nomura*'s voice overwhelmed her. 'Take amah for boy. Go! *'Kudasai!* His eyes popped with rage.

Despite the fear flaring in her, Peggy stared him down. After a moment, *Nomura's* face transformed. He was smiling again, bowing ironically, indicating the door, and almost whispering the word '*Onegaishimasu.*'

Downstairs in the hall, *Zhang* stood to one side, cradling Jonny. The toddler was bundled up like a baby rabbit, all fur, and woollen mittens. The rest of Peggy's household staff were wiping their eyes and moaning, 'Missy go, missy go.'

Bowing, they placed their hands in Peggy's. There was no hugging. She knew there was nothing she could do for them, and she didn't want them to assume there was.

She turned to the garden boys: 'Lin Wei, Lin Na – please fetch trunk topside, in Missy's bedroom.' The young men shuffled off.

She knew that December temperatures in Shanghai could drop as low as 2c. Today, it was a more bearable 8c, but outside she could see a sharp wind ruffling the night's snowfall.

Peggy had kept on her woollen slacks. In the upstairs bathroom, with *Nomura* standing sentry and her body electric with apprehension, she had changed into a warmer shirt. Over the shirt, she'd pulled a Fair Isle sweater. 'Is this my going away outfit?' she wondered silently, raising a half smile to quiet her nerves. Now she took a tailored black coat from a closet in the hallway, shrugged into it, then adjusted a cherry red cloche hat to protect her ears. Her fur-lined boots felt warm and sturdy.

Her staff, faces tragic, continued to stare at her as she stood at the door, waiting for the trunk. She tried to avoid their eyes, but she could sense their anxiety. Asians, she'd been told, were impassive, but she'd learned how to read the signs.

Minutes later, the twins staggered down the stairs with her trunk.

'Missy, Missy, bye-bye! Little Jonny, bye-bye!' her staff chorused.

Peggy clasped her hands at the tip of her nose and bowed to them. She scrunched her face, denying her tears. She turned and led *Zhang* – Jonny in her arms – past the guards at the door, past the carved sign stating, '32 Bubbling Well Road', and towards whatever future waited.

ENGLAND

PEGGY STEELE
Derby 1935

Peggy Steele never watched cricket – unless her brother, George, was playing. She was thirty years old, single, and running her own hairdressing salon. She was feeling good about her life – sitting on the grass, tanning her legs – when Stanley Parker came ambling towards her.

'He does amble,' she thought, glancing at the approaching figure. For some time afterwards that's how she would think of Stanley after that first meeting – a man who went through life at his own pace.

Peggy's brother captained a local cricket team – 'George's Boys' – on summer Sundays. The field was a green space near the River Derwent. The land abutted a dozen allotments that had been staked out in the late nineteenth century. The Victorian council had built the terraced houses for families they termed 'the working classes'. The council believed that the small plots might compensate for the lack of gardens.

On that June day, Stan Parker came over to where Peggy Steele sat.

'Hello,' he said. 'I'm Stan Parker, one of George's mates. All right if I sit here?' His hands full, he gestured at the grass with an elbow.

She raised her head, shading her eyes, unable to see more than a blur. She was half-annoyed by the interruption but intrigued by the stranger's arrival. Her brother had never mentioned anyone named Stan Parker.

'Of course. Here, I'll make some room.' She wriggled on the rug, creating a space.

'If it's difficult, I can go somewhere else.' The man started to move away.

'Please, that's fine.' She patted the rug and put down her book of Yeats's poems. 'I'm reading, but of course, you may sit here. I'm Peggy, Peggy Steele,' she nodded but didn't extend a hand; she hadn't decided whether she wanted him to get too comfortable – 'but if you know George, you'll know that.'

George's friend had a plate of sandwiches in one hand and a bottle of lemonade in the other. He wobbled down. She noticed that his grey trousers had cuffs that were marked by dried mud, and despite the lack of rain for weeks, he hadn't bothered to brush them. In comparison with Peggy's fresh summer frock, smooth bare legs and black and white, open-toed shoes, Stan seemed scruffy – even for a local cricket match on a hot day. Only his accent marked him for better than a roughneck.

'So, you're Peggy,' he mumbled through a mouthful of egg. 'I wonder why George has never introduced us?'

Peggy pushed a lock of hair from her eyes. 'No idea,' she paused. 'But pleased to meet you, Stan. And you know my brother, how?'

'We did sea cadets together. George got seasick. They kicked him out.'

She laughed. 'I remember that.'

Stan had brown, thoughtful eyes set in a face that, she guessed, had spent much time outdoors. His complexion was too unlined to be weathered, but the elements had given his face a worldliness that, she thought, made it interesting. She decided that he wouldn't keep his thinning hair for much longer, but his voice was warm and his gaze steady. And he had, she decided, a gentle air.

He glanced at some sheet music she'd left lying on the grass.

'What's this, then? You're musical?'

She grabbed the sheet and nestled it in the folds of her dress. She could feel the blush as she said, 'Oh no, no. My church choir is putting on a musical comedy at the end of the month.'

When she told him that she owned a hairdressing salon, all he could say was, 'Well, well, aren't you the Christmas cracker – full of surprises!'

'Midland Bank owns the salon. I impressed the bank manager – Mr. Wreston-Harbor.'

Stan grinned, 'What a perfect name for a bank manager – unimprovable!'

'Ee, you're right,' she agreed. They laughed together; their eyes remaining on each other for a moment.

'I liked Mr. Harbour; he's all for women getting on in the world. He has two daughters himself, one at university.'

'Ah, a modern father.'

Peggy told Stan that she called her business the Sadler Gate Hairdressing Salon and located it – despite the higher rent – in an historic area of Derby city. 'It's only my assistant Margery Jeffry and me, but we've got enough customers to pay off the loan. We'll be all right.' Her voice brightened. 'I love to style hair.'

Peggy lowered herself on to her elbows and closed her eyes for a moment. When she opened them, Stan was looking at her reclining figure. She saw him look away.

'Well, I can see you're proud of what you've done.' he said, scanning the field. He drank some of the lemonade.

Soon, Peggy gave up the pretence of being a spectator. Her elbows were cramping. She allowed her head to fall back on the rug.

The sky was a white tent. Birds rested, only butterflies trembled through the air. The sound of leather on willow – ball connecting with bat – underscored the sunlit inertia of a village cricket match, even one played on the borders of a great industrial city.

Moments later, a cloud covered the sun. Peggy sensed, as much as saw, the change of light. Shadows fell on the scene, creating a chiaroscuro landscape. The cricketer's flannels, set against the penumbra, became white flags. The shift in light brought Peggy upright. She turned to Stan. 'The grass has changed colour – it looks almost like charcoal in the deep boundaries.'

'Rain can't be far away.' He paused and seemed to be considering his next words. 'You said you like to style hair. I'm trying to find a job, something I can really like.'

She hugged her knees and smiled, 'Finding a job can't be hard for a young man.'

'Thirty-five's not so young. My Pa calls forty 'the foothills of middle age.'

He told her that, since the age of twenty – when he first went abroad – he'd been working on freighters in the Far East. The posting had been as an Able Seaman. 'I like being a nomad,' he told her. 'I don't like to owe anything to anyone. But my pa doesn't think much of my attitude – he thinks it's all too casual for a naval man – but then he's from a different generation.'

Peggy raised her eyebrows, saying nothing.

He studied her. 'How about you, Peggy, a woman with her own business: Is it that important to be with a man who knows where he's going?'

She shrugged and looked away.

He went on talking: 'For my pa, the 'Charleston' is typical of what's wrong with my crowd – foot loose and fancy-free, he says. Ha!' She sensed his frustration.

'Oo, but I love the Charleston!' Stan didn't smile, and her remark didn't break the tension as she had hoped it might.

After a moment, Stan spoke again. 'This world depression got as far as China. Even the cargo ships got fewer and fewer. I could see I'd be extra cargo before long.' He pulled at a blade of grass. 'I cleared out and came back to Blighty.' He snorted, 'But there's nowt, here. We need one of those new deals that the Yanks have got – a politician with some vision, like that FDR chap.'

'Well, his wife is behind all those changes – women's place in the world; she's the kind I admire. American, of course – not stuck in the past, like us.'

'Well, whatever you want to call it, and whoever's responsible, we need something like that for our blokes.'

She was relieved to hear clapping from the men on the field. She never enjoyed talking politics, maybe because they rarely did at home. Her father was scathing about politics and said, 'it attracts the criminal classes.' Now she had an excuse to move – the players were walking towards a hut on the edge of the field.

She stood up and reached for his hand. 'Come on, cheer up! Let's have a cuppa at the club house. George will be ever so pleased to see you.'

Stan didn't take her hand but stood up awkwardly, balancing the plate and the bottle of lemonade. He rocked back on his feet. She thought he might lose his balance.

'Can you wait a minute, please?' he said.

'What is it?'

'I can get a bit dizzy if I stand up too quickly. I'm sorry.'

'Oh dear, that's a worry. What does the doctor say?'

'Nowt.' He laughed, 'because I haven't asked him. I know what the trouble is.'

CLEW PARKER
Derby 1936

Days shortened. From Russia's Ural Mountains, winds brought freezing weather into the English Midlands.

Peggy was preparing to leave for the day when – as though borne on the northern gale – the salon door opened, and a tall man in an overcoat seemed to blow in. The man struggled to shut the door. He was stout, but his height dispelled any impression of excessive bulk. He pressed back his shoulders, his chest high; she thought, 'a military man.'

The man's features were big, handsome ('like Tyrone Power,' she decided), his pale grey eyes made more striking by the contrast of his dark eyebrows. The black overcoat was cashmere, the wingtip shoes were army-bright.

The visitor introduced himself in a rumbling voice that bore no trace of a Derbyshire accent. His smile put her at ease before he spoke.

'Good afternoon. I am Clew Parker, Stanley's father,' he said. 'And you, I assume, are Miss Peggy Steele? Stan's told me about you and your salon.' He pronounced the last word in the French way. 'I was rather hoping we might have a quiet chat at the end of your day, but I can see you're ready to go home. Can you spare me a little time?'

She smiled. 'Of course. How do you do, Mr. Parker.' She removed her hat but kept her coat on; it was Friday, and she tried to get home in time to give Father Kelly his glass of sherry and the family contribution for St Agnes.

He removed his coat and gloves. They shook hands. 'Excellent, excellent. At last, I have the pleasure of meeting Miss Peggy Steele of the famous Sadler Gate Salon.' Was that a wink, she wondered?

She blushed. 'The salon?' She echoed his pronunciation. 'Not famous at all, sir.'

'Oh, come now: a friend of my wife's, Genevieve Mansergh, tells us you take very good care of her.'

'Well, that's most kind of Lady Mansergh, I'm sure.' Then she thought 'I'm sure' sounded common, or as if she was putting on airs, or both. She gestured again, pointing to the two upright chairs, wishing that she'd made more effort to improve the reception area. They sat.

'Miss Steele, let me tell you why I've come. This will be a difficult conversation – one that I have rehearsed in my mind many times – but it is one we must have.' He leaned forward, looking at her so intently that she feared what he might be about to say. Her hand went to a lock of hair that she always twisted when she felt nervous.

Unsmiling, he said, 'My wife and I don't believe that Stanley, without any employment, is in a position to pay attention to a young lady, let alone support one.'

She was relieved; *is this all it was?* Peggy raised her hand to stop him from saying more.

'Mr. Parker, I'm doing a good job of supporting myself. I also take care of the needs of my parents. I need no one to support me.'

Clew Parker sat back.

'I see.' He paused and steepled his fingers. 'Well, my son tells us he loves you and that you are just the kind of girl he should marry.' He chewed his lip in a way that reminded her of Stan. 'Is he alone in that intention?'

Peggy blinked. Barely six months had passed since she had been seeing Stan, and here was his father asking if she might be interested in marrying him.

'I am very fond of your son, sir, and it is possible that we may marry at some future date, but Stanley, as you have pointed out, is without a job.'

'I have to say, you're very frank, Miss Steele.'

'I know of no other way, sir, but do call me Peggy.'

'Peggy, it shall be!' He smiled with a soft clap of hands before continuing, 'Stanley is now thirty-five and seems determined to "plough his own furrow" – as the saying goes.'

He coughed, flicked his trouser leg, then leaned forward again. 'I understand your situation, and it is noble of you to care so much for your parents. But as three people who care a great deal about Stanley, adding his mother to that equation, we must contrive to put my son into a situation where he can improve himself to a point where a wife and family are a realistic possibility.'

Peggy hesitated while she unravelled his last sentence. She frowned, wondering how best to respond.

'I see,' she said carefully, 'but Stan's first task is to get a job, whether or not he marries.'

'He must get a job, certainly. However, Peggy, my wife and I believe our son is ill-fitted for the commercial world. Stan needs support around him – an institution, such as the Navy, can offer.'

'You know Stan didn't like his time in China?' She held his gaze.

He looked surprised. His voice rose, 'Nonsense!'

'He said his life as an Able Seaman didn't challenge him. He saw life as an officer much more appealing, but he's aware that if he stays at sea, he needs more qualifications.'

'Well, of course, but…'

'But he dislikes exams and lacks confidence in his ability to pass them.'

Clew Parker sat back, his eyebrows raised, lips curled in a reaction that Peggy hoped was admiration.

He drew a deep breath. Speaking slowly, he said, 'He has confided in you in a way that he hasn't confided in me.' He shook his head. 'Stanley is more capable than most chaps of getting his Mate's ticket. He just needs to believe it about himself and know that people who care about him believe it, too.'

Peggy pressed her lips together, keeping a straight face when he said 'chaps.' Clew Parker pronounced the word just as Stan always imitated: 'chee-aps.'

'Let me be precise, Peggy: clearly, my boy can't sit on his hands in Derby. As I've said, neither his mother nor I can see him succeeding on Civvy Street. These are hard times in Britain, and I think our little friend, Herr Hitler – despite the soothing words of Mr. Chamberlain and, for heaven's sake, our present King – plans to make it harder.'

Clew Parker got up and crossed to the window. He turned to study the salon. He eyed the three hairdryers on their rolling stands and the ceiling to floor mirror that covered one wall. He looked approvingly at the freshly laundered robes hanging on racks.

'You're an exceptional young woman, Peggy Steele. And Stan seems determined for you to be together. I approve, if that matters. You, of course, hold all the cards, but if you're as fond of him as you say you are, then I hope we can co-operate in getting him a posting as an officer. But he's in no position to bring that about without my help.' He added, almost as an afterthought. 'As his father, you understand.'

He appeared to take a deep breath, sat down opposite her, and continued. 'I've always wanted Stanley to follow me to sea, as I'm sure he's told you. Sadly, he failed the Royal Navy's medical exam.' He paused as if considering his next sentence. 'If he hasn't already told you, it's important that you should know: Stan was born with a hole in his heart.'

Peggy was stunned. Why hadn't Stan told her? He'd never told her about failing the Royal Navy medical; in fact, she remembered he had said that he'd never applied – obviously, too embarrassed to speak the truth. Why had he hidden the news of his weak heart? Stan's father was looking at her keenly, waiting for her reaction.

'That's terrible news, Mr. Parker. I've known about his dizzy spells, his sleeping bouts, and headaches, but I always thought it was the stress of finding a job.'

'Hmm, I wish it were so temporary, Peggy. No, the shortness of breath has been a factor since he was a boy. He was never one for robust sports at school. And this foggy, smoggy climate doesn't help.'

He clapped his hands. 'But we're all facing the reality of it – his mother, Stan, me. Nothing medically can be done, but if he isn't under too much pressure, Stan will be all right.'

'But as you've said, sir, his medical condition will limit his prospects of employment – as it did with the Royal Navy.'

Clew Parker pulled his chair closer. They were at eye level.

'It's true. But one of the few advantages of age is that it confers old friendships with people in high places.' He hunched forward. 'I may be able to get a posting for Stan, even though he's not qualified. They'll insist that he have a Mate's ticket, and, dear Peggy, we shall need you to persuade him to sign up for the extra study that will entail. It's nepotism, of course, but that's how it works, sometimes, in this little world of ours. But if Stanley ever finds out we cleared his path – well, he will be very, very unhappy. He'd prefer to think they spotted him as leadership potential so remember – don't let on.' He grinned as if they were conspirators.

'Peggy, I believe that, together, we can arrange a good position for Stanley, one that will place him in a position to offer you marriage.' He tipped his head. 'In case you become more positive about that.' Peggy noticed that the sentence was more a statement than a question.

After he'd finished speaking, Clew Parker waited. He seemed to study his crossed knee, occasionally glancing up. After half a minute had passed, Peggy spoke: 'Please be assured I want to help him.' She looked at the man opposite. 'As a first step, he might be willing to study for his Mate's ticket. And I've found out that there's a training course in Liverpool he can join.'

'HMS Conway – I know it.' Stan's father sat back in his chair. 'Well, well, it seems as if you're thinking ahead of me. Are you making Stan your mission, Peggy?' His eyes twinkled, and he put a hand over his mouth but not before she saw the small smile.

'Mission? No, Mr. Parker, I wouldn't put it quite like that.' But at the same time, as fond of him as she was, she knew that Stan was not instinctively ambitious. The insecurity she sensed in him was different from her own self-confidence and sociability. She knew that Clew's son was going to need a push or two before he realised the rewards of ambition. Now she could help him without making any binding commitment.

Stan's father looked around the room. 'What about all… this?'

She followed his gaze as he waited for her answer. She faced him, smiling. 'Let's take this idea one step at a time, shall we, Mr. Parker?'

He pursed his lips. 'Of course, of course. Naturally, the two of you must talk some more. These are life choices. Dear Peggy, you must forgive me if I seem to be taking charge, but I want only the best for both of you. Believe me, when I tell you that, should you decide to go abroad – despite your obvious success – your life will be infinitely better than it is here.'

Peggy decided not to respond to the suggestion of going abroad. For now, helping Stan to get a job would be enough.

They got up together, both sensing their business was done. Clew Parker put his hands on her shoulders. 'I can assure you, Peggy, that being abroad is always better than being in Britain. And most importantly, if we do go ahead with this, I shall arrange that Stanley earns enough to provide a sufficient allowance for your parents.'

She could see the affection in his eyes. She was warming to this resolute man, so different from her ruined father. At the same time, she would not place her future in his hands.

'Can we keep this talk between us, Peggy? I shall tell Stan we've met, and he'll just put that down…' he grinned '… to me being a Nosey Parker! My son will be so happy to know that I like very much what I've seen of you – and that he has my full approval. I'm sure his mother, Rose, will be an eager supporter, too. You must meet her – she's already said she must meet the young woman who has stolen Stan's heart.'

He smiled again as he turned and opened the door. 'Goodbye, my dear; I can't tell you how pleased and happy I am to have met you.'

Clew Parker wrestled the door open, braced himself against the rioting weather, and was gone.

As the door slammed shut, Peggy realised she had made some sort of pact with Stan's father.

A PROPOSAL
Derby 1936

From the moment he picked up the London postmarked envelope on the hall table, Stan had the feeling that the day would be exceptional. He passed the letter to his father.

'I never doubted it.' Clew Parker's eyes scanned the letter and hugged his son, a rare gesture. 'Your Mate's ticket – now Blue Funnel will be darn lucky to have you.' Clew waved the letter in the air. 'On Sunday, you must take your Peggy for a run in the new Morris. I shall tell your mother – I know she'll be delighted.'

Peggy had been apart from Stan for several months; she knew he'd been studying for his Mate's ticket on Merseyside. Before travelling to Liverpool – where he stayed in Conway's student quarters – Stan told her about a meeting he'd had in London with a Blue Funnel director named Pennington. He chuckled as he told her, 'He's actually my godfather, but he's done bugger all for me until now.' Pennington had explained that, if Stan was interested and free, there would be a commission for him in China. 'But Pennington said it would be critical for me to get better qualifications – and it seems that's not open to negotiation.'

Peggy knew that when Clew Parker told his son about Pennington and the opportunity at Blue Funnel, it would get Stan's attention. On his return from the meeting with his godfather in London, Stan told Clew that he intended to study and apply for his Mate's ticket; Stan didn't mention the fact that, some weeks earlier, Peggy had planted the idea of studying on Merseyside.

By then, Stan and Peggy had been 'walking out' for over a year. Peggy knew the man was in love with her; he had told her that she'd given him a purpose in life. Stan loved her, however, in a way that she couldn't match; he didn't *excite* her in the way her sophisticated friend, Amy, told her she should be excited; they'd never did more than kiss and cuddle. Stan seemed satisfied by their adolescent fumbling.

She knew she wanted Stan to make more of himself – that's how their friendship had begun, but the – was it a 'plot?' – with his father seemed to be assuming a momentum of its own.

That Sunday morning – under a sky her brother George called 'weepy' – she'd been looking out for Stan from her window. He'd called her salon earlier in the week to say he had some news, and he would call for her on Sunday.

'Is it good news, Stan?' she'd asked, clutching the phone, nervous.

'Now, now, be patient, Pegs: I'll call for you at ten-thirty on Sunday.'

She was surprised to see a small green Morris, obviously new, pull up outside her parent's house. A minute later, she was running down the garden path.

She ducked her head to see Stan at the wheel and squealed with delight as she got in and closed the door. 'What have you done to deserve this?'

'You mean Pa lending me his new car? It's 850 ccs, and he paid almost one hundred pounds for it, brand new. He's barely driven it himself, but he let us have it today because I've passed all my exams. I have my Mate's ticket.'

Her eyes glistened as she pulled him towards her across the seat. 'Oh Stan, I just knew you could do it. I'm so happy for you.' She kissed his cheek.

They both felt very grand travelling in the little Morris. 'What are these?' Peg said as she reached up.

Stan smiled. 'They're to keep the sun out of your eyes when you're driving – they call them visors. And this is the first car to have them – though they may not get much use.' Stan nodded at the road towards Matlock, where bruised clouds writhed in a racing sky – portents of an unpredictable day. Stan said he had planned a picnic in the Elizabethan Garden at Chatsworth House. Peggy knew that they would have to resign themselves to eating sandwiches, probably in the shelter of their tiny car.

He beamed at her from the driving seat. 'I can't tell you how happy I am at the sight of your grand little face after those dreary weeks in Liverpool.' Leaning over, he squeezed her shoulder, 'This is such good news, Pegs. Blue Funnel say they'll start me as Second Mate. Then I can work my way up from there.' Peggy giggled at his high spirits. 'This is the Merchant Navy, ducks,' he said. 'They don't ask you who your people are like they do in the Royal Navy.'

Peggy thought, 'No, especially if you don't know you would never have had the interview except for your father's connections.'

Out of the corner of her eye, she saw Stan looking thoughtful before he added, 'But it's a big decision, isn't it? To go back to China, I mean.' Stan wiggled his eyebrows like Groucho Marx; she sensed he was trying to keep the conversation light.

Peggy didn't reply, and she suspected her silence would upset him. She knew – because he had told her so often – that she had all the qualities he desired in a woman: beauty, energy, independence, and an ambitious – almost reckless – spirit. He was singing her praises again as he drove. 'Since meeting you, love, I've felt capable of being so much more.' He flicked a sideways glance at her. 'It's not just the idea of pleasing you – although I'd be lying if I said that it wasn't a part of it – but I didn't want to reach forty without any proper qualifications. The opportunity with Blue Funnel could not have come at a better time.'

Again, she didn't respond. Stan changed gears to take a tight bend. Then Peggy, staring at the road ahead, said, 'If you think China is right for you, Stan, then that's the only decision.' She took a deep breath. 'You loved your time in the Far East – it was the people you worked for that you didn't like.'

She knew he'd be disappointed by her reply, but she needed to separate his ambitions from her own. She needed him to understand that her support for his career was unrelated to anything she might want for herself.

By his tone, she could tell he was trying to maintain his enthusiasm when he said, 'If I work hard, I'll soon be an officer – thanks to Pa. He knows a lot of important people; he always says, 'It's who you know…'

'It's not just that, Stan,' she said. 'You're the one who's studied, you're the one who's earned his Mate's ticket, you're the one who's acquired the skills and experience. It's *what* you know *and* who you know.'

'Well, I know ships, Peggy, and that's the job.'

'Of course, you do, love.' She felt his shoulder press against her.

An hour later, they had parked the car some two hundred yards from the main gates of Chatsworth House. They sat munching their cheese and tomato sandwiches while the wind rocked the small vehicle. An instant later, a burst of sunshine lifted the gloom. 'C'mon, love,' Stan said. 'It's another day for an hour or so. Let's make the most of it.'

They took their chances in the elusive sun. Peggy liked to walk at a quick pace, but as usual, when they walked together, she slowed down for Stan.

After a quarter mile, he reached for her arm. 'Peg, can you wait a moment, please.'

He pulled her towards him. She had a moment of alarm, sensing he wanted to discuss something important. She was right.

'I think we should get married.'

She couldn't look at him without betraying her feelings. She squeezed her eyes shut.

'Are you all right? Oh dear, are you in pain, Pegs?' He half laughed. 'It's not that bad, is it?'

She moved her head a fraction but said nothing. Half a minute passed. Eyes closed; she tilted her head at the sky. Thoughts bounced through her mind: she had released more than ambition in Stan. Yes, he wanted to go back to China with a proper job – but he wanted her with him.

'Why are you hesitating?' She could hear the doubt lifting his voice.

She decided to ignore his questions by asking another.

'Aren't the Japanese fighting the Chinese? My dad tells me the Japanese are pushing towards Shanghai all the time.'

'Oh, that will blow over.' He smiled. She sensed he didn't want to lose the momentum of his proposal. 'The Japanese and the Chinese have been warring for hundreds – even thousands – of years.'

She shook her head. 'But you want me to leave a country that may go to war, for a country that's already at war.'

She could almost see the anxiety rushing through him, colouring his face.

He dropped her hands.

'Peggy: You've often said we don't know enough about each other to get married, but we like being together, don't we? In China, we'll be free of brothers and sisters – yes, I know I don't have any – but I know they're always bothering you. And we won't have mums and dads always being around when we want to be alone.' He took her hands again and placed them on his hips. 'Pegs, I want us to be together, to be better off, and have children and be happy. Is that too much to ask of the woman I love?'

He pulled her towards him and started to whisper in her ear.

'Now I'm going to tell you something: I've been saving it – you know, like a secret weapon – but this is a huge decision for you, and I realise that you must have all the facts.'

She doubted if there was anything Stan could say that would weaken her resolve, but she was intrigued. His eyes – now soft with love – looked directly into hers. She felt the intimacy of his hands on the back of her neck.

'Look, love: Blue Funnel told me the job – which I'm confident of getting – comes with a house – a big one, a family home! My pa confirmed all of it. It'll be a grand life: you'll have five servants, and – and, well, you'll have everything you need.' He put his arms around her. 'Darling, it's a new life, a giant step that we could never take here. And you'll be completely safe, I promise you, because our home will be in the International Settlement – that's a neutral zone where Britain, the USA, Russia, France, and so on – are independent of the Chinese and the Japanese.' He stepped back and looked into her eyes. 'Imagine all the fascinating people you'll meet, Peggy.'

She was torn. Living in the way Stan described would give her a life so different that it strained her imagination; she couldn't conceive of it – a house of her own, servants, a garden.

She looked at her shoes. 'I won't have my salon, Stan. And my mum and dad… you know how much they depend on me.'

He closed his eyes, his head drooped. She knew how her objections must be disappointing this sweet, lovely man.

He shook his head. 'That damn salon.'

'I've told you. I love my little business, and it's doing so well.'

'But it's just a job, isn't it? That little shop can never give you the life I can give you.' Shaking his head: 'I'm sorry, that was unkind of me.'

She bit her lip, too upset to respond.

He put his arms around her and hugged her hard. He swayed with her as if they were dancing. 'Anyway, it's high time I had a proper job. All the things you said that first day we met, at the cricket. You spoke about me making something of myself?' He smiled. 'Sweet Peggy, you're the one who's made me see that. This is our chance.'

He dropped his hands and looked into her eyes. She saw his determination. He nodded – it seemed to himself – as he spoke.

'I shall go back to Shanghai and take a commission with Blue Funnel. I have a few more weeks training on Merseyside, and then I shall be off – unless you can give me a reason to stay for a bit longer.' He smiled at her with all the warmth and love she knew he felt.

If only she could feel the same.

Sitting on her bed that night, in the room she shared with her sister Connie, Peggy considered her unchanging life in Derby. She knew her father's health would worsen, and he would die; her siblings would find partners, marry, and have children; her widowed mother would live with one or other of the families until she, too, passed away; and Father Kelly would continue to expect his donations for St. Agnes. Even her salon, as much as she loved the independence that its small income gave her, would remain a financial struggle.

All choices had consequences. But, she thought, they were still *her* choices. Unlike her father, no one was ordering her to 'hold the line'. A searing but brief anger filled her for submitting to everyone's needs but her own.

How would her life with Stan be different? There was one thing of which she was certain: in China, she would not be burdened by the expectations of family or class. Even so, the prospect of marriage to Stan didn't fill her with joy, although he was a decent man who adored her. Yet she, who wanted so much to look after herself, was tired of looking after others. She knew she had an inability to share herself openly with anyone because that would mean giving someone else control over her happiness. All indications were that Stan accepted her as she was. By marrying him, she would take care of Stanley; and he would make sure she – and, more importantly, her family back home – were looked after.

She undressed and brushed her teeth. Minutes later, she was deep in the large feather bed. She wanted to be asleep before Connie came up.

As she closed her eyes, she remembered the only occasion when Stanley had asked, 'Do you love me, Pegs?'

'You're the best.' She told him. She had never lied.

DAD'S WAR
Derby 1936

Peggy's father, Arnold Steele, was a casualty of chemical warfare, and suffered from a range of nervous disorders: he'd forget how to form sentences; he always felt confused and anxious; sometimes, he would have bouts of unproductive vomiting. She had learned that these symptoms were classed, in medical terms, as neurasthenia – a mechanical weakness in the nerves. Her mother, bewildered and frightened, called his chronic illness 'Dad's nerves'.

As a child and later, as a young girl, Peggy spent many hours with her father, fixing any small problems on the two Rolls Royce cars that he maintained for the Duke of Devonshire. The Steele family lived on the duke's Chatsworth estate. Peggy's mother, Annie, worked as a cook in the duke's household. Peggy's father instilled in his daughter the belief that there was nothing that should be off-limits because of her sex. He made sure she spent time with the farm manager. She learned to deliver foals and calves, and to observe the planting and harvesting routines. Her Dad had once introduced her to the duke – something he'd never done with his other children. Dressed in a worn checked jacket and old corduroys, he had knelt to her level and gravely asked, 'And how, sweet poppet, will you change the world?'

Peggy had blushed. 'I don't know, sir, but I'm going to.'

Born in 1905, Peggy was nearly ten years old when her father went to war. She missed him, and her schoolwork suffered. She longed for his return and, after four years, he came home. He was placed into a classification called the 'walking wounded'. By chance, he was scheduled to return on her fourteenth birthday. She put on her prettiest frock, handed down in fair condition from her eldest sister, Connie.

The day was a dark one – clouds low, capricious rain. Peggy sat by the kitchen window, knowing her mother and father would come down the path at the side of the house. The front door was rarely used, as her dad said:

'only for Christmas Day visitors, or for the King, who disna' come around as often as he used to.'

She heard the slam of a car door – her mother had ordered the luxury of a taxi to fetch the two of them from the hospital.

'They're here!' Peggy called out to the house at large, but when she stepped towards the kitchen door and opened it a crack, she stopped. Annie Steele had emerged on to the path. She saw that her mother was holding the arm of a stooped man, his head and one eye bandaged, shuffling forward.

Peggy fled.

Out of the front door she went as George, Richard, Ina, Connie, and Nancy ran down the path to greet their father. A minute later, she was on Richard's purple bike, tears and rain streaming down her face, cycling five miles against the lashing wind. She hid in the allotment's shed for hours, howling her grief into the creosote-soaked wood. For four days, alone, she mourned the death of the father she'd known.

A month later, she and her father made peace with each other. Two more years would pass before Peggy accepted that the broken man who had returned from the war had once been the prince of her life. On her sixteenth birthday, she left school, determined to live life on her own terms.

After that, Arnold's sickness occurred randomly in the form of fits. When he had one of these episodes, Peggy's mother would say, 'Everybody upstairs, please, Dad's having one of his turns.'

One quiet evening – there were maybe three or four a week – her dad told her about an episode in the Great War. She knew he had never talked to anyone in the family – including her mother – about that haunting time.

Arnie – the name his pals gave him – never said why he chose that evening to speak so openly. She guessed it was because in the previous week, he'd attacked Annie, blacking her eye.

That night, some days after Stan's proposal, Peggy walked into the kitchen at the rear of the cottage; a fire was spitting in the grate. 'Is that you, Win?' Her father always called her a version of her baptismal name, Winifred, Winnie, or Win.

His chair, a striking leather piece at odds with the other plain furnishings, was tilted to one side. The piece had been presented to her father by the ducal family when he returned from the war. One of the chair's legs had broken some months ago when her brother George, a heavy young man, had sat on it; Arnold Steele was perched on it now, at an angle both comical and sad.

Peggy crossed the room and shovelled more fuel on the fire. When she stood up and turned around, she saw that her father was rubbing his eyes. 'What is it, Dad?'

Crouched forward in his broken chair, staring at the worn carpet, he began to talk.

'I'm so glad to see you, Win.' He tried to wipe away his tears with the cuff of his coat. 'Sorry I'm like this but it's been a bad few days for me…' He looked at her, his face hollowed with pain '… for all of you, I know.' He shook his head then folded his arms, collecting himself. 'I'm so sorry, love – for you, but mostly yer mam. It's the first time I've ever laid a hand on her. I shan't blame her if she wants to send me back to Longshore.'

Peggy knelt beside him, her head on his knee. She knew about Longshore Lodge, where he'd been treated with other casualties of war. She'd heard the hospital was well-equipped for treating physical wounds, but she also knew Longshore had no expertise in what doctors were now calling 'shell shock', or 'combat stress'. Medical men had agreed that for her father and other sufferers, the symptoms would end in an early death.

Despite the lack of a cure, the family had been told that it helped veterans to be able to talk – or 'expatiate' as the doctors called it – their experiences. Arnold never wanted to talk about what he had seen. Peggy sensed that tonight would be different.

'It all came back to me this afternoon. Sometimes the guilt does that to me. About how I treat yer mam. When I have one of me rages.'

Peggy moved nearer, hugged his knee.

He spoke again. 'We were trying to hold this bloody patch of trees near bloody Dellville.' He unfolded his arms and lifted his hands – two fingers of the left hand had been shot off – and moved them up and down as if he were holding a vase. 'That's all it was – a flaming bunch of trees! They never told us why – they just kept shouting, 'Hold the line! Hold the line!'

He squinted, remembering.

'Twere near Dellville,' he repeated. 'Dead horses were round us – from the cavalry, don't you know? And at night, the rats came and fed on them, and our dead mates, an all. The stench were so bad you could bloody *taste* it. That smell were like an octopus: it went up yer nose and sent its fingers into every bit of yer. And the rain – the rain went on, day in, day out, and through the night, an all.'

He reached for the top of Peggy's head. 'I'll tell you, darlin', I don't need to go to hell; I've been there.'

He sat back again. 'We were with the South Africans.' His head flopped back, and he closed his eyes. 'Bloody hell, those buggers could fight! Oh, sorry, love.' He patted the top of her head. 'They had their darkies with 'em an' all – though they never gave them rifles. Funny that; they never trusted them blacks with guns. They were lovely fellers, the blacks, and we were all on the same side.' He shook his head. 'Never knew why. They just did supply stuff at the rear.'

He frowned, remembering. 'Any road, there were even some Chinks there!' His eyes lit up as a memory sparked. He sniffed. 'That's right! Government got in 'undreds of Chinamen to pull the dead off the battlefield.' He shook his head. 'Sixty thousands of our lads knocked out on the first flaming day – twenty thousand of 'em dead and gone.'

'Imagine', he paused, imagining: 'You're a young lad – never been further than Peckham – you go to France to fight for yer country – you get killed by Germans – and then you're buried by a bloody Chinaman.' He puffed his cheeks. 'How's that for a game of soldiers, eh?'

His effort to laugh drew a wet explosion from deep in his lungs. In seconds, the ragged laugh became a sob. The coughing and laughing, and sobbing gripped him for nearly a minute, but he held up his hand when Peggy tried to comfort him.

When the cough had done with him, he touched an eye with the cuff of his jacket. Again, he bent forward.

'Anyway, there we were when this yellow mist starts comin' in from Jerry's lines – the ruddy thing slithered along the ground like it knew it were evil.' He stopped for a moment and wrinkled his nose. Peggy knew he was back in the trench. 'Real peculiar it was. We had'na any idea… smelled strange – like mustard and horse radish.

'Any road – too late – those of us what had gas masks put them on – those what did'na have them were told to piss on their handkerchiefs and put them on their faces… well, weren't many lads what done that!

'Next thing, we could'na breathe – eyes stinging, nose running… all of us blithering about in them stinking rat-filled trenches… then I saw all them blisters popping up on me 'ands.'

Staring at his disfigured left hand, he made a fist of it and ground it into his stomach. He uttered a long, low keening sound that lasted almost a minute. She reached up for his hand, but he held it tight against his stomach.

'Oh dear, lass, oh dear. It was right bad y'know?'

'Stop, Dad, please stop.' Peggy lifted herself to sit on the arm of his chair, which set it to wobbling again. She placed an arm around her father's thin shoulders; she thought that 'expatiating' was doing him no good at all.

'Away with ye, darlin'.' He nudged her and drew in a deep breath. 'There's no need for all that soppy stuff.' He wiped his eyes and nudged her again. 'But afore ye go and get me another bottle o' Guinness, I just want ye to know – and I know it's not the first time I've said it – how much it means to me that you've taken over the family. It were just too much for yer mam.'

Peggy looked at his rheumy eyes. 'Come on, Dad, don't keep saying that. Everyone helps.'

'I say it because I mean it, love. You've taken care of everybody – including that great lump of a brother o' yours, George – ever since you was a little 'un, when I got called up.' He patted the top of her head. 'You were born to take care of folk, Win, you really were. I don't know what we'd have done without you.'

A WEDDING
Derby 1937

Peggy married Stanley Parker in January 1937, a few weeks before her thirty-second birthday.

The small church, St. Anne's Catholic, might have seemed romantic on a sunny, even cold, day but the Peak district had delivered chilly, biting weather that Saturday.

Peggy had two bridesmaids – Margery Jeffry, who had been hired by the new owners of the salon – and her friend, Amelia Jane.

Her father was back at Longshore, too ill to attend the wedding. Her brother George, who had driven her thirty-five miles from Derby, walked her down the aisle. Her other brother, Richard, and her nephew, Martin, were ushers.

As Peggy started the short walk to the altar, her two bridesmaids followed; they were holding colourful bouquets of mixed freesias and wearing dresses of pale yellow. Their bare shoulders looked raw with cold.

Her mother, tiny, was wearing a brown dress and a scraggy fur with fox eyes that – as a child – had scared Peggy. A few old school friends and customers had come with boyfriends or husbands – the men squeezed into too tight jackets and mismatched trousers.

Peggy saw Clew Parker standing alongside his son at the end of the nave. Her new father-in-law wore a dark blue suit cut, she guessed, by some Savile Row tailor to show off his tall figure. She was expecting Stan, in his naval uniform, to turn around as she walked up the aisle on George's arm, but he didn't.

As she came closer, she could see a woman sitting in a pew to the right of Stan's father. She wore a hat so ornate that Peggy guessed it might have covered most of the cost of the simple wedding. Only when the woman turned and smiled did she recognise her customer, Lady Mansergh. Peggy's spirits lifted when the woman gave a discreet wave.

Peggy knew that Rose Parker would be absent; two days before the wedding, a letter had arrived from Clew Parker. He wrote that he looked forward to the ceremony but would have to apologise for his wife's absence; 'It's her nerves,' he explained.

Peggy had her reply delivered by hand to the Parker home in Dronfield.

'Dear Mr. Parker,' she wrote. *'I am in receipt of your letter for which I thank you. I, too, look forward to seeing you on my wedding day. Please convey my regrets to Mrs. Parker. Stan, obviously, would have preferred to have his mother present at the ceremony. For my part, please assure your good wife that I shall take good care of her son.'*

To her surprise, Rose Parker wrote back; the letter reached Peggy the day before the wedding.

As she read the two short sentences, Peggy was glad she had opened the letter in the relative privacy of her bedroom.

'I hope you make a happy marriage, Peggy Steele, now that you have Stanley for your husband. But he will always be my son.'

CHINA

ARRIVAL
Shanghai 1937

Peggy was unnerved by her first sight of Shanghai. Growing up, she had never been further than the English seaside resort of Skegness, close to Derby. She was nineteen before she saw the sea for the first time.

'Look, *liebchen*,' said the young woman at her side. They were on the top deck, leaning over the side as the shoreline slid by. A river breeze played havoc with their hair but took nothing from their enthusiasm: they were both desperate to see the landfall of China for the first time.

Peggy had been given a berth on a Blue Funnel cargo liner, the *Tantalus*, from Liverpool to Shanghai. She and her companion had shared a cabin. From the moment she met her, Peggy liked and admired Natasha Pavlovich – or 'Tash', as she liked to be known. Tash, a young artist, was a Russian who had fled Byelorussia, the smallest of the Soviet republics, in 1934 – the year that Stalin began his purge of Trotskyists.

Natasha had told Peggy – in a voice that seemed almost bored – that Stalin wanted to confine Socialism to Russia while her parents, like Leon Trotsky himself, wanted a non-stop, worldwide revolution. Refusing to recant, her father and mother had been executed by the secret police – taken outside to die in one of the NKVD's mobile gas units. Hours before, her mother and father had watched their two daughters being raped by prison guards. Other dissidents stood by, too frightened to act. Their mother collapsed, banging her head on the stone floor until she bled. Her father faced the wall and shrieked, hitting his head repeatedly with his fists.

That night, Tash's sister, Nadia, had wrapped a sheet around her neck and, from the top bunk, had leaned into the air. Natasha, waking, had found her sister's body twisting in front of her.

Natasha, Peggy soon realised – as the young Russian talked about what had happened – had an ability to embrace suffering as if it were her due. She told Peggy that the rapes 'meant nothing: I placed myself elsewhere because these low creatures were victims of their own instincts. One of the young men who raped me helped me to escape; it was crazy – he handed me his gun and asked me to shoot him.' She shrugged. 'And I did. And then I ran away to England.'

'And then?' asked Peggy.

'I decided to place the past in the past: I sailed to China.' She added quietly, 'And here we are.'

Despite her lack of anything more than a few clothes, three boxes of charcoals, and two sketchbooks, Natasha survived. She owed her survival to fluency in Russian, French and English. Nearly six feet tall, the young woman was a striking figure. She walked gracefully on long, slim legs and possessed a *gamin* quality, an impishness mismatched by her height. Peggy – as attractive as she was – envied Tash's angelic face, framed by black, pixie-cut hair. When Tash's dark eyes looked into hers, Peggy felt they might reach to the back of her head.

They were from different worlds, but Peggy soon came to adore Natasha with a purity that felt right. The twenty-five-year-old's vivacity was a magnet for men. Yet she was dismissive of lovesick suitors: 'I have discovered that men are like dogs, *liebchen*, with more brains but less loyalty.' There would be no shipboard romance for Tash.

Now, as they looked at *Shanghai*'s Bund unfolding before them, Tash said, 'This is why we've come to the Paris of the East – that's what they call it, you know.'

The *Tantalus* continued to shunt up the river while the great city unspooled its carpet of sights, noises, and smells – like offerings from some seventeenth-century explorer. The insistent wind tugged Peggy's coat; Natasha, as usual, preferred style over good sense and was resplendent in one of her three outfits – a lime green skirt with a bright floral jacket. As ever, she looked dramatic and gorgeous.

As Peggy gazed from the deck, she knew that life in Derby had not prepared her for the towering concrete of the buildings on the Bund. Tash – who seemed to know all the landmarks – pointed out the Peace Hotel, the Bank of China, the Customs House, and the Cathay Mansions.

'So many Chinamen!' said her companion, pointing to the ants' nests of Chinese swarming around the docks. The men wore an assortment of clothing to protect them against the river winds: scarves, hats, and caps of every kind.

The noises, too, were unlike anything Peggy had experienced on the streets of Derby. As her ship pulled into the dock and the toiling turbines hummed and hissed into silence, their mechanical sounds were replaced by the shouts and screams of arguments on the quay below. Fidgety Chinese men, pigtails swinging, dressed in black jackets and trousers, shouted, and tussled with each other. Each man was trying to find the best spot to help disembarking passengers.

Every smell resisted definition. Peggy tried to isolate the more intrusive of the odours: Rotting garbage; industrial effluent; urine; fecal matter; sweet and sour food odours; garlic, boiled rice – an organic conflation of things eaten or released from bodies. She felt overwhelmed by the smells enveloping her – some pleasant, some revolting but all sensually potent and – there was only one word for it – exotic.

Peggy, holding her nose, turned to see Natasha standing with her eyes closed. The young emigre seemed to be inhaling every molecule of the foul air.

'Ooh, heck Tashie, you like this smelly place?' Peggy had never felt the need to speak anything other than in her normal way with her new friend. She had never tried to sound posh, as she felt she had to be with Stan's mother.

'*Bien sur, c'est fantastique!*' Natasha threw back her head, her eyes sparkling with wonder.

Peggy shook her head and laughed, 'You're a funny one.'

Tash's energy and appetite for life were undiminished, or so it seemed to Peggy. As the ship's ropes snaked to the quayside, Tash announced, 'I'm hungry for the great banquet of China.'

Peggy smiled. She loved the girl's excitement about everything, and she would miss it. Hoping the answer would be positive, she asked, 'Do you need somewhere to stay, Tash?'

'Non, merci, ma Cherie,' she smiled. 'I have family here. I will be fine, but we will see each other again, non?'

After hugs and kisses, Tash went below to get her luggage.

Peggy stayed on the deck for another quarter-hour, thoughts swirling: the journey into this vast continent had begun, and she would be voyaging with Stan into married life. She must be sure to not let marriage extinguish her; she must stay in control and yet let life live itself. And Stan: How would he be as her husband? She knew him to be a kind and gentle man. Would China change him? Would she grow to love him in the way he loved her?

She walked the deck for a few more minutes. England, her family, seemed so very far away. The thought of her aloneness made her reach for breath; she clenched and unclenched her fist. The palpitations eased.

The deck was busy with crew, and she had to weave her way between the sailors – some of whom made it clear she was in the way. Ahead, an officer snapped to attention, opened a door and gestured to the stairwell. She smiled at him, nodded, and went inside.

'CHINA STAN'
Shanghai 1937

Still on board the 'Tantalus' but packed and ready to disembark, Peggy spotted Stan on the quay, waving enthusiastically. Two months had passed since they'd seen each other – the week of the marriage.

Her new husband ran halfway up the gangplank to greet her. 'Sweet Peggy, oh, my darling, it means so much to have you with me in this wonderful city.'

She thought how healthy he looked: handsome and dashing in a way that made all men look good in uniform. His overcoat was open, and it pleased her to see that he'd lost some weight around his middle. Her apprehension of their reunion as man and wife melted when Stan wrapped his arms around her. The feel of his uniform, the rough fabric of his Navy-issue coat – the *maleness* of him dispelled some of the alarm she'd felt when the '*Tantalus*' was steering through the swarms of sampans and junk boats on the river.

They kissed briefly, both conscious of the need to clear a path for others pressing down the gangplank.

Stan seemed to know several of the Customs officials. Because of his ability – which she hadn't expected – to talk to the men in their own language, they swept through formalities, but it was still mid-afternoon by the time they emerged from the Customs Hall. Three shockingly thin men – 'coolies' Stan called them – hauled their luggage to a large car. Peggy, who knew her cars – because her brothers worked tirelessly to maintain theirs – recognised the highly polished, pearl grey vehicle as American, a Packard.

She also noticed that Stan walked briskly, business-like; the ambling pace had gone.

The Packard's uniformed driver had a broad smile. Later, Peggy would learn the smile was as permanent as his nose. The man rushed forward, ordering the three coolies to store the bags in the car's boot.

'This is Han, Peggy, our driver.' The smiling, black-clad Chinese raised his cap and bowed. He opened the car door for her.

'Sweetheart, we could have taken a taxi.'

Stan laughed. 'Pegs, you don't understand: Han is our driver; this is our car.'

She was surprised to be climbing into the large sedan. 'Do Second Mates usually have a car?' she asked. 'Don't you have to be a Captain for that? How have you've managed so well without me?' she grinned, her eyelids fluttering with every question; she was intrigued by Stan's change in status.

Her husband joined her in the warmth of the back seat. 'Actually, I look after the Packard for my boss, his nickname 'PP' are his initials – Peregrine Pennington. I'll tell you about him later – he's the one I met in London, you'll remember. He lives between here and Blighty, and he likes to have a car available. To be frank, though, he seems to take taxis when he's in Shanghai. The car is virtually ours – and Han, too.' He reached forward to tap the driver on the shoulder, 'Right, Han?' *Han* raised his thumb, 'Yes, sir.' Stan looked back at her. 'And Han speaks rather passable English, right, Han?'

'Good English, yes sir, Captain Parker.'

'Captain?' Peggy whispered. 'Since when?'

Stan shook his head and put his fingers to his lips. 'It makes Han feel good to call me that.'

Peggy arched her eyebrows. 'Hmm. And I'm sure you haven't corrected him?'

Stan winked and kissed her cheek.

The big car moved slowly through a scrum of rowdy Chinese, who were pulling rickshaws and wheelbarrows, manhandling crates, and packing cases. Their shouts were interrupted only long enough for them to hawk or spit; Peggy was reminded how distant she was from the civility of her salon.

'My God, these coolies never stop yelling!' Stan leaned across her to roll up her window, but it did little to reduce the din.

'Why do you call them that?'

'What, coolies? I honestly don't know. That's what they've always been called.' Stan leaned forward and tapped the driver's shoulder. 'Han, why do we call these chaps coolies?' he waved his hand at the men surrounding the car. Peggy noticed that he now pronounced the word 'chaps' like his father.

'Mean slave, Captain, labourer. Fetch, carry – dock man.'

Peggy frowned. 'And do the coolies mind being called 'coolie'? Don't they have names?'

Stan grunted softly. 'I doubt anyone has ever asked them their names – unless you own them?'

'Own them?' She turned to him, incredulous.

Stan pulled a face. Peggy, he remembered, had been something of an agitator for equality – often talking about how women shouldn't be in second place. Stan knew she was likely to be incensed by some local mores – the way most Europeans would refer to 'Coolie Number One' or 'Coolie Number Two' when asking their servants to perform some task – 'Coolie Number Seven, open the windows.'

He reached for her hand, anxious to put her mind at rest. 'Pegs, you'll soon understand that customs are very different here. Shanghai's a colonial outpost and, despite the outward signs of modernity – well, socially, time has stood still for the locals. You'll have to take it as you find it.'

He tried to change the subject. 'You've seen Pa? He's well?'

Peggy turned to him and nodded. 'Clew is as fit as ever. He took me to lunch the day before I left. Your mother didn't come, but that won't surprise you.'

He put his arm around her and snuggled closer. 'No, no surprises there.'

Stan remembered what his mother had said on the morning of his wedding: 'You could have done better for yourself, young man.'

While Stan discounted most of his mother's negative judgements, occasionally, he wondered if marrying a woman of equal social class might have suited him better. But what would such a woman have seen in him – a low-ranking merchant seaman, newly returned from a shady life in Shanghai?

Whereas he and Peggy had much to prove, together.

He gave her his brightest smile. 'I have to say that things *are* going rather well, ducks.' He squeezed her hand. 'When we were back home, I told you that Blue Funnel has been on these seas for more than a hundred years.' He crossed his legs, adjusting a crease as he did so. 'For instance, when I tell people I'm with Blue Funnel, I get flattering looks. The Chinese respect our firm's willingness to be with them for the long haul.' He chuckled quietly, his voice lowering, as he nodded towards *Han*. 'They seem able to overlook the fact that since the Industrial Revolution, we Brits have always had an appetite for any venture that yields a high return on capital.'

He looked at Peggy, but she was staring out of the window. He wondered if she was still mulling the last conversation, perhaps preparing a list of questions to ask him when they got to their new home.

RUMOURS OF WAR
Shanghai 1937

The crowds were thinning as the Packard moved away from the Bund and headed west. Stan pondered how much should he tell his bride about the mood in Shanghai?

Rumours of war were everywhere. It was now less a question of how much he should disclose, more a question of how much she might hear, anyway – on the streets or from other expatriates. The fears that Peggy had expressed that afternoon near Chatsworth House were crystallizing. Stan knew that, within days, his new wife would realise that she had stepped into a world – his world – that she could have avoided by not marrying him. There was little he could say or do to reassure her. What he was not ready to reveal, until surer of his information, was that today, this very afternoon – the Japanese were capable of invading, and owning, *Shanghai*.

Above the rumours roiling underground, the city remained what it had been for centuries: a place where men met to discuss business and, if adept at bluff or negotiation – depending on how you defined it – made their fortunes.

Stan lowered his shoulder so that Peggy could rest her head. Soon he felt her low breathing

The previous month – alone and frustrated that Peggy wouldn't be with him for another ten days – Stan had crossed the city to the *Hongkou* area. He was interested in visiting 'Little Tokyo', an area where most Japanese businessmen were concentrated. He'd wanted to find out how small firms handled their freight needs – maybe there would be business for his ship, the '*Shenkin*'. He was aware of the rumours that Japan's *Kempeitai*, its secret police, had agents and double agents planted in the town. He made Han drop him at the edge of the township and, in mufti, continued on foot.

He called on *Gong Husong*, a Chinese he knew he could trust. *Gong* was the brother of Able Seaman *Jiang Husong*, who worked with Stan. Big and fleshy for a Chinese, *Gong* had close-set eyes – a stereotype which, had

Stan not known him better – would have made him wary. But the man was as solid morally as he was physically; Gong was no double agent for the *Kempeitai*.

That evening, they went to a local restaurant that *Gong* knew well. The staff made a fuss of them both, delighted that their regular customer had brought a foreigner with him. They sat at a wooden table near the kitchen, which, *Gong* pointed out, was something of an honour – the reverse of western restaurants where, Stan knew, dining near the kitchen signalled low status. There was no menu. *Jiang's* brother recommended that they order steaming plates of *xiaolong bao*, with sides of boiled *bok choy*. Stan nodded approvingly; it was not a time to argue about food, and, anyway, he liked *bok choy*.

Gong's giant frame engulfed a wooden stool as he sat down. A log fire blazed in a corner, but they both kept on their coats. The steamy, aromatic food soon warmed their vitals. Stan used chopsticks to lower the pork-filled dumpling into a sauce and then, also with chopsticks – Stan had always found this part difficult – he opened the top of the dumpling and poured in more of the sauce from a small porcelain spoon. For every single dumpling Stan manoeuvred into his mouth, he saw *Gong* demolish three.

'I have bad news,' the Chinese said, speaking Mandarin as he chewed his fourth dumpling. Stan waited while the big man took several gulps of his beer, brewed by the Germans near *Tsingtao*. 'This,' *Gong* said, holding up the bottle, already half-empty, 'is giving me many secrets. Last week, I eat here with senior Japanese naval officer, Matsui Komamato. We drink many bottles, but he is small man, and I am...' he hesitated, smiled, 'how you say,' he broke into English, '... big ferrow. Beer take long time to make my head crazy.' He reverted to Mandarin. 'But Matsui get crazy very quick. He tells me good news for him, bad news for...' he pointed to Stan and then *Gong* tapped his own chest. 'Matsui say Japanese will own Shanghai by summer.' He reached for his fifth dumpling.

'Around August, then? We have maybe a few months?'

Gong shrugged, 'Maybe August. He just say by summer.'

Gong ordered more beers and two heaped plates of shrimp. The tiny shrimp were followed by large bowls of rice; Stan knew that rice, traditionally, was served at the end of the meal to ensure that no guest left the table hungry.

Shortly before eleven o'clock, Stan paid the small bill, and they left.

As he walked back to his rooming house, having decided to avoid the ostentation of a hotel, Stan realised that his own contact – *Gong Husong* in *Hangkou* – had better sources than Chinese Army Intelligence.

The following day, back in the city, Stan told Rollo Vigne at the British Consulate about his conversations with *Gong* in Little Tokyo. 'Oh, let them have a go at each other,' said Vigne. 'It's just Jap on Chink, nothing to do with us.'

Stan, appalled by the man's insouciance and casually expressed racism, telegraphed his findings to his London boss. In a rare moment of censure PP, who had been irritated to learn of Stan's trip to Little Tokyo, telegraphed back, 'stick to your knitting, old chap. Such matters are so far above your paygrade, they have snow on top.'

Chastened but determined to nourish his budding interest in geopolitics, Stan understood the Chinese and Japanese had been sharing the same city for years – there were twenty thousand Japanese residents in *Shanghai*. He knew that the Japanese felt so secure that their Navy had moored its armoured Japanese cruiser, the *Izumo*, on the *Huangpu* River. The crew – and Stan thought this weird – had joined crews on a neighbouring French flagship by celebrating Bastille night with Japanese fireworks.

Shanghai locals thought such behaviour normal, but in the face of it, how could he convince Peggy that, despite apparent serenity, life would become more dangerous? How could war break out when two ancient enemies were sharing the same city? Most importantly, how could he give her an explanation of why the tectonic plates of Far East politics were shifting beneath them?

Officially, it was accepted that the two races would have to engage militarily as they struggled for dominance in the city. The Chinese knew that the Japanese had already conquered *Beijing* and *Nanjing*. But would their ancient enemy dare to storm *Shanghai* – the fifth largest city in the world?

To Stan, the situation was made more perilous by the fact that the Chinese themselves were divided. Nationalist leader *Chiang Kai-shek* had instituted gradual modernizing reforms to unify China. But in the countryside, he was confronted by *Mao Tse-tung's* Communist thugs. In dozens of villages – with Moscow's backing – his Red Army was starting to sew dissent among the farm workers. *Mao* played what he'd heard

Pennington call 'a long game'; a country as vast and as dispersed as China could not be changed in a year or two. The first job was to make the peasants aware that society could be changed, but it would take time and their willing co-operation.

Chiang's challenge as one of the two great leaders of China was to divide his attention between the other leader, *Mao*, and the Japanese, who were acquiring more territory and power every day.

At some point, *Mao* and his ally, *Chou en-lai*, realised the growing threat from Japan. The warring Chinese agreed to an uneasy truce with *Chiang*, deciding there was little point in fomenting a civil war between them when the prize – China itself – was hijacked by their mutual foe, the Japanese.

As ever, politics was creating odd bedfellows.

In the stew of these events, Stan sensed the political and military temperature rising. Nor did he or his expatriate friends applaud the appointment of Chamberlain as British prime minister. Stan worried that Chamberlain's resistance to confrontation and his misreading of Hitler's intentions to dominate Europe – coupled with America's isolationist policies – could leave *Shanghai* on its own, at the edge of the world.

Stan thought these incidents underscored the artificiality of the situation in *Shanghai*; to him, it didn't add up. How could he begin to explain these bizarre events to his bride?

But with this bright, beautiful woman at his side, Stan decided it would be unfair to share these fears with her. He would continue to stress the positive side of life in a city that, he could sense, was already working its magic on her.

THE PARKER HOUSE
Shanghai 1937

Stan turned in his seat, gently moving Peggy's chin towards him. He kissed her softly on the lips. Her eyeballs, when her eyelids fluttered open, were red with disturbed sleep.

'Darling, you must try to stay awake, or you will never sleep tonight.' He squeezed her hand. 'Let me tell you about our new home.'

Peggy sat up, her attention sparked. 'Ooh, yes, please.'

'Well, I'm not going to spoil any surprises, but I think you'll be rather chuffed with our digs – they're a bit of a step up from HMS Conway.'

She sighed. 'Oo, er, I shan't forget those trips to Liverpool to see you on that ruddy awful training ship.' Stan paused, reminding himself she'd have to rid herself of those provincial responses. He smiled.

'Well, my darling, you'll know you've earned your reward the moment you see our new domestic arrangements. They're another example of how well the firm treats its incoming people.' He winked at her. 'Even the desk pilots at our Shanghai office treat the naval men with deference. For example, I have a shoreside batman.'

'A what?'

'Exactly. A fellow at the office who takes care of anything you or I need – like a butler.' As she shook her head, he continued, 'His name is Hopton.'

'Weren't you at school with a Hopton?'

'God, your memory! But no, that was Heesom – though Hopton reminds me of some of the boys at Repton. Hopton's a pimply, moon-faced man in his late twenties, with a rather unfortunate chin. He's a scholarship boy from Teesside and quite proud of it, I'd say. The man's always blinking – a bit like Stan Laurel – you know, the thin one from Laurel and Hardy? He has those oyster eyes, his nose hairs need clipping, bad haircut; his clothes smell of nicotine, and his breath…' Stan paused to draw in a breath '… could stop a train.'

'Does he have a wife? Sounds as though he needs a wife to take care of those details, as I do with you, my darling.'

Stan snorted and squeezed her hand, 'I've coped rather well without one, haven't you noticed? But I doubt Hopton has a wife – he's what nowadays they call a confirmed bachelor.'

Stan said that he'd soon detected the source of Hopton's nicotine odour: a smoking Meerschaum pipe. 'He got the habit at Malvern – his scholarship got him there. Seems the school permitted the prefects to smoke, but it was never encouraged.'

Peggy smiled. 'Boys playing at being men.'

'Exactly.' Stan paused and leaned forward. 'Another fifteen minutes, Han?'

'Yes, Captain, fifteen-minute, chop-chop.'

'Chop-chop?'

'Cantonese for 'hurry, hurry' – very important words in China.' He grinned. 'Anyway, I asked Hopton a bit about the house: he said the fellow who designed our house was a Bavarian, Joshua Madel, a German Jew. Madel knew that Nazis didn't believe a Jew could be a German – Arab versus Aryan, and all that. Far-thinking Jews came to China to get away from the Third Reich; they were given a haven by the Sassoons – Baghdadi Jews themselves – and people like Madel made new futures here.'

Peggy interrupted him. 'And that's part of why I didn't want to leave my family. Remember our argument at Chatsworth? Now Germany is getting ready for war: rounding up Jews, making them wear armbands.' She shook her head in disgust. 'God knows...' her voice trailed away.

Stan considered that this was a moment when he might share some of his misgivings about *Shanghai*. He decided there would be a better time.

***

The Packard was now free of the crowds and was picking up speed along a tree-lined boulevard, the car's suspension gliding them over bumps and potholes.

A few seconds later, *Han* spoke, 'One minute to go, Captain.'

Stan whispered in her ear. 'I'll be frank, Peg, I *do* feel uncomfortable with the level of attention I'm receiving here. All this palaver – the house, the car, the driver – seem more than a Second Mate deserves. On the other hand...' he arched his eyebrows and pulled his mouth down, as if to say, 'why argue?'

'Well, your pa did say life here would be better for us.'

'Yes, but this,' he spread his hands out. 'It's invigorating, certainly, and wait until you see the house they've given us.'

'No buts, darling. All you or, rather, *we* must prove, is we're worth it.'

The Packard swung into a circular driveway. 'Home, Captain.'

Peggy, stepping out of the car, was stunned by the size of the property, which looked wonderfully grand in its architectural permanence, imperially white in its confident stance. There seemed to be a mass of windows – always her way of gauging size – four at ground level and six on the upper two levels. Behind her, she heard Stan say, 'thank God for servants, eh?'

Overwhelmed, she could only follow Stan when he took her through the rooms: a living room, study, dining room, five bedrooms, and three bathrooms. Then Stan – speaking Mandarin, she assumed – introduced her to a team of five servants who, in addition to *Han,* the driver, would run her household: an *amah,* houseboy, cook and two gardeners. They all stood to attention when they bowed to her in the biggest kitchen she'd ever seen.

Peggy had barely caught her breath before Stan swept her upstairs and uncorked a bottle of champagne; he appeared to do the act with a flair that suggested it was something he did every evening.

She looked at him over her glass of champagne. 'Why does this evening have the quality of a dream? Please don't pinch me, Stan, because I want it to last forever.'

They were standing on a verandah that led off their large bedroom. The wind had dropped, and the air had warmed. Twilight had brought out the fireflies; they sparked elusively in the soft air. Derby seemed another existence.

'Oh, Stan: I can't believe the change in you since we left Derby.' She threw her arms around him. 'And now the change in our life – all this. Heavens! What does Blue Funnel do for you when you make Captain?'

'It's this country, my love. I'm back in my water – or the China sea, to be more accurate. This I where I was born to be.'

She laughed, "and this is how I was born to live.'

That night Stanley was sweet and understanding of her fatigue as they embraced in a huge bed.

WAITING
Shanghai 1942

Leaving the Parker house to the Japanese invaders, Peggy led her small entourage across Bubbling Well Road towards her neighbours, the Trenchers. As always, she was aware of the giant camphor trees, standing like charcoal sentinels. She wondered when she would stand again under their summer shade.

Sometimes, when the wind was pungent with river smells from the Huangpu, Peggy could hear the exuberance of the crowds in the Nanking Road. This morning, though, the silence sat like a cat.

Peggy joined her neighbours in a small bus shelter on the other side of the road. Tom's wife wiggled her wheelchair to make a space for Peggy and Zahn, who was holding Jonny. The two garden boys held on to the trunk, their faces troubled.

As soon as he saw Peggy, Tom Trencher exploded with anger. 'My God! And you, too?'

Peggy nodded. 'They burst in an hour ago. I'd been given some warning by Vigne at the Consulate; I didn't realise they were evacuating the entire Settlement. The soldiers allowed me one trunk plus a few bits and pieces. Again, they gave no explanation, other than to say that, because they had won the war, everything now belonged' she raised an eyebrow, 'to the glorious Nipponese people.' She turned to Zhang, giving her a small smile. 'They told me my staff would have to stay, except Jonny's amah, Zhang.'

'Any indication of where they were taking you - us?'

Peggy shrugged. 'The colonel said we were being taken to a place called a civilian assembly centre.' She paused. 'And he took our British passports.'

'Christ-on-a-bike!' Tom swore. 'My God, I can't believe this is happening.'

Peggy raised her hand, suggesting that the two gardeners should go. The young men put down the trunk, gave a deep bow to their mistress, and set off at a lope towards the city centre. She wanted to hug and thank the young men for their loyalty, but she knew that such displays of affection between employer and employees was forbidden. Of all her staff, she would miss 'the garden twins' – as she called them – the most. They shared her love of everything growing and green; they had been raised in such a place – a remote tea plantation in the low hanging fog of Hunan.

'Not sure your coolies will be any safer in the city,' Trencher was saying as he looked at the retreating figures. 'The Nips are everywhere. Maybe looking alike will spook the Japs – put a jinx on whoever kills them, ha!' He barked his staccato laugh.

Peggy didn't smile. 'Not all Chinese are 'coolies', Tom; you can't put them all into the same box. Would you do that to Americans? The twins were my gardeners and very respectful – as we were with them.'

Her neighbour snorted. 'Of course, Peggy.' He smiled at her indulgently and turned away but not before she saw his raised eyebrows.

Chao-xing, Trencher's much younger Chinese wife, reached for Jonny. The toddler gurgled and made a noise that sounded like 'ching-ching' as he held up his arms for her. In the summer, when Peggy permitted it, *Zhang* took Jonny to the Trencher's house where the toddler and the childless Chinese played for an hour on the sunlit lawn.

Peggy looked across at Tom, walking in a small circle, kicking snow impatiently. After meeting him for the first time at her friend Natasha's party, Peggy had tried to like the middle-aged American and, while she had respected his willingness to stay with his handicapped wife, she always felt uneasy in his company. She had soon realised that Tom was an unpleasantly ambitious man. She'd decided that the American resented Stan's 'Britishness', his chauffeur-driven car, their larger house and all the things that Americans – she assumed – saw as evidence of status. And most annoying of all, she suspected, might be Tom's realisation that such symbols seemed little to Stan.

Peggy bent down to kiss *Chao-xing*, already snuggling with Jonny. 'Peggy,' she said, and smiled sweetly as if this wasn't a day that likely would change their lives profoundly. Peggy wondered if *Chao-xing* would ever lose her Buddhist composure.

More flurries of snow began to fall. Peggy looked up, her eyes streaming in the cold air; through a glazed film she saw a sky of dull grey, stretched tight against the chance of sun. Tom cut into her thoughts.

'Christ, this brass-monkey weather is freezing my blood; I swear my goddam circulation has stopped.' Almost casually, he added, 'Stan not back yet?'

'No. He only left a few days ago. Otherwise, he would be here with me, don't you think, Tom?'

'Does that mean Stan has swapped sides?' Tom's curt question brought her back to the present.

Alarm flushed her face. 'What do you mean?'

Trencher looked away as he spoke. 'We know he was training the Japanese. He mentioned he might at that dinner we had at the Palace hotel.'

Peggy felt *Chao-xing*'s eyes on her. There was a short silence before Tom continued: 'Pennington, his liaison, boss – whatever you call him – told our people about the "training";' Peggy could hear the parenthesis in his voice. 'I mean, we're supposed to be allies, right? We appreciated the information. But to us at the American Consulate – Stan helping Ohta Tang?' The question hung while Trencher paused. 'Pegs, it's obvious that the Nips are not going to let Stan back into Shanghai – especially when they realise he's betrayed…'

'*Betrayed?*' Peggy felt her cheeks burning. 'What's that supposed to mean?'

Tom continued, his voice soothing. 'I was about to say "betrayed them – in a way – because that's how Stan's disappearance could seem to the Japanese. One minute he's there, training them, then he's gone. The thing is, Peggy, your husband has got himself stuck between two stools and – hey, I don't like to say this – maybe he's fallen into the stool between.'

'Wait a minute, Tom. Stan left about four days ago. It's not unusual for him to be away – often for two weeks.'

Peggy felt too angry to say more. But Trencher continued to speculate.

'Look, Pegs, Stan must have known that you might be interned – that's always been on the cards. The Blue Funnel Line was put in mothballs last month, the staff repatriated on Blue Funnel ships. Any staff that stayed behind will be interned.' He gave her a puzzled look. 'But your Stanley seems to have disappeared just as hell broke loose. Good timing, no?' His watery blue eyes searched her face. 'Does he *know* what happened this morning? Do you – do we – even know where he is?'

Peggy's voice rose. 'How could he know what's happened? He's away on a trip and, as per protocol, he couldn't tell me more. How could he know we'd be invaded – God, evicted – today? Don't be ridiculous, Tom.'

'Pegs, he works for Admiral Tang. You mean to tell me that Tang wouldn't tell Stan about the evictions – so that he could alert his family.'

Peggy drew her breath in; Trencher had a point.

Tom nodded vigorously with the certainty of his next words: 'I'll tell you why: because the man who controls all Japanese forces south of Peking has no idea of the whereabouts of Stanley Parker.'

'How do you know that?'

'Let's just say I'm sure he doesn't know.' He gave her a grim look, conveying, 'it's obvious.'

In fact, Tom was not sure, but the likely story was that *Tang* hadn't been able to reach the Englishman. That would be why Peggy received no warning of the invasion of the Settlement.

What were the Brits up to? This was why Washington distrusted them – always off on little adventures, trying to prove an independence of action that they didn't have. What could Stan have dreamed up that was so important he would leave his wife and child to the mercies of the enemy?

Peggy was wondering how much Tom knew. Why was Trencher questioning Stan's patriotism? Surely it must be more than a clash of male egos? And he'd be annoyed that Stan's activities excluded him. She reminded herself that Tom envied her husband's progress, despite his lack of academic credentials. But Peggy had decided – from the moment she arrived in the city that, despite his father's quiet patronage and her own encouragement – that 'China Stan' was a self-made man.

She stepped closer to Trencher, resisting the temptation to stick a finger in his chest. 'Why are you talking about betrayal, Tom? As far as Stan is concerned, he's just doing another job for Blue Funnel.' She drew a deep breath. 'I can't see *you* training fifteen Japanese officers for six weeks.' She paused. 'That takes a certain kind of Englishman.' She stressed the last word as she looked into Trencher's eyes, untroubled by their blueness. 'I know my husband, and I know he would never do anything dishonourable. I'm sure he helped the Japanese because he knew that if he didn't train them, his competitors – Jardine's – would.'

She paused before giving him a hard look. 'As an American, you must appreciate commercial necessity more than most.'

'But you weren't happy about it.'

'In what way?' Peggy sensed that Tom was determined to continue needling her.

Jonny's whining broke the tension. He wanted his bottle, and he knew where to find it. He waved one arm at *Zhang,* 'Mook? Mook?' The two Chinese women passed the boy between them, and the *amah*, holding the toddler close, gave Jonny his formula. Tom's wife had kept the bottle warm in her coat.

Tom would not be distracted by Jonny's contented sounds. 'Ma'am, it was clear that night – what, five or six months ago – when we all dined at the Palace – that Stan's plan to train the Japanese was all news to you.' Peggy saw a smirk flash across his face. He looked down at his wife, who was watching them. 'I said to Chao-xing as we left the hotel, that I'd like to be a fly on the wall when the two of you got home.' His wife, who hadn't missed a word of their exchange, nodded. Tom pressed on. 'But I guess you kowtowed.' He used the Chinese word for obeyed. 'You knew that Stan would do what was needed to advance his career.' He shook his head and stepped away.

Peggy thought, 'I was right: this is what it's about – pathetic male envy.'

Tom had become engrossed in the hedge bordering the pavement. He pulled a leaf from the privet and appeared to study it.

After a moment, *Chao-xing* tried to break the tension: 'As I say, you will make your peace about not seeing your husband again.'

Peggy shook her head vigorously. 'Nonsense, Chao-xing! Of course, I shall see him again. He hasn't abandoned us.' As she said the words, her mouth was dry with suppressed panic; she was thinking, 'of course, Stan has abandoned us.' But she was saying to *Chao-xing:* 'He will find us. Stan knows what he must do. And when he's done it, and this wretched war is over, we shall be together again.' She stopped, doubt flaring. 'Maybe before,' she added, more to herself.

Chao-xing closed her eyes and steepled her fingers. Peggy thought, 'if you start chanting, I'll smack you.'

She wedged her cloche hat tighter, trying to cover her ears so that the vice-like cold wouldn't bring a migraine or worse. She watched Trencher kneel in front of *Zhang*. Jonny, content again after his milk, giggled as Tom tickled his nose with the leaf.

Trencher stood and looked up the road to the East. Without glancing at the quartet huddled on the bench, he said, 'And so we wait for whatever it is to take us to wherever we're going.'

A MAJESTIC BALL
Shanghai 1937

Peggy soon adjusted to her new life, and to Stan's frequent absences. His freighter steamed up and down the coast for a week or ten days, and then Stan would be home again, always bringing her a gift.

At one point, she had to say, 'Please, Stan, no more rice bowls! We could entertain an army with our crockery.' Next, he'd bring her Chinese fans in bright colours until she said, 'I have to be with you if you buy me a fan, love.' Finally, she said, 'Stan, darling, it's enough that you come back to me; really, that's all I want.' Touched by her remark, he stopped bringing gifts.

As the days became warmer, Peggy explored the neighbourhood on foot and rickshaw, or with *Han* in the Packard. She visited scores of little shops, the financial lifeblood of the city, on the Nanjing Road. On these trips, she was intrigued by the banners hanging from every store front – 'says name of store, Missy,' explained *Han*.

Peggy relished the appetite-arousing smell of foods, hearing the shouts of hundreds of Chinese hustling at their store fronts, or running helter-skelter through the streets. At times, the *foreignness* of Shanghai overwhelmed her. Derby was the only city she had known; if she'd come from London, she may have been less dazzled by its novelty. And, for the first time in her life, she became aware of how the colour of her skin set her apart from 'the natives' as Stan, much to her dismay, occasionally called the Chinese. Although the locals stood to one side when she approached – a custom that embarrassed her – she also knew that, without their deference, she would have made no headway. After an hour, exhausted, she would reunite at an agreed spot with *Han*. He beamed, always relieved when he saw her.

Three weeks after she'd arrived, Stan asked her if she'd be interested in taking elocution lessons.

She cocked her head. 'Why, what's the matter with the way I talk?'

He hugged her. 'I love your Derbyshire accent, ducky. Here, people are from everywhere. Being from the north of England is no crime.' He paused, and she could see him searching for words; she wondered if he was trying to be diplomatic.

'Well, I never thought of myself as a criminal.' She raised an eyebrow to let him know she was teasing.

'It's more to do with expressions.'

'Like?'

'Like "bloomin' heck" and words like "ruddy nuisance" and "bloody hell".'

'I've never said, "bloody hell"!'

He hugged her closer and chuckled. 'No, you haven't, darling. But I think it's only a matter of time.'

'Sounds as if you think those expressions make me working-class.'

Stan looked puzzled. 'The fact that your people are working class is nothing to be ashamed of.'

'I'm not ashamed,' she snapped. 'Better than sitting on your bum and living off what your parents or grandparents have chiselled out of poor people.'

He released her. She saw him shake his hands in the air, feigning helplessness as he walked away

Two days later, Peggy received an envelope addressed to 'Second Mate Stanley Parker and Mrs. Parker.' She saw the Blue Funnel Crest and opened the envelope. She removed a thick, embossed card that read:

The Directors of Blue Funnel Line invite
Second Mate Stanley Parker and Mrs. Parker
to a Spring Ball at the Majestic Hotel
on the second day of April,
one thousand nine hundred and thirty-seven.

Peggy had never seen an invitation so formal. She took deep breaths. This would be her first exposure to *Shanghai*'s high society. After Stan had told her that her accent needed some changes, she was at once nervous and thrilled as she studied the invitation. They would be at the ball together – Stan told her he would be 'shoreside' that week. He guessed he'd also be on the lookout for any missteps.

Briefly, she considered how their relationship was changing; now she was the uncertain one, depending on Stan to tell her how to behave. Part of her understood why that made sense, but part of her also resented it.

During her first week in the city, exploring the area around the Bund, *Han* had driven her along some of the neighbouring streets, or '*lus*'. Peggy remembered passing a towering building; 'Majestic Hotel. Famous,' *Han* had said without further explanation. The hotel stretched across several blocks.

Peggy had read as much as she could about *Shanghai* as soon as she arrived in the city. She was well versed in the lore of the Majestic Hotel. In 1924 a Spanish architect had converted a large house – owned by a European who had the Shell concession for China – into one of the world's leading hotels.

Within months, the massive ballroom became the heart of *Shanghai*'s social set. At various times, the hotel drew famous guests like Charlie Chaplin and *Chiang Kai-shek*, who made the hotel the venue for his wedding ball.

Within weeks, Peggy fell in love with her new pulsating city. *Shanghai*, with its smells, its noises, its people, spoke to Peggy in a language that the locals couldn't – or didn't care – to hear.

At the same time, the young woman from Derbyshire – almost subconsciously – was refashioning herself. 'Yes, Peggy Parker,' she'd say when introducing herself, liking the way the words rolled off her tongue. 'From England,' she'd reply. If they were English and probed, she might add, 'I grew up on the Chatsworth estate.'

As they dressed before the ball, Peggy swirled around in a new powder blue gown, 'And now I shall be dancing at The Majestic – in the ballroom where Douglas Fairbanks and Mary Pickford dared to do the Charleston; where Charlie Chaplin and Paulette Goddard waltzed while her mother chaperoned.'

She turned to her husband and saw his small smile.

'Golly, Pegs, you soak up everything. How do you know all this stuff?'

'You're just like my family, Stan. They'd say, 'You've always got your ruddy head in a book.' She paused; her one eyebrow raised: 'That's how I know all these things.'

Stan was easing into the jacket of his dress uniform. She felt a rush of affection for him. Crossing the room, she kissed him on the nose. 'Oh Stan, thank you for this wonderful new life you've given us.'

He frowned. 'I want you to be happy, Peggy, that's all. Then I can do my job without worrying.'

As Peggy fixed her hair, she wondered when Stan had become so serious about himself. At times, he seemed almost arrogant and needed very little reassurance from her on any topic. But she asked herself: wasn't that what she had hoped for? Part of her admired his newfound firmness; another part of her resented that his independence lessened his dependence on her.

And Stan seemed to know so much about China – she guessed that's why she'd heard some people refer to him as 'China Stan'. His occasional asides on history or current affairs quickly turned into monologues that could have a dampening effect – on company, or even on a rare supper for two in the French Quarter. Had they been in Derby, she would have said something, but she'd decided she wouldn't subtract anything from his new confidence.

She wondered if Stan missed her when he was at sea. He never said so, and his new, off-hand attitude was a marked contrast to how he had admired and complimented her before they were married. In small ways, she noticed that his need of her was waning – 'just a tiny bit', she reassured herself. Their lovemaking had diminished, which didn't trouble her as she'd always found the sex side of their marriage an ordeal. Stan's behaviour in this and other respects, she supposed, was the natural evolution of their marriage. 'But' she thought, 'we've only been married four months; isn't it a bit early for that?'

In a letter to Connie, she had tried to give her sister some impressions of *Shanghai*. She'd also mentioned that Stan seemed to depend on her less.

'They're all lovely, to begin with,' Connie replied. Unable to imagine a life so far from the familiar, and she hardly commented on *Shanghai*. She reserved her thoughts for the change Peggy saw in Stan. Her sister had said she was planning to marry a man named Ernest Palmer, a textile designer, and she had no illusions about the fickleness of men: 'I mean, soon as I accepted his proposal,' she wrote, 'it was as if Ernie clicked off a switch marked Marry Constance Steele. He just gave up.' She added a PS: 'Remember how he wrote those poems to me? Now he's off 'avin' pints down at the working man's club.'

An hour later, she and Stan stood at the edge of the Majestic's vast dance floor. Peggy was daydreaming; she was imagining *Chang Kai-shek* and his new bride mingling with their one thousand wedding guests in the same room.

Champagne glass in hand, Stan drew her back to the present. He was nodding towards an overweight, middle-aged man hurrying towards them. 'Here comes the director who interviewed me in London. The man with the Packard. I told you that he's the one who lets us use his car. He's regarded as a big man on the China coast – the title they give to anyone of consequence – Peregrine Pennington. That's why he's called PP.'

'That's rather unfortunate,' said Peggy, with a giggle brought on by her third glass of champagne. Stan didn't smile.

Peregrine Pennington marched up to her. The Englishman had a broad, meaty face, a moustache, and big ears. Unusually large and ravaged by rosacea, his nose defined him. In days to come, talking to Stan, she'd sometimes refer to Pennington as, 'the man with the rosy proboscis.'

At that moment, she was thinking, 'So this is Stan's godfather, the man his father connived with to bring Stan into Blue Funnel – my co-conspirator.'

Pennington's eyes were small, fudge-coloured. Now, she felt those eyes measuring her.

'My dear young lady, may I introduce myself? Peregrine Pennington – I'm Stan's godfather, as he's doubtless told you.' He beamed. 'I insist you call me PP. And let me say immediately how thrilled we are to have you join the Blue Funnel family.' His moustache jumped up and down as he talked. She noticed that, even when he wasn't talking, it quivered.

Pennington made a deep bow and turned to Stan. 'My dear godson, what a ravishing bride you've brought with you.' The older man again scanned Peggy up and down with a look just short of bold.

Peggy smiled sweetly at Pennington. 'I came of my own accord, I promise you. The opportunity was too good to miss.'

'Ah ha! That's the way to think. Say 'yes' to everything. Excellent, excellent. Shall we dance, Mrs. Parker – may I call you Peggy?'

'Of course, PP!' she beamed. He led her onto the dance floor at speed. She wondered if he had a dance card and a certain number of wives to accommodate in one evening.

They had taken no more than two dozen steps of a foxtrot before Pennington said, 'Well, my dear, Shanghai: Thoughts?'

Peggy's attention at that moment was on 'PPs' bushy moustache, which seemed to be a landing strip for something tiny and green; she hoped it was part of an olive.

'Thoughts. Yes, Mr. Pennington.'

'Oh, please, PP.' He tipped his head and winked.

Peggy summoned a serious look. 'PP, sir, I've never lived in such a grand house as the one you've given us...' Pennington smiled self-deprecatingly. She looked around '... and this hotel's not too shabby, either.' She saw Stan's boss look puzzled and realised he didn't understand the turn of phrase. 'I mean it's, it's wonderful. I've read so much about it. I can't believe I'm here – dancing where Douglas Fairbanks danced.'

Pennington gave a wry grin. 'Well, I'm no Douglas Fairbanks, of course, although you are a more than pleasing substitute for Mary Pickford.' He punctuated his remark with a huge guffaw before swinging her around and heading in the other direction. 'No, my dear, actually I meant what do you think of Shanghai, your husband's posting, etcetera? Can we do anything for you?'

Not waiting for an answer, Pennington pressed on, 'Stan has been on post for only three or four months, Peggy. He came out here on my recommendation, but already he stands out. Do you know why?' Peggy sensed that he was not expecting her to answer. 'The quality that makes your Stanley exceptional,' he went on, 'is his ability to get the best out of the Chinks.'

He paused to lead her through a corner turn. 'I say, your footwork, madam: truly outstanding; ha, ha.' His face was pink with exertion. She could see the dampness on his shirt front.

'You must know Clew, his father? He had the same gift, an extraordinary ability – even as a Commodore – to get on with men of any colour or rank. That's how I met him, as a young trainee in Singapore. Absolute charmer, Clew, and a Damn. Fine. Officer.' He punched out the last three words in case she might question Clew Parker's character. PP executed another turn with more flair than was necessary.

'Well, with your Stanley, the little fellers over here respect the fact that he's already been on the China coast – off and on – for, what, almost twenty years? No wonder they call him 'China Stan'. Most importantly, he can speak fluent Cantonese *and* Mandarin – which is more than most of us can say.' He chuckled and leaned into her in a discomfiting way. 'I've always believed that God is an Englishman, and if you shout loud enough in English, well...' he paused '... Johnny Foreigner should jump, what?'

He pulled her towards him again and his body odour, though faint, was disagreeable.

Pennington was almost whispering again as he said, 'We're watching Stan carefully. In fact, we're giving him every chance to hasten his progress. And I can tell you that his flexibility in languages extends to his sensible approach to any new challenges – if he sees that something will work, he will, as they say nowadays, 'have a go.' He grinned. 'In that sense, you are a good match. Stan's openness to new ventures is a formidable gift, and I suspect you have it, too. Such talents are useful to the firm in strange times such as these.'

At that moment, Peggy was wondering if Pennington's expectations justified the fact that Stan was not being treated like any other Second Mate. She suspected there was another agenda, but she had no idea what it might be; there were too many 'perks' being lavished on them both and Stan – as far as she was aware after less than three months in *Shanghai* – had not done enough to warrant them. She had been with her husband long enough to guess that 'a word' had been whispered to someone high up at Blue Funnel's London headquarters. Peggy was sure that Clew Parker, the Commodore, would not countenance his son falling short in front of his former colleagues. She had a good idea that Stan had been set up to succeed.

Well, if that were so, Clew could depend on her to do her bit.

The music ended, and, by coincidence or design, they found themselves in front of Stan. In the five or so minutes they'd been dancing, a small group had gathered around her husband.

'I say,' said Pennington, loud enough for the people to hear, 'It looks as though we might have missed China Stan giving a talk on local customs.'

Stan beamed at them and opened his arm so Peggy could snuggle against him. 'Not at all, sir. I was just explaining the etymology of the word 'coolie'. Peggy asked me to explain it on the very day she landed in Shanghai. I looked it up and was telling these chaps about it.'

Pennington frowned, looking at Peggy. 'Coolies? Not something you should worry your pretty head about, my dear.'

Something in PP's tone irritated Peggy. She hated to be patronised, and here again, it was happening. Should she speak? Did the fact of being Stan's wife render her silent on a topic that had nagged her for weeks?

She took Stan's hand from her waist, holding it tight as she looked around the group. Then she focused on Stan's boss.

'Mr. Pennington, don't you find that a lot of the people in the Settlement – and I don't exclude us – think the Chinese are not worth tuppence – Coolie Numbers One, Two and Three – heck, they don't even have *names*. People seem to treat them like a bunch of peasants. But from what I've seen so far, the Chinese keep the whole ruddy thing afloat – even though the Japanese are at their bloody throats.'

'Well, no one trusts the Japs,' said one of the men in the group.

Peggy nodded. 'Fair enough. Who does? I'm sorry, I didn't get your name…?'

The man shook his head, clearly not wanting to identify himself to the VIP from London. Peggy saw his partner tug at his elbow and thought, 'we shan't hear much more from him.'

Stan's hand was tightening in hers as she talked. She became aware that her voice was relapsing into her Derbyshire accent.

'I can understand their distrust of the *Japanese*,' she stressed the last word to show she disliked the way they were spoken of as Japs. She again addressed Pennington directly. 'But I wonder, sir, do they trust us, their colonial masters – as I've heard us called?'

The group looked to Pennington for a response. The man looked uncomfortable and touched his moustache. Stan may have sensed the tension because he deflected the question. Looking at his godfather, he said 'This is all new to my lovely bride, sir. The concept of master/servant is something she's never encountered before.' He turned and beamed at her, but Peggy saw his eyes: Stan was seething.

Pennington spoke, and all eyes moved to him. 'Stan's right, of course. Some people can be a little patronising, although I'd wager they're not even conscious of it.' He paused. Peggy noticed his eyes were not on her but moved between Stan and the group. 'I would say,' he spoke slowly, 'that the term master/servant connotes a difference in social levels,' he pushed out his chest as he added, 'which, of course, is unignorable.' He paused. 'But I would suggest that "teacher/pupil" might be more accurate.'

Peggy said, 'I see, so our one-thousand-year culture has much to teach a three-thousand-year culture?'

Pennington's cheeks were flushed. Like spectators at Wimbledon, the group had looked back and forth during the exchange. Pennington drew himself up and said, 'I don't know what they taught you at your local school, dear Peggy, but English civilization didn't start with William the Conqueror.' Peggy again noticed how his eyes avoided her. Pennington nodded, said, 'Stan', and left.

Peggy could almost feel the hush as the group started to disperse. In less than a minute, she and Stan were left standing alone. Peggy yearned for a friendly face, if only Natasha was here.

Stan dropped her hand. 'We should talk.'

'For heaven's sake, Pegs. He's my bloody boss. You can't sound off to senior people in Shanghai as if you're gossiping at your salon.' They began to walk towards the bar.

Peggy took some deep breaths, acknowledging the anger rising in her body. She took a glass of champagne.

'Maybe you've had enough?'

'I've had enough of being treated like a naughty ten-year-old,' she shot back before gulping her drink. Beneath her anger, though, was the sickening feeling that she had failed. She should not have spoken as she did. She had annoyed Pennington, and she had embarrassed Stan. She had learned enough in the last few weeks to interpret the meaning of 'the Company line'; in future, she, too, had to 'hold the line'.

'Peggy, I told you on the first day: things are different here. People behave differently.'

He put a hand on her arm and, through tight lips, said: 'Come, others are looking at us.' His arm circled her waist. 'Now dance with me, and we'll try to look like any young married couple who are still madly in love.' He squeezed her waist, but she knew she'd hear more about how to behave as Mrs. Stanley Parker.

Two hours later, as she took off her gown in their bedroom, she said, 'Stan: remember when I told you I would never be one of those women who would freeze you out because of some imagined hurt; and that you would always know what I thought because I would tell you?'

'Uh, oh – what's coming?' Stan said.

'Seriously, darling, I feel I failed you tonight, and I want to be sure you can make it up with Pennington.'

'If there's an apology in there somewhere, I accept it. But Peggy, PP's an old buffer with antiquated ideas. Yes, it's important that I stay on his right side. It's also important that he likes you and sees you supporting me. As for the others in that group? Look: expats are the worst kind of snobs; I've heard people say that lots of them know they wouldn't have been successful in London, New York, or Paris, so they came to Shanghai. Now they lord it over new people – not just the Chinese – and pretend they are their social betters. It's all rubbish, of course. But …' He started to take off his shoes.

Peggy said, 'but it's important that I'm seen to be supporting you. And that's why I want to return to the matter of self-improvement.'

'Ghastly American term.'

'That's as maybe, but I realise you were right: I need to work at my accent and – oh, so many other things.'

Stan smiled, crossed the room, and hugged her as she stood in her satin slip. He nuzzled her. 'Oh, this is… so nice.'

And so began a series of coaching sessions with a former English teacher named Lance Hoblock from Harrow school. It was open knowledge that Hoblock had been asked to leave Harrow under mysterious circumstances, but he was renowned as the best man in *Shanghai* to teach 'RP', or 'received pronunciation'. Allergies meant that Hoblock sniffed a great deal, but between sniffs, he explained that 'RP' was the kind of English spoken by a handful of people in the south of England; for some illogical reason, he said, but probably related to snobbery, it was the pronunciation that many expats aspired to use. After completing Hoblock's elocution course, however, Peggy was able to recite all the verses of Hilaire Belloc's poem, 'Matilda'.

Stan was still laughing when Peggy finished her recitation. 'Brilliant, Pegs! You're a natural – and so many words to learn.'

She grinned. 'It took a lot of practice – bloody 'ell!'

He threw his arms around her as he continued to chuckle.

'And one more thing, Stan: the sniffy Mr. Hoblock has recommended I also take a course in *tai chi* to improve my balance and deportment.'

Stan held her at arm's length. 'Pegs, there are no half measures with you: that all sounds marvellous.'

NATASHA
Shanghai 1937

Six weeks after the ball at the Majestic, another invitation arrived. She and Stan had been asked to a party at Natasha's new home. 'Sorry to take so long to be in touch, liebchen' she had written, 'but now I am settled in my own apartment. I long to see you. You absolutely must come to my party. We will dance and sing and have fun.'

Peggy was peeved when she heard from another 'Blue Funnel wife' that Natasha had a lover, Pascal Casanova. Peggy remembered how close she and Tash had been on the ship; surely an event as important as a new lover might have spurred a call between the two of them?

The name 'Casanova' sounded ridiculous, but Peggy was surprised to learn that, as a surname, it was common in Corsica. She'd heard the man was 'stupendously rich' and owned an import and export business founded on wines, mainly brandy.

Peggy – bored by the dog days of summer sliding by – felt buoyed by the invitation to see her young friend. The party would be a pleasant change from meeting the new, mostly older, friends she had made in the Settlement.

Ten days before the party, she and Stan were sitting on the verandah of their new home, enjoying a pre-lunch gin and tonic.

'You must go, Pegs. Natasha's bound to have asked our neighbours, the Trenchers. It would seem odd if you weren't there. I'm relieved to say that I have a long run to Qingdao in Shandong, so I shall miss it. But as you know, I'm never much company at these affairs.'

Peggy had not told her man about her friend's new life. Stan could be strait-laced and judgemental, and the news that Tash was a 'kept woman' would have upset him.

'Well, then,' she said. 'You better brief me on the Trenchers. I've only waved at them.'

'Oh, that's just being very English.' He said 'This isn't Surrey, where it's permitted to cross the road to avoid your neighbours – except at

Christmas,' he chuckled. 'You'll have to jump on the expat carousel soon; Natasha's party will be your chance.'

He paused. 'Ah, yes, the Trenchers.' He scrunched his nose before continuing. 'Well, I suppose we shall have to have them over soon, but I'll tell you my impressions, I hope, without prejudicing yours."

Stan paused, his head moving side to side, considering. 'I understand that Tom is liked by his colleagues at the American Consulate. Honestly? He's a bit of a… what we used to call a *mamamouchi* – less important than he thinks he is. Apparently, he asked to be billeted in the British sector – rather than the American. Seems he'd told his Consul General that Oxford had given him more *cultural empathy* with Brits. I must say I hadn't noticed it. All we English ask of anyone before forming a friendship with any class or nationality, is that they be funny, engaging – and not take themselves too seriously.'

Stan turned towards her. 'In my dealings with them, I've found that most Americans find it hard to be flippant, to banter without purpose – I know they're reared on this nonsense of being exceptional, and they can't understand why we Brits – who *know* we're exceptional – can afford to laugh at ourselves.' Stan snorted. 'Tom is damn clever – no one gets to Oxford at fifteen by being a slouch – but he's lacking those subtler qualities.'

He looked at her, seeming to nod at the acuity of his observations. 'I don't have to tell you, Pegs, that there are pools of nuance that Tom will never paddle in, no matter how much time he spends with English people.'

Peggy shrugged, 'I have to say that the American women I've met here are all pretty nice people'.

'Oh, I agree, I agree,' said Stan, raising his hand in protest. 'As a tribe, if that's the right word, they're a lot nicer than the Brits. That said, if they were more articulate, they'd probably be as mean as us; but they're not, so they aren't.' He reached across to touch Peggy's arm. 'But Tom's not all bad, quite the reverse, in fact. I'll tell you the story Trencher told me about how he met Chao-xing, his Chinese wife. The tale may give you a glimpse of what he's really like.

'How can I put this? Tom had invited me for cocktails at the Pacific Hotel. I'd just been a few weeks with Blue Funnel and, whenever I had shore leave, I tried to meet as many of the locals as possible. I knew Tom was with the Americans, and he seemed the right contact to have.'

Stan was quiet for a moment. 'When I met Tom, he was fifty-three. Now, Pegs, you know I'm not mad about being around older men – they reminisce too much, and most of them seem to talk down to me. I've always thought that the generation gap goes up rather than down.'

They watched a heron float by, then land at the edge of the ornamental pond in the far reaches of the garden.

Stan was talking again, 'Everyone in the diplomatic service knew Tom's history – you know how they gossip – that Chao-xing's family and friends had tried to stop her from marrying such an old man. By then, I'd got used to the open way that Tom shares confidences – which I truly do not like, but…' He paused, wrinkled his nose before continuing. 'But that evening, totally unprompted, Tom told me how he'd first met her. Later, I wondered if he was trying to make sure I heard the right version.' Stan shrugged.

Stan affected an American accent…

'I'll tell ya, Stan, Chao-xing was frickin' amazing, an absolute knock-out. No red-blooded guy – even a stuffed shirt like you – could have said no. Sure, she was twenty-five years younger than me but so what? Well, it took me under five minutes to unhook her from that fatso. I mean, the – guy – was – a – whale!"

As Stan continued, caught up in his imitation of Trencher, Peggy smiled. She preferred this version of her man: playful and less serious about himself.

'Tom told me that, apparently, Chao-xing's girlfriends had raised the topic of the age difference with her. One friend – her best friend – had said that, as a Chinese, it was fine to venerate ancestors, but no one expected you to marry them.

'Tom just laughed when he told me that. And then he said Chao-xing's parents were both – how did he put it? Oh yes, 'as dumb as a box of rocks.' Stan chuckled. Her family warned her that she'd be pushing Tom around in a wheelchair in a couple of years. But, as Tom pointed out, God had other plans.

'Chao-xing began to show the first signs of multiple sclerosis: first an inexplicable fatigue, then small difficulties with speech; a numbness in the extremities. Soon she was in a wheelchair. She was twenty-eight and on a long, slow ride to death.' He paused 'And Tom was devastated. He asked me, "What was I supposed to do? There was no way I was going to leave her".'

Stan raised his shoulders and, as he exhaled, he sighed deeply. 'Surprising everyone, he married her.'

Peggy raised her eyebrows. 'Well, he did the decent thing; a lot of men would have bolted.'

Stan frowned. 'Pegs, he was in love; it makes men do strange things.'

'But she's handicapped – what sort of physical life can they have?'

'My dear Peggy, there's more than one way to skin a cat.' Stan rose and, as if shaking off the seriousness of their conversation, said, 'Talking of which, shall we see what Wang Fang has made for lunch?'

She laughed. 'Don't be silly.' She punched him playfully as they went inside.

Tash's or, more accurately, Monsieur Casanova's 'palace of sin', was situated in an elegant, three-story building on *Nanchang Lu*, abutting *Fuxing* Park.

Tash greeted her at the double front doors of the penthouse. Natasha twirled her around. 'I love what you're wearing, *liebchen* – after all, why should we all wear dresses?' Peggy wore a pale blue striped top with flared grey slacks. Stan, who usually took little interest in what she wore, liked the outfit and called it her 'Katherine Hepburn look'.

Her tall friend looked as slim and as glamorous as Peggy had ever seen her. The artist wore a black, backless dress that displayed her toned arms and splendid back. The dress was short enough to show her tanned, gleaming calves to stunning effect.

In the hallway, Peggy was astonished to see the number of drawings that Tash had produced in so few months. Some of the results were evident as she entered: a striking mural of the Bund, a drawing – ominous-looking – of the Peace Hotel that, Natasha said, would be placed in the hotel's reception area. Peggy knew that Tash worked only with charcoal on paper – no oils, pastel or watercolours. The work was arduous, intense; Natasha had to wear overalls, gloves, and a mask to prevent her inhaling the charcoal dust.

'Now Peggy,' she said. 'You must understand this is a furnished apartment. Furnished by a Corsican with more money than taste. I would hate you to think these pieces are representative of my taste – God, no!'

'Am I going to meet your new man?' Peggy asked, hoping not to be fobbed off with some excuse.

Tash shrugged. 'He's in Europe. He's rich and boring and at his best when he's not here. Really, darling, there's nothing more to be said.'

As she looked around the entrance hall, Peggy realised that her knowledge of furniture styles was limited. 'Well, Tash, this is lovely.' Peggy ran her fingers over the top of a small desk in the entrance hall. A display of pink China roses rested on the surface, festooned in a large blue bowl.

'Ah, you spotted one of two decent pieces: that's a Quarti desk, and there's a lovely Eileen Gray cabinet in my bedroom. Frankly, *Liebchen*, after that, it's just a style I'd call "rental drab".'

She led Peggy down the hall to another set of double doors. 'Now my friends,' she said, 'are rather more interesting than my furniture.'

They entered a drawing room filled with forty or so people, and a hubbub of voices. Shards of dying sunlight fell across the carpet. Cigarette smoke rose in lazy swirls. At a bar in the corner, uniformed men stood languidly, being served cocktails from an array of gleaming bottles by a tall Chinese dressed in a black tuxedo. Large sofas and soft-looking chairs were dotted about; a few older-looking people sat, but most guests stood in clumps of noise, talking or laughing with what struck her as determined gaiety.

The crowd seemed to turn as one as they watched Peggy and Natasha walk to the centre of the room. Peggy smiled nervously, hoping she wasn't thought of as some special guest; Natasha immediately made it clear that she was.

'Everybody, this is my dear and special friend Peggy Parker. Peggy and I came over together on the "Tantalus". You must show her why you're the sort of people I would have as friends.' Peggy saw Natasha give a mock glare to the assembly.

There were a few muffled cries of 'Hi, Peggy,' 'Ni ha', and 'Bienvenue!' She had a moment to see that most of the women wore cocktail dresses; a few were in slacks. The men – how easy to be male, she thought – were either in military uniform or dark suits.

Peggy took in the room: she could smell cigars and perfume and food; silent Chinese waiters slipped through the crowd with trays of canapes. From a corner of the room came Sinatra's plaintive voice singing, 'Where are you, where have you gone without me?' The song wrapped around her, bringing the idea of Stan. She was surprised to find she wanted – as much as the thought irritated her – to have the comfort of a husband at her side. Like the ball, here she was again, feeling as though she was expected – if not to perform – at least to behave flawlessly among strangers. Then she realised that not all of them were strangers. She recognised Sue and John Lang, a married couple she'd met at one of the many Consular receptions. She knew she'd be more anxious if Stan were with her. Tonight, if she was going to cock-up, she'd do it all by herself.

Artworks filled every wall; it seemed as though Casanova had bought all his mistress's drawings: Shanghai night scenes, the Suzhou Bridge, rain-slicked streets, umbrellas, traffic lights, children running, more bridges, the Bund, a flash of blue sky – the entire range of her friend's talent. Natasha's art demanded active looking and a responsive eye. She would try to study the drawings later. Peggy had always felt that the young woman's creativity was an extension of her personality: hyperactive, sexy, omnivorous of the senses.

Someone across the room beckoned to Natasha. Her hostess left Peggy's side after whispering, 'Here's Tom Trencher and his wife; I understand you two are neighbours?'

Trencher was built close to the ground with a wrestler's rounded shoulders, and what Stan would have called 'agricultural hands'. The man himself might not have been taller than five and a half feet.

He had dark, wavy hair that began in the middle of his skull; Peggy thought his hair seemed like a wig that had slipped. His eyes, set in a round, unlined face, were a watery blue, as if he'd been crying – a direct contrast to his overt manliness. A moment later, her hand seemed to be attacked by his; the grip was unnecessarily forceful, making no concessions to her sex.

'Welcome, Peggy. Tom Trencher, token American, at your service.' He looked behind her before asking, 'Is Stan shipside somewhere? We had him over for tiffin, you know.' His wet eyes creased. 'Liked him. Of course, he's been around for a while, and I knew him before he got elevated to Blue Funnel.' He swelled his chest in an exaggerated way, as if to imply that Stan had gone up in the world.

'Yes, he's away, Tom,' Stan had asked her to be vague if people asked his whereabouts. Trencher raised his eyebrows, but she said nothing more. 'And thank you for having him over,' she smiled politely.

'No problem. Come and meet my Chao-xing.'

CHAO-XING
Shanghai 1937

Chao-xing was seated in her wheelchair. She wore a black silk cheongsam. Her youth made her seem an effortlessly beautiful woman: her complexion was like pearl, her classically straight black hair so long that it hung over the chair's arms. As Peggy's eyes took in the wheelchair, her immediate thought was 'tragic'.

Tom's wife had soft brown eyes, and now they appraised Peggy. Chao-xing extended a hand, fingers curled and limp. 'Hi, and welcome – though this is not my party.' When she smiled, her eyes seemed to close.

The 'hi' was held a moment too long, almost drawled. Peggy took the woman's fingers into her hand. For a second, she wondered if the other woman might feel as nervous as she did.

Tom said, 'Chao-xing, this is our new neighbour, Peggy Parker, Stan's wife. He's the guy who's with the Merchant Navy – Second Mate – that right, Peggy?'

Irritated by his introduction, Peggy's eyes crinkled. 'For now, yes.'

'But you are so lovely,' the Chinese said. 'I am sure you are his first and only mate.'

Peggy laughed. 'I certainly hope so.'

Chao-xing's laugh was a trill. Peggy knew that birds and telephones trilled, but she had never heard a human do so. The Chinese woman's trill was a high, quavering sound, truly bird-like, the last quaver left hanging. 'Hee, hee, hee, heeeeee.'

Peggy decided it was her only obvious flaw.

Tom interrupted *Chao-xing*'s trill. 'I shan't ask you, Peggy, for the hundredth time – what you think of Shanghai, because this place is impossible to dislike. I'll ask you something much more important: what would you like to drink?'

While *Chao-xing*'s husband went to fetch her a gin and tonic, Peggy stood awkwardly next to his wife's wheelchair. None of the etiquette books she'd been reading since her arrival had covered 'Talking to Chinese Woman in Wheelchair.' Peggy banished the thought as unkind and, determined to treat Tom's wife as she would any other human being, she said, 'Thank you so much for having Stan to your home.'

With a quick movement of her wrists, the Chinese swung her wheelchair round to face Peggy. 'Stan is an absolute charmer.'

'What may I call you? Chao? Chao-xing?'

The woman nodded. 'Chao-xing will do fine but be sure to pronounce it Chao-shing. You'd be surprised how the 'x' throws off many people – the 'x' is simply pronounced as 'shee.'

Peggy scanned the room while *Chao-xing* chatted with another woman on her left. She spotted a tall man with ecru-coloured skin and jet black, swept-back hair that seemed too long to qualify him as a Consulate employee. His eyes flicked towards her, held, then returned to the blond woman standing next to him. Whoever he was, he looked foreign in a room filled with foreigners. If, later, Stan had pushed her for a description, she would have to say there was something – what – 'dominant' about him? Whatever his appearance, she decided – quickly and without reason – that he was the most interesting-looking man in the room. But that thought was immediately leap-frogged by another: 'I'm married, why am I thinking like this?'

Chao-xing's voice cut into her thoughts, 'I see you've spotted Marcus. He's quite a dish, you must agree.'

Peggy blushed, thinking, 'I must be more discreet with these sharp-eyed Chinese.'

Tom's wife persisted: 'Come, come, my dear, don't be coy; Shanghai runs on alcohol and adultery.' She raised a hand to her mouth. 'Oh, my dear, I am so sorry – I'd forgotten you're just married.' She trilled so loudly and for so long that Peggy decided it must have been a genuine mistake and not an attempt to embarrass her.

But her remark wriggled into Peggy's mind and was not unpleasant.

Chao-xing was saying, 'Natasha chooses her friends carefully: no racists or bigots – a few Communists and Nationalists, a sprinkling of military.' She paused. 'What would be a collective noun for a group of military men I wonder?'

Peggy was nonplussed. She hadn't been in *Shanghai* long enough to handle this kind of small talk. *Chao-xing* saved her embarrassment. 'Ah, I think a pride of officers, perhaps?'

Peggy smiled. 'Perfect!'

'Oh, you've spotted their arrogance, have you? I mean the Japanese – strutting around our city as if they already owned us.' *Chao-xing* twisted her head. 'Ah, here's Tom, bearing gifts.'

The American, all smiles, handed them their drinks. 'And has my bride been giving you her rapid-fire opinions?' he asked. He kissed his wife's head as he bent down to give her a glass of what looked like orange juice.

Chao-xing looked up at Peggy. She winked. 'It's a screwdriver, and Tom, bless him, is very generous with other people's vodka.'

A waiter walked by offering a tray of vol-au-vents, angels-on-horseback, pigs-in-a-blanket.

'Peggy? Chao-xing, darling?' asked Tom as the waiter paused in front of them. Both women shook their heads, but Tom reached for a pastry. Examining the canape before popping it into his mouth, he said, 'Ah, must say I'm a sucker for the hyphenated snacks of the expat cocktail circuit.'

Still smarting from Trencher's referring to Stan's rank – correctly but unnecessarily – as 'Second Mate, Merchant Navy', Peggy, overcoming her nervousness, said, 'I can't place your accent, Tom. Help me.'

'Well, I'm from the eastern end of Long Island, the better end? My village – hamlet, really – is about a hundred miles from Manhattan, twenty miles south of Montauk.'

Peggy shook her head uncomprehendingly. Trencher smiled. 'Don't worry, a bunch of people can't place my accent.'

Chao-xing spoke up. 'How about you, Peggy? A home counties girl – or do I detect a slight breeze from the north?'

Before she could marvel at the woman's insight, some impulse made Peggy turn away to see the dark-haired man coming towards them – the 'dish' that *Chao-xing* had mentioned. As he neared, she smiled; he grinned. She would know who he was in less than ten seconds. Suddenly, Natasha was standing in front of her, a little old lady at her side.

'Peggy, I'd like to introduce you to Lady Gwenyth Smythe. Lady Smythe is the doyenne of expat ladies in the Settlement.'

Dressed in black, a colour that served to emphasise the large spider brooch on her flat chest, Lady Smythe was a pencil of a woman. Strong features sagged in a once handsome face. Instinctively, Peggy gave a small curtsey.

'How charming,' said the little woman.

'You're from Derbyshire, Natasha tells me.' Her voice was carefully enunciated, BBC-ish.

'We are – from the Chatsworth area.'

'Hmm, is that so?' The older woman paused. 'I know it well. When we were still part of civilization, my husband and I spent the occasional weekend with the Devonshires. Do you know the duke?' She stepped closer and her eyes, which had twinkled a moment ago, focused like x-rays.

Peggy fought her instinctive feelings of unease when faced by someone so obviously entitled. She thought, 'I can either wilt, or I can brazen this out.'

'Oh, I've known the duke since I was a child. Only last month, Genevieve Mansergh and I bumped into him at Sadler's Gate in Derby.' She paused. 'Perhaps you know Lady Mansergh?'

'I don't believe I have had the pleasure; the Manserghs…' She paused, thoughtful, 'are they the Royal Navy Manserghs?'

'They *are* Royal Navy people, as is my father-in-law, Rear Admiral Clew Parker.'

Gwenyth Smythe eased back. 'Oh, how jolly,' she said. Well, let me welcome you to Shanghai on behalf of the Ladies Settlement Improvement Society. I shall see you receive an invitation to our next meeting. A pleasure to meet you, Peggy dear.'

The little woman turned to Natasha, who, taking her cue, led her away – but not before she had raised a thumb behind Gwenyth Smythe's retreating back.

***

'Marcus Carter!' Tom's wife trilled with delight.

The man appeared to have come from nowhere as he bowed to kiss *Chao-xing* on the cheek.

'Ciao, Chao.' Peggy felt a thrum of power around him.

Chao-xing looked at Peggy. 'He's the only one I allow to say 'Ciao Chao' when he greets me. Not even Tom is given that liberty.' Rising, Marcus Carter lifted his dark green eyes to Peggy.

'Peggy Parker. At last, I can say "hello". I would have come a moment ago but, odd though it may seem, it was important for you to meet Lady

Smythe; she pretty much runs the Settlement – or likes to think she does – I can't imagine there would be any other reason for Natasha to bother with her.' His laugh went straight to his eyes, which were bright and mirthful. 'I saw you at the Majestic ball – at a distance, I have to say – but I would never forget your hair. I'm extremely glad to meet you, at last.' He smiled. When he spoke, his voice was deep, warm, and the tone, she could tell, was interested. 'I wish I'd introduced myself.' He made a small bow. 'Marcus Carter – from the British Consulate. I've met your husband Stan, of course; he often pops into the Consulate.'

Marcus Carter, she realised, would be a head taller than Stan. He practically loomed over Tom Trencher. Stan had never mentioned him.

'Hello, Marcus,' she said. Something was going on in her legs, a softening. 'You should have come over and introduced yourself at the ball. Stan may even have mentioned you once or twice,' she lied. 'I'm pleased to see you here. I hardly know anyone.'

She thought how open his gaze was, unfiltered – genuinely glad, as he'd said, that she was here.

'Yup, Marcus is our new boy,' Trencher cut in. 'Our man from India. You're not drinking, sport?'

Chao-xing said, 'Tom, you know perfectly well that Marcus never touches alcohol.'

The tall man chuckled softly. 'May I join the conversation – as I seem to be the subject of it?'

Trencher looked at Peggy as he gestured at Carter with his thumb. 'He's head of Chancery, but although he's from Delhi, he ain't no chancer. Ha!' No one laughed. Peggy had the feeling that Tom felt upstaged by Carter. Trencher struck her as the kind of man who didn't like the spotlight moving away from him; like a small boy, he needed constant attention.

From across the room, there was a burst of laughter among the Chinese officers. As Tom moved aside, Peggy saw Natasha, who, it seemed, had caused the laughter.

Carter was looking at her again. She felt herself blushing. Her legs seemed on fire. What was this? 'What are these feelings?' she thought. 'I'm a married woman.'

'Isn't Tash remarkable?' Carter tilted his head in the direction of the laughter. Peggy saw Natasha in a knot of blue uniforms. 'You must have had great fun with her on the "Tantalus".'

Trencher's voice, drawing their attention back, cut into his remark. 'Well, Natasha's getting laughs out of General Feng, and that has to be a good thing for all of us.'

Carter explained to Peggy that *Feng Yuxiang* was known as the Christian general. 'He was a warlord in the north before *Chiang Kai-shek* recruited him. The legend is that after he converted to Christianity, he baptised all his men with fire hoses. Apparently, he's such a zealot that when they march into battle, he makes them sing "Onward Christian soldiers".'

Peggy laughed, and Carter joined in, seemingly pleased at the effect of his words.

'No, really, it's true,' said Carter.

Peggy was aware that *Chao-xing* was watching them as they laughed.

They were still laughing when Natasha came over. 'Well, this seems to be a party that I'm missing.'

Peggy said, 'Marcus was just telling me about the Christian General.' She nodded her head towards the Chinese officers.

'Oh, he's a darling. But I wouldn't like him to be angry with me. He might have to punish me.' She rolled her eyes coquettishly. 'Now, you must all have a spoon. The *piece de resistance* is about to arrive.'

Earlier, Peggy had spotted an odd array of several dozen glasses with spoons in them. As Natasha left them and walked across the room, someone turned up the volume of the gramophone. There was a sudden blast of the thirteen-year-old child star, Judy Garland, singing 'Stompin' at the Savoy'. At that moment, four Chinese manservants entered the room, each carrying a huge silver bowl above their heads. They moved swiftly to a large rosewood table. Before the bowls had come to rest, a spoon-waving crowd, chanting 'Sa-voy, Sa-voy' in tune with the music, surrounded the servants. With some difficulty, the Chinese, their mission completed, slipped away. They left the Europeans, laughing and jostling with good-humoured greed, to plunge their spoons into the mounds of caviar. Peggy had once tried caviar and had decided that the appeal of the sturgeon's salty roe was resistible.

As others scrambled around the silver bowls, she watched the Chinese officers move to one side. General *Feng* looked on quizzically as the Westerners agitated for position, spooning in the black delicacy. *Feng* caught Peggy's eye and smiled, his eyebrows raised, as if signalling, 'what's the fuss?'

Peggy turned to see Marcus Carter staring at her. His mouth mimed 'crazy' as he tipped his head from side to side. She knew his look was only for her, and it made her breath scatter.

Peggy left the party after an hour and a half but only after she'd engineered a chance to talk alone with Marcus. She wanted to dance with him, to know what it might feel like. He had pleaded 'two left feet, I'm afraid, but let's chat a bit more. Let me get you another G and T.'

'I'll go with you,' she'd said, not wanting him to be diverted by other guests. They stood at the bar while he ordered her drink and a lime juice for himself. She saw others approaching and said, 'Let's get back to our corner, and you can tell me how India came into your life.'

She was surprised at her boldness, but she hadn't talked to an intelligent man since Stan had left on his latest trip. This was a party – she might never see this man again, she lied to herself.

A minute later, alone again, the buzz of the party behind them, he'd looked at the ceiling before answering her question about India. He clenched his jaw, and she wondered if he was embarrassed by the question.

'Not at all. It's a long story, but here's the short version: my great, great grandfather, Miles Wilberforce Carter,' – Peggy smiled – 'I know, I know – everyone called him 'Wilbur' – was an adventurer who went to India in 1790 and married a local maiden in Delhi. They had a son, my great grandfather Taj, and he came to England and married a woman named Stella St Clair. They also had a boy, my grandfather, Roger. In 1845, Grandpa Roger met Rab Berriam, an old school chum, and Grandpa thought their names lent themselves naturally to an undertaking business: Carter and Berriam. Apparently, it still gives a good living.'

He stopped talking and grinned until Peggy could stop giggling.

'Then my grandpa, the undertaker Roger – who also played the organ – met and married one of his choristers, Candice Keynsham. They soon had a child, also a son, and they named him Gabriel – don't ask me why. As I understand it, Gabriel – my father – was a bit of a tearaway: he went to France, met a woman named Hortense, put a croissant in her oven and, at the very turn of the century, out I came – a little darker than expected. After all, it had been four generations since Wilbur went native.'

Again, he paused until Peggy stopped laughing. 'And that's the short version?' she spluttered.

'Well, you did ask. That's how India came into my life.'

'Well, well – and how did you find out all this, this history?' she beamed.

He shrugged. 'Went to India myself some years ago. Part of my degree at Bristol was as an archivist. I just love walking into a forest of family trees.' He smiled. 'And then I joined the Indian Civil Service in Delhi – I can get by in Japanese, Mandarin, French, and passable Hindi – that seemed to help. A wonderful chap named Vishal Tandon took me under his wing and trained me. Tandon's sponsorship brought me to an interview at the Foreign Office, and they sent me to Shanghai. That was two years ago.'

Marcus stopped talking and looked at the ceiling. Finally: 'But Delhi… Delhi was – is – oh, such a wonderfully maddening place: all-consuming, intoxicating, ravishing… crazy! Filled with heady scents and perfumes and contradictions – a real woman of a city.' His eyes were empty of insinuation as he looked at her; even so, she felt drawn by the sensuality she heard in his descriptions.

Peggy felt she needed to change the subject, and she began to tell him how intrigued she was with the politics of the moment. She was worried she might say something foolish, but she ploughed on. As she talked, his listening seemed so acute she could almost hear it. His green eyes watched her mouth, his aura subsuming her own.

'China has always had interesting times,' he said. 'When someone says, "may you live in interesting times", it's said to be an ancient Chinese curse. Its etymology has never been proven, so I shall simply say: Peggy, you've arrived in Shanghai in interesting times. We should all pray it's not a curse.'

'Oh dear, that's troubling. Is that why you've been sent here, from India?' She thought that whatever had motivated her country to send him here, she was glad. 'Is there going to be a war?' She looked into his eyes, trying to sound as matter of fact as possible.

He shrugged but didn't answer her question. 'We just need the largest consulate we can afford; it's not a full embassy, you know.'

'I didn't know. But I never wanted to come to China, anyway.'

'You don't like Shanghai?'

'Heavens, no, I love it. But I do feel it's like a big shiny apple with a horrid maggot inside.'

He stepped back.

She scrunched her face. 'It just feels, well… false.' She paused, wondering whether she should be completely frank. But she felt so comfortable in his presence that she chanced it: 'Heck, Marcus, I'm a working-class girl from the Midlands and here I am in a big house with a car, a driver, servants. And everyone pretending there's not a war going on around us.' She looked up at him. 'False.'

Carter was thoughtful, studying the rim of his glass. 'Look, Peggy, the Japanese haven't officially declared war because they don't want to provoke the West. At least, not until their forces are ready and can take the offensive. We think their high command in Tokyo is confident that, although there's ten Chinese soldiers for every Japanese one, Chiang's nationalist army will be no match for their forces. After all, the Japanese have been trained by Germans – and they have superior artillery.'

Peggy frowned. 'Gosh, now you *have* frightened me.'

'I'm sorry, Peggy, perhaps I shouldn't have said that.'

She put her hand on his sleeve.

'No, no, Marcus. It's important that I know what to expect. Stan has always told me we'll be safe.'

'Stan is right. In the Settlement, you should be safe. But every war is unpredictable.'

Peggy realised her hand was still on his sleeve. She took it away, and they stood for another minute, saying nothing. She felt that they both wanted to say more but couldn't. She guessed that Marcus was cautious because of his job. She didn't want the evening to end, but anything beyond small talk could lead nowhere. Or somewhere she dared not go – should not go.

'I hope we'll meet again,' he said, when she said that she had to leave.

'Of course.'

Marcus kissed her on both cheeks. 'Oh, I like that European way of saying goodbye,' she said. 'In Derby, we only kiss one cheek.'

'Well, then I'm glad I met you here – and not in Derby.' He grinned and winked.

'Mmm,' she said, and gave him her best smile.

She chatted to a few more people before she sought out the Trenchers. She was promising to meet them again when Tom said, 'Hang on for another fifteen minutes, Peggy, and we can give you a lift home.'

'That's a kind offer Tom, but my driver is downstairs.'

'Oh, right. I forgot. You got a chauffeur.' He pronounced it *'show-fah'*; Peggy spotted a flash of resentment.

Natasha appeared next to them. She was like a will o' the wisp at her own party.

'Oh, you are thinking of leaving, my darling?'

'I *am* leaving, Tashie. Thank you for giving me the chance to meet *Chao-xing* and Tom and so many other new people.'

'I don't think you met many others. You and Marcus seemed to be in deep conversation.' She gave a sly wink.

This time she felt both *Chao-xing* and Tom's eyes on her.

'He was telling me I have arrived here in interesting times.'

'Ha!' Tom sniggered. 'He's got a point.'

Peggy waved at the remaining guests as she left. Her eye caught Marcus, and he waved back. For a moment, it seemed as though he would approach, but someone called him away.

Natasha took her to the door. Peggy was sure that they both felt the static between them.

'We couldn't talk,' Tash said.

'No.'

Natasha turned and hugged her. 'My darling, all will be well. We shall have coffee at Bonheur soon. Thank you for coming to my little soiree. I think you like Monsieur Carter.'

Peggy smiled, kissed Natasha's cheek, and left.

MARCUS CARTER
London 1935

Piccadilly on a fine May morning: A touch breezy, black cabs belching blacker fumes as two pretty girls – emerging from Green Park Tube station – take notice of thirty-five-year-old Marcus Wilberforce Carter, recently landed from India, as he strides southwest towards Hyde Park Corner.

He had dressed carefully: a white shirt that set off his dark good looks, a purple tie, a cream-coloured tropical jacket, charcoal grey trousers, and a foldable Panama hat that he'd paid far too much for on Jermyn Street. He wished to project the picture of a well-travelled gentleman – without appearing foreign – among the push of Londoners emerging from the Underground. He remembered Vishal, his Delhi chief, once saying, 'most women will try to catch the eye of a handsome man.' He felt his care with dressing had paid off – he became aware of several women taking sidelong glances.

As a boy growing up in the London suburb of Kingston-upon-Thames, Marcus had asked many questions about the 'Indian bit' of their family history. 'I'm not sure it's even true,' said his mother when her son confronted her with paperwork from Somerset House that proved the Indian link. Marcus – a natural student – had spent hours in its draughty rooms, making notes from the registries of births and deaths.

Marcus had no mind to argue about incontrovertible facts. He despaired of his parents' lack of curiosity; he knew his father had been a rebel in his youth, but the 'catastrophe' – as he called it – of a forced marriage because of a child had quenched any ardour for adventure.

'Oh yes, Gabriel's wings have been clipped,' Hortense Carter would explain to anyone who asked about their life in suburban Kingston – 'no more *Hindu Kush* for my sensible husband.' Marcus hated the smug look that accompanied such remarks. As a growing man, he found his parents to be an embarrassment: What other schoolboy had to suffer a mother and father with French accents and a ghoulish undertaker's business? By the age of twenty-seven, he had a first-class degree from Bristol university in politics, philosophy and economics, and a minor as an archivist. He couldn't wait to leave England. He sailed for India in 1927.

He was soon hired as a lecturer at the University of Calcutta; there, he had made no attempt to deny his Indian heritage – indeed, he boasted about it. He suspected that his beige complexion and language skills made him an exceptional candidate. A year later, he was accepted by the prestigious Indian Civil Service.

At the end of three years, Vishal Tandon notified him that he'd recommended him for a more senior position. A few weeks later, Marcus received a letter advising him that his next posting was 'imminent'. He would be contacted by the Foreign and Commonwealth office. And now he was back in London for the first time in over three years.

Puffy white clouds chased each other above Green Park on that May day as Marcus crossed to the northern side of Piccadilly. In front of him was the Naval and Military Club, more generally known as the 'In and Out'. The nickname referred to the tenure of men in the armed forces. Marcus skipped up the steps to the entrance trying to quell his anxiety.

'Lovely day, sir, but rain by the weekend, I fear.' The cliché about the weather came from a cadaverous steward as he led Marcus down a short corridor to an oak door. 'Sir Gerald is expecting you,' said the man with a twitch of lips, before slipping away.

Marcus stepped into a vast, high-ceilinged room. The gloom in one corner made it difficult to see if that part was occupied. He noticed the windows had been shuttered – he assumed to preserve the shelves of books where now – his eyesight adjusting – he could see a shadowy figure. Marcus turned back to the door and gave it a hard knock.

'Come!' came a voice. Marcus looked in that direction as the shadow moved and became a tall man, shoulders as stooped as a heron's, walking towards him. The man emerged from the gloom of the far room and into the pool of sunlight where Marcus stood.

Sir Gerald Choate wore a well-cut, black double-breasted suit, a high-collared pale blue shirt, and an eye-catching MCC tie. Marcus estimated the man might be in his late sixties.

'Ah, Carter! What a pleasure to finally meet you. I hear great things.' Choate extended a hand. 'I'm Gerald Choate.' Age had turned his eyes a veiny blue but time had not softened the fierceness of their gaze nor the strength of his handshake. Choate's eyes looked at Marcus from a lined, saturnine face. The senior diplomat presented a forbidding figure; Marcus was determined not to be intimidated.

'Sir Gerald. Delighted, sir.' Nodding his head towards Choate's colourful MCC tie, Marcus chanced a personal remark: 'Ah, you're a cricket fan, sir.'

Choate flipped the tie 'Oh, the old bacon-and-egg?' he said, referring to the red and yellow stripes that gave the tie its nickname. 'Yes, I'm hoping to see the South Africans play against us at the end of June.'

Marcus nodded. 'Five five-day tests – that's an arduous agenda, sir.'

Choate shook his head. 'Heavens, no, I shall only bother with the one at Lord's.' His blue eyes pierced. 'And you, Marcus: Watch much cricket?'

Marcus chuckled, 'Not at all, sir. Too complicated for me.'

Choate gave him a rueful smile. 'Ah, but you've done your homework, I can tell.'

Marcus tipped his head in assent, thinking, 'The cunning old bugger's got my number already.'

Choate gestured towards a leather chair that faced bright sunshine gathered from three deep sash windows. Marcus sat.

The tall man moved across to a butler's tray and poured two glasses of sherry. 'Fino acceptable?' he asked without turning around.

'I don't take alcohol, sir.'

Choate's head whipped around, 'Really? How extraordinary.' He nodded and returned to filling his own glass. He said, 'Water? Coffee? I can't promise it will be quick.'

'No, thank you, sir. Everything is fine.'

'Splendid, splendid.'

Choate sat down on a small couch opposite, his arm resting lightly on the back of it. His blue French cuff with its small gold link almost covered a Rolex watch with a worn strap. Marcus spotted the class-signifying signet ring on the small finger of Choate's left hand. A synapse fired; he remembered telling an English visitor to remove his 'pinkie' ring before entering a bar filled with West Virginia miners.

Choate coughed. 'Um, it says in your file that you spent a sabbatical in West Virginia,' Choate looked puzzled. 'Enlighten me.'

Marcus took thirty seconds to assemble his response. He looked at the ceiling to imply that he was giving the question deep thought; in truth, he was trying to quell the vertiginous possibility that the man might be a mind reader.

'My uncle Bryn was a miner in South Wales, sir, back in 1913. In fact, it was one of the largest coalfields in the world...'

'Yes, yes, but you: why were *you* interested in coal?'

Marcus realised he had been stopped from sounding boring and that Choate had no time for family anecdotes.

'I wanted to study the political attitudes of the American miners to see if they were different from the Welsh. It was my dissertation: 'Occupational malcontents: from Wales to West Virginia.'

'Pah! I could have told you that all those types are Communists – all filthy, all angry...'

'With respect, sir, I think we'd all be of a different political persuasion if we had to spend eight hours crouched in the dark, hammering away at a hard coalface.' As he said it, Marcus knew that he might have just wiped off the table whatever job they had in mind for him.

Choate turned his head away to study the park behind him. Marcus wondered if the diplomat was trying to control his irritation at the young man's remark or was seeking a subtle way of ending the interview. A minute ticked by. Marcus worried whether he should say something. He kept quiet.

The silence was broken by Choate saying, in a newly soft voice, almost to himself, 'It lifts the heart to see Spring trying to get a grip on those plane trees; how green they're becoming. You weren't at Cambridge, eh?' He asked the question in the same soft tone as he turned to face the young man. He seemed to re-focus his eyes, peering at Marcus across the short distance between their chairs.

'No. Bristol, sir. PPE and Archivism.'

'At Cambridge, it might have been PPE and Anarchism.' Choate snorted, his keen eyes still on Carter. 'Not so many Communists at Bristol, I'd wager.' Marcus shook his head. 'You see, old chap, Cambridge seems choc-a-bloc with Communists. All of them reading Orwell, who can't seem to make up his mind about anything. We have a few suspects at Cambridge – dots on the radar – but nothing that we can, as yet act on.' His sentence ran on into, 'You're not queer, are you? Homosexual, I mean.'

'Sir?'

'No, of course you're not. I can tell. Forgive me. It's just that your interest in the discontented: miners, suffering Indians, etcetera, suggests the sort of liberals who fall into socialism and communism – the difference between being slightly pregnant and pregnant.'

Marcus tried to laugh carefully, wondering if the attempt to do so sounded artificial, but he didn't intend to offend the veteran diplomat.

Choate nodded, signalling he didn't disapprove of Marcus's incredulity. 'I know it sounds bizarre, but those nancy boys make themselves vulnerable to compromise, to blackmail. We can't have that in the Service.' he slapped his leg. 'Anyway, to business: I thought it best we meet away from Whitehall. People can be so damnably nosy, especially when they see a strange face in the corridors. Odd, really, considering our business is diplomacy and discretion. But there it is.' He sipped his sherry, then flashed a smile so sudden that Marcus might have missed it.

'I shan't bugger about, old man: We need a Head of Chancery at the Shanghai Consulate, and you are a leading candidate. You come highly recommended by the Indian service – a country certainly top of the class when it comes to shifting paper and admin. I'm told you acquired a great deal of experience working in Delhi with old Tandoori…'

'Tandon, sir.'

'Yes, yes, I know his name,' his eyes closing, his voice patient. 'But here he's known as Tandoori – for short.' He pressed on, 'First-class chap, you couldn't have done better.' A sudden smile creased his face. 'I've heard it can be tricky keeping those Bombay ducks in a row,' His eyes pierced. 'But I suspect your drop of Indian ink did you no harm.'

Choate paused, letting the remark sit between them. 'Got on well with them, did you?' he added.

Marcus knew Choate's reference to his bloodline was a deliberate goad, as was his use of the nickname 'Tandoori' for a man who he had learned to respect and admire.

Choate looked at him through hooded eyes. Carter stared. Finally, he said, 'I got on well enough. I got the job done… sir.'

His host smiled – almost affectionately, it seemed – and Marcus was annoyed to realise that his imperturbability had impressed the older man.

Choate continued: 'You did splendidly on your training; it always sorts out the men from the girls.' He sipped his sherry then twisted the glass as he studied its contents. 'Mm, rather good, this one.' His eyes creased as he smiled. Marcus watched for any mocking look about his abstemiousness.

There was none.

'I'll be frank: The Foreign Office wants to put you on a fast track before somebody else steals you. And we can't have you sitting about getting bored.'

'Well, that's pleasing to hear, sir.'

This time Choate beamed, baring a row of uneven teeth. Marcus assumed dentists hadn't seen much of Gerald Choate.

The diplomat leaned forward to offer a cigarette from a silver case. Marcus demurred. Choate continued, 'In the words of the late, great Cecil Rhodes and your former masters in the Colonial Service: would you be interested in becoming a tool for extending the frontiers of civilisation?'

Marcus smiled. 'The answer to "would I be interested?"' said Marcus, 'is yes. As you can see from my papers, though, my practical experience has been limited.'

Choate said nothing. His eyes closed again, and, for a moment, Marcus thought the man might be dozing.

Marcus had found that, in most circumstances, people preferred to talk about themselves. He wondered whether Choate would be an exception.

'How about you, sir? May I ask if you served abroad for the Foreign Office?'

Immediately, Choate sat up, animated. 'Of course, of course. I did a tour in Kenya in twenty-five, shortly after we established the colony. Like the Masai, we FO people must drink the blood of Africa or, anywhere abroad, if we're to be taken seriously.' He paused and looked at the ornate ceiling. 'All I remember of it now was that we spent hours driving through the bush in ramshackle lorries.' His eyes crinkled, 'We called it the African massage.'

A short laugh became a wheeze. Marcus waited for Choate to recover. 'While I was there,' he continued, pulling a handkerchief from his coat sleeve, and dabbing his lips, 'everyone was a little – what did they call it? Ah yes, "bush happy" – especially the women.' He stuffed the handkerchief back in his coat cuff and, for half a minute, considered his long legs, stretched out in front of him.

Marcus waited, unsure if Choate was about to reminisce; unsure if he had been offered the position.

Choate looked up: 'Let's move to matters more current: Am I right in saying that all you know about the Far East is what you've read, plus a couple of Fu Manchu films?'

Marcus nodded, 'That would be a fair description of Marcus Carter, Orientalist.'

Choate chuckled, sat back, and studied the younger man. Displayed in the strong morning light, Marcus had no place to hide. He stared back.

Choate crossed the room and poured himself another sherry. He waved the decanter at Marcus then put it down when the younger man shook his head. As he walked back to his chair, Choate asked, 'Seriously though: How much do you know about our worthy Oriental gentlemen – currently – I mean?'

Marcus pushed out his lower lip, 'I know about as much as the man on the five thirty-seven for Weybridge.' He shook his head, 'I'm not privy to anything outside the public domain.' He gave Choate a lopsided grin. 'If it helps, I like the food.'

'Ha!' the older man exclaimed. 'Well, old chap, it's rather more than that – though I know you jest. We tolerate the Chinese; they're a passive bunch – after all, we've encouraged their opium habit for long enough.'

He leaned forward. 'The Japs, unfortunately, seem incorruptible. They're full of fire and brimstone – Knights of Bushido – that kind of thing. No, the Foreign Secretary doesn't like the way the Japs behave towards us. Halifax finds them impertinent.' He gave Marcus a sharp look. 'You're aware of the hatred between the Chinks and the Nips, yes?'

'The Sino-Japanese war?'

'Exactly. Through most of this decade – although the hatred goes back for thousands of years – they've been hammering away at each other. This latest war – like so many wars – started with a minor incident. The Japanese were on manoeuvres in North China when they lost one of their men. They wanted to look for him in Chinese territory, but the Chinese refused to give permission. Shots were fired, and before you could say "Charlie Chan", all hell broke loose. And since then, it's got worse.' He waved a finger in the air. 'You must understand that the Nips think the Chinese are no more than smelly peasants. In fact, the Japanese even look down on us Brits, which strains one's reasoning.'

Marcus didn't like to hear bigotry and found it rarely stood up to intelligent questioning. He leaned towards Choate and asked, 'What have we done to earn their contempt?'

Choate paused and closed his eyes. Marcus guessed he was not expected to question opinions.

Seconds later when Choate looked at him again, the older man said, 'God knows! They suspect we favour the Chinese, which is true, and they know that if the war in the south gets more serious, we would protect their enemy. That makes us their enemy. Also, we commit the crime of being foreign; we're all "*gaijin*" to them.'

'So, matters could get tricky.' Marcus said, unsure of what might be expected of him in China.

Choate drained his sherry. He studied the empty glass, then gazed at the ceiling.

'Tricky? They already are, old man: Hitler marching all over Europe, boasting that his Third Reich will last a thousand years. And if Japan sees what we permit Adolf to do, then they'll make a grab for the Dutch East Indies – Java, Sumatra, Malaya – they need the rubber and the oil. That means they won't have to rely on the United States for anything. In fact, some of Halifax's people think the Nips might even take on the Yanks.'

'And that would put all our people out there, and the Dutch, at risk.' Marcus said it more as a statement than a question.

'Absolutely. Whitehall is almost as worried about that part of the world as they are of Europe.' Choate opened his cigarette case again. 'They've asked me to ensure that we have the best possible people over there. Hence you.' He gave Marcus a wide smile, his teeth a panorama of decay. 'Carter, old boy, we shall want you to stay close to anything or any person who seems suspicious.'

Choate paused and pursed his lips. 'There's an American named Trencher who seems to spend a lot of time with our people. Got a Chinese wife. I'm sure there are others who may be a bit fishy.' He looked away. 'I'll get one of our people to give you a full briefing so you can get familiar with the political nuances – that'll be your bailiwick as Head of Chancery. Make discreet enquiries. Get the word back to us.' He nodded to himself.

Marcus flared his nostrils, drawing in air. He realised that he was facing the start of a new life. His body buzzed with excitement.

'You see, old boy, this job could be more than changing cutlery for chopsticks.'

Choate lit another cigarette. The smoke caught his eyes, forcing him to squint at Marcus.

Marcus beamed – excited, happy; it seemed the job was his. 'It will be a privilege to get in the thick of it, sir.'

'That's the attitude.' Choate slapped the arm of his chair and stood up.

Marcus had the feeling he'd passed some kind of test that had nothing to do with the tests he'd written two years previously – yet, somehow, was as important.

'When can you be ready to leave for China?'

'Almost immediately. I'm staying with a friend at Albany.'

Marcus got up and gave the senior man a level gaze.

Choate extended his hand and said, 'You seem just the fellow we need, Mr. Carter. I'm not permitted to have personal views, but Churchill – who is the best politician we have – is sure war is coming. We need to get Chamberlain out of the way and prepare for battle.'

Marcus smiled, his chin out, and bowed his head a fraction. 'Right, sir. To arms!'

Choate smiled appreciatively. 'Good man.'

Marcus Carter sailed for *Shanghai* on July 4th, 1935.

TYPHOON
Shanghai 1937

Leaving Natasha's party and stepping into the avenue, Peggy was surprised at the change in the weather. A blustery wind was coming from the northeast. For the third time since leaving Natasha minutes ago, she cradled the thought of Marcus Carter.

Her driver opened the rear door of the sedan. Settling in, she said. 'Home, Han.'

'Of course, Missy. Different route is okay?"

'Why different?'

'Missy, gunfire coming from Bund.'

'Of course. Whatever you think is best, Han.'

'Thank you, Missy.'

Peggy settled into the back seat and closed her eyes, playing with the memory of her conversation with Marcus. What was this attraction she felt for him? Was this the 'squirmy-squidgy' feeling that her friend Amelia Jane talked about – these cartwheeling thoughts, this clenching-unclenching in her tummy? She had to be careful: One of her core beliefs was that experience followed thought – she was comfortable with her thoughts, but she was wary of becoming them. She had to be vigilant that her thoughts didn't evolve into plans, that plans didn't warp into actions. Wasn't emotional infidelity the forerunner of physical infidelity? She had to neutralise the magnetism that she felt pulsing between her and the man she'd met tonight. She knew that there were only two ways to do that: surrender or flee. *'Don't see him again,'* a voice in her head commanded. Yet in the closed world of expatriate life in Shanghai, how would that be possible?

At Natasha's party, after her initial nervousness, she realised how free she felt without Stan – the same feeling she'd had before she met him – a free agent. With him, she didn't feel herself to be the person she was without him. The thought arrived with stunning force: she realised she had married

Stan for a new life – the adventure of China – rather than for any love of him. Meeting Marcus showed her what she missed with Stan. If she had to choose between Peggy Parker, the wife and Peggy Steele, the woman, she preferred the latter.

These feelings, she realised, had surfaced for the first time that evening. What had happened? Marcus Carter had happened: With Marcus, she had been open to every sensation.

She guessed there would be other social evenings like tonight – but not always with Marcus present. She remembered what Father Kelly had said to her in the confessional when she was sixteen – hormones bouncing inside her – 'the devil only goes where he's invited, Winifred.'

Her thoughts revolved fruitlessly until *Han* interrupted them: 'Must stop, Missy, soldiers at roadblock.'

Peggy felt a twitch of alarm. She realised that they had been travelling east for six or seven minutes on Avenue Edward VII, the border between the French Concession and the International Settlement.

'Well, if they're Chinese, that's all right, isn't it, Han?'

'They not Chinese, missy – Japanese. Han talk with them.'

The Packard rolled to a stop. Three soldiers came forward and screamed at them in Japanese.

Han, oddly calm, turned to face Peggy. 'Best follow orders, Missy.'

As she was about to exit the car, one of the soldiers pulled open the back door and hauled her out.

'Do not touch me! I am a British citizen from the International Settlement.' Peggy pulled her arm from his clutch and turned her back to him.

The Japanese slammed his rifle butt into her back. She fell heavily in the road, her right shoulder crushed between the tarmac and the weight of her body. She shouted with pain. As she hit the ground, she felt, more than heard, something click in her right shoulder.

***

Two miles and fifteen minutes away, Colonel *Feng Yuxiang*, seated in the back of his military vehicle, was humming a Christian hymn. His car, a 1930 Armstrong Siddeley cabriolet, was escorted by four outriders – two in front, two behind – all riding British-made Triumph Bonneville motorcycles. The motorbikes, moving at slow speed, were difficult to control in the restless wind. Behind the motorbikes were two Chinese Army Jeeps.

After another mile, the front right outrider raised his arm and brought his motorbike to a halt.

The General leaned forward. The outrider wheeled his bike back and said something to the general's chauffeur.

The chauffeur turned around to address the General in Chinese.

'Enemy roadblock, sir. Six Nipponese.' *Feng Yuxiang* grunted.

'We kill them?' The driver waited for an order.

Another grunt, then the general agreed. '*Hai!*'

The chauffeur turned back to the escort. '*Hai!*'

The two Jeeps that had been escorting the General's small convoy, accelerated around the black cabriolet. Seated in each Jeep were three heavily armed military police. The drivers of one of the Jeeps conferred with the outrider who had brought the convoy to a halt. The Jeep's driver gave the General's driver a thumb's up. Both Jeeps roared off in a northerly direction.

Peggy lay helpless but conscious on the pavement. She tried to achieve some leverage from the arm underneath her but, despite a nervous effort to push down, her arm seemed to have the firmness of a noodle. She howled again as pain stabbed her.

The Japanese stood over her, arguing.

'This is my punishment for wishing for a life without Stan.' she was thinking. Her Catholic-driven, God-centred guilt arrived, as punctual as ever. 'This is what life is like without a man to take care of me, to protect me.' Contradicting her thoughts of minutes ago, she muttered into the tarmac, 'I married for protection at moments like this.'

She heard the throb of engines as two Jeeps swept into the clearing, the occupants shouting and firing. Each Chinese soldier was armed with a sub-machine gun. Peggy flattened herself on the pavement. The Chinese continued to fire, and from her position, one eye pressed against the ground, she watched the six Japanese soldiers spin, jerk, and collapse.

Next, a car entered the area. More gunfire popped. The soldiers in the Jeep were standing up in the vehicle and firing more bullets into the bodies of the Japanese; there were six of them lying there, faces bloodied. A whistle blew three times. A gust pulled the kepis from the heads of two of the corpses and sent the little caps bowling down the avenue like skittish kittens.

She recognised the General from Tash's party as he climbed out of the car. Peggy eased herself, groaning all the while, into a sitting position. The General walked over.

Wincing, Peggy looked up and gasped, 'General Feng, thank you. I think your men may have saved my life. And my driver's.'

Feng frowned. He hunched his knees and, looking closely at Peggy, spoke in his poor English. 'Is fine. We do nothing. Good luck to find you. I remember from party. You talk to Marcus Carter. I ask him about you. You, Missy Parker.' Peggy nodded. 'You need go hospital? We take you.'

Peggy staggered to her feet, groaning from the flashing pain in her right shoulder. She leaned the left side of her upper body on *Feng*.

'You must go to hospital, Missy Parker. Maybe something broken.'

'Thank you, General, the soldier just knocked the wind out of me.' She was saying 'no' to a General; what would Stan have thought? But British stoicism was bred into her. 'I shall be fine in the morning,' she said, trying to smile.

'Then we take you home, Missy Parker.' He nodded towards the six soldiers. 'These poor souls finished.' He barked orders to his men, she presumed to clear the dead bodies.

Fifteen minutes later, in the back of her car, Peggy was still recovering her breath and, with each bump of the car, trying to suppress the fierce jabs of pain in her shoulder and down her right arm.

'Slowly, Han, slowly.' She had never raised her voice to him.

'Sorry, sorry, sorry, Missy.' She could see his tear-streaked face in the rear-view mirror. She knew he would feel responsible for the events of the past hour.

Han, aside from feeling contrite, was disappointed that it was a dark and stormy night. He had wanted his friends and neighbours to see him in the Packard – accompanied by four motorcycle outriders – driving down Bubbling Well Road.

Outside, the warm wind buffeted the car; Peggy saw the trees bend with its invisible force. The streets were deserted. Each lurch of the car made her wince, but her head was filled with the image of one man's eyes.

Four miles away, at the Bund, on the Japanese cruiser *Izumo*, the ship's steel spine creaked at its mooring. First Mate *Kyoto Zakura* turned briefly to address the officer: 'Typhoon coming, sir. Bad.'

First Officer *Matsui Kamomoto* replied, 'But good for us, Zakura. Chinese cannot fly airplanes in typhoon.'

'Chinese cannot fly airplanes in good weather or bad weather, sir.'

Laughter gripped them for a moment. After a minute, recovering himself, *Kamomoto* wiped his eyes. Then *Zakura* turned around again and, eyes miming terror, looked at his senior officer. Once more, they both convulsed. The wind caught the sound and took their laughter down the *Huangpu*.

THE MORNING AFTER
Shanghai 1937

Peggy woke at 6 a.m. to the rattle of loose window shutters; she 'emerged' more than woke, for she had been half-conscious for five hours; now she was fully conscious – such was the jagged transition from sleep to wakefulness.

Gingerly, she eased herself down from the big double bed. She'd had to spend the entire night resting on her left side; even so, the slightest movement delivered a slice of pain to her right shoulder and forearm. Whenever she had the urge to rest her right arm on her right thigh, she took her left arm across her body and, avoiding as much pain as she could, she lifted the right arm and placed it on her right thigh. The change of position served for a few minutes before, again, she had to adjust her body.

Pushing on her left elbow and using her abdominal muscles, she eased herself upright. She shifted her legs over the bed and placed her feet on the carpeted floor. She scooched herself into a sitting position. Using only her thigh muscles, Peggy stood up. For a moment, she took four deep breaths to recover from the effort of the last two minutes. She walked to the bathroom and, balancing with care, sat down. She urinated and was relieved to see her water had the healthy colour of straw. The rifle butt had not hit her kidneys.

She got up and turned to the mirror. She was appalled, almost frightened, by the woman who stared back at her. Her right eye looked as though someone had punched her, the socket red and half-closed. There was a reddish patch above her eyebrow where, last night, she had fallen on the tarmac. But it was the area around her right shoulder that caused her the most distress: from shoulder to wrist and under her breast were angry bruises – blooming in varieties of black, blue, and indigo – all tinged on the edges with a yellow discoloration. 'I've been hit by a bloody lorry,' she said to herself, realising how much trauma her body had suffered.

Shock stole her saliva. Dry-mouthed, she lurched back into the bedroom, faint from what she had seen. She took the carafe of water from the bedside table and, not bothering with a glass, drank deeply. She sat on her bed, closed her eyes, and took a dozen deep breaths.

Peggy knew her staff must not see her in this condition. She also knew they were too respectful to comment on her appearance. Two months ago, she would have told them exactly why she looked as she did, but now she knew better. 'Never explain, never apologise – especially to the staff,' Stan had told her within days of arriving. Nonetheless, she spent nearly an hour on her make-up and then, barely satisfied with what she saw, she went downstairs to face the day

In the living room, she pushed out the shutters with her left hand and looked out on a scene transformed overnight.

Bubbling Well Road appeared as though a hurricane had hit; in fact, its junior cousin – a typhoon – had brought havoc to the manicured neighbourhood. The camphor trees gave no sign of vulnerability – their massive trunks seemed set solid for millennia; Peggy knew that storms made trees take deeper roots; like strong people, she mused. She watched as tree branches dipped and swung with the wind. Around these sentinels, though, leaves and broken branches piled up and danced: crates, newspapers, shopping bags, garbage bins, a pram, broken rickshaws, bedding, clothes – presumably from snapped washing lines – even an upright piano. Packs of Chinese foraged through the debris.

The typhoon had blown in from the north-western Pacific. Stan had told her that was the region where typhoons were born – as unpredictable as they were frequent. When Peggy, leaving Tash's party, had been surprised by the wind that forced branches to dip and leaves to scuttle, she hadn't realised it was the disaster's advance guard.

As she surveyed the avenue below, the voice of *Zhang*, her personal maid, came from the door: 'You okay, Missy? House okay. I check. Big typhoon.'

'*Shi, shi.*' Peggy knew the Mandarin for 'yes.' She used the word 'shi' a lot, often when she didn't know what was being asked.

She turned around to face the *amah*.

Zhang's eyes widened, but she made no comment and turned away. Peggy called after her, 'Zhang, what is Chinese word for 'typhoon?' She knew she was pushing the limits of Chinese etiquette, but she was also intrigued by the servant's apparent indifference to her appearance.

Zhang, turning back, tried to stifle a giggle. 'Typhoon *is* Chinese word, Missy. Maybe Mandarin or Cantonese? Maybe Taiwanese?'

Peggy laughed softly, conscious of the pain in her ribs caused by the smallest movement. 'So English word for "typhoon" is Chinese word, "typhoon".'

Zhang paused as she parsed Peggy's words. Her eyes darted around the room, avoiding Peggy. Finally, she smiled, nodded, and said, 'Very good, Missy, I make breakfast.'

Peggy had seen no reason to tell her maid about the incident with the enemy on the previous evening. Her staff was worried enough about the increasing presence of Japanese military on the streets in greater *Shanghai*. They felt safe in the Settlement and never ventured beyond its boundaries; the fact that her brush with the enemy occurred within those boundaries would create a pandemic of fear among the Chinese service staff.

She knew she could have been raped and killed if it hadn't been for the General's intervention. Surely Stan would have heard about the typhoon; surely, he would have been *in* it? It seemed absurd that he couldn't arrange a secure line.

Downstairs in the dining room, she was surprised to find she was hungry. But then she remembered that she'd eaten nothing at Natasha's party. She had taught the cook, *Wang Fang,* how to make scrambled eggs. Catching the cook's eye, she made a whirring gesture with her hands. Then she took slices of bread and placed them in the toaster. *Wang Fang* nodded; message received.

'Zhang, please ask Han to bring the car to the front door.' Peggy said twenty minutes later, eggs demolished.

'Missy go out today? Bad weather Missy, better stay homeside.'

'No, I am going out, Zhang. Go shopside, Nanjing Road.'

Zhang's disapproval was obvious, but Peggy already had learned to ignore the woman's tendency to control her. Peggy wouldn't admit to herself, and certainly not her servant, that her main reason for going out was to distract herself from waiting for Stan's call.

Han, too, was concerned. "Missy must go Nanjing Road shopping? Bad weather today. Typhoon.'

'Yes, Han. Yes, yes, yes – *shi, shi, shi* – I can see that.' She was getting impatient with all the Chinese solicitude.

DEATH ON THE BUND
Shanghai 1937

Peggy settled into the Packard, and within thirty minutes, they were in sight of the Bund. The dramatic weather placed the sedan into a dark tunnel of rain; occasionally, a barrage of gusts rocked the car from side to side.

'There, Missy!' *Han* shouted. Her driver pointed to a rickshaw floating into view ahead of them, some twenty feet in the air. Han swung left as the rickshaw shattered on the street behind them. Peggy began to wonder if the servants were right; perhaps this had been a bad idea. Then she began to spot Japanese soldiers crouching in alleyways and lurking on rooftops.

'Japanese everywhere, Missy – bad times – we go home now?'

'Just to the Bund, Han, then home.'

There were a few other cars on the road, most of them official-looking – black, seeming sinister, and the occasional military vehicle. Every time the Packard lurched or hit a pothole, she gasped from the pain in her shoulder. Peggy assumed the Merchant Navy number plates prevented them from being stopped by the militia. Then she remembered that it hadn't stopped the ambush on the previous night.

She spotted a group standing in a row down one of the alleys. There was a burst of distant machine-gun fire, and, like marionettes, the group fell to the ground, their strings cut by some unseen hand.

She was about to tell *Han* to turn around when she saw a crowd lining the balustrades that faced the *Huangpu* River. There was another cheering group less than a quarter mile to her left, packed around two great *Shanghai* hotels, the Cathay and the Palace.

The wind seemed to relax. The rain turned off with the efficiency of a faucet. The typhoon appeared to have moved on or, she thought, was simply gathering breath.

Han cheered, 'Look, Missy: Chinese air force bombing Japanese ships.' Peggy could see nothing but a front of black clouds.

Han began to hum, then sing, his voice growing in strength as they neared the promenade overlooking the *Huangpu*. Peggy knew the tune – *Wang Fang* often hummed it as he worked in the kitchen. But it was out of character for *Han* to start singing in the car. Peggy thought the tune sounded like a marching song.

Han was singing with full-throated joy. He brought the car to a halt at the edge of the crowd. She was impressed that the Chinese were braving the weather, holding on to each other and the stone balustrades as the typhoon roared back into full strength, sucking, and eddying around them. It seemed as though the people around them would brave any setback, so intent were the Chinese masses to see their forces attack the Japanese defences.

Han turned around to face her, his eyes brimming – she could tell he was much affected by the moment. 'So happy, Missy, so happy I sing today. My great uncle Tian Han write this song three years past. Song called in English "March of volunteers". Uncle Tian, great poet, sometimes call his song "March of Self-righteous Army". Make Han very happy to sing his great uncle's song.'

The mob in front of them seemed emboldened by the arrival of the big car. When *Han* tooted the horn, the crowd parted to let the Packard purr forward. Smiling faces pressed against the windows, waving at her in the back seat. People yelled, 'hurr-hah, hurr-hah.' There were thumbs in the air and laughing, faces – shiny with rain – the crowd pleased to be sharing the moment with a foreigner.

Peggy leaned forward to see the panorama of the river. Six months had passed since she and Natasha had steamed up the *Huangpu* on the '*Tantalus*'. And here she was again, this time something of a witness to history; she thought; 'Oh, if my family could see me now.'

Han pointed: 'There, Missy!' She could pick out specks of planes as they emerged from the roiling whorls of black clouds. The planes came closer, some of them banking north towards the *Suzhou* Creek's confluence with the *Huangpu*; Peggy assumed the sketchy Chinese Intelligence had been informed – as Stan had told her – that the bulk of the Japanese fleet was anchored there.

When the leading planes veered north, the second wave of Chinese aircraft released their bombs. None of this ordnance hit the Japanese destroyers, but a half-mile downriver, a Shell tanker exploded in a burst of flame, the sound reaching them seconds later. From Stan, she'd heard about a Chinese cable-laying ship moored near the gas tank – she saw that the ship, too, caught fire. Half a minute later, the ship whooshed into the darkening sky. The sea morphed into a crimson mirror.

Peggy began to realise that the Chinese air force, if this was what it was, had erred in making the assault. Stan had been worried about their capabilities from the start. He'd heard that the Chinese pilots had been trained by Italians – 'better at fusilli than fighting' was his scornful verdict.

In the river in front of them, geysers of water spouted as they watched more bombs land harmlessly in the water.

Peggy muttered, 'this is an unfortunate, pointless event.'

Nonetheless, the crowd cheered as each bomb hit. They continued to sing their anthem, some of them mock marching to the tune, bending into the wind. Little boys and girls strutted and weaved around their parents, saluting each other, giggling, and singing.

Moments later, the Packard vibrated from the rumble of anti-aircraft fire. To her right, the huge anti-aircraft guns of the cruiser *Imuzu* rose like disturbed beasts. They began to bark fire at the Chinese planes. Panicked, a half-dozen of the attacking planes released the remainder of their bombs, banked, and retreated to the east.

Han began to understand what was happening. 'They send bombs too soon, Missy. This bad.' He turned around again to look at her. This time, she could see that his tears weren't of joy. He looked mortified, embarrassed perhaps, by his country's ineptitude.

'Look, Han!' *Han* turned back to see what she was seeing. The wind, its intensity reborn over open water, was pushing two of the dropped bombs towards the shore at a height of five hundred feet. The bombs continued to descend as they approached, seemingly directed at the Packard. There was nothing she could do except, instinctively, to duck. Hysterically – she was terrified – she had a memory of Amelia Jane's standard joke when a Chinese waiter brought her order and asked 'Duck?' she'd duck.

Eyes tightly closed, mortal fear displacing her pain, Peggy scrunched into the space between the seats, her hands over her head. She heard the bombs scream above her. She raised her head and looked from the rear window at the crowds gathered near the hotels. She saw the first Chinese bomb explode on the Cathay Hotel. Seconds later, the second bomb blew apart the neighbouring Palace. Bodies, or parts of bodies, spun in the air.

'We must help, *Han*,' she screamed at her driver, 'we must help.'

AFTERMATH
Shanghai 1937

'It was a mistake, Pegs!' Stan was protesting on the telephone, hours later, his voice rising, 'Their war is not with us. The Japs respect the Brits if they respect anyone. For them, the enemy is – and always has been – either the Koreans or the Chinese, or both.' As ever, he couldn't tell her where he was.

Two hours had passed since she'd witnessed the fiasco and the carnage at the Bund. Despite her protests and her suggestion that they drive to the hotel area to see if they could help, *Han* was desperate to return to the haven of Bubbling Well Road. 'Must keep Captain's missy safe. This my orders. Always keep Missy safe – that is what Captain tell me.'

Peggy was taking the long-delayed phone call. She'd told Stan what she'd seen that morning, and he was explaining his understanding of the events.

'But the planes were Chinese, Stan, Chinese!' her voice rose to match his; what she had just witnessed had cancelled her attempt to stay calm.

'I know what happened, Peggy, and I'm more than relieved that you're okay.' His voice softened. 'The Chinese planes were hoping to bomb those Jap destroyers on the Huangpu. They should never have taken off in that typhoon, but they needed the element of surprise.'

'Instead of which they surprised themselves – and us, on the Bund,' she said pointedly.

Stan ignored her sarcasm.

'Madame Chiang Kai-shek authorised the mission,' he said. You've read how tough she can be, and she felt her husband was waiting too long to act. The planes dropped altitude and reduced speed, but they didn't adjust their bombsights. Result? Disaster. And an unintended attack on the Bund, the Settlement.' His voice seemed to contain a chuckle when he added, 'Anyway, it was mostly Chinese who were killed – and the Chinks are pretty fatalistic about death.'

'Why does it matter less that they were Chinese, Stan? They were humans, people, children – and the bombs found them here, in the

International Settlement. And anyway, how do you know all those details?'

Stan ignored her question. Instead: 'Do you want to leave Shanghai and go home to your family?'

'Do you *want* me to leave?'

'Oh, let's not play that game, Peggy. I just want you to stop worrying. I've told you many times…' She heard his voice take on the patronising tone he'd used occasionally since she'd arrived in China, '… the Japs would never think of mounting a full-bore attack on the expats. Remember what Wavell said on the radio?' He imitated the military man's deep voice, "The Japs are sub-human specimens who can't form a fighting force, blah, blah, blah." And that was a year ago when he was here in Honkers. I reckon if our field marshal tells us that, we must take him at his word.'

'But what if we should have a child?' She knew she might sound hysterical, but the thought was never far from her. She continued, 'If you're at sea, I won't know where you are or how to reach you…'

The phone hummed in her ear.

'Stan?'

His voice was soothing when he spoke again: 'Really, Pegs, there's nothing for you to be concerned about. As I told you before you left Blighty – these yellow fellows have been at each other's throats for centuries. Do you really think I'd have asked you to follow me here if I thought you'd be in any danger?' She could hear the smile in his voice when he added, 'You know I don't tell you where I'm going because it protects you not to know.'

Another pause.

'Now, go and have a pink gin, play a record by that new Sinatra fellow – the chaps here play his records all the time. And when he sings "Yours is my heart alone", think of us, ducks. Remember, I'll be home in a week, and then I'll show you how much I love you.' The line clicked.

She held on to the phone, thinking, 'but what if we did have a child?'

Their love making was infrequent, not simply because Stan was often at sea. Peggy disliked the thought of making a baby and then giving birth to it – but she still wanted a child. Stan was dead set against adoption, 'We don't know where the child comes from,' he argued. But Peggy found the sex act painful.

She preferred to cuddle in bed with Stan but being like most men – or so she imagined, her experience was limited – she sensed that Stan always wanted more.

'Don't you like to do it?' he'd asked a month ago.

'Yes, sometimes. But I prefer to be close.'

'What could be closer than, you know, what we're supposed to do?'

'I don't know, maybe because we're supposed to do it. I don't need anything more than this.'

Despite her dislike of what was required to have one, Peggy knew that only a child would make them feel like a proper family. She sensed it was her fault that she had not fallen pregnant; 'was something wrong with her?'

She put down the phone and, feeling faint and in need of a cup of tea, perhaps a biscuit, she headed for the kitchen. Before she could leave the drawing room, however, the phone rang again.

***

'Did you forget to say you love me and miss me?' Her voice was soft, seductive.

A voice, deeper than Stan's, said, 'Apologies, Peggy, it's not Stan – it's Marcus Carter, wondering if you got home safely last night and if you're aware of the bombing on the Bund this morning? I fear the Palace and the Cathay are pretty much destroyed.'

She swallowed, trying to find her voice. 'Marcus, how very kind of you to call. You're right. I thought it was Stan, that he'd forgotten something – we've just talked.'

'Not at all. After you left, Tom told me that Stan was at sea. I expect he called to see if you're okay.'

'Who – Tom?'

'No, Stan.'

'As I say, he's just called.' She almost blurted, 'I am not at my best now.'

'Of course, I shall get off the line immediately. But just wanted to be sure, absent a husband, that you are fine.'

She paused; *'Should she involve Marcus in her life in this way?'* He seemed genuinely concerned, and she knew the story would get back to him, but that was different from encouraging his direct involvement.

'Well, last night we were ambushed by some Japanese soldiers…'

'Good God, Peggy!'

'… but General Feng's bodyguards took care of the situation. Honestly,

Marcus' – how she loved to say his name – 'it sounds worse than it was. And this morning?' she continued. 'Yes, my driver and I witnessed the bombing.'

'Oh, Peggy! You're in the thick of it.'

'Really, Marcus, you don't know me at all, but there's one thing you should know: I'm very capable. Stan knows that, too; that's why he can leave me on my own for weeks on end.' Peggy had not intended to sound arrogant, but a few moments later, she was worrying about the pause at the other end of the line.

Finally: 'So there's nothing I can, or should, do?' His voice was tight.

'Absolutely nothing. But thank you, Marcus, for ringing, and for being so concerned.'

'Of course, think nothing of it.' His voice was back to its original tone. 'I should stay inside today, Peggy, if I were you. You might get blown to Wuhan. Do look after yourself, although it seems a bit superfluous to say that.'

She managed a soft laugh. 'It's nonetheless welcome. Goodbye, Marcus'

'When…'

She put down the phone. She knew what his question would be.

THE BUS TO FU-XING
Shanghai 1942

First, Peggy heard shouting: 'Ikimasu! Ikimasu!' The high voices belonged to three small figures. They were running alongside a clanking vehicle approaching from the east.

'Ah, at last.' Said Tom Trencher.

The runners were shouting, 'Let's go, let's go' in Japanese, as if they had some part in the day's drama. A yellow bus materialised out of the snowy gusts, trailed by a truck.

The vehicles stopped less than a quarter mile away, where another group waited. Their shapes came and went as the snow swirled around them.

Two adults and two children disappeared into the bus before it shuddered forward again. As it approached, they could see that the roof of the leading vehicle was piled high with luggage. The trailing truck, too, held more trunks. The small convoy moved towards them.

A Japanese soldier straddled the cargo on the roof. He held a rifle and used the weapon to sweep back and forth across the empty street. Now and then, he would scream at the running boys. They laughed.

The convoy came to a crunching halt in front of them, the engine sighing then ka-thumping over and over with a grinding, unpromising sound. Peggy saw the name on the side of the bus, **FU-XING MISSIONARY SCHOOL**. Then she saw, on the driver's window, a crudely written placard. Two lines were scrawled, the top one in Chinese characters and under it, the translation: **FU-XING CIVILIAN ASSEMBLY CAMP**.

The young runners collapsed into the snow, laughing and chattering. A moment later, they were making snowballs. Tom said, 'Those kids are Chinese. If they carry on like this, all three of them will be dead by nightfall.'

A soldier – he looked no more than sixteen – stepped from the front door of the first vehicle. Holding a clipboard, he shouted, 'Five-three-one-two one adult British, one child British; five-four-one-nine, two adults British!'

They were unprepared for what happened next: the soldier on top of the bus fired a shot into the air. He was pointing his rifle at *Zhang*, who had retrieved Jonny from *Chao-xing*'s arms.

'She no stay! Leave boy! You go!' the Japanese shouted at *Zhang*.

The *amah* looked at Peggy, her eyes pleading. The servant had cared for Jonny since the day Peggy and Stan had brought him home from the hospital.

Zhang started to wail at Peggy. 'Ay Yee, ay Yee! Missy, please, I have no place. House gone; family gone. You, Jonny, my family now.'

Peggy held out her arms for her son. 'It's all right, Zhang. I'll talk to the soldier.' The *amah* handed over Jonny. The little boy was trembling, his legs kicking. Peggy knew that, disoriented and frightened, Jonny was about to erupt in a tantrum.

Peggy looked up at the soldier. 'Sir, please let *amah* stay bus-side. She come with me. She has no family. We, her family. I can pay.'

Tom Trencher, showing his identity papers to the guard, called to her. 'He's not interested, Peggy. She's Chinese – she's the enemy. We're all the enemy.' He was struggling to get *Chao-xing* out of her wheelchair.

The soldier with the rifle screamed at Tom in Japanese.

Tom froze; he had no idea what the soldier had said.

Chao-xing, leaning on Tom's shoulder, erupted into a babble of Japanese. Her face twisted with fury; her words were directed at the man with the rifle. Peggy realised the young woman was using outrage and anger to intimidate the soldier. Then *Chao-xing* pulled off her glove and pointed at her ring finger. Peggy assumed she was explaining her status as Tom's wife. The soldier looked away, saving face, then raised his arm, signalling for the couple to proceed.

In the moments that it took for this exchange, *Zhang* continued to wail. Two more Japanese swung down from the luggage truck and, in one movement, gripped the cabin trunks and swung them up to rest on top. The men climbed back, sat on the trunks and, pointing forward, yelled, *'Ikimasu!'*

The bus engine revved, but the vehicle didn't move.

The soldier on the roof, panicked by the distractions, aimed his rifle at Peggy as she stood waiting to get onto the bus. For a fraction, her heart thudded to a stop. She saw the rifle swing some six feet to her right. *Zhang* was kneeling like a supplicant, her face shiny with tears. 'Missy, please, Missy. Ah Ni, Ah Ni. Love you, love you.'

Peggy's breathing raced up her throat as the moment turned to tragedy. She wanted to scream 'no!' but all her voice could produce was a groan. Instinctively, she cradled Jonny's head with her hand, pulling him close. A rifle cracked, and, over her little boy's curls, she saw *Zhang*'s head turn into a bloody knot. The *amah*'s body fell back into the snow.

'Bus! Bus!' the soldier yelled at Peggy.

Peggy went rigid. Jonny, too, seemed in shock, burying his head into her shoulder, moving it round and around, as if he was trying to enter her body. She could see that the three boys who had run beside the bus were now silent, too scared to move. Figures hunched, each with hands over their eyes, or mouths, or ears – like creatures out of legend.

Peggy looked back at *Zhang*'s body – her blood already staining the snow – willing the Chinese to get up, and knowing the wish was futile.

The soldier was peering at them over the edge of the bus, waving at her with his free arm, gesturing her into the transport. Jonny clutched her coat, eyes wild. His wail turned into a high scream, his little fists hammering into her chest, legs kicking; she realised the toddler wanted to go to his *amah*. The snow swirled around them.

'Sh, sh, shush. It's all right, baby.' Her instincts surged back, and, hardly believing she could do it, she began to hum. Slowly, Jonny's legs stopped thrashing. Like a fish, he took little gulps of air, the trembling eased, and, although the tears never ceased when she gave him his pacifier, he sucked it: 'mm, mm, mm.' Jonny's body shivered and heaved in bursts, his head continuing to swivel back towards *Zhang*'s corpse before he rested it on Peggy's shoulder. She knew the two minutes of crisis had passed.

At that moment, the sound of two gunshots – *thump, thump* – fired slowly and, it seemed, almost thoughtfully – reached her from her house across the road. Peggy knew then that Lieutenant Nomura had executed the house boy *Wu*, and the cook, *Wang Fang*. She realised the Japanese had killed three of her six servants; only *Han* and the two garden boys had escaped.

The soldier on the roof was still looking down at them, but his eyes were on Jonny. Her heart tripped: was he going to steal her child? But the Japanese smiled and gestured. 'Go, go,' he said in a normal voice. Again, the driver revved the engine. The bus creaked forward a few inches then stopped.

As she stood in a shroud of snowflakes, she felt panic move again from her chest to her mouth. She was about to vomit. Peggy took a huge breath of icy air. She began to repeat the phrase that Arnold Steele had drummed into her since she was a little girl: 'Steele by name, steel by nature; Steele by name, steel by nature.' The panic eased.

Clutching her son, she climbed onto the bus.

STAN RISES
Shanghai 1937

Stan's career soared in China. He had been assigned to a freighter named the 'Shenkin', a ship with a range of twenty-three thousand miles – enough for a freighter to steam up and down the nine thousand miles of China's coastline. The 'Shenkin' travelled from the Bohai Sea in the north down to the Gulf of Tonkin in the south.

The merchant ship loaded and unloaded freight at *Shanghai, Canton, Ningpo, Fuchow* and *Amoy*. Stan knew that the ports – *Shanghai* being the biggest – had historical significance. The 1842 Treaty of *Nanjing* – a huge humiliation for China – had given Britain 'favoured nation' status in all the five Treaty ports. ,

The British had always viewed opium as an important source of tax revenue. Much of the drug came through the ports patrolled by the '*Shenkin*'. Smuggling was rife, and pirates feared the sight of the '*Shenkin*', Stan on the bridge with megaphone in hand, as he ordered them in English and Mandarin to 'HEAVE TO!', WEI GAN!'

A scarcity of good naval officers in China at that time – many of the senior men already preoccupied by the growing threats in Europe – worked to Stan's advantage. He'd had more than twenty years of experience in the region. The years plus his innate sense of destiny – making China a dominant force in the twentieth century – made him feel exceptional.

Stan felt vindicated by his decision to return to the Far East. He worked with a crew of thirty men on the '*Shenkin*' – twenty-five of them Chinese – and his fluency in the local languages improved by the day. A few of the deckhands were from Hong Kong; to them he spoke the more tonally complex Cantonese – to the rest, Mandarin. The skill gave him an advantage over his peers. He could give orders to his men in their own language – English or Chinese – and they obeyed. His fellow officers, some university men, deferred to Stan because they could see how the crew, by nature argumentative, became cheerily compliant when Stan joined in their banter.

The officers, some of them outranking him – rather than feeling excluded – respected the Second Mate's ability to balance authority with good humour.

On board, Stan wore authority like a second skin. As the year passed, he felt a liminality growing within him: the uncertainty he'd felt only a year ago – that he couldn't cope in China without Peggy – was fading. Ambivalence about his ability to manage his new powers – so much more than those of an Able Seaman – disappeared shortly after he stepped aboard. Within hours, as the ship took the retreating tide down the *Huangpu*, Stan felt himself to be 'master of his fate, captain of his soul'. Never a religious person, Stan nevertheless knew he was experiencing a rite of passage, one from which he felt certain to emerge whole.

On the '*Shenkin*' Stan was promoted from Second Mate to First. As he turned 38, Stan earned his Master Mariner's ticket; he became Chief Officer of the '*Shenkin*', one rank below the Master. As Chief Officer, he was in command of the loading and unloading of all freight; but Stan was more than that – everyone knew he ran the show.

The skipper of the '*Shenkin*', the master, and the man Stan reported to, was a boozy Welshman named Watcyn Williams. Because of Stan's language skills, Williams would always ask his Chief Officer to mediate disputes within the crew. Given his predilection for whisky, the Welshman spent most of the time in his cabin, drinking, sucking his teeth, and playing solitaire. When he did roam the decks in search of something to do, the big, awkward Welshman lived up to the nickname given him by his officers: '*Watcyn-I-fuck-up-next?*'

As he pushed through the ranks, reports of Stan's leadership skills filtered back to London. His growing reputation compelled his London bosses to agree that his progress was, as one of them put it, 'meteoric'.

The British War Office at Whitehall, while preoccupied with the war in Europe, was troubled by not knowing enough about what was going on in the Far East. Diplomacy wouldn't permit them to make a full-frontal assessment; they would have to infiltrate in other ways. Shipping lines, they decided, were a good place to start, and they turned first to the Blue Funnel Line, where their freighters gave official access to ports. As was often the case, 'one or two people knew one or two people' at the shipping line. The Board of Blue Funnel, aware of Stan's rising star and family connections, decided to enlarge Stan's remit. PP would be their emissary in asking First Officer Stanley Parker to accept an expanded assignment.

Halfway through that year, on one of his visits to *Shanghai*, PP gave Stan dinner at the Astor House Hotel. The previous year, while Stan was waiting for Peggy to arrive, PP had scolded his godson for his secret trip to the *Hongkou* district. Stan worried that he was to be reminded of his error because the Astor House also was in the same district but better placed on the Bund. In fact, conversation at dinner that night turned out to be more consequential.

After the waiter had cleared away the remains of their *cremes brulee* and left them with coffee and brandy, Perry Pennington said, 'Our London people want to expand your mission, Stan.'

Stan was quick to react: 'Sir, I'm very happy on the 'Shenkin' and both Peggy and I love Shanghai.'

Placating Stan, Pennington waved his hand in the air. 'Steady, old man, steady: Nobody has talked about your leaving Shanghai or the "Shenkin". No, no, no.' PP drew a deep breath and leaned across the table. 'It's clear to my colleagues in London that you're more interested than most in what's going on between the Japs and the Chinese. My annoyance about you sneaking off to Hongkou was only because you did it without consulting me.'

Stan leaned back, thinking, 'Here we go,' but before he could say anything, PP continued, 'And that was only because Hongkou was already something I intended to talk to you about.'

Stan raised an eyebrow.

'Yes, dear boy, we want to use your exceptional knowledge of the region, your languages, and your gift of mixing with all sorts – just like your father – to find out as much as you can about Japan's intentions. London believes war is inevitable. Hitler is hungry for conflict, and the Japs are more likely to be his allies than ours.' He winked. 'The Japs share more with the Germans than a noticeable lack of humour. We need people deployed in this area who can be listening posts.'

'You want me to spy on the Japanese?' Stan was taken aback. 'Why wouldn't the British Secret Service take that on, sir – MI6, I mean?'

For a moment, Pennington looked uncomfortable. Stan knew that PP was not a man who welcomed challenges to what he thought of as his good sense; he preferred conversations to be opaque, or at the very least, oblique. For half a minute, Pennington took his eyes off his guest.

Stan watched as his boss surveyed the richly furnished restaurant: the Astor's multiple balconies in their excessive shades of pink; chandeliers from overhead beams that supported a glass ceiling which, at that hour, was shafted through by sunlight. Finally, PP turned his gaze back to his godson.

'You're correct. By rights, MI6 should take it on, but to say they're light on Chinese or Japanese speakers would be an understatement. There are two so-called linguists I'm told: one a Wykehamist who speaks Mandarin and Cantonese languages with a Belgravia accent; the other, who may be a crypto-Communist, has yet to earn the full confidence of the Service.'

Stan looked across the table, worried at the turn of conversation.

The older man gave him a baleful stare, 'Stanley, you understand this idea comes as something of an order from London?'

Stan tightened his mouth. 'Well, I'll do what I can, but there are no Japanese on my ship, so I think it may be a case of slim pickings on the espionage front.'

PP shook his head. 'Stan, please don't talk of...' he paused, '*espionage*; it's simply a matter of keeping your eyes and ears open when there are Japanese about.' He stopped to fuss with a cigar; Stan demurred.

A minute later, through a haze of Cuban smoke, PP said: 'For example, your Chinese crew? They must mix with the Japanese when they go ashore.'

Stan suddenly realised how much London had detached PP from shipboard life.

'Good God no, sir. The Chinese stay away from the Japanese as much as they can; the fact that they look similar... well, so do the Scots and the English... but they couldn't be more different in culture and temperament.' Seeing PP's disappointment, he added, 'but I'll put the word out. Jiang Husong would be a good place to start.'

'Where's that?'

Stan rubbed his mouth so that PP wouldn't see his smile. 'Jiang is the brother of Gong Husong, the man who guided me around Hongkou – Jiang is one of my Able Seaman on the Shenkin.'

'Excellent, excellent,' said PP, not in the least embarrassed by his confusion.

Stan looked closely at Pennington. 'Sir, you'll have to give me some indication of what I should be looking for.'

'Everything, everything; we're particularly interested in their plans for war. We both know that the Japanese are itching for a reason to strike another blow on China's mainland – especially as they've now got a foothold in Manchuria. Chiang had asked us – and Washington, of course – to co-ordinate with his people so we can enlarge our pool of intelligence.'

'Why Washington? The Americans aren't at war with anyone.' Stan decided to risk PP's discomfort one more time.

His boss nodded, then looked away before saying, 'True, but they have bases in the Far East, and one wouldn't need to be a genius to suspect that Tokyo covets them.'

'Hmm,' mused Stan. 'And the last thing America needs is the wrong war in the wrong ocean at the wrong time.'

'Precisely.'

'Well, sir, I'm honoured that you've given me this responsibility – even though it's a bit off my patch.'

Pennington leaned back. 'Blue Funnel thinks you are more than capable of meeting this mission.'

The older man leaned forward, as if about to share a confidence. 'I feel lucky to have hired you, Stan, and, given who your father is, your patriotism has never been in doubt. Now we can put your abilities to work.' He smiled and nodded enthusiastically.

He waved at a waiter for the bill and then leaned again towards Stan. 'This is strictly a need-to-know mission, Stan,' he'd said. 'And I can't think of anyone, not even your' – he paused – 'charming wife – with whom you should discuss it.'

PEGGY RISES
Shanghai 1938

Peggy had made friends with several Navy wives. Stan's growing reputation in the firm had been confirmed by these women – some of them, she was sure – envied her. The wives were dubbed – rather annoyingly, Peggy thought – 'the Blue Funnels', or worse, 'the Funnels'. When Stan forgot how the name irritated her, or simply to tease her, he'd say, 'Pegs, when are you having the Funnels over for lunch?'

In addition to elocution lessons and *tai chi*, Peggy had learned to play bridge. This new skill added to her confidence in an environment so markedly different from what she might, laughingly, have called her heritage. She'd eavesdrop on the women gossiping while she supervised lunch preparations. She heard one say, 'You know all the officers call him "China Stan"?'

Another woman said, 'Oh, Paul is so jealous that he can speak all these Chinese languages; apparently, his crew adore him.'

Sometimes one of the wives would say, 'How's the skipper?' and it would take Peg a moment to realise she was asking about Stan, and not his captain.

But some time passed before she could display the same self-confidence around expats as Stan did. If, sometimes, someone thought that Peggy might not be everything she pretended to be – well, in *Shanghai* she was one of many.

Even so, when Stan was away, she'd sometimes stand in front of the bedroom mirror and recite 'Peter Piper picked a peck of pickled peppers' or 'how now brown cow'. Only once or twice did she feel melancholy, concerned that she might be burying her true personality. Those moments of *tristesse* – another new word she'd learned – never lingered.

Slowly, as she groomed herself to be the equal of her social set, Peggy began to blossom.

Thuyen Nguyen, her *tai chi* master, was delighted that she practiced the exercises with Jesuitical zeal: Peggy loved the aura of calm that was a by-product of what he called 'the form'. Thuyen Nguyen connected her with a French woman named Louise Lecours, a 'deportment mistress'. Within weeks, she noticed heads turning when, with new confidence, she strode into *Shanghai*'s best restaurants. 'You must change the room when you walk in,' urged Madame Lecours. Peggy felt she did exactly that.

Her social life was moving to another plane, and slowly, with Stan's support and the admiration of new people, Peggy became a well-known member of the expat community.

Part of her growing popularity stemmed from being a regular broadcaster on the Settlement's local radio station, XCDN. Peggy, by instinct an actor, voiced the role of Dorothea Brooke in 'Middlemarch', and 'Miss Pym' in 'The importance of being Ernest'. These radio dramas were broadcast to satisfy the middlebrow cultural needs of the British expatriate class. After a year, the station's general manager, a former BBC producer, realised that this vital, charming woman was, as he once told her, 'a diamond in the rough.' The ex-BBC man gave Peggy a ten-minute segment of her own. The monthly monologue, promoted as 'Peggy's Pot-Pourri', was a light-hearted assembly of news and gossip about the capital. Two months later, she was thrilled to hear that 'Peggy's Pot-Pourri' was being relayed to Europe by Voice of America.

When she and Stan talked about their new life in China, Peggy concluded that it mattered less that theirs was not an 'emotionally intimate' partnership – a phrase she'd seen in Redbook, an American magazine. What mattered more – and she sensed Stan's tacit agreement – was that they were supporting each other as they grew professionally and socially.

Despite this upward momentum in their new lives, Peggy felt that many reasons – undefinable, almost mysterious – were conspiring to make she and Stan more successful than they had dared hope. As a new decade – the Forties – began, Peggy knew she had been freed from her homeland's clasp of class. China had given her the chance to become what she always had dreamed of being: an independent, twentieth-century woman.

And then she became pregnant.

GISELA EBBECKE
Shanghai 1940

Disliking sex but still wanting a child, Peggy heard about a doctor from Munich, Gisela Ebbecke.

The gossip among the women of the Settlement was that the half-Jewish doctor had emigrated from Europe because she feared the anti-Semitic policies of the Third Reich.

Whatever the reason, a year later, the bulky, middle-aged German Jew was bustling around the Shanghai General Hospital as if she owned it. Gisela Ebbecke's revolutionary surgical techniques were said to enhance fertility by diagnosing and dealing with any physical obstructions in the body, especially those related to conception. Peggy made an appointment to meet her.

Dr. Ebbecke was stout and unattractive by the standards of the day – which favoured petite, pretty women like Peggy. Ebbecke was a large woman – not fat, but big-boned. Even her facial features seemed overdrawn: lips too thick, eyes too wide – as if she had arrived at puberty and had continued to grow in all directions without leaving her acne behind; her complexion was ruddy and pitted. There was no Mr. Ebbecke.

Peggy, however, liked the woman's Teutonic briskness; she felt confident in her hands. After a preliminary examination and some basic tests, Peggy subjected herself to a small operation that, Doctor Ebbecke said, '*vill fix all ze troubles inzide.*'

For a few weeks afterwards, Peggy and Stan found that their attempts at making a baby were so painful that they had to stop. Peggy had to ask Stan to be patient with her. 'This is just making a bad situation worse,' Stan said as he turned away.

She was near to tears. 'It's bad for both of us, Stan.'

She could sense his head rolling back and forth on the pillow. 'Let's be truthful with each other, Pegs: our love-making is pathetic – even on the rare times it happens. The fellers on the ship tell me that even bad sex is good. But not for us, it seems.'

She propped herself on one elbow and stared at him. 'You discuss this with your...' she paused, 'mates?'

He wouldn't meet her eyes. For a few minutes they were silent until Stan said, 'Of course not.'

A few weeks later, when the pain had faded, Peggy asked *Wang Fang* to prepare Stan's favourite English dinner: roast beef, Yorkshire pudding, and Brussels sprouts. The dessert – or 'pudding' as Stan insisted on calling it – would be the one his mother had made when he was a boy – bananas and custard.

Peggy didn't like pandering to Stan, she hated any role that smacked of 'the little woman at home' – it ran against her nature – but this time, she reasoned, the cause was indisputable.

Wang Fang, excited by the prospect of cooking a special dinner for 'the master', came to Peggy in some distress at lunchtime: 'Missy, no cow, no cow for tonight. Only dak dak – duck.'

Peggy was unfazed. 'Then duck it will be, Wang Fang. Your duck is always very good.'

The evening was a success. She asked the staff to lay a table on the verandah. The moon was high and full, and Eddie Duchin's piano – Stan's favourite – tinkled quietly in the background. If anything, she worried that Stan might find the dinner a little contrived, but she could see how happy he was. *Wang Fang* wore white gloves to carve the *dak* meticulously and, drizzled with his plum sauce, a secret recipe from his village at *Tong Li* – they easily demolished three-quarters of the bird.

During the meal – while Stan drank two bottles of *Tsingtao* beer – he talked about voyages on the '*Shenkin*', the war in Europe, and his days at Repton. Peggy enjoyed the way she had learned to be present without paying too much attention to his words. At midnight, they drifted off to bed.

Three months later, she was able to tell Stan. 'I am with child, o master.'

Stan beamed, 'Well, fuck a duck.'

'Indeed.' They burst out laughing and hugged.

The baby, an eight-pound boy, arrived one week earlier than expected. Stan was away on a trip to *Ningpo*, a port in southern China.

Barely conscious after thirty-six hours of labour, Peggy – red-eyed with pain from the forceps delivery, her pelvis torn and bruised from the delivery

– shouted, 'Where is Doctor Ebbecke?'

The pink-cheeked English attending nurse, her lapel badge identifying her simply as 'Morton'. had arrived that week from London. Again, Peggy shouted, 'Where is my doctor, Morton?'

With a prim smile, the nurse hushed her, 'Sh, sh, sh, Mrs. Parker. Dr. Ebbecke is conducting an operation on another woman. Exactly like the one she performed on you, enabling *you* to have *your* child.' She walked over to Peggy's bed before saying, 'I venture to say we should all be grateful for Doctor Ebbecke.'

Peggy, wincing, raised herself on her elbows. 'Well, Miss Home Counties – or wherever you came from – I venture to say – find my bloody doctor now!' She fell back on the bed, exhausted.

A quarter-hour later, the large figure of the doctor appeared at her bedside. 'My poor little canary,' she said, looking at Peggy's white, pain-filled face. Peggy was angry and frustrated. 'Where were you? This was my Calvary!' She was close to shouting. 'How could you leave me alone with this child of a nurse?'

'Es tut mir leid. I am sorry, Frau Parker. I told you that the Caesarean would have been better, but no, you said you had to be in control, and this…' she shrugged, palms upturned, '… is the result.'

Ebbecke reached for her hand, but Peggy pulled away. Dr. Ebbecke's voice hardened. 'Don't blame me. Blame your husband. He is lucky to take both of you home. Tell him you must never have another child. You are not made for this. She turned at the door to look at her patient, a small white ball scrunched between the sheets. 'Men and their appetites,' she said. She repeated the phrase with Germanic emphasis – *'Manner und Ihr appetit.'*

Three days passed before Stan arrived to take her home. He was appalled to hear how she had suffered. 'My poor darling,' he said. 'I feel so useless.'

She held the newborn tightly as Stan placed her in a wheelchair and pushed his little cargo to the front doors of the hospital. *Han* had brought the car around and stepped forward to take the wheelchair. He bowed, his face creased with smiles. 'Missy, Missy, good Missy. Now we have little Master. Good, good.'

While Stan took Jonny, Peggy eased herself into the back seat of the Packard then held her arms out for Jonny. 'I just wish you had been with me, Stan – not in the room, they wouldn't have allowed that – but, you know… near.'

Stan made no apology but looked at her in the back seat. 'Just rest, my darling. Han will drive us home safely and carefully, won't you, Han?' Stan tapped Jonny's nose. 'I'll hold my son.'

'My God,' he laughed nervously, 'he's so tiny… and these little fingers – he has fingernails… unbelievable. What a precious little chap!'

Peggy smiled at Stan from the back seat as he stood, seemingly mesmerized next to the Packard, with the child in his arms.

'Are you happy, Stan?'

'Oh, Peggy, yes. Most certainly, I'm happy.'

'It's a wicked world we're bringing him into, the poor, wee laddie.' Peggy said, frowning.

Stan rocked the bundle for a moment, still gazing at the son in his arms. 'We will keep him safe.'

Finally, he looked down at Peggy. 'Won't we, love.' There was no question.

THE BUS TO FU-XING
Shanghai 1942

No one greeted Peggy when they stepped inside the bus on the way to the camp, Jonny in her arms. She scanned the two dozen or more people on board. They were a mixture of adults and children sitting in silence. Children were distributed in various positions, oddly quiet; smaller ones sat on their parents' laps, others crouched on stools in the aisle.

Filling the air was the sour fetor of baby shit and urine. Jonny's little head swung from side to side, his button of a nose crinkling with disgust. 'Poo, mummy!' He blurted his favourite new word.

Peggy guessed that not all the smell was caused by the children. The breath-catching fug, she thought, was partly due to the fear of what might happen next. Even the icy chill couldn't sanitise the air.

She recognised some of the people from the Settlement: Willy Allen and his White Russian wife, Marina; John and Sue Lang with their two children. There were some officials she recognised from cocktail parties at the consulates: a curly-haired Englishman named French, and a bearded South African engineer whose name, she recalled, was Tony de Bruyn and, sitting next to him, a beautiful American with long grey hair.

Peggy acknowledged those she knew, however vaguely. The women smiled back, but the men stared ahead or sat with bowed heads. She looked around for somewhere to sit. Tom avoided her eyes. A mother told an older child to vacate a seat so that Peggy could sit with Jonny on her lap. Peggy mimed 'thank you' and sat down. The Trenchers sat behind her.

They exited the gates of the International Settlement. Flags – the Union flag, the Tricolour, and the Stars and Stripes – hung limply. She thought, 'Even the flags have surrendered.'

Their vehicle stuttered past the gates with a grind of gears. Chinese workers, watched by soldiers, began to hack down the flag poles. No one looked at the bus as it passed.

She hugged Jonny to her. 'Daddy go shipside?' He gave her such a sweet, questioning smile that her eyes filled with tears. Again, he asked, 'Daddy go shipside?' It was the phrase Stan always used before he went to his vessel.

'Yes, darling. Daddy go shipside.' She kissed his dark curls. Soon Peggy felt Jonny slipping into sleep, the episode with *Zhang* seemingly buried in his innocence. She closed her eyes, only to succumb to more thoughts sliding into her mind: what if Stan *had* disappeared? Once his link to *Ohta Tang* was severed, there would be no way for him to have advance notice of their capture. Quite the reverse, in fact, *Tang* would be happy to keep Stan in the dark. She and Jonny would become the Admiral's bargaining chips. They would forever be in jeopardy, their future in the enemy's hands. Despair consumed her.

'DAY OF INFAMY'
7th December 1941

The 'day which will live in infamy' – as American president Roosevelt called it – dawned clear in the city.

Peggy and Stan were five thousand miles west of the Hawaiian target, bisected by the international dateline. It was December 8th, 1941, in Shanghai when news of the catastrophe chattered through on the teletype to the British Consulate.

Because of the time difference, Peggy and Stan were unaware of the attack when they set out for Stan's ship.

The plan was that *Han* would drive them along *Nanjing Xilu* to a shopping area near the Peace Hotel. If there was time, they agreed they might have coffee at 'the Peace', as locals called it. Afterwards, they realised the irony of the choice. She and Stan had almost completed their shopping – they were still furnishing Jonny's nursery, even though he was nine months old – and, after coffee, they would take a taxi to the *Huangpu* district. There, they would board a *sampan* to the '*Shenkin*'.

Before they could enter a store, however, the thud of bombs reached them from the Bund. They heard the sudden barking of anti-aircraft fire. 'That's Archie,' said Stan, using the sailor's shorthand for an anti-aircraft gun. Panicking Chinese began to scatter, rushing past them, around them. Many of them were yelling the panicked cry of all Chinese, 'Aye-yee, Aye-yee.'

Peggy was alarmed at being so far from Jonny. The last time she'd witnessed an attack was nearly four years previously, during the Battle of Shanghai, when the Cathay and Palace Hotels had been bombed in error by the Chinese Air Force.

Now a mother, Peggy's feelings were of a different order when the guns boomed. Four years ago, everything had been an adventure. Now she was a lifeline to her son – her existence was his existence. Her emotions belonged to someone else, or so it felt, as the artillery threw death into the sky.

'Get home as quickly you can, love. I've no idea what this is about, but that bombing is at the port.' He turned and hugged her. 'Hurry – and trust no one. Go to Watcyn's and Zofia's – you should be safe there. I must get to my ship.' He kissed her cheek and then was swallowed into a scrum of yammering locals.

Stunned and bereft of help in the middle of a bombing raid, Peggy stood for a moment, taking deep breaths. After a moment, she began to push her way back through the *melee*. She realised that the 'bamboo wireless' – as they called the informal information network among the local population – was already humming with warnings.

Hectic, the Chinese were running everywhere. Peggy could almost smell the fear from their bodies. People bumped against her, scrambling to return to their homes and families. The locals knew that to stand still would mean being shot in the streets. As a European, a '*gaijin*', Peggy hoped she was unlikely to be stopped as she moved west along *Nanjing Xilu*, away from the Bund and towards home.

Within fifteen minutes, rickshaws were clattering along the pavement, loaded with pieces of roped-together furniture. Scores of sobbing, yelling, screaming people surged about in the avenues on either side of her. Meanwhile, above the mayhem, distant shelling competed with the shouts of the victorious Japanese – 'Banzai! Banzai*!*'

As she struggled through the clogged streets, Peggy remembered how, months previously, Stan had asked her if she wanted to return to her family. She had resisted the idea. He reminded her that all British armed forces had been evacuated from Shanghai to Hong Kong. American civilians in the Settlement had been ordered to leave the country. Now it was too late.

Peggy believed – like the ten thousand expatriates who had remained in Shanghai – that her status in the International Settlement would protect her from the invaders. 'If we stay together as a family,' she had told Stan. 'I just know we'll be all right.'

Pushing through the babble of sweaty, panicked citizens, she was thinking, 'Why was I so stubborn, when all Stan cared about was our safety?' And the next minute, she'd shift the blame: 'Why didn't Stan insist that we leave?'

She felt hot, frightened and spent as she hurried west. The road had narrowed, making her passage even more cramped, but after a quarter-mile, it debouched into the calm of Bubbling Well Road. She could still hear shouting and gunfire, but the sounds were not close enough to feel threatening.

Her escape from the mayhem re-established her sense of control; she knew what she had to do.

The Parker House – even she had learned to use that term for her home – seemed deserted, the servants gone. All except *Han*, who was polishing the Packard. Her driver saluted as she walked up the driveway.

'Missy walk?' he said, his eyes wide with alarm.

'Zhang?' There was no time for niceties.

'Upstairs, Missy, with Master Jonny.'

Peggy raced up the stairs to Jonny's nursery. She found him in his cot, asleep and *Zhang* behind the cot, on her knees, praying. She remembered Clew's only utterance on the matter of religion. 'By all means, pray,' he had said, 'but when you get off your knees, hustle.'

'Come on, Zhang, chop-chop. Wrap Jonny in blanket.' *Zhang* snapped into action.

A phone was ringing in Peggy's bedroom; she dashed there and picked it up.

'Second Officer Chris Hall, here, Mrs. Parker,' said an English voice. 'Is Stan still with you?'

She explained what had happened: that they were on the way to the ship when the bombardment began. 'He should arrive at any minute,' she said.

'Good man,' said Hall. He added, almost casually, 'I hope he makes it through this mess.' A pause. 'Mrs. Parker, the Japanese have attacked the Americans in the Pacific, at Pearl Harbour. They've already bombed one of ours on the Bund – the gunboat 'Peterel' and a Yank ship, the 'USS Wake'. Poor chumps had no idea they were going to be hit. I should think Pearl Harbour brought this on – a co-ordinated attack – clever little bastards. I hope that…'

The line went dead

Peggy collapsed on the bed, shivering with despair, absorbing the news, her breath quickening. The drone of aircraft reached her. If the Japanese were at war with the Americans, she realised, their neutral status in the International Settlement would change – perhaps immediately.

Seconds later, a hunk of metal ruptured the wall above the bed. On the ceiling where the metal had embedded, Peggy watched, as if it were in slow motion, tentacles of black cracks forming. Immediately part of the ceiling opened up. She leaped off the bed as a chunk of plaster fell where she had been sitting. She was shaking. 'What shall we do, Stan?' she asked the empty room.

She yelled, 'Front door with Jonny, Zhang. Now!' She knew they had to leave the house.

Han had anticipated her. The Packard was purring in the driveway. The car's trunk was open, and *Han* stood at attention, ready to load any luggage. But there was none. *Zhang* had packed a few necessities into a hold-all. They took the bag into the back seat with them.

Jonny was squealing with excitement, his chubby little legs jack-knifing with joy in his portable bed. *Zhang* lifted him into the car with her. Jonny, unaware of the danger, was thrilled by the diversion.

Stan's skipper, Watcyn Williams, kept an apartment at Eden Gardens, a few miles north from Peggy's on *Jiangning Lu*, towards the Jade Buddha temple. In the summer, when the heat of July could be so stupefying that it banished all reason, Peggy would ask *Han* to drive her to the temple. In the cool interior, she took pleasure reading, or simply sitting on a bench, watching the saffron-robed monks flow by while Buddhist worshippers prostrated themselves in front of the gigantic jade Buddhas. At that moment, she wished she could summon that tranquillity.

As *Han* drove, distraught Chinese tried to stop the car, often running in front of it screaming unintelligibly.

'What are they saying, Han?'

'They want us to help them.'

Peggy understood their desperation, but she was resolute. 'Don't stop, Han, chop-chop, chop-chop!' she ordered.

'Look, Missy!'

She turned to her left, where *Han* had pointed. As they drove past, she saw that Japanese soldiers had lined up four or five Chinese in a line. 'Chop-chop! she urged *Han*. She had seen one street execution and didn't need to see another. She knew what would happen next. Above all, she did not wish to draw attention to the Packard.

The car accelerated.

'Why they not stop us, Han?'

There was the occasional thump of a body and an angry yell as they slowly moved north on *Jiangning*. Han knew that any accident would be devastating; he would have to stop the car, a mob would form, there might be blood. He had to be determined but aware of likely consequences should he become impatient.

'Missy, me think they not want attack foreign people. But soon, Missy. Friends have told me this.'

Then they were passing buildings in the French Concessions. She thought briefly of Natasha but dismissed the idea of help: Tash was young, single, and resourceful – she'd find a way. There was no time for diversions. Keeping Jonny safe was all that mattered.

A few buildings in the Concessions had already been reduced to rubble. The Japanese seemed to have dropped bombs all over the Settlement. Later, she heard that these hits were not from the enemy's planes but from the tiny, ill-trained Chinese air force.

When they reached Eden Gardens, Peggy asked *Han* to find a sheltered place to park the car and then to go to his family. 'Missy, maybe Captain Parker need me. I wait here with car?'

'As you wish, Han.' She didn't have time for debate; if *Han* put duty above family – so be it.

Zofia Williams met Peggy at the door of the apartment. The captain's wife was a thick-waisted Serb. Peggy had always felt, on the few occasions that she'd seen her – in Peggy's early days in the city, they'd had lonely tea parties together at the Majestic Hotel – that Zofia possessed an innate stoicism. As a child, the woman had been through many changes of fortune in her Balkan homeland.

Her face that evening was red with excitement as she ushered them in. 'Mein Gott, what times, what times!'

'Stan said he'd told you to come to us,' she said, kissing Peggy's cheek and taking Jonny from a shaken *Zhang*. 'We'll make the boy some porridge. Go to Watcyn – he's in the living room,' she called over her shoulder as she took Jonny and the *amah* into the kitchen.

Peggy found Stan's commanding officer slumped on the couch. Williams, in his early fifties, looked ten years older; he was the kind of man who wore his life in his complexion. From the moment she had first met the splotchy-faced Welshman, Peggy had concluded that years of drinking were now exacting retribution. Watcyn's skin was like a purple roadmap.

Now Williams stared at her, unseeing. Peggy knew Stan's skipper had probably been drinking since morning when the news of the attack came through. He broke out of his thousand-yard-stare before speaking. 'Hello, Peggy. Oh, it be a mess, I'm saying. We're well pleased ye came. Stan's bound to call again. We'll put Union Jacks and Saint David's flags to cover the car. Stick it in the garden, so they know there are Brits and the Welsh here!' He chuckled. 'This'll be over in a couple of days.'

Peggy wondered why the Welshman thought the Union Jack and the Welsh flag could withstand Japanese bombs better than bricks and mortar. And what did he mean by 'a couple of days'? British arrogance, she decided, knew no limits.

The phone rang. 'Must take that, darlin.' Orders from the new owners, I'll be guessing.' He grunted as he pulled himself off the couch, swaying slightly, and left the room.

Peggy poured herself a small glass of neat whisky. When Williams weaved back into the room, he nodded approvingly at the glass in her hand and said, 'That was Stan, your man. Seems he can't get through to your digs. He wants you to know he made it back to the ship. And now he knows you're safe.' He gave her a weary smile. 'Would have let you talk to him, but the Japs may be listening, and you might say too much.'

He called out, 'Zof! I have to get back to my command. Stan's told me we've got orders to take the ship to Kobe and collect supplies for our new masters. The Japs gave him a password to use at roadblocks near the docks. I have it, and I'll use it if I have any problems.'

Peggy said, 'Han can take you, Watcyn. He needs something to do.' She knew Stan's skipper was unfit to drive.

Williams lowered his voice as he turned to Peggy. 'That's so sweet of you, my dear. Seems as though the wee Japs had this well planned. But we must obey. From now on, it'll be Heil Hitler – Tora, Tora, Tora, hey?' He shook his head. 'What a bloody brew!'

JAPAN RULES
Shanghai 1941

The day after the Pearl Harbour attack, Peggy heard that the Japanese had entered all the Shanghai banks, the embassies, and the great business houses. They sealed all of them and stopped all commercial activity.

'It's been a co-ordinated invasion – no doubt about it,' Rollo Vigne told her when he phoned from the besieged British Consulate.

Vigne sounded outraged, as if the Japanese didn't know the rules of cricket. 'But we're holding things together, and we're trying to behave as if nothing too serious has happened. The blighters stormed into our clubs while members were dining.' Disgust was blended with contempt in his tone. 'They have absolutely no idea how to behave.

'Bill Thurber was dining at the American Club.' Vigne rushed on: 'Bill said that they marched him and other members across the street. Luckily, he had the presence of mind to hold on to his martini…' he allowed himself a small chuckle, '…it takes more than an invasion to separate an American from his martini, but still… the Japs made the Americans – despite slaughtering thousands of them at Pearl – salute the Rising Sun. My God, they raised their bloody flag over the clubhouse. Outrageous scum!'

Peggy closed her eyes as he spluttered down the line; she knew his rage had no purpose.

When she thought Vigne had finished his rant, she asked, 'And Marcus Carter?' she hesitated. 'Is everyone else at the Consulate accounted for?'

'Marcus? Oh, we're all fine. Do you want to talk with him, Peggy? He's in with the CG at this moment, but I can tell him you called.'

'Heavens no, Rollo, don't disturb the Consul General. I just wanted to be sure everyone was safe.'

'Absolutely, ma'am. But I shall tell Marcus you called. Must go. Look after yourself.'

He was gone before she could ask him not to tell Marcus she'd called. 'I'm such an idiot!' she said to herself. She felt like some whimpering schoolgirl. What had the man done to her to make her act so out of character?

Soon all cars owned by expatriates, or their firms were confiscated. A week after *Han* had driven Williams to the '*Shenkin*', the Japanese found the Packard where *Han* had hidden it. People had seen soldiers drive it away, they told him; they were puzzled when *Han* wept.

Han told Peggy he would leave. He looked anguished as he explained that, without the car to maintain, his life had no purpose. He said he would go back to his family. Peggy had nothing to offer him except four weeks' wages. She watched *Han*, shoulders slumped, walk down the driveway.

After a few days, Peggy, like every expatriate, was commanded to wear a red armband, making it easier for foreigners to be identified in the event of greater chaos. For security reasons, foreigners were not permitted to work; foreign-owned stores were shuttered.

Then came a comical turn of events: The occupying force ordered that Britons needing new clothing would be restricted to buying them from the sole Chinese tailor trading in the Settlement. The tailor's customers discovered that the man's supply of material was limited – corduroy jackets and trousers in two shades only. Anyone with any fashion sense would have to be prepared to meet another expat wearing an identical outfit.

Japan ruled.

AN OCCUPIED CITY
Shanghai 1942

A late summer evening in Occupied Shanghai. Stan and Peggy were at the Palace Hotel, handsomely restored after the bombing on 'Bloody Saturday', five years previously. They shared pink gins on the hotel's verandah, watching the sun bloat before it slid away on the west side of the city. A few minutes before eight-thirty, they stepped into the hotel's lobby, ready to greet their dinner guests, the Trenchers, and the Vignes.

'I cannot believe that these little yellow men have vanquished the British Empire,' hissed Roland Vigne as they began eating their appetizers of shrimp and salad. A Chinese waiter filled their glasses with a chilled Chablis; nothing indicated he'd heard the Englishman.

Peggy shook her head at Vigne, incredulous. 'For heaven's sake, Rollo, I wish you'd stop pretending that we Brits have some sort of divine right to tell other people how to behave. We're visitors here – tenants – we don't own every stone.' From across the table, she saw Stan raise his eyebrows – a private communication that could only mean, 'easy, Peggy.'

The table fell silent. Glasses were lifted.

Allegra Vigne said, 'Good for you, Pegs. Rollo needs a good spanking.' Rollo pursed his lips and looked across the room, feigning boredom.

Stan had made himself the nominal head of the round table. Peggy sat opposite him. Rollo was on Peggy's left and Tom Trencher on her right. Stan had seated *Chao-xing* on his right and Rollo's wife, Allegra, on his left. Peggy had taken at least a half-hour to plan the seating – she knew that Stan could be very particular about where his guests sat, and how that governed what he called, 'the dance of conversation'.

At some point, Stan had decided that Rollo and his wife, Allegra, were too young to be compatible as regular friends even though only a decade divided them. 'We can be friendly, but nothing says we have to be *friends*,' he'd decided. Peggy realised her outburst was unlikely to ever make them friends; now, even 'friendly' might be a challenge for Rollo.

She felt a small twinge of contrition as she thought about the young diplomat sitting beside her. Vigne was engaged in a soft conversation with *Chao-xing*. Peggy knew that Rollo (Dragon School, Oxford, a stint in Burma) had 'legacy preferment'. In colonial office language, this meant he would be advanced quickly in his career because Rollo's father, Sir Rupert Vigne, was a Permanent Secretary in Whitehall. Peggy, who believed people should be judged on their merits, hated such practices. In her view, that kind of nepotism maintained the status quo. She had persuaded herself that Stan's 'perks' were of a different order; whoever had granted them expected something in return – the nature of which she had yet to identify.

Vigne seemed furious with the way control of *Shanghai* was unfolding. To support his reactionary views, Rollo was now announcing – rather than saying – 'I believe the Japs plan to take over the Maritime Customs. *They* will decide what goes in and out of *our* ports.'

Allegra Vigne, staring at her husband, protested, 'Oh darling, can we talk about something else?' She seemed to be aware that Rollo was readying himself for a polemic.

'Ally cat', as Rollo called his young wife, still radiated the vibrations of the promiscuous games mistress she had once been. Peggy knew that five years previously, Rollo, attracted by Allegra's bosomy charms and the freedom with which the pretty girl dispensed them, made sure that he benefited. He impregnated Allegra on the pretext of getting her a job interview for the GCHQ, the nexus of British military intelligence. Allegra left her post at Cheltenham Ladies College and married Rollo. The job at GCHQ never materialised, leaving Allegra to sit alone in her Surrey cottage awaiting motherhood

Peggy had heard that Rollo's father, Sir Rupert, was not best pleased with these developments. As punishment, he arranged for the newlyweds to be shipped off to China on, as he told his son, 'The road to redemption'. *Shanghai* also had the advantage of being a less public place for the birth of Sir Rupert Vigne's sooner-than-desired grandchild. The baby, Regina Fuchsia Vigne, was born three months after their arrival in the city.

Stan, fingers steepled, now considered Allegra's objection. Peggy saw him turn to Vigne's wife with a kind but dismissive smile.

'Wait, Allegra.' He winked at her. 'Frankly, if you're not angry – as Rollo most certainly is – you're simply not listening.'

He tapped the air in the direction of the younger man and said, 'But I submit that you, Rollo, have been misled. You see, Vigne, they are no longer – nor have they ever been – *our* ports. Peggy – perhaps with too much zeal – just made the same point.' He paused. 'As a matter of fact, the Nips have asked me to train their officers in Customs protocols, marine surveying – that kind of thing.'

There was a shocked silence. Even Peggy, although having been scolded by her husband, wondered if Stan was simply trying to be provocative.

Again, Vigne's eyes widened. 'Surely you won't do that?'

'I haven't accepted. I may not. First, I need to discuss it with Peggy.' Peggy tried not to look surprised, but she was stunned to hear that Stan might help the Japanese. She had no time to regain her composure before Vigne addressed her directly.

'Well, Peggy,' he said, staring at her and giving his best impression of a menacing look. 'You mustn't let Stan do this. To me, it smacks of consorting with the enemy.'

'Oh, I'm sure our Chief Officer can make up his own mind,' Allegra interrupted. She looked at her husband. 'But it's charming, don't you think, Rollo, that Stan cares what his wife thinks.'

Peggy turned to smile at the man on her left. 'Don't worry, Rollo,' she said, 'Stan and I will do whatever serves our family best.'

'And the country, too, I hope,' said Vigne to the table at large, sitting up in his chair, shoulders back, as if to emphasise his opinion.

'Exactly, China,' said Stan.

'That's not the country I meant.'

'I know what you meant, Rollo.' Stan spoke softly. 'But we have new masters now, and if shipping comes to a halt because Customs can't clear it, who does that serve? Your family? Our Chinese family? Our Japanese captors?' He shrugged, his hands expansive. 'The fact is, we all need fuel and food; we all need to keep trading if the world is to go on spinning.' He paused to sip his Chablis. 'Sorry, old chap, but it seems to me that we have to take a pragmatic view.'

From Peggy's right came Tom's American voice: 'Well, Stan, you've got to watch out with these little guys. They're clever bastards. Caught us off guard at Pearl.' He addressed the table. 'America thinks it's too big for the small fry to try. But we took a beating, and they've *gotta* be coming for us in Shanghai soon.' His eyes swivelled back to his host. 'Whatever you decide, just watch your back, Stan. Folks tell me they're cunning little buggers – as you Brits say. They've been working with China since… since forever. Now they've got a chance to grab what they can. Why should they watch us take the pickings, huh?' He looked across the table at his young Chinese wife. 'Am I right, or am I right, sweetheart?'

Chao-xing smiled as if her husband had disclosed a great mystery. She sipped her wine. 'Yes, Stan; dine with a long spoon.'

Vigne looked at his plate. 'Well, I don't know…'

'No, you don't,' said Stan. Peggy knew he was irritated. Stan turned his attention back to Allegra.

'Now Allegra, what good films can you recommend?'

***

An hour later, flexing the eight cylinders of his Chrysler Airflow along the Bund, Tom Trencher was saying, 'Strange that Parker wants to work for the Japs, no?'

Chao-xing glanced at him from the passenger seat. 'I'm not sure 'wants' is the right word. It doesn't sound as though he has much choice.'

'That's how he's positioned it – the idea, I mean – but maybe he wants to get close to them, find out what they're thinking.'

His wife snorted. 'That's not difficult to figure out: the Japs want world domination.'

Tom glanced back. 'And is that such a bad thing? The Americans have it – why shouldn't the Japs?'

She frowned. 'Tom, when you say things like that, you seem to forget I'm Chinese. The Japanese have started by trying to dominate us. And remember, the Americans didn't start a world war to be where they are.'

Later that night, having settled his wife in her room, Tom nursed a small glass of bourbon in his study. He stretched out on the chartreuse-coloured chaise longue, the only piece of furniture he'd kept from his parents' Long Island beach house. He'd peopled the shelves with his books from Oxford; they were the only personal items that gave the smallest clues about a man who, at age nineteen, had won a first-class degree in Philosophy, Politics and Economics.

Sometimes Tom wondered why he'd accepted the offer from the State Department. Given his spectacular academic record, his final interview was with the Secretary, Henry Stimson. A Harvard man, Stimson wondered why Tom had chosen to go to Oxford when his alma mater, he thought, gave as good an education.

'I wanted to get out of America. I'm not sure you can influence foreign policy if you haven't been further than Miami.' Tom was on safe ground; he knew that Stimson had worked in France and the Philippines. Months later, he heard that Stimson had pushed for Tom to get the China posting. When the Japanese invaded Manchuria, using it as a staging post for their military harassment of China, he'd admired Stimson for refusing to recognise the change of regime. Tom believed that he and his boss, though separated by many levels of hierarchy and thousands of miles of ocean, had similar ideals.

He decided that with Stimson as his champion, there was a clear path ahead; in headier moments, he speculated about being the youngest-ever Secretary.

Now he scrunched into the chaise longue and thought about Stan Parker.

He tolerated the Englishman because his Consulate General had told him to stay close to the machinations of the Merchant Navy, Blue Funnel, and Stanley Parker – a man, he'd been told, who was 'cutting a swathe' through the shipping company. The State Department suspected that the British government's attitude to their merchant fleets was more liberal than Whitehall's link with the Royal Navy. Was it possible, Washington wondered, that a blind eye was being turned to cargo that the Americans would have impounded? 'State' would expect him to be even more vigilant after learning that Stan might supervise the Japanese as they learned the centuries-old protocols.

Tom knew, however, that he had got as close to Parker as was possible. He also knew that, despite his close attention to British social mores, the Englishman's air of command, his apparent need always to have the last word, would prevent them from being confidantes. Aside from being white men in a foreign land, they had nothing else in common. Their meeting at the Palace hotel three months ago – when he'd told Stan how he'd met *Chao-xing* – had never developed into anything closer. Tom soon realised that Stan had met him as part of a programme of 'getting acquainted' with the locals, or in Tom's case, the neighbours.

And Stan was away so much, Tom mused. Every ten days or so, at an early hour, Tom would see a black Packard pull up outside the Parker house across the road. Minutes later, Parker, in his naval uniform, would walk down the driveway and slip into the front street with *Han*, his Chinese driver. After Peggy arrived from England, Tom would see her – attractive, vivacious – leave the house, also in the Packard. Sometimes she'd wave.

His speculation moved to the evening's dinner table conversation. Tom sensed it revealed Stan's high regard for the Chinese. If he were to shorthand Parker's attitude for his Washington masters, he'd say, 'Stan Parker is what you'd call a *China-for-the-Chinese man.*'

Which made him wonder why the Englishman was so ready to help the Japanese. Unless – he swirled the last sip of the bourbon in the glass – he was also helping the Chinese.

He wondered if the Japanese had considered the possibility of this before they asked for Stan's help.

Whether they had or not, he thought Stanley Parker needed watching.

He downed the last of the bourbon and climbed the stairs to his room.

AN ARGUMENT
Shanghai 1942

As was their custom, the Parkers reviewed the evening when they arrived home.

'I wish you'd given me some warning,' said Peggy over her shoulder as Stan unzipped her. She sat down at her dressing table and started to remove her earrings.

'There was no time. Admiral Tang called me this afternoon as I was about to go to the hotel to meet you.' Stan moved to the bed to remove his shoes. His face was ashen, his shoulders slack. 'God, I'm buggered!'

He took a few deep breaths and stretched his arms before speaking again. 'Tang's in charge of all Japanese ships in Shanghai. His officers respect me. They know I've been in China for almost twenty years. That means a lot to the Nips.'

She could sense that an awkward conversation was simmering: She had grown increasingly worried about Stan's health.

'May I be frank, Stan?'

He gave a lopsided grin. 'You've never been anything else, Peggy.'

'Seriously, sweetheart, this job you're about to take might kill you. You'll be doing it in secret, and that's bound to add to the pressure.'

'What do you mean "in secret"? Blue Funnel knows what I'm doing.'

She raised an eyebrow. 'Sweetheart, I may have been born yesterday, but I wasn't born last night. Are you telling me that PP hasn't asked you to get as much as you can out of the Japanese while you collab-, I'm sorry, while you co-operate with them?'

If Stan felt insulted by her slip of the tongue, he didn't show it. 'Well, they do expect me to keep my eyes and ears open.'

'Exactly, they've asked you to spy on the Japanese.' She let the phrase hang between them before she went on.

She said the next sentence at the mirror; she was too nervous to say it to his face. 'It's crazy: A man with a hole in his heart doing the kind of work that could give him a heart attack any day.'

Stan looked up with a start as Peggy swung around to face him. She had to look into his eyes before going on.

'Seven years ago – shortly after we'd met – your father came to my salon, uninvited. This was the day after I'd spoken to you about getting your Mate's ticket; it was sheer coincidence – if you believe in that kind of thing – which I don't.' She looked at him intently, willing him to hear her out. 'I'd never met your Pa before, and we got on straight away. Together, we agreed that you needed a push to get you out of Derby. We felt you had to go back to sea – where you could flourish. That was when Pa told me about your heart; he thought I should know.'

Her voice rising, Peggy went on: 'But this is different: now you tell me you've agreed to do this spying job without discussing it with me – the person who cares for you a million times more than any of those fat prigs at Blue Funnel.'

She couldn't help the tears pricking at her eyes, knowing they were not of regret but of anger. She drew a deep breath to quiet her shaking body. He had to know why she felt so angry that he'd excluded her from what might be a life-changing decision.

'Do you know how you *got* this commission, Stan?'

'What do you mean?' His face flushed. 'I got my Mate's ticket. I went to London and had an interview. They liked me. They offered me a position.' He rubbed the back of his head – a sure sign he was becoming impatient. 'What did I miss?'

'Stanley, would you even *be* here if it hadn't been for me and your Pa pushing you?'

He shrugged and turned away. 'Oh, you and Pa didn't think I was capable of planning my own future, is that it?'

She crossed to him and took his hands and pulled his so he faced her. 'Darling, your Pa and I both love you, and we wanted you to feel fulfilled by what you were doing. Of course, you interviewed well. All we did was nudge you into it.' She made him turn to face her. 'And look at you now: a brilliant Chief Officer – virtually a Captain – and a big man on the China coast, as people like to say.' She winked at him, wanting to pull him back into her affection.

He looked miserable and lowered his head as he spoke. 'Of course, I haven't forgotten your support, but I was the one who spent four wretched months in Liverpool, who sat the exams, and passed. And, by the way, I do remember your telling me that – when you supported me.'

'And I still support you, darling; I hope you'll always welcome my support.'

Stan still refused to look at her. She continued, maintaining the softer tone. 'As far as I can tell, your physique is just about coping, but these new challenges are going to place a big strain on you. Already you're beginning to look worn and…'

He dropped her hands. '… and you don't have to worry about it.' His voice got stronger. 'I'm not a flaming invalid, Pegs. This is an important commission; Blue Funnel are backing me. It's a clear crack at the top.' He shook his head. 'PP says I shall have my own command by the end of the year. You must trust me to know what's best for our family.'

She couldn't bear to look at him when he wore that stubborn look – face set, lower lip jutting, eyes angry. She knew he was trying to hold himself back.

She softened her voice. 'It's not just about what's best for you, me, and Jonny. It's what's best for you – Stanley Parker. What if your heart can't take it – leaving you as half the man you were? And, yes, of course, I'm worried it will leave Jonny with a disabled father – and me with a husband who's not all in one piece.' She spread her hands, 'All for what? So Blue Funnel can give you more commissions, more responsibilities?'

He didn't reply, so she went on. 'And what of your reputation, Stan? Your father's name? What if others – not that I care for Vigne's opinion – but there may be others who think you're being disloyal.'

She realised that his decision to work with the Japanese was the result of him becoming so confident in his new position. The days were over when he would heed her advice. She didn't know how to end the quarrel – and she knew it was a quarrel more than an argument; logic didn't come into it, this was a battle of wills.

Through clenched teeth, he answered: 'Well, tonight, I didn't say what I did just to squash that young turd. Yes, I *do* think I should help them,' he continued. 'I spoke to Andy Tudhope at Butterfield and Swire, and they think it would be good for Blue Funnel. Andy will get the Consul General to clear my position as 'expediting officer' to the Japanese. Everyone's aware that if we help the Japs, they will give our freighters preferential treatment. Anyway, if we won't help them, they will find someone else who will - Jardine's, for example - our biggest competitor. Frankly, I'd rather keep the control. I've already told Ohta Tang that we'll co-operate. It's war, Peggy; sometimes you must sleep with the enemy to smother him.'

'You mean like Chamberlain tried to sleep with Hitler?' She shook her head. Stan had won. She made one more throw of the dice. 'Talking about it with me is just a formality, isn't it, Stan? If Blue Funnel and the Consulate approve, my opinion doesn't count?'

'Of course, your opinion counts, but when you married me, you married my job. You must know that.'

'I see; I gave up my job to be the servant of yours?' This time it was a question. For a second, she wondered if she should open another rabbit hole in the argument. She was so upset that she continued before he could answer, knowing it might be wrong of her, but he could not be allowed to lord it over her this way.

'Dearest Stan, let me tell you why this plan with Tang worries me: I understand that, for the moment, the Japanese are our masters. But you'll be collaborating – not simply co-operating – with them if you train them to run our Customs and Excise.'

He turned around to face her. 'But Jardine's…'

'Yes, I know, you don't want your competitors to have an advantage. But at what price?'

She could see her attitude was continuing to upset him; she rarely questioned his decisions, especially since she'd joined him in China.

He stood and continued to pace the large bedroom. There was a purpose in his stride that made her know he'd made up his mind.

His hands waved agitatedly, as if he wanted to push the argument, and her, away.

'Turning down this offer will do nothing for my reputation. Pennington was my champion in London, and he still is in Shanghai. PP sees this – and other assignments – as a leg up.'

He looked up at the ceiling for a moment, as if considering whether to appease her or not.

'Pegs, this must stop. I'll make it simple: if I don't take this job with the Japanese – because of some lame excuse about my health or my principles – Blue Funnel will shove me into some backwater – tabulating shipping schedules or quarter-mastering the stores.'

He wriggled out of his dress shirt, and for a moment, his voice was muffled. 'When I was on the Conway training ship in Liverpool, they drilled into us that if the highest aim of a captain was to preserve his ship, he'd never take it out of port.'

He tossed his shirt into the laundry bag.

'Peggy, I don't want to be that captain and, believe me, you don't want to live with such a man.'

He turned and looked at her through hooded eyes, bare-chested, hands on hips.

Peggy made as if to speak, but he put up his hand and shook his head. 'Uh, uh, uh. End of story.'

THE BUS TO FU-XING
Shanghai 1942

Her seat on the bus was hard, and Jonny's weight and constant restlessness didn't make the journey any easier. Forty minutes later, her child was struggling in her arms, grunting, whining, trying to wriggle free.

She couldn't let him totter around the bus. She guessed her son, who had learned to walk six months previously, couldn't understand why his mother wouldn't let him get down from her lap.

'Be still, darling, please.' She kissed the top of his head, remembering the unique smell of his fontanelle when they first brought him home. Now he was her little boy, toddling from room to room and, when *Zhang* brought him to her in the morning, upsetting her breakfast tray with a gurgling shout.

But *Zhang* was dead, her body icing, rigid in a snowy coffin. At the time of the shooting, Jonny had screamed, 'Zhang! Zhang!' When his sobs had turned into a strangled, 'Uh, uh, mama, mamaaa.' She had told him, her voice catching, 'Zhang go bye byes, sweetie; Zhang go sleepies.' For how long would Jonny's age protect him from any memory of the incident? She had no idea.

To appease his restlessness, she bribed her son with a biscuit. Finally, he curved himself into her. The movement of the bus, though uneven, again lulled him to sleep.

She turned in Trencher's direction and asked, 'Any idea where this Fu-xing place is?'

There was a smattering of laughter from people seated nearby.

'No Fu-xing idea, Peggy.'

The laughter increased, and then someone began to sing. 'It's a long way to get to Fu-xing, it's a long way to go.'

Another male voice joined in: 'It's a long way before I'm Fu-xing, the one girl that I know.'

'Now, now chaps,' came an upper-class voice. She smiled to herself when she heard the pronunciation as 'chee-aps'. 'Less of that, please.' He continued. 'There are women and children aboard.'

The singing stopped, but a few people continued to snigger or hum.

The creaking bus bumped its way through every pothole and bomb crater. The suspension groaned. There was an ominous knocking sound coming from under the floorboards.

An hour had passed since they'd left the Settlement. The awful smells had increased.

'I say,' called the same male voice. 'We must stop to relieve ourselves. We are Her Majesty's subjects. We are not animals! There are children here. Have a care, man.'

Another voice, with an Irish lilt: 'For the love of God, will you no talk to the little Nip, so he understands?' The voice rose: 'Shitty, shitty, shitty – now, now, now!'

The Japanese driver yelled back, 'Hai! Hai! Hai.'

'Christ, it's *Hai, Hai* to everything,' said Tom. 'They say that even when they have no idea what you're asking for – just because it's safer than saying no.'

Another voice, overhearing him, said, 'Not so dumb, then.'

Peggy half-turned and said, 'Actually, Tom, Stan says "Hai" doesn't mean "yes" – it just means "I have understood what you have said." There's no guarantee at all that the driver will stop the bus before we get to Fu-xing.'

'Well,' answered Tom, his eyes narrowing – was it disdain, she wondered? 'I know that. And if Stan says so, it must certainly be true.' Peggy ignored the sarcasm in his voice.

She'd noticed the resigned look of the other men when she got on the bus. Their brief attempt at humour – singing a ribald song – had been the only sign of the spirit they once possessed. While the women looked ahead – read, knitted, or fussed with their children – the men studied their hands, or sat with their arms crossed, looking out of the window, staring into the middle distance

She knew they probably felt useless, embarrassed by the sudden erosion of what she'd heard called their white saviour complex – the feeling of being 'the finest men of the Empire' – as the London 'Times' had once described them. The Colonial Service might have told them about their 'civilising mission' – to develop and protect the indigenous population –

but it had, literally, exploded in their faces. Almost overnight, they had become victims, human chattels of the Japanese, a race of men they despised.

Adding to their sense of guilt – and this, she thought, was how Stanley would have analysed it – was the feeling that they had betrayed the local people. He'd once told Peggy that some expats felt that if the Japanese ever took over the country, the Brits would have placed the Chinese at the mercy of another Oriental power, one that was determined to kill their men and rape their women.

How easy, she thought, to allow their defeatism to affect her, to *kowtow* – Chinese fashion – to her captors. But no, she had Jonny, her investment, to worry about. She would raise him to be ready for the hard, brutish world that was waiting. She would not raise him to be a reed in the wind, so dependent on status for his self-confidence. She had not suffered to bring him into the world as a weakling. But one question nagged at her: did Jonny know how much she loved him – did her little chap know that all her dreams were invested in the small defenceless form on her lap.

OHTA TANG
Shanghai 1942

A few weeks later, Stan came home from a late meeting at the Consulate. He told her that Ohta Tang had invited the two of them to dine with him and his senior officers on Saturday night.

'Seems our people have put my name forward as someone who would be willing to help them.'

She tried not to say it, but she couldn't help herself. 'Not a lot of competition, I imagine.'

Stan seemed to ignore her remark. 'Tang told me he's making up his mind over something and, as he put it, 'it is hard to remain enemies when you've broken bread together.' Stan paused, smiled, 'He's an unusual fellow, Pegs, and he can come across as domineering. I think that's his rank and the Japanese top-down style of leadership – he's the master, and everyone else is there to serve him.'

Peggy raised her eyebrows but didn't reply.

Stan found reasons to enthuse: 'But the man is highly rated in Tokyo. He has command of twelve warships, all moored on the Huangpu. We'll be on their new battleship – well, it's not new: it was the 'Osaka', but they've refitted it with a few more armaments, better officer quarters – and they now call it the 'Nanjing'. I can only assume that the Japanese derive some pleasure – what do the Germans call it – *schadenfreude*? Yes, maybe they get schadenfreude from commandeering a Chinese freighter and making it a kind of battleship, and now their flagship. It's not truly a fighting vessel – more a floating HQ while they're in port.'

He saw the reaction on Peggy's face. 'Well, they and the German have a lot in common,' she said. 'After all, they are allies. Why don't they call the flagship "Rape of Nanjing"?'

Jaws clenched, Stan crossed the drawing room and poured himself a whisky. He didn't offer Peggy a drink.

'Well, your new friend sounds perfectly awful, but if it helps you, I shall keep an open mind,' she said. 'But I still think it's gambling with Fate to spy on these people.'

'Peggy! Please stop saying that.' Then, very slowly, he added, 'If I help them, that's the key assignment. Any information I pick up on the way is a bonus.'

Two nights later, Peggy found it strange to be greeted by their Japanese hosts as they stepped aboard the newly named '*Nanjing*'.

Stan, aware of the Japanese insistence on punctuality as a sign of respect, made sure that they arrived precisely as eight bells sounded.

Peggy knew that, traditionally, Nipponese men and women did not eat together – women served, men ate. As Stan's wife, she knew she had been paid a compliment by being invited to dine with male officers.

'Peggy, please be aware that when the Japanese talk, some of them will pause between thoughts and ideas. It's considered ill-mannered to interrupt with your reply until you are certain they have finished. Often the pauses can last longer than we, in the West, are used to – so just be aware.' Stan raised his eyebrows as if to indicate it was not an option to make such mistakes in etiquette.

She had given more than usual thought to what she should wear. Stan told her there would be no other women present, so there was no need to dress competitively, as did most white women in *Shanghai*. The warm air suggested something backless to her, but there was the problem of her freckles. Freckles were an oddity in the Far East. To clear-skinned Asians, a white, auburn-haired woman with freckles drew unwanted stares – she was even more an alien, a *waiguoren* or *laowai*.

Finally, she settled on a simple black dress. She powdered her bare shoulders to mask her freckles and wore a light grey silk scarf – its pattern a mere hint – across her back. The scarf, while adding flair, also served to hide her freckles; they were almost invisible under the scarf and swirls of auburn hair.

Peggy had sculpted knees and slim legs. She would like to have shown more of what Stan called her 'assets', but she made sure the hem ended just below her knees. She chose a lipstick more aggressively red than usual – she thought the colour had a 'take me seriously' look about it. She thought it important that *Ohta Tang* realised he was not meeting a simpering Japanese female.

When *Han* opened the door of the Packard, seagulls' cries and the smells of the *Huangpu* river rushed to meet her. Peggy looked up at the palace of lights that was the ship. All sense of intimidation left her. She knew she presented an alluring, confident figure. She looked, as her Irish mother would have said, 'grand'. She was thirty-eight, in excellent health, with a handsome Chief Officer husband and a sweet baby. 'What more could a woman want?' she thought as she reached for Stan's arm.

Admiral *Ohta Tang* – barrel-chested, walnut-faced – was waiting at the top of the gangplank. She guessed he might be in his early sixties. He looked at Peggy with black eyes, revealing nothing of his thoughts as he faced an attractive European woman. He immediately moved into a deep bow. She knew *Tang* would not cause offense by taking her hand.

'Missy Parker, we honoured to have your serene presence on our humble ship. We borrow this unworthy vessel from Blue Funnel Line,' he paused before adding, 'and will give back one day.' Tang chuckled.

The Japanese was wearing a splendidly cut uniform. Double-breasted, the jacket hung easily on his shoulders; beneath his chest whatever girth he had was disguised by the rich black material and the tailor's skill. *Tang*'s Imperial Japanese Navy clothes – bemedaled, elegant – were a statement of power. Stan's well-worn Merchant Navy outfit was a poor contrast to *Tang*'s uniform. Whatever cologne *Tang* was wearing was just short of intrusive, the scent subsumed by the smells of the ship – the tar, the ropes, the river.

Tang chuckled, bowing again, the second time not as deeply as he looked at Stan. 'Parker-San, I do so appreciate your acceptance of our simple hospitality – and at such short notice.'

Stan smiled and nodded. 'We both are truly looking forward to this evening, Admiral.'

Tang led them through a narrow passageway. The comforting fragrance of boiling rice – the signature aroma of China – wafted through the corridor. She knew her way around the '*Osaka*' – mentally, she refused to accept the vessel's new name – because she had dined on the freighter a number of times. On earlier occasions they had been the guests of the Blue Funnel captain, Ben Clayton. Stan had told her that Clayton had requested re-assignment with his family to Hong Kong. 'Ben's there now,' Stan had told her. 'Skippering a desk until this show is over.'

A table for eight had been laid in the Officer's Mess. Glancing around the familiar room, Peggy saw that *Tang* had changed one key feature.

Clayton had indulged a fondness for George Stubbs's reproductions of horses; they looked appropriate against the wood panelling of the officers' mess. Peggy saw they had been removed.

In their place were woodcut prints by *Katsushika Hokusai*, the eighteenth-century Japanese artist and printmaker. Peggy was familiar with the works; they could be found in many restaurants and tea houses in *Shanghai*. The full suite of thirty-six 'Views of Mount Fuji' hung on the walls of the Officer's Mess. Peggy thought the delicacy of the scenes were too feminine for a room that smelled of stale cigar smoke. This, however, was a male domain; her views on décor would not sit well.

'Please,' said *Tang*, gesturing her to a chair to the right of him. Stan sat at his left.

'Tonight, Missy Parker, your food will be best in China.' When he smiled, his eyes became slits and disappeared into his cheeks. 'Japanese food much lighter than British food, much better than primitive Chinese food.' Again, a short chortle.

He clapped his hands and five officers, wearing full dress uniforms, filed into the room. They announced their names and rank as they bowed to Stan and Peggy; she made no attempt to remember the details.

Tang said, 'Let us sit.' Moments after they eased into their chairs, the burly admiral raised a small ceramic container of sake. He gestured for them to rise.

'A toast, please: to Emperor *Hirohito*.' Stan and Peggy rose, paused, sake in hand. *Tang* saw their hesitation and added, 'And to your King George number six – so far away but, I am sure, close to your hearts.' No chuckle this time, but Peggy noticed his impish smile. The eight diners drank the sake. Over the past few months, Peggy had learned to enjoy its warmth and fragrance.

When the sushi was served, Peggy noticed a marked difference in eating behaviour: the Japanese smacked their lips, made appreciative grunts; she and Stan ate quietly. Occasionally, Peggy would stop to nod her pleasure at *Tang* but never for long enough for him to feel she wanted to engage. There came a moment towards the end of the meal when *Tang* squared his shoulders, as if readying himself for more serious discussion.

He turned to Peggy. 'Perhaps you are wondering how I speak such good English, Missy Parker?' His officers turned their heads towards the guests. Peggy realised every conversation at the table would be a public one. She smiled and nodded: 'I do wonder.' *Tang* continued: 'A drill sergeant at the English military college where I studied your language and the strategy of great British battles, once said to me' – here their host lapsed into mock Cockney. "of course, Mister Tang, you are the Other." He paused, and again chuckled, 'or "the Uvver", if I am to be precise about his pronunciation.' He smiled at his guests, including his officers.

Tang paused to take a sip of sake. Then his voice quickened. 'After a few weeks at the college, I realised that this "othering", as I call it, of non-Caucasians is a particularly British habit. We Asians understand why such half-educated Britishers – like the sergeant – place themselves above us – the people they call the Other. For them, the ruler has always been white. The Caucasians assume that simply by *being* white – no matter how low their rank and their intelligence – they will always be the ruler. And *we* shall always be the Other.'

He paused. 'But to understand "othering" does not make it acceptable, does it?' Silence followed his question.

Tang's voice hardened. 'This is one reason of many why we wish to throw out the white imperialists. We accept that the British dominated the nineteenth century, the Americans this century – the twentieth, but the next century, surely, will be the Asian century.'

He smiled, but his face wore a puzzled frown, as if anyone might doubt their ascendance.

Tang's black eyes scanned the room. There was no trace of a smile as he added, his voice softening. 'And Japan will lead this change. We started with Manchuria – now we will take all of China. No one can stop us.'

Tang stared down at Stanley. Peggy knew that face: her husband's jaw flexed with suppressed anger. His lips were white from the pressure of remaining silent.

Perhaps realising that Stan would not rise to the bait, *Tang* continued. 'That poor sergeant, what could he know of Japan?'

Tang passed a wine decanter to Peggy, but both she and Stan declined. He gave them both a piercing look. 'Now to more important matters.'

TANG TRIUMPHANT
Shanghai 1942

Tang squared his shoulders once more. He was back in hectoring mode. Stan was right – the man needed to dominate.

'Japan today is a modern state with superior technology in weapons, vehicles, and strategy. And one day, we will turn these wartime advances into peacetime advantages for all people in the world.'

Tang had started to nod affirmatively as he talked, as if agreeing with his own words. The gesture seemed to convey, 'Listen to me, this is important.'

'Japan welcomes everything that is new; we want to learn, to progress. But China is like one of your British aristocrats: old, feeble, passive. The Chinese think we are – what is the English word? Brash. Yes, we are brash – like a young son: kick out the old man, throw away the old ways and take the castle.'

Tang looked almost mischievously at his officers. 'What does China have?'

The men waited for half a minute, and then they did so on cue, chorusing five Japanese words:

'Jinko!

Gohan!

Ocha!

Abura!

Wa!'

Three of the men burst into giggles. Peggy realised that *Tang* and his officers must have played the game before.

The admiral held out his hands to his men, as if in gratitude. 'Exactly!' he said, before translating: 'People, Rice, Tea, Oil, and Space.' He rubbed his chin and then let his arms float as if he were conducting an orchestra.

'But Japan has four words for "space" and "wa" is just one of them. The word "wa" represents the space between people. Sadly, the "wa" between Japan and China is very tense. I will return to that problem in a moment.'

Peggy's heart sank; bored by the conversation and *Tang*'s delivery, she stifled an urge to say, 'Must you?'

Tang shook his head again; he looked puzzled. 'But China now? In past century the opium drug that British forced on Chinese made them soft, weak, and poor. Chinese have lain down with foreigners. They have welcomed western imperialists. Shanghai is world's biggest brothel!'

He glared at his officers. 'This brings great shame to all Asians,' he added, his voice rising.

The men nodded but did not look at their leader. Peggy thought the admiral's implication was that his men's occasional visits to *Shanghai*'s numerous brothels had, single-handedly, destroyed the Chinese and Japanese empires.

Then *Tang* sat back, narrowed his eyes, and asked: 'How do Chinese see us?'

Another pause. Peggy sensed that *Tang* was interested, again, in answering his own questions.

'Chinese people see Japan as modern, but,' he pinched his finger and thumb together '… small, small. They see us like – excuse me, Missy Parker – like the shit of seagulls, stuck on our tiny islands.'

There was another pause while *Tang* studied the ship's beamed ceiling.

'Like Chinese, we Japanese have people, rice, tea but – important difference – better people, better rice, better tea!' He chuckled.

He nodded as he said, 'What we expect here in China is Sokk-sen, sokk katsu; quick war, quick settlement.'

Suddenly, he stood up, his chair screeching as he did so. He was looking directly at Stan as his voice rose, 'What Japan now needs…' he opened his arms wide '… is "abura" and "wa" – oil and space! Why? Because Chinese population is ten times bigger than Japan's, but China's space is twenty-five times bigger. His voice was deep, angry when he added, 'This not right!'

He brought his gaze back to his Western guests. His next words seemed to hiss from his mouth. 'Corrupt China has too much space, but we – glorious Nipponese empire – have too little space.' He drew a large breath. 'As I have said, this makes the space between us very tense.'

He paused to turn and look intently at Stan, shooting each word at him as he banged the table: 'What Japan must have – more space. And if we do not have oil because America stops us… then Japan will *fight* to have more oil.'

The admiral poured himself more sake and sat down.

***

The air pulsed with male static. Peggy watched Stan, waiting for him to respond. She guessed the Admiral knew that he, *Tang*, was the most senior Japanese for a thousand miles; perhaps that fact had given him the license to break a historic and cultural convention: never to abuse a guest.

Stan waited a moment to be sure that *Tang* had finished speaking. Then he smiled, stayed seated, chin on his fist, and looked at the admiral. When he began to speak, Peggy was surprised to hear it was in the tone of voice that he used with her in bed: warm, soft, seductive.

'Tang-San, firstly, my wife and I must thank you for this exceptional meal.' Stan raised his arms to include everyone at the table before again resting his eyes on his host.

'And I regret your obvious agitation at the perceived differences between China and Japan. I have to say, though, that every aggressor, since war began, would prefer to have, as you say, 'Sokk-sen, sokk-katsu' – a quick war followed by a quick settlement.' He tipped his head, raised an eyebrow. 'But I do not have to tell you, a great warrior, that quick wars and quick settlements depend on the strength and tenacity of the enemy.'

Peggy noticed that all of *Tang*'s officers, though she was sure they understood very little of Stan's words, seemed gripped by his gravitas.

Stan paused, then smiled as he continued.

'Admiral Tang, we come from a small island, too. We understand why you feel you need oil and more space. In the last century, as you know, Britain found more space by moving into other countries. This was how we spread our culture and our practices. This is how we became *Great*... Britain.

'We built institutions – law, medicine, religion, railways, postal systems, education, civics. In the process, these countries became our colonies. Yes, we took their raw materials for our industries, and we did not treat all the people in a way that we should have. But some people's lives we did improve.' He grinned before adding, 'And we taught them English, and democracy, and how to file documents. And, of course, we taught them something they still find difficult.'

Tang raised an eyebrow.

'We taught them how to queue,' said Stan.

Tang chuckled as Stan continued, his voice becoming flat, hard.

'However – in what you now tell me is a desire for more space and oil – Japan has chosen to attack – without provocation, the most powerful nation on earth. As I understand it, you took this unfortunate step to give you access to the wealth of the countries to your west, and to China – a country, by the way – and we both know this – that Japan has coveted for centuries. Also, by making new alliances with fascist governments in Europe, we must assume that Japan also has territorial ambitions beyond the immediate,' Stan raised his eyebrows. 'We have yet to see if your decision to achieve more space, done in this manner, was a wise one.'

He folded his hands on the table to show he had finished speaking.

Tang's eyes became slits. Then he gave a raucous shout of laughter. 'Ha! You English say so little, mean so much. I also learn this at military college.' He nodded, it seemed to himself.

Tang was studying Stan's face, as if making up his mind about her husband. 'We Japanese do not easily give trust, Parker-*San*. We have a proverb: 'when you see a stranger, suspect him to be a thief.'

Stan raised an eyebrow at the implication.

Tang continued, 'My men tell me you have been in China for some years.'

Stan nodded, 'Since nineteen twenty.'

'Ah so. Then I must assume, as the British say, that you have been "tatamised" – that is to say, it is second nature for you to take off your shoes when you enter a man's home or your own.'

'That is true.' Stan said.

Peggy knew it to be a lie. The only time that her man took off his shoes at home was to exchange them for a pair of ratty old slippers, or to get into bed. She let it pass.

'You are becoming less "namban", *Tang* went on, 'less of a Southern barbarian. You are less "gaijin" – an outsider – and more like us, more "doho". This is important for us, for me especially, Parker-San, because Japan is looking for a "nagai tsukiai" with you – a long and trusting relationship.'

He glared at Stan. 'Such a relationship, though, must be based on the understanding that we have won, and you have lost. Is that understood?'

Stan bowed his head as if honouring the Admiral's words.

'That is understood, Tang-San. As your own Lao Tse has said: 'we are but pebbles on the Tao, the way.'

'Good, good,' said the admiral. He rubbed his hands and called for cognacs, whiskies, and cigars.

'Ah, serene Missy Parker, we glad you with us because this evening I give important news concerning your husband.' She saw Stan's head rise inquisitively. *Tang* turned to the officer sitting on Peggy's right.

'*Masataka-San*, please.'

At the start of the evening, *Kurihari Masataka* had announced himself as captain of the '*Nanjing*'. A slim-hipped man with a face pink and what Peggy called 'chimpy' – as though evolution had not quite finished with him – *Masataka* kept his eyes on Stan as he addressed him. Occasionally, he flicked his eyes at *Tang,* but his attention was fixed on the Englishman.

'Chief Officer Parker, we very happy you agree to train our officers in customs and exercise…'

'Excise!' *Tang* cried.

Masataka corrected himself. 'So sorry, honourable admiral. Excise!' He bowed deeply to his superior officer and then at Stan before continuing.

'First Officer Parker, good friend of Japan, we thank you for agreeing that glorious Nipponese empire is now master of all China.' He paused. 'This very good.'

The officers around him nodded and clapped softly. The admiral beamed. Stan sat stone-faced.

Peggy was baffled: was that it? The whole evening had been designed to humiliate her husband.

Tang rose as *Masataka* sat down. He looked directly at Stan and spoke in the deep voice that Peggy had noticed he deployed for formal statements.

'Honourable Parker-San, if you are to work with Captain Masataka, you must be equal rank.'

He raised his glass of cognac, and his officers rose. He nodded at Peggy, implying that she should be standing with the others. Peggy stood up, reaching for her water, glad she had declined a liqueur.

Tang raised his hand as Stan made to stand up. 'Please, Parker-San,' he said. Her husband stayed seated, suddenly the focus of all eyes.

Tang's impish grin was back. 'Chief Officer Parker in British Merchant Navy,' he said, 'I now promote you to Honourable Captain in Imperial Japanese Navy.'

STAN, TEACHER
Shanghai 1942

Stan told Peggy that, when he reported their dinner conversation to Blue Funnel, they were amused. Stan told her that Pennington had laughed: 'He said that Tang is a wily old dog, and the title was his attempt to embarrass us by giving me a Japanese rank. PP said I should – and these are his words – 'train the little buggers, and we'll have you back on the "Shenkin" in no time.'

The training course kept Stan home in *Shanghai* for a month. Peggy and Jonny delighted in having him at the Parker house for the few hours he could spare, but most of the time he was working along the Bund, supervising *Masataka* and his team.

The two leaders worked every day in close quarters, and a friendship emerged naturally. Stan and *Masataka-San* – as he asked to be called – had a hot drink together at the start of the second week of co-operation. Sharing the acorn-based coffee substitute was a routine that Stan had initiated to get closer to his colleague. Stan always paid for their drinks; *Masataka* never offered.

On the first day of their second week of collaboration, the Japanese officer showed him pictures of his family back in *Osaka*. Stan learned that the Japanese captain was also a new father: a son, *Isoruku*, had been born a year after Jonny Parker.

'My son, very good boy.' *Masataka*'s English, while not as fluent as Tang's, was good enough for casual conversation. 'We name him for great Admiral Isoroku Yamamoto, hero of Pearl Harbour.'

'Yes, Masataka-San,' Stan said with the slightest of smiles, 'where nearly three thousand Americans died, many of them asleep in their bunks on a Sunday morning.' Stan added neutrally: 'My wife and child were nearly killed in Shanghai.'

'True. War is bad.' *Masataka* continued in a dispassionate tone. 'That is why we must end war quickly. Admiral Yamamoto always planning, always want to end war quickly. Admiral Tang also say he hate war and very angry when Americans bomb Tokyo.'

Pennington had told Stan that the Japanese believed the Americans would never bomb the mainland from the vast trenches of the world's biggest ocean; they had promised their people that the war would never come to their shores. The Japanese military had never imagined that sixteen B-25 bombers, waddling into the air from a ship moored six hundred miles from Tokyo, would bomb their capital; it was a major psychological blow.

Facing *Masataka* with a sympathetic smile, Stan said: 'America slapped the face of all Japan when they attack Tokyo.' He held his hands up as if protesting. 'I say this as an Englishman, you understand, not as an American.'

The Japanese nodded, acknowledging the difference.

Stan pressed his point, trying to draw out the younger man: 'Soldiers like us, Masataka-San. I understand that Admiral Yamamoto must respond, or he lose much face.'

'Hai! But I have given Admiral great face by honouring him with the name of my son.'

'That is so, that is so.' Stan, diverted for the moment, nodded, and threw his arm around the young Captain. 'I understand this. But surely Japan must do more to strike back?' He topped up the other man's tin cup from a small urn.

Masataka continued. 'Hai. Now Yamamoto, commander-in-chief of combined fleet of Nipponese Navy, will travel far to slap Americans.' He stopped, looked at Stan. 'Not slap. More.'

'Punch?'

'Hai! Punch! In face.' *Kurihari Masataka* laughed happily, proud to boast of the strength and extent of the Japanese forces.

***

Stan was exhausted at the end of each day. The mental concentration and physical effort that he had to invest in the marine surveying aspect of the work, as well as the attempts at espionage – pretending to be someone he wasn't – took its toll on his nerves.

Every day, Stan had to walk ten or fifteen miles – followed by the Japanese trainees and an interpreter – around the ports along the *Huangpu*, and sometimes as far north as *Hongkou*. Together, they inspected a score of freighters for their seaworthiness and safety. They reviewed cargo transportation methods; they ran engines to identify flaws; operated on-board cranes; tested the stress levels of hulls.

On most evenings, Stan came home to shower and to spend ten minutes playing with Jonny. Too often, Peggy found that both her men had fallen asleep over whatever picture book Stan was reading to his son. On those nights, Stan was too tired to eat. Peggy would take her supper out to the verandah and eat alone, the fireflies her only company.

STAN, 'MOLE'
Shanghai 1942

Towards the end of the induction process, Stan and *Masataka* would finish the day with a beer at one of the many harbourside bars. Stan encouraged the naval officer to talk about the deployment of the enemy's forces across China.

'Since Nanjing, war goes well for Japan. True, bad things happen there.'

Stan said, 'Like taking heads from bodies, raping children, and burning Chinese alive?'

Masataka looked away, and Stan wondered for a moment if the man was embarrassed.

'War is bad, bad, Parker-San. And Americans now make the war go on long time.'

'But Masataka-San, Japan must expect America to fight back when they attacked Pearl Harbour.'

The Japanese officer studied his beer. 'Yes, but Americans and British now fight together; we hear American president and British Churchill very close. They think they can win war.'

This was the first indication Stan had received of a wavering in Japan's resolve. He understood the view of events came from only *Masataka* but the captain, clearly, was *Tang*'s favourite officer; Stan wondered if it was possible that *Masataka*'s resigned attitude extended to others in the Japanese command.

'You think Americans will make war longer if they win in Pacific?' Stan knew he was risking exposure when he asked such direct questions.

Masataka replied, his voice laced with anger: 'Imperial Nipponese forces will win Pacific. Japan never surrenders.' Impatient, he gestured with his bottle. 'More beer, Parker-San.'

Stan wondered if *Masataka*'s simplistic view of an assured Japanese victory had any value. He'd heard that America was mobilising rapidly and was supplying vast amounts of armaments and ordnance to the Allies. Also, he knew that the Japanese had not expected the Americans to open a new front in the Far East with such determination. Bombing Tokyo, while not significant militarily, was a terrible blow to the morale of the Japanese nation.

Stan reported to PP on Yamamoto's intention to administer 'a punch' to American forces in the Pacific. The American naval command had gambled on the Japanese fleet heading for the outlying islands where, at Midway, their own fleet was centred. Their calculation, plus Stan's sketchy confirmation, proved to be correct. Their readiness and the deployment of supporting forces under Admiral Nimitz blunted the Japanese attack.

All of these activities meant nerve-wracking work for Stan. Only the enthusiasm of his Japanese officer-students and their obvious thirst for knowledge of harbour administration, made the work satisfying. Stan also gained some pleasure from the occasional misdirection he gave *Masataka*.

Importantly – as he told Peggy one evening – he was opening a theoretical savings account with the enemy.

'It's what I call a "scratch-my-back" arrangement,' Stan explained to Peggy as they sat one night on their verandah. Stan had lived long enough in the East to understand the concept of *"on* and *giri"*. He told her why it was important: 'The Japanese, more than the Chinese, believe in the value of friendship within business. There is a lot of giving and receiving of favours; they believe such behaviour feeds personal connections. Superficially at least, I've tried to achieve that with Masataka, and he's told me that Ohta knows and appreciates it. They see the *"on* and *giri"* in my actions. I am helping them; one day they will have to help me.'

'When?'

'That I'm not sure about, but the moment will come.

Peggy agreed. 'Oh, I think it will, too, if these customs are central to what Tang said when you signed up for this – his wish to have a *nagai tsukiai*, a long and trusting relationship – with you, Stanley Parker.'

'Well, when you put it like that....'

'... I do, love. And you must, too.' Peggy reached for his hands. 'None of us knows when the *"giri"* will happen, but when it comes, we have to be ready...'

'... and clear about what we want,' Stan finished for her.

***

In *Shanghai*, the expat community had come to accept the sight of Japanese soldiers on horseback, swords clanking at their sides, riding through the International Settlement. Schools, even private ones, were guarded by Japanese soldiers with pistols and guns.

'Why?' asked Peggy. 'What are they expecting – a sudden invasion by the British Expeditionary Force?'

'It's for show, darling,' Stan explained. 'They want everyone – including the children – to know they are the ones to be frightened of.'

'Well, they certainly frighten me.'

'Then they've made their point.'

While no foreigner could leave China legally, no one had any idea what was to become of them. Stan refused to speculate when Peggy asked him. Rumours were circulating that camps were being built on the edge of the city. As the summer steamed on, a sense of helplessness began to infect expatriate life.

That month though, Stan was still busy with his mission for *Ohta Tang*, instructing *Masataka*.

Peggy knew that Stan enjoyed the assignment. The task had brought out his penchant – a rather pedantic one, she thought – for explaining ideas to the uninitiated. Stan often talked about being a civilising influence on 'the other', even when it was the enemy. A memory fragment of their dinner with *Ohta Tang* came back; the Admiral knew about 'the other'.

After the month it took to train *Tang*'s officers, Stan resumed his routine of taking freight up and down the China coast on the '*Shenkin*'.

Everyone on Stan's ship knew that the value of their cargo had been assessed by Stan and acquired by the Japanese Navy. Stan led the same crew: Watcyn Williams and his officers were practical men; they understood why Stan had done what he had done. They knew their survival depended on him.

Stan could never tell Peggy where he went, or for how long he would be away: one morning he was gone and then days – or weeks – later, he was back.

At those times, in the long afternoons or nights when she was alone, she nursed the memory of her evening with Marcus Carter. She reminded herself that it had not been an intimate *dinner a deux* but rather, a conversation on the edge of a room full of people, mostly strangers. Then why did the evening feel so – she struggled for the right word – *personal*? Maybe it was because the room and the crowd seemed to melt away, leaving only the two of them, their eyes, and the electricity between them.

She tried not to think about whether she might meet Marcus again. Never a romantic, she nonetheless knew that if it occurred, it was simply what was meant to happen.

***

One night – although at the time she was not to know it was their last evening at the house – Peggy put Jonny's iron bath in front of the fireplace in their bedroom. The little boy loved bathing in front of a fire as it crackled behind a protective iron screen; he'd giggle when the water hissed as he splashed it on the flames.

Peggy still marvelled that she could have a working fireplace in the bedroom. As a child, she had shared a room with her sister Connie, both of them squealing on winter mornings as they slipped out of their warm feather bed and placed their feet on the ice-cold linoleum floor.

That final night, Stan smoked a cigar and watched as Peggy washed her slippery, laughing boy. She turned to Stan and thought how happy he looked. 'You two are peas in a pod,' she said.

Later, in bed, she nudged Stan awake. 'Love, I'm terrified I'm going to have a little sister for Jonny.' He assured her that it was impossible – though later, she wondered how he could be so sure. Being Catholic, she refused to use contraception, so their love-making was a fumbled, hazardous business for Stan. And a hurried, painful episode for her.

He turned to hold her in his arms, her head tucked under his chin. 'Look, ducky, I know you're concerned about the pickle we've found ourselves in. However, I know you and little Jonny are safe here. I just have this run to the north, and I'll be back in no time.'

She wrestled away and looked up, shocked. 'You have to go away again? You told me that after Pearl Harbor the Japanese would see us as their enemy. How much longer before they come for us?'

He smoothed her frown. 'They won't – come for you – I mean. The Settlement is like a sovereign state.' Peggy put a hand to his lips.

'But,' she protested. 'They've attacked a country, America, that is *allied* to our sovereign state, Britain.'

She knew she was right. Finally, Stan said, 'Well, I do have this connection with Otah Tang. That has to mean something.'

She turned away. 'That compromises us, don't you see? Getting special treatment from Tang is the last thing we need. I hope to God he doesn't try to step in.'

He eased away, his voice hardened: 'There you go again, imagining a situation that may not happen.' She knew he was weighing arguments that might pacify her.

A minute later he said, 'Look, Pegs, you're here, you're safe. At the very worst, I can steam back here within a few days. Things will work out now that the Americans are committed – it may take a while – but I just know it.'

They had stayed awake, talking, until the eastern sky brightened. Then she laid out breakfast on the upstairs verandah, a habit they'd started whenever Stan was home. She knew the routine; he would board a launch to his ship, and the freighter would catch the early tide.

As he stood up from the breakfast table, she asked him – later, she would never know what prompted the question – 'Have I been a good wife?'

He came around and held her close, 'None better.'

The door hushed behind him.

RENDEZVOUS
Changsha 1942

Three days later, Stanley Parker was one hundred and twenty kilometres south of Shanghai.

He was navigating the 'Shenkin' towards the East China Sea. In a few days, he would be meeting a senior Chinese officer. The Chinese Nationalist Army wanted proof that the man helping their enemy in Shanghai was 'credible'; they believed that could be achieved only by meeting him.

A frigid north-west wind from Manchuria pushed the freighter down the Yangtze. The flow of China's longest river that morning was, as the captain liked to say, 'lumpy'. When Stan was an Able Seaman, one of his favourite duties was steering the ship; this morning, his mind spinning with plans, he'd told AS *Jiang Husong* that he would like to take the wheel.

Why Foochow?' Watcyn Williams addressed his First Officer as they stood on the bridge of the '*Shenkin*'. Because Williams knew nothing of Stan's secret assignment for Pennington, the Welshman was puzzled. 'We put into Foochow two months ago. Why are we going in again?'

Stan had rehearsed his reply: 'Sir, I think we'd better start throwing in a few surprises. When I was working with Masataka – you know, the Jap they asked me to tutor on Customs protocols – he said they were surprised we never caught the ports off guard by arriving without notice.' Stan raised his eyebrows at his skipper. 'We have a roster, and we stick to it.'

Stan paused to gauge the distance that separated the '*Shenkin*' from an Italian tanker steaming up on their port side. He'd learned to give the ships of Japan's ally a wide berth – many of them were not skilful navigators; Stan mused that finding a new landmass in the fifteenth century and thinking they'd discovered India would take a long time to live down.

Stan turned to his Captain. 'I thought we'd start the new random pattern with Foochow,' he said. 'And, by the way, I've never taken the '*Shenkin*' through the Straits of Taiwan.'

Williams nodded, smiling. 'Not got a sweet cariad squared away there have you – in Foochow, I mean?'

Stan laughed. 'Now what would a sweet Welsh cariad be doing lifting her skirts in Foochow? Ah, no sir – no sweetheart. But I am going to ask you for a twenty-four-hour pass.'

Williams wouldn't be put off. 'Ah ha! There is a little lady somewhere…'

'That's for me to know and you to find out.' Stan said, although he felt uncomfortable laughing with Williams in a male, conspiratorial way.

'But on the other matter, Captain, I'll be surprised if you and the lads *don't* find a stash of drugs – when they don't expect us, the Foochow people may not be as clean as they seemed to be in November.'

After the Captain had gone below, Stan headed into the open sea. Alone on the bridge with only *Jiang Husong* behind him, he recalled his conversation with Pennington a few weeks previously.

'They want you in Chongqing.' PP had announced when they had last met for dinner at the Astor Palace, which had become Pennington's favourite rendezvous. 'Chiang has established his new headquarters there.'

***

Stan had agreed to meet with an – yet unnamed – officer who was reported to be close to *Chiang Kai-shek*. Stan's only condition was that the meeting took place in *Changsha*. The month before, the Chinese had won the city back from the Japanese. 'Changsha is halfway between Chongqing and Foochow,' Stan explained. 'Unless we meet somewhere in between, like Changsha, I can't be away from my ship for that long.'

'I can see that you don't want to arouse suspicion,' Pennington frowned across the table. 'But I'll have to give them a jolly good reason for setting conditions – especially for you to meet in Changsha. They're still recovering from pushing the Japs out of that part of China – a situation, by the way, that could change at any time.'

'I know, I know. But sir, if Tang ever finds out I'm meeting the Chinese...' Stan looked directly into Pennington's eyes. PP looked away.

'Your father would never forgive me.'

There was a short burst of laughter from Stan. 'Ha! That's the least of my worries.' Pennington raised his eyebrows but said nothing.

The Chinese objected at first but finally agreed to meet Stan in

Changsha. For secrecy's sake, Stan would have to take a long train ride to the city; for the Chinese official, it would be a three-hour flight.

Stanley Parker had done his homework: a train left *Foochow* at noon every day, travelling all the way to *Chongqing*, but making its first stop at *Changsha*.

***

The train he boarded was a remnant of China's attempt to destroy as many railway lines as they could – they were intent on slowing the advance of the Japanese, who were desperate to conquer China's interior. The train looked like a 'remnant' too, thought Stan as he walked down the dimly lit, draughty corridor. He didn't wish to arouse Watcyn's suspicion by carrying an overnight bag; he'd taken only a briefcase with an empty manila file and, underneath it, a toothbrush and a clean white shirt.

With effort, he pushed open a stiff carriage door and was hit by a burst of chatter and a strong smell of incense. The incense failed to cover the reek of sweat and garlic, caused by a group of Chinese workmen who were squashed together on two bench seats. Stan counted nine of them.

Shocked at the sight of him, the men stared. He was relieved to be wearing a sports coat, trousers, and a grey Trilby – a British naval uniform would have made him a marked man – not, he thought, that a Caucasian in civilian clothes wouldn't arouse comment.

He stepped into the compartment. At once, all the Chinese stood up. Stan was annoyed by this custom, practiced throughout China – Caucasians were immediately associated with authority, trouble, or both. He patted the air with his hand, gesturing for the men to sit; slowly and one by one, they did.

The men made space for him against a window. Giving his companions a broad smile and repeated '*xie's*' to thank them, Stan wedged into his seat.

He resisted the urge to talk Chinese with the men. He had a great affection for the Chinese people – their patience and resistance throughout so many wars; their ability to survive all kinds of pain and hunger; their sense of humour. But he knew that if he engaged with them, any conversation would be tomorrow's gossip. Perhaps his presence already was the topic of the day: they would think it odd enough that a pink-skinned man in a funny hat was travelling with them.

***

By twilight, the locomotive was straining through mountain passes. Through half-closed eyes, Stan saw that they were passing monolithic blocks of stone, with trees clinging to the rockfaces. The mountains looked like the raised fingers of giants. 'Giants in a giant land,' he thought. He wished he was more relaxed; he felt drowsy but on his guard. He kept a mantra running in his head: mentally intoning 'Endure, endure' to survive the journey and – to remind him why he had agreed to this odyssey – 'For King and country.'

As each hour passed, the fug around him grew thicker. Five of the nine men were smoking pipes, and four were pulling on inexpertly rolled cigarettes. The compartment was unheated. Opening a window to disperse the fug was unthinkable. By midnight, when he would have been grateful for even some broken sleep, several of the men pulled out an assortment of cloth bags. Strange smells came from small bundles wrapped in bandanas and old newspaper. From the bundles, the men pulled pieces of meat and dried fish, plus small patties of rice. One man had a wedge of dark bread and something unidentifiable other than for its rank scent.

Two of the older men staggered across to Stan's seat to offer him some of their food. Stan shook his head, again patting the air, as of to signal, 'It's okay.' He then pulled a bulky muslin cloth from his briefcase.

Now he had the attention of the whole carriage. Some of the men near the door stood up, the better to see what he had inside the muslin. Stan opened the package to reveal two thick rolls of salami. Holding one in each hand so all the men could see, he resisted saying, 'Ta-ra!'

The Chinese were now giving him hand signals and questioning looks; the message was clear: famished they might be, but they wanted to know what was in the salami. He couldn't resist responding, to do so would have seemed odd, even haughty. The men were jabbering with speculation. Stan rummaged his brain to remember the Chinese word for the ingredient. He remembered but decided to enact it: standing up so he could flap his elbows, Chief Officer Stanley Parker made the sound of a quacking duck. The men burst into high-pitched laughter. '*Dak, dak!*' the men chorused, nodding merrily.

Stan carved several generous pieces from one of the salamis and handed them to the two older men. The men bit the slices and passed a portion to others. Stan smiled inwardly, wondering if this was communism in action. If so, he thought, it was time for capitalism to reassert itself. He cut more slices and passed them around, saving two pieces for himself. The men nudged each other as they ate, grunting with satisfaction. His gift was a success.

The intensely flavoured sausage, scant though it was, made him sleepy. He dozed, despite the jolting of the train, the men's babble, the smells, the fug.

A few hours later, the vibrations in the wooden seat indicated that the train was making a long descent from the mountains. *Changsha* sat on the alluvial plain of the *Xiang* river. Stan could understand how the Japanese must have found it hard to overwhelm a city situated on a river and surrounded by mountains.

The men started to chatter. The word '*Changsha*' was repeated frequently. As the train slowed, only Stan prepared to leave. As dawn began to reveal the riverine landscape, the train rumbled into the city.

The nine peasants nodded at him; some stood, attempting to bow as he squeezed his way to the door. Grunting, Stan pushed it open and stepped into the corridor, turning to wave goodbye. Nine lined, brown faces grinned and nodded at him. One man quacked, then another; then they all quacked. Stan quacked too, through his laughter. The sound of '*dak, dak,*' followed him as he searched for a way out of the train.

STAN, AN AGENT IN THE FIELD
Changsha 1942

As he stepped onto the platform, a Chinese man of about thirty years old came towards him. The stranger wore a black suit, white shirt, and a bright red tie. The man scanned him without embarrassment then, with a dip of the head, he asked, 'Lin?' Stan completed the password: 'Yutang.' The suited man said, 'I am your contact. We have a car for you. This way, please.'

When he followed his 'contact' into the street, Stan could see the effects of the recent battle for *Changsha*. Looking up and down the pavement, he saw bombed buildings, burnt-out cars, upended rickshaws, humps of clothing that might have been bodies – foraging dogs acting as their sentries. Smoke from a few dying fires etched gray lines into the pale sky. Stan's senses were dominated by the smell of rotting human flesh.

Changsha had history. *Mao Tse-tung*, a name that meant 'to shine on the East', had owned a bookshop there. The shop had become a nexus of propaganda, financed by the Russians. Always a bookish man, *Mao* found it a congenial job and an excellent spot for forming liaisons. Then a lusty twenty-seven-year-old, he preferred the company of women; he was more committed to bedding the young women of *Changsha* than in studying the new philosophy of Communism.

Stan had always been intrigued by *Mao Tse-tung*. Being in *Changsha* evoked a thin memory of how the rising Chinese star had come to the city, intent on helping other young men overthrow the 260-year Manchu dynasty. Like young men everywhere, they believed they had better ways of running a country. As a sign of their seriousness, all of *Mao*'s friends cut off their pigtails. If they encountered resistance from others, they cut off their pigtails, too. A year later, a Republic was declared.

The Russians had taken note of the radical teenager – they had received a good report of him from a party fund-raiser whom they respected. Being surrounded by so much Communist Party literature soon influenced the ambitious Chinese: *Mao* became convinced that Communism was the first original idea of governance in a long while. The young revolutionary also thought Communism might be the ideal instrument for reforming the ancestor-worshipping people: one ideology, one China.

Stan's thoughts of revolution were interrupted by the man in the suit: 'We are still clearing the bodies.' He remarked. 'If you had come last week... well, you would not have come.'

They had walked some hundred yards from the station. A large black limousine sat at the curb ahead of them. When they were thirty yards away, its engine fired. As they came close, the suited man opened the rear door of the car and gestured for Stan to enter. Dialogue from an Edward G. Robinson movie zipped across his mind: 'never get in the car.' Stan got in the car. The door closed behind him – apparently, he was to be alone with the driver. Stan looked across the street. A group of Chinese were gawping at them.

The man in the suit knocked on the driver's window. The driver lowered the window. The suited man leaned into the car, looking at Stan in the back seat. 'The driver will take you to the airport. At the airport someone will meet you and take you to your meeting. The flight from Chongqing landed twenty minutes ago. You will not be asked for the password again. You have been vouched. Good day, sir.' The young man's garlic breath lingered in the car for the next ten minutes.

As they drove, fatigue fell upon him like a cloak. Stan mused that the subterfuge was everything he disliked about the world of espionage: Passwords and black cars, men in suits who had no name – or had been ordered not to give it. What would Peggy think if she could see him now? Would she be proud of him? Or would she, like him, find the episode ridiculous?

He had found it hard not to tell her about this aspect of his job, this secret work. Peggy disliked duplicity of any kind and, although she had accepted his association with *Tang*, he had to wonder if the anger she felt that he was – as he had put it, 'sleeping with the enemy' – was outweighed by the pride she felt in dining with a Japanese Admiral.

He realised that both were equally susceptible to status and flattery – Stan because he wanted to live up to his father's ambitions for him – Peggy because she wanted to outgrow her roots.

He'd been impressed by how his bride had blossomed in *Shanghai*. The guilt he'd felt by taking her away from her provincial life, had melted when he saw the enthusiasm with which she embraced her new *milieu* – a word she loved to say.

He had recovered from his irritation about Peggy and his father colluding – if that was the right word – to get him the China posting. He liked the idea that these two people wanted him to succeed. When he had first met her, he had no doubt that Peggy wanted more for him than he wanted for himself. He admitted, though, that he was beginning to enjoy the feeling of success. Where he had doubts – and still had them – was if his wife's wishes were driven by love for him or by her own ambition. He had the feeling that his lessening dependence on her troubled his wife: after all, hadn't he told her he couldn't do the job without her? But he was discovering that he could.

Then why this feeling that he had triumphed in every part of his life except marriage? He and Peggy had become supremely good friends – they both thought of themselves as the other's best friend – and yet he felt that they had never achieved the closeness that should bind them – even while doubting that such fusion might need physical intensity to produce it. But otherwise, how could intimacy be achieved?

He was convinced, after three years of courtship and just a few months of marriage, that sex was more important to him than to Peggy. On board ship with other men – on the few occasions that he allowed himself to be drawn into late-night conversations – Stan learned he was not a member of a minority. Many married men felt equally 'undernourished', as one young officer described it, before going on to say, 'Surely one of the advantages of being stuck with one girl is that sex is always available.'

'That's right,' said another. 'If you go to the biscuit tin, there's always a biscuit.'

Watcyn Williams closed the debate in high humour when he said: 'Lads, you only stop masturbating when you're divorced.'

A half-hour later, Stan was sitting in a windowless room. He had been ushered there after arriving at the gates of the military airport. The room's furniture was sparse: a pine table and two facing bentwood chairs, once bright red – China's 'lucky' colour – but now chipped and faded. Brown-

and-white linoleum covered half of the concrete floor. Walls were bare – except for one decorative touch: a curling, fly-specked calendar from the previous year, 1941. As he looked down at his knees, Stan noticed two fleas jumping, then settling on his trousers. He assumed the room wasn't often used.

Again, he thought about his wife and child. As usual when away, he had not spoken to Peggy for a week. She had no idea where he was. *Tang* had promised always to tell him if any situation in the Settlement became dangerous; that was the great benefit of his work for the Admiral: the guarantee of his family's safety.

He breathed deeply, preparing his mind and body for the interview with some faceless military man. He became aware of a faint smell of duck salami. Another five minutes passed before a door opened, and a short, middle-aged Chinese strode into the room. He was in uniform and alone.

Stan recognised him at once. He leaped to his feet, and remembering he was not in uniform, restrained a salute. Instead, he bowed. 'This is a great honour, General.'

ARRIVAL
Fu-xing 1942

A pale sun was touching the horizon when their transport pulled up in front of a pair of iron gates. The jolt woke Jonny, who strained to see what was happening. Two soldiers pulled open the gates, and the ancient bus inched through.

The vehicle jolted forward again, then laboured up a hill for a few minutes until a long, three-storied building came into view.

'Fu-xing used to be a school.' Tom snorted behind her: 'Christ! Imagine having to say you went to the Fu-xing High School.'

Chao-xing whispered something to him. He chuckled as he turned to Peggy. 'Apparently, Fu-xing means "renaissance" or "being reborn". Hell, I can think of better reincarnations.'

The main building looked less like a school than a mansion. Peggy was surprised by the size of the structure. Five floors high, the main section was a mass of windows; the dying sunlight had set the windows ablaze from lines of golden panes. The frontage was a set of four pillars, making an odd blend of Greek and Fascist architecture

Peggy thought the place looked much better in appearance from what she had imagined a concentration camp to be: a set of wooden huts. Then she remembered the Japanese had never expected to be housing the entire expatriate community of *Shanghai* in its camps, but now they were forced to deal with the ten thousand or so who had stayed behind in the city. *Fu-xing*, rumour had it, was supposed to handle fifteen hundreds of them.

As she gazed at what was to be their new accommodation, she heard someone say, 'well, this could have been a lot worse.'

'No,' she added to herself. 'This will be bad enough.'

Reality was reasserted by a large sign that stated:

'This compound is now the property of his Imperial Majesty.'

As she climbed down from the bus, Jonny started struggling; again, he wanted to walk. She had potty-trained him early, and now she took the opportunity to take him behind a tree.

Although the camp was on higher ground, for some reason the snow had not reached where they were. Jonny squatted, smiling as he enjoyed the act of shitting in the open. He giggled while she held his hand, then she wiped his bottom. Looking around, she saw small white flags of toilet paper among the grass. She added to them.

Peggy feared the future that she felt was creeping towards them like some terrible beast: To herself, she muttered, 'In the name of God, how can we live like this?' Again, she looked at the building while fear came into her bowels and slithered around her stomach, sex, and throat. She found it hard to draw breath. She hugged Jonny to her breast, sobbing.

'Mama? Don't cry, mama.'

His words brought her to attention, dispelled the moment of self-pity.

She sniffled and held him closer. 'It's all right, sweetheart. Mama's here.'

To the right, a quarter mile away, she spotted another five wooden constructions. Were they the barracks for the Japanese guards?

Behind her, she saw others climbing down from buses into the field. The area was dotted by tufts of brown grass, newspaper pages, packets of shit, bottles, and cans. People collected their baggage from the trunks, thrown to the ground by the guards. Some of the bags had burst, scattering pyjamas, trousers, pants, books, underwear. Women scrambled to retrieve their possessions, heads bowed, humiliated by the mess.

As she stood clutching Jonny, Peggy overheard one mother say to her two small daughters, 'Everything is tickety-boo, my darlings. You must think of this as an adventure, like "Swallows and Amazons".' Her voice, inflected with the clipped enunciation of a BBC announcer, made Peggy feel at once proud and hopeless. When would such people allow reality to bite?

CHIANG-KAI-SHEK
Changsha 1942

Chiang Kai-shek smiled. 'Please, please sit, Chief Officer Parker. Or should I call you, "Mr. Parker", as you are not in uniform?'

'That might be correct, sir,' Stan said, taking a deep breath. 'Sorry, General but...'

'You had no idea you were meeting me? Neither did I. Well, until yesterday. Then I was told the purpose of your coming here was for us to reassure ourselves that you believed in our cause. That you are not one of Tang's agents.' He stopped and peered carefully at his visitor for what – to Stan – seemed like an age but was probably no more than fifteen seconds.

Chiang moved slowly around the room, as graceful as a cat. Stan sat still, eyes front. He was sobered by a glance at *Chiang*'s face: he reminded him of Doc Skellorn, a teacher at Repton, who had tried to drill the Periodic Table into a room of raucous youths. Stan knew that this stern-faced man had millions of men under his command – the entire Chinese Nationalist Army. He hoped he would pass *Chiang*'s evaluation.

Still affected by meeting the head of the Chinese state, thoughts twisted in Stan's mind: he, Clew Parker's son, was being vetted by a living legend. Then swiftly came another thought: No, he Stanley Parker, Chief Officer of the 'Shenkin', was about to have a conversation with *Chiang Kai-shek*, known as the Red General, head of the Nationalist Party of China.

Peggy would be astounded if he was ever able to tell her.

Chiang was saying, 'Well, if we want to make sure you are our man – then who better than I to do that?' He glared at Stan, who wasn't sure if the look was genuine or mocking.

As *Chiang* stood over him, he sniffed the air. 'And have you brought me some...' he sniffed again, 'salami?'

Stan stifled a laugh. 'All gone, sir, shared with some very hungry men on the train from Foochow.'

'Ah, pity. I am famously regarded as an ascetic. But one of my failings is the love of salami. He sniffed again; 'and moreover, if I'm not mistaken, this was duck salami – my absolute favourite.' He gave Stan a thin smile.

Stan nodded, 'I am so sorry, Sir: I know your countrymen would have given up their share had I told them it was a gift for the Red General.'

Chiang's eyes narrowed, either from suspicion or disguised humour. 'Of that, Mr. Parker, I have no doubt.'

Chiang eased into the chair and fixed his eyes on the Englishman. 'But to business: tell me what you've derived from the philosophy of Lin Yutang.' Stan blinked, caught unawares by the question. The General smiled, and his grey eyebrows shot up: 'It was *your* choice of password, Mr. Parker.'

Stan realised that *Chiang*'s English was impeccable; even so, as a courtesy, Stan said, 'We can talk Mandarin if you prefer, sir.'

'I prefer English. Continue: Lin Yutang?'

Stan blinked, paused, then said: 'It's strange. I thought of Lin Yutang a few times when I was with some excellent fellows on the train from Foochow.'

'Excellent fellows – in what way?' *Chiang* cocked his head, his eyes refocusing as he studied Stan.

'They were all scamps.'

'Ah, Yutang loves scamps; why did these men remind you of scamps: did you like them? Were they amusing?'

Stan was aware he was being tested, but he knew enough of Yutang's ideas to reply. Even so, he paused again as he collected his thoughts.

'They seem untroubled and free,' he paused. 'And curious.'

'… About you, I suppose.'

'No, sir, they were curious about what my salami was made of.'

Chiang snorted. 'Ah ha! I would have known, just from the aroma. But tell me more.'

Stanley continued, glad that he had won the General's attention. 'As Lin Yutang says, our playful curiosity – early man's ability to turn over a stone – even to inspect each other's ears – was a sign that we came from an instinctively curious root of mankind's tree. Evolution's greatest gift – to free the hands – led the emerging human biped, falling from a branch, to follow the route of the semi-upright orang-outang, rather than the quadruped baboon.

Chiang curled his lips appreciatively, 'You are curious, too, Mr. Parker.

A touch of the professor, perhaps?' The Chinese smiled teasingly. Stan remembered Peggy's quips about his tendency for pedantry.

Chiang said, 'Now these men on the train: You must have talked to them a lot to be able to judge their character. Was that wise?'

Stan shook his head. 'To be honest, sir, I wanted to talk to them – my Mandarin, even my Cantonese, is good enough – but I didn't want to be the topic of conversation across Hunan province. So, no, we spoke little.'

Chiang nodded, 'What else?'

Stan realised the test was nearly over. 'General, were they unpredictable? I truly don't know, but as I took note of their carefree attitude to life – true scamps, every one of them – I concluded that they had managed to retain their...' Stan paused, unsure whether he should continue.

'Yes?' *Chiang* was looking at him keenly, but Stan was aware the military man had relaxed – Stan's answers seemed to have put him at ease.

'Well, retain their individuality – at a time when China is threatened by Communism.'

Chiang Kai-shek clapped again. "Excellent, excellent! The scamp's qualities: curiosity; humour; unpredictability; and individualism.' *Chiang* took a deep breath and looked around the small room. 'And that is why, Mr. Parker, I wish the Chinese nation to retain those qualities and not be submerged in the groupthink – I believe it's called – of Communism.' He added, 'I think this room was designed by a Communist: very efficiently organised, but soulless.'

'And windowless,' added Stan. 'To keep out enlightenment.'

Chiang nodded, his face signalling that he was happy to make the acquaintance of the Englishman.

Chiang slapped his knees and stood up. He began to pace; cat become tiger. 'You may know that many people, including my own commanders, have criticised my decision to kill the virus of Communism in China before driving out the Japanese. But I realised – when I called Mao Zedong and Zhou to a conference at Mount Lu – what, five years ago? I concluded then that any alliance could only be a pragmatic solution. They are totally committed to making China a Communist state when the Japanese have gone.' He stopped circling and looked directly at Stan. 'My conundrum is this: do I join the Communists to get rid of the Japanese? Because if I do, I will be hastening my country's retreat from democracy and freedom of thought.'

The silence lasted for over half a minute, both men weighing the same dilemma.

Stan broke the quiet. 'Ohta Tang and the Japanese are equally committed to victory. We have a huge fight on our hands.'

Chiang suddenly lifted his head, eyes shining with resolve. 'But we now have our allies, the Americans and your people, the British.' He held his hand up. 'tell me about Tang. How well do you know him? And what did he ask you to do for him?'

The next ten minutes were taken up with Stan's description of the dinner conversation on the '*Nanjing*'. He knew that *Chiang* would want to know what he could tell him of the Admiral's goals – what informed them, and any plans he might have for fulfilling them. He also told *Chiang* about his work with Captain *Masataka* and Stan's sense that Japan's Admiral *Yamamoto* wanted to wage a bigger war with America in the Pacific.

Chiang interjected: 'Huh. I know Isoruku Yamamoto; we studied at the war college outside Moscow. He was then – as he is now – a man whose reach exceeds his grasp. But he has a formidable navy, and he thinks unconventionally, unlike his peers in Tokyo. His flaw is that he has no idea of the strength and resources of the Americans; it may take a year or two, but Japan will lose the war in the Pacific.'

There was a soft knock at the door. The General walked over. Stan heard a muffled conversation, then an explosive '*Tamada!*' – from *Chiang* as he shut the door. 'Tamada', Stan knew, was the worst swear word in Chinese, the equivalent of the Anglo-Saxon 'Fuck!'

Chiang sat down again, his face drawn. 'I have very bad news, Mr. Parker: our enemy has heard you have – they say – "defected". They do not know your exact location, but they know you have left your ship in Foochow. The worst news is that they are rounding up all expatriates in the International Settlement. It distresses me to tell you that your family is being taken to a concentration camp.'

Stan's mind reeled. After twenty minutes of thinking about how he could reverse the course of events, discussing options with *Chiang*, this news pushed the matter out of his hands.

'Parker, you must return with me to Chongquing. The matter is beyond your control,' *Chiang* stood up. I am most terribly sorry that this misfortune has come about because we asked you to come here. But now that you *are* here, we must use your intelligence and familiarity with the Japanese to help us understand Tang better. You can bring some needed – what shall I call it – detachment – to our deliberations in the strategic command. And we shall ensure that you play an important part in hastening our victory over the invaders.' He gave Stan a gentle smile. 'And returning your family to you.'

Stan barely registered any of these assurances. He was appalled at what might be happening to Peggy and Jonny. My God, he thought, this was *Tang*'s revenge? This was not how Stan had seen the *on giri* arrangement unfolding.

Despite fears for his family, he remembered that Peggy was the most self-sufficient woman he had ever met. Recalling her actions, the day of Pearl Harbour, he knew his wife was fearless, even formidable, in emergencies. From experience, he also knew that if she ever felt weak or helpless, she would deny it – to herself and to others. On a separate track, he'd concluded some time ago that this lay behind her fear of intimacy; intimacy required vulnerability. Her new situation would challenge her to the limit. If anyone could welcome such a test, Peggy could.

There was no alternative but to stay with *Chiang*. He wondered what would happen to Watcyn and the crew of the '*Shenkin*'. Captain Williams would be ordered back to *Shanghai*. There was no alternative for Watcyn either, the seas were all under *Tang*'s control. The captain would be interrogated, painfully, to find out how much he knew. If the Japanese finally concluded – without killing the poor Welshman – that he was ignorant of the plan, he would be released. And doubtless he would hate Stan to his dying day.

Another knock, this time more assertive, took *Chiang* to the door again. This time he threw the door wide. 'Ah, you're here and, I hope, ready to return home to Chongqing.' *Chiang* ushered a figure into the room. 'Alena, we have an important addition to our team, Mister – or now can I say it? Chief Officer Stanley Parker.'

As *Chiang* led the newcomer into the room, Stan noticed immediately that the woman was taller than Peggy. Next, Stan was struck by her unusual looks. Her auburn hair – like Peggy's, he thought – was shot with red and pulled severely into a ponytail. Her face had a delicate blend of Asian and – was it Slavic – features? Her figure was lost inside a military-style black leather overcoat, buttoned to the throat where – the only concession to colour – she sported a pale blue silk scarf. Stan guessed she might be in her early thirties. She crossed the room towards him, her quizzical eyes taking in the length of him; the eyes, he noticed, were an extraordinary colour: chartreuse. Stan's hand was taken in a warm, strong handshake. From behind her, he heard Chiang say, 'Please meet my chief of staff, Alena Zoltan.'

PEGGY ADRIFT
Fu-xing 1942

Peggy was feeling adrift. Her busy, useful life in Shanghai – supporting Stan while making a new life for herself – and everything associated with that life – already was embedded in memory's amber. Was she ready for this new chapter: were any of them?

People milled about in a vague formation, searching for order. 'Ah, so British,' Peggy muttered, 'if you don't know what to do – queue.' She had counted thirty-two buses and trucks parked in a semi-circle at the top of the hill. As they moved forward, more yellow buses continued to lumber through the gates. When they halted, dozens of people clambered from each vehicle. They carried suitcases, clothing, assorted bags – an army of bewildered refugees. Peggy saw many of them spinning round and around, trying to make sense of their location before walking unsteadily across the grass to stand in front of a row of fifty or so Japanese soldiers. The men stood at ease in front of the pillared porch. Their bayoneted rifles were on full display.

'Sweet Jesus,' She heard Tom's voice behind her. 'There must be over a thousand of us here. Where in God's name will they put us?' *Chao-xing* sat in her wheelchair, eyes tightly shut, shaking her head.

Dusk fell rapidly and, within minutes, the figures around her became shadows. A car horn parped through the muted burble of voices. The shadows turned towards the sound. Surging through the gates, its headlights arrowing into the fading light, came what must have once been a white Rolls Royce. Now the big car was covered in dust and smeared with grime and mud. The big vehicle was followed by a small Peugeot van, like the ones that delivered bread in the city. Peggy watched the convoy come to a halt. Immediately, harsh floodlights clanged on, displaying the scene.

'My Christ, what's this?' whispered Tom behind her.

Using her arm to protect her eyes against the burst of light, Peggy could barely make out the number plate on the Rolls: 'CG1.' The Japanese 'rising sun' flag flew from its bonnet. Some of the crowd, like Peggy, were aware that the Rolls had been the Consul-General's car. To her left, she heard a male voice mutter, 'Cheeky buggers.'

The driver got out and opened the rear door. A Japanese soldier, wearing multiple decorations, emerged.

Another man, in khaki fatigues and a *kepi*, clambered out from the small van and opened the back of it. Two Great Danes, one grey, the other black, bounded out, cocked their legs in unison to vent powerful streams of urine on the wheels of the Rolls Royce. There was muffled giggling from a few of the children. Their business done, the dogs loped to either side of the much-decorated Japanese soldier. Their great heads levelled at a fraction above his waist. Like sentries, they surveyed the crowd.

'On behalf of divine Emperor Hirohito,' said the man with the megaphone. 'We who will serve you, say welcome – to – Fu-xing.'

His eyes ranged the mute, sullen crowd of Britons. 'Britishers and other prisoners of glorious Nippon, I say hello.'

He smiled at the large crowd and continued to wave his megaphone. 'You know what means Fu-xing in Mandarin?' There was no response. 'Fu-xing is good word, means "rebirth". Everybody now has chance to have rebirth as glorious sons and daughters of Nippon. You are good Fu-xing people.'

No one laughed. Peggy realised that the new man hadn't made the connection with the English word.

The man continued. 'My name is Commandant Riku Ushiguro. I am senior officer at camp – Commandant.' He beamed at his audience before continuing, 'This is now your Fu-xing home.'

'Too bloody right, mate,' a male voice uttered from behind.

A few snorts of laughter came from the huddled foreigners. Peggy wondered if *Ushiguro* was asking himself why these conquered people could find humour at such a moment.

It became the Japanese was wondering about something else: 'How will we find room for you?' he asked the crowd. 'This is what you must be thinking. You can see that this is a fine building. We have commandeered it from imperialist western owner for you, our Western guests. You must all fit into this building – over one thousand.' He gave a huge grin. 'I think you prisoners think of many ways to make Fu-xing better.'

'We are not prisoners,' she heard Trencher mutter.

Ushiguro turned his attention to the children – there were several hundred of them – at the front of the line. 'You children will like fields at Fu-xing. Lots of room here. We have twenty-eight acres – to live, work and play.' He paused and turned to his dogs. He rested his hand on the head of one of them. 'Ushiguro have no children. These my children.' He bowed to the black one, 'This Mister Tokyo,' and then turned to the grey beast. 'And this Mister Kyoto.' He looked at a group of children. 'I give present to first boy or girl who tell me what is clever about these names.' Again, he paused, almost as if expecting applause. He pointed to the huge dogs: 'My children.' The children chattered. The rest of the crowd was silent.

He stepped forward to spread his free arm expansively while he continued to use the megaphone. 'Boys and girls can play cricket here, beloved English game.' He smiled and cocked his head. 'I think cricket very inscrutable game. You say Japanese inscrutable. Maybe cricket invented by Japanese?' He paused, then cackled joyously. Again, silence.

His voice hardened. 'You not forget you prisoners here. Try leave Fu-xing? We shoot you.' His voice rose, he scowled at them. 'This important! Children also must know this important. Mummies and Daddies tell them this important.'

Again, he stared directly at the children. They stared back, attentive but seemingly unafraid. 'Stay away from fences – then you make Japanese guards happy; children happy; mummy and daddy happy. We all happy.' He nodded approvingly, then pointed to the building, gesturing them to move.

'Now go make Fu-xing new home. My guards take you.'

As if to the crack of a starter's gun, the crowd pushed forward towards the building. Peggy stepped around the detritus at her feet and moved forward.

Tom and *Chao-xing* were about twenty feet in front of them when she heard Tom call out, 'All together now: "Oh, when the saints, come marching in...."' Tom began to sing in a voice of such surprising richness and rhythm that, within half a minute, more than a hundred voices picked up the words of the new marching song from the American South.

Peggy's eyes filled with tears; it was the tune that Stan often hummed as he shaved.

***

Peggy picked Jonny up as she moved forward. She tried to feel positive.

She remembered that the main drawback about their rented house in *Shanghai* was that it had never felt like home. What she missed most were: the big, airy rooms; the devotion of her household staff; *Han,* her driver; and the bizarre excitement of living in a war zone. She accepted that the house had given them an enviable launch into married life rather than some plodding existence in a Derbyshire suburb.

At that moment, it struck her that even life in a row of identical houses, along a rain-streaked English street, seemed wonderfully more attractive than the life she and her son faced in *Fu-xing*.

Did Stan even *know* where she was? Although she'd never allowed herself to feel depressed, current events were testing her mental strength: she was a woman, alone with a child, imprisoned by an occupying army in a foreign land. Was this the fruit of her need for independence? How much worse could it be?

If Stan could make his way back to *Shanghai*, would he be able to use his friendship with Admiral *Tang* to find her? As quickly as she had the thought, she dismissed it; it was fantastically improbable that *Tang* would help them. If the Admiral knew that Stan had gone AWOL – and he must know, otherwise why had they been arrested like everyone else? – the Japanese would put Stan into prison or even execute him. Another thought: Had the Consulate been given details of the location of each expat? If Stan could escape Tang's clutches and find his family that way – would his firm have influence?

'Honestly, I don't know Peggy,' Tom Trencher had answered in the bus when she asked the question, looking away as if he didn't care – Why should he? she thought. Her goal now was to survive the camp until the war was over. Then they would be reunited with Stan. Nothing was more important than being a family again.

As she turned these thoughts over in her mind, she realised that they had been waiting in the line for over an hour to get her papers checked. She had lost sight of the Trenchers.

The guard at the main entrance was studying her three cards, checking them for verification. He consulted a list, made marks with a pencil. The Japanese pointed to the picture of Stan. 'Where this man?'

'My husband not here. Me not know where husband.'

Jonny, in Peggy's arms, saw the soldier pointing at the picture of Stan. He smiled: 'Daddy go shipside.'

The soldier stared at Jonny, 'Hai, hai…' Then to Peggy: 'Daddy go shipside? Maybe Daddy go home-side. Clever fellow.'

The soldier chucked Jonny under the chin. Immediately, Peggy pulled the boy closer. 'Go!' said the Japanese, angered by her reaction. He turned his attention to the next person.

They pushed their way into the building's interior. Nobody eased back, even when they saw her carrying a child. An intimidating wave of sound crashed around them. The din – a battle of decibels – would become the permanent background noise of *Fu-xing*. It was the sound of a thousand and more voices, talking too loudly, in a dozen languages.

She stepped into a space that was vast – perhaps double the size of a football field. Peggy had to look at the ceiling to gauge the room's scale. Facing her, she could see only rows and rows of ragged sheets that might once have been white. The grey linen was suspended from long poles that had been fixed horizontally some fifteen feet from the ground, and secured on opposite walls. The room smelled like an airless laundry.

She struggled through the crowd for five minutes. Everyone seemed to be searching for other people, or a place to settle. Peggy arrived at the first row of sheets. She lifted a sheet that indicated an entrance. There were strangers inside, unpacking, getting themselves straight. They didn't look up.

Peggy paused. She assumed people worried that she and her child would add to their disarray, would steal the little space they thought they'd secured. She dropped the sheet and moved on.

Her son was transfixed by all the activity, by this new world he had entered. He kept pointing and saying, 'Look, Mummy, look!' his head swivelling back and forth, putting added pressure on her arm.

Peggy pulled aside every third or fourth sheet – the sheets formed an entrance into what passed for a room. She poked her head inside. She noticed that the bed frames were covered by thin, horsehair mattresses. Peggy calculated that the arrangement would yield no more than forty square feet for each individual.

Twenty minutes later, when Peggy was a third of the way down the large hall, she stepped into another sheeted room.

'Sorry, love, these are all taken,' said the woman inside. She looked as though she'd been punched in the face, her features were like a Picasso sketch. 'The others will be here in a minute,' she said, her mouth firm. 'Best go further down, eh?' The three men in the section didn't look up. They continued to unpack.

Fighting an anxiety that was making it hard to breathe, Peggy again shunted forward for another twenty minutes, looking from side to side, searching for anyone she might recognise. She peered into section after section. She was greeted by the same sight: strangers struggling to settle into their accommodation. All gave her surprised, hostile looks.

Usually, when she walked anywhere in the city with Jonny – carrying him or pushing him in his pram – strangers would stop to talk with her, admire him, ask his age. Here, everyone ignored them – even mothers with children. Every inmate, it seemed, had bigger concerns.

Peggy was exhausted and close to tears. She sensed the suck of negative energy. Jonny, now bored with the newness of his surroundings, had become miserable and whiney. He felt like a sack of potatoes on her arm.

A few minutes later, she pulled aside what seemed like the two hundredth sheet and found Tom Trencher stretched out on a bed. *Chao-xing* sat in her wheelchair, her eyes closed. Peggy's face crumpled with relief, tears threatening. Familiar faces – even Tom's – meant safety, the comfort of a shared language, even a kind of friendship with relative strangers.

There were three other beds in the small space, all empty. Too tired to speak, Peggy flopped down on the bed. As she collapsed, the small explosion of creaks made Tom sit up. 'Oh shit, Pegs, in all this craziness, I forgot about you and Jonny. Jesus, I'm sorry.'

Peggy rolled to one side on the bed, allowing Jonny to slip from the crook of her arm.

Her elbow had locked. Slowly and painfully, she began to straighten it.

'Tom, how could you leave Peggy?' said *Chao-xing*, her eyes now open, her head shaking in annoyance. 'I apologise, Peggy. This entire removal has been such a trial, hasn't it?' she said.

Tom's wife reached out for Jonny, 'Here, darling.' Tom passed the little boy into *Chao-xing*'s outstretched arms. Jonny whined for a moment at being separated from Peggy but soon started to bounce on *Chao-xing*'s thighs. 'So much energy!' the Chinese said. 'Please give me some of your energy.'

Trencher removed Peggy's shoes and started to massage her feet. She sat up in protest at the intimacy. He shook his head, 'No, Peggy, lie down.

This is my penance for forgetting about you.' He winked theatrically, 'And for swearing at you.' She yielded to the bliss of the massage.

'Never fear, Pegs,' Tom said with an impish grin. 'The Seventh Cavalry will soon be along to fix things.'

A minute later, Peggy tapped Tom on the head. 'Thank you, that helped.' She wriggled into her shoes.

Peggy got up and stepped into the next unit. Coats and luggage were piled onto two beds. The next moment Tom was whispering in her ear, 'We're bad people; we parked some of our stuff here, but the beds are free.'

'Bless you, Tom. Oh God, I never thought I'd be so grateful for so little.' Peggy examined the area for her and Jonny.

Her world was continuing to somersault. She knew she was at the end of her endurance. She was among people she barely knew, sharing this new existence in the most intimate of circumstances. She needed to bathe, to change her clothes. Such necessities now seemed to be luxuries – all out of the question. Again, it became difficult to breathe; again, she asked herself, 'how could my world have changed so much?'

Tom was suddenly behind her, his hand on her shoulder. 'I know Pegs, this is a huge mess. But we've gotta beat them. We mustn't let these little shits break our spirit. Marcus will see to it that they don't get the better of us.'

The rush of oxygen that came with his words made Peggy realise how tense she had been seconds before. When she spoke, she tried to sound casual.

'Marcus made it to Fu-xing?'

'Marcus? Hell, the guy *asked* to come – wanted to make sure the Japs had made it decent enough for you Brits. I'm sure we'll see something of Marcus before we hunker down this evening.'

Peggy was both reassured and annoyed to realise that Tom had guessed she might be surrendering to the hopelessness of *Fu-xing*. But with this news about Marcus, she must not make her happiness too blatant. She must change the subject.

She blinked away tears as she turned around. 'Oh Tom, it's Jonny, not me, that I care about. What has he – or any of the children here – done to deserve this fate?'

Tom shook his head, putting his hands on her shoulders and fixing his watery blue eyes on hers. 'I don't know, hon. But I do know that action is the only way to fight this situation.'

Peggy managed a weak smile. Trencher was a man, for all his faults, and although he was *Chao-xing*'s husband –she needed a man to share her fears.

Tom was saying, 'I'll bring Chao-xing into this spot with Jonny and leave a few things on our beds to establish territory. We need to make it obvious that all four places have been taken. Come, if you can bear it: you and I will go in search of food.'

FOOD
Fu-xing 1942

Minutes later, they were lifting aside more sheets as they headed towards the end of the sleeping section.

As they weaved through the beds and the people, all Peggy could think about was the fact that Marcus was here. For months, she had struggled to keep him out of her thoughts. She had known how much pressure Stan had been under, and she felt – in some mysterious way – that clutching the thought of Marcus made Stan more vulnerable. But now, now he was here. And Stan, as usual, was away.

The clamour of voices around her tugged her back to the present moment. The talk seemed more like a panicked jabbering – in English, French, Russian. Peggy realised that nobody had privacy. Those who were not sitting were busy making beds, throwing stained blankets over stained mattresses. Every available space was filled. Large cupboards had become sleeping quarters.

Everyone looked fearful, protective of each little space.

'God! This is bloody madness,' said Peggy as they pushed forward. 'I'm sorry, Tom, if I've seemed crabby. I'm exhausted and frightened and very grateful to be with you and Chao-xing.'

He threw his arm around her. Tom was not a tall man, so she found herself looking down at him – an odd sensation. He hugged her hard, and she looked away, embarrassed by her flash of weakness.

'Heavens, I'm being such a *girl*. Sorry, Tom.'

'Perfectly understandable, hon,' he said. 'But unexpected, even so. I mean, from strong, resourceful Peggy. Come on, we need to get some food into you.'

The last, eighth section, had a sign pinned to a sheet. It read **'Unattached women with children.'** The section was larger than others they had seen. Guiltily, Peggy wondered if this was where she should be. But she preferred to be with people she knew.

There were a dozen women milling about. An older child, about fifteen, sat on a bed reading to younger children. The girl looked up at Peggy, she asked, 'Hello, may we help you?' Her smile was so warm and innocent that Peggy found herself at the edge of tears as she shook her head in reply. The girl was reading '*Swallows and Amazons*' to her little audience.

She looked around and saw the woman with the BBC accent that she had seen near one of the buses. Tall and thin with well-cut black hair, the woman must once have been beautiful, but now her complexion was crisscrossed by a patina of tiny worry lines. She wore black slacks and a red blouse under a black cardigan. Peggy realised that many of the women had put on their best clothes for the trip to the camp; but hadn't she? She heard another woman, carrying a tray of tin mugs, say, 'Hilary, where shall I put these?'

The Hilary woman seemed to have taken charge: she was handing out blankets and chatting with the women around her. She could have been preparing for a church fete. Again, Tom's hand was on her shoulder. 'We must press on, Pegs.'

Five minutes later, they came across a family they both knew. The man was trying to hang up a sheet to shield their area from passers-by. She remembered seeing them on the bus, and here they were again: John and Sue Lang. She had first met the couple at the British Consulate. The event was a reception, held on the Queen's birthday – at the time, Peggy thought how ludicrous. She wished she could be there now, sipping Pimm's on a green lawn, swapping inanities with a clamour of chattering Brits.

The Lang children, Diana and David, were playing pat-a-cake. They looked at Peggy and Tom without recognition before continuing their game. John Lang, who Peggy had always thought of as good-looking as Clark Gable, spotted them and called out: 'Hello, Tom, Peggy – isn't this marvellous!' He raised a dark eyebrow; his look was ironic.

Then Lang seemed to study her more carefully, 'Peggy what are you doing with that bounder, Trencher? Where's Stan?' She shook her head, and he gave her a look that blended surprise with disappointment. 'Oh, bad show. What happened to our sailor boy?'

Peggy raised a hand, palm towards him, cutting off further questions.

Tom called out, 'Stan's at sea, apparently. Chao-xing's back at home base…'

'Home base?' Lang looked puzzled.

'Tent City, our quarters, looking after Peggy's boy.' He jerked his thumb behind them. 'We're as good as can be expected – as guests of the divine Emperor.'

Peggy felt sickened by the male show of normality.

'Come on, Tom, let's get that food.' She realised she hadn't eaten since they'd left Bubbling Well Road. She'd taken some food to keep Jonny content but nothing for herself.

They waved at the Langs and tried to move forward again. All around them were lines for bedding, medicines, and food. Peggy was conscious again of a humming in the fetid air, like some magnified tinnitus – it was the thrum of more than a thousand fearful strangers,

Tom whispered: 'The gossip is that our jailers have provided no clothes, no shoes, soap or toilet paper, no disinfectant or mosquito nets. One of the chaps told me there wasn't even any cooking utensils.' Tom shook his head. 'It's almost as if these bloody Nips never thought they'd get this far – catching us and then having no place to put their new enemy.'

They managed to scrounge three discoloured blankets that smelled of damp. They rejected the yellow pillows they were offered. There were no sheets.

'Now, food!' said Tom, pantomiming the signs of hunger.

They found another queue; the odour of something being cooked suggested that there might be food at the end of it. The aroma of the food did nothing to arouse Peggy's appetite; it smelled rank, unpleasant – as if it had been left standing out for too long. There were flies – not a swarm – but enough to be a worry.

After another fifteen minutes of shuffling forward, they reached the hulking figure of a man in a grey apron. He was so large that his neck had disappeared into his chest and shoulders. Huge hands were using a ladle to put a grey substance on small piles of rice in tins. There was also an assortment of mismatched bowls. The fat man's two black eyes studied them briefly.

'ID?' his eyebrows, suspicious, raised with the question.

They showed their identity cards. The man used the ladle to push forward two of the containers. On each bowl, he placed a thin slice of bread. Peggy noticed the crusts had been sliced off. He saw her staring at the bread. 'We spent the first hour cutting the green mould off the loaves – they'd been left in the damp – but the congee should be all right.' He shrugged.

Peggy knew about congee: rice that had been boiled to a tasteless mush in 'congs', or big metal bowls. Her servants ate congee morning, noon, and night and *Wang Fang,* her cook – oh, so long ago, she thought – tried to make her like it. He was unsuccessful. She doubted whether congee had any nutritional value. 'At least it will fill Jonny's tummy,' she whispered to Tom.

'The meat: what is it?' asked Tom, pointing to the dark lumps on top of the congee.

'No idea, mate.' He stirred the contents of the tureen. 'The Japs started us off with rice and some vegetables. From what we can make out, this is the Fu-xing diet. We're calling it SOS – same old stew.' He nodded at Peggy, 'That's putting it politely, miss.' He scooped a chunk from the tureen and sniffed it. 'Best guess? Chinese street buffalo, or maybe greyhound – the Japs got into the kennels at the track.' He pointed to the congee under the meat. 'Even so, you want to watch that congee because you might find more protein in it than you bargained for.' He gave a sort laugh then looked at Tom, 'Know what I mean.'

'What do you mean?' Peggy frowned.

Tom touched her elbow. 'I think the chef here means the food may contain some foreign material – mice droppings – who knows?'

'More likely weevils, sir,' said the man behind the tureen, his eyes only on Tom. Peggy wondered why Tom's American accent gave him rank. Even in these desperate circumstances, differences prevailed.

'Buddy,' said Tom. 'We're gonna need another two bowls of this glop – one for my wife,' he nodded his head back, 'and' – he nodded at Peggy, 'one for her son.'

Tureen man shook his head. 'Well, sir, by rights, you should have brought your wife's ID card to prove she's here and has your name.' He turned to Peggy. 'Same for the little man.'

Tom sounded irritable. 'C'mon buddy. It'll take more than an hour for us to get there and back.'

The man was cowed by Tom's raised voice. He looked down at the big bowl. Peggy could tell he was deciding how not to lose face. 'Well, as it's the first night an' all, I'll overlook it. But next time – every time, in fact – bring your ID to the food line.'

He began to fill the two additional bowls. And in a friendlier voice, he said, 'I think the Japs have been storing this – whatever it is – for a year while they've been deciding what to do with us.' He barked a phlegm-filled cough. 'Probably be easier to poison the lot of us.' He choked and spluttered for a few moments without turning his face away. He set down the two bowls on the counter.

Leaning back, he stuck an upraised thumb in the air. 'But soon we'll be preparing our own food. I think the little buggers expect that. And it'll be a darn sight safer for us than this crap.' He smiled at Peggy, 'If you'll excuse my French.'

Juggling the four bowls, Peggy and Tom threaded their way through the squash of beds, all pushed together. Unusually, the sheets suspended from above had been tied back, opening up the area.

A woman's shriek cut the air, followed by a foreign voice shouting, '*Christos*, you cannot take this bed! It is *my* bed. I only left it to fetch the revolting thing in this bowl.' The shout came from a tall, slender woman, her face bright with anger.

'My God, it's Natasha!' said Tom.

NATASHA
Fu-xing 1942

Peggy called out: 'Tash! Tash! You're here. I can't believe it.' Natasha Pavlovich shrieked with obvious joy as she scrambled between the beds, her arms wide for an embrace. Peggy held up her bowls of congee, fending her off. The two women kissed.

'Liebchen, das ist wunderbar!' she exclaimed. 'How happy I am to see one polite English person among all this... these... these peasants.'

'And Tom!' she hugged him. 'Oh, we are all here together. That is so lovely! But where is Stanley – and Jonny?' She peered at Tom, holding him at arm's length, as if he might have something to do with Stan's absence. 'Tom?'

Peggy found herself able to laugh. 'Jonny is fine – he's back on our patch – you know, where we've managed to make some space for ourselves.

'And Stan's at sea.' Tom added.

Hearing him say it, Peggy felt a stab of regret, almost embarrassment. 'Tash, we have no idea where my husband is.' She gritted her teeth. 'But Tom is being a wonderful help. Now he has three women to look after. Do you have *any* idea how happy that makes the old rogue?' She winked at Tom, hoping her remark didn't seem cruel. She was rewarded with a smile, and realised the American thought he'd been complimented.

Peggy turned back to Natasha. She said, 'Well, darling, it would seem you've lost your place in the sleeping queue. You had better come with us, and we'll see what we can find for you. I expect Jonny has gone to sleep on an empty tummy, but he'll be thrilled to see you in the morning.'

The trio found their way back to their quarters. Many people sat with bowls on their laps. They didn't look up as Peggy's group passed; they seemed to be too engrossed with their congee. Was this their new sense of community, Peggy wondered – strangers blending with the background when seen for the second time?

'Here's our little bit of heaven, Tash,' said Tom.

Jonny was asleep in *Chao-xing*'s arms. 'Natasha!' the Chinese smiled with pleasure. 'Now we can have parties, and all will be well.'

They all laughed and *Chao-xing* passed the sleeping boy over to Natasha. Tom's wife whispered that she'd used the wheelchair to move back and forth; the regular movement had been enough to send the little boy to sleep.

Peggy turned her attention to the two bowls of congee that they'd brought back. She spent several minutes sifting through the sloppy gruel. She extracted a few tiny weevils. Eventually, she decided that the food wasn't contaminated beyond weevils or, if it was, she would never find the source. For a moment, she debated waking Jonny to feed him but decided against it; hunger would wake him eventually. She set aside some of her own congee for Jonny in case he woke in the night. She gave the second bowl, under protest, to Natasha.

Without utensils, she used her fingers to eat. She tried not to think about the squishy substance in her mouth. She closed her eyes, shivering as she swallowed.

Peggy could hear the Lang children, a section away. They were singing nursery rhymes and playing pat-a-cake, which seemed to be the only game they knew.

John Lang, it seemed, had swapped his family's location for something closer. *Chao-xing* explained, 'He said he'd rather be with PLUs – people like us – than surrounded by hoi-polloi. Anyway, the people they swapped with were thrilled to be closer to the food – God knows what they eat at home if they enjoy this filth.'

Chao-xing nodded in the direction Peggy and Tom had come from: 'The Langs are fetching food for their kids.' She smiled, 'I said I'd be mother to all of them.' Peggy sensed that the childless woman was enjoying her duties.

Tom was pulling another bed into place alongside Peggy's. 'Right-o,' he announced. 'We now have a bed for our gypsy princess!' Peggy wondered why Tom was trying to impress a woman who wasn't a stranger. She guessed it was in his nature to flirt.

'Mind if we join you for supper?' John Lang stepped through the opening. 'Oh, hello Natasha, Not quite your scene, I imagine. This is hardly party hearty, is it?' Not waiting for an answer, he moved into their space. Sue Lang, her eyes smarting from the cigarette between her lips, crowded in behind him with her two children.

Five of them – Peggy, Natasha, and Lang's wife plus the Lang children – spread themselves across the two beds. Chao-xing looked comfortable in her wheelchair. Jonny continued to sleep in Natasha's arms. Tom and John Lang stood while they ate. John Lang raised his bowl towards the boy in Tash's arms. 'How I wish I were he,' he said. But Peggy noticed that Lang's eyes were fixed on Natasha's legs.

MARCUS CARTER
Fu-xing 1942

'Hello, everyone.' A man's voice, distorted by a megaphone, broke into the buzz of conversations. 'May I say a few words before you all turn in?' An hour had passed, and, as best they could, they were readying themselves for bed. The time was a few minutes after ten o'clock.

Peggy, though aware that Marcus was in the camp, was still shocked to see him standing on a table forty feet away. She studied his face and bearing anew because, given her feelings for him at Natasha's party, she had ensured that they never met alone again. Yet it seemed unbelievable now that – bar a few cocktail parties where she'd avoided him – that they had not seen each other for such a long time. Her stomach still burned when she looked at him. She was astonished to find that whatever feelings she'd had then were still dormant. Her body stirred as she studied the man across the room.

'My name is Marcus Carter. I'm the new Head of Mission at the British Consulate.' He paused while his eyes ranged the room. Peggy looked down, blushing, in case his gaze discovered her, and he reacted.

Marcus went on: 'Less than a week ago, as I think most of you know, our Consul-General, Sir Jeremy Birkbeck, was interned at another camp. In the absence of Sir Jeremy, I have been appointed Head of Mission…'

He grinned, looking down at the children near the table before adding '…which is Foreign Office code for boss.'

He held his shoulders back as he talked, in a way that conveyed confidence, even dominance. Part of this effect was created by his stance on the table, but Peggy got the sense that much of this was innate; it was who he was.

As she watched him – between the heads moving back and forth across her vision – she wondered: why do I care again about the impression he's making – not just on me, but on all the people in this room? The room had hushed; all eyes were on the man on the table. She guessed that most people had become aware of his physicality, the authority of his presence.

'Ladies and gentlemen, boys and girls: it's fair to ask, do I – do we –

still have a mission? We do, for as I see it, the first and most important thing for you to do is to think of yourselves as part of the British Empire, currently located at Fu-xing Civilian Concentration Camp.' He paused for a moment. 'Note that I don't call Fu-xing a civic assembly area. Forgive me, children, but this is a bloody concentration camp! We are not – and I repeat this – we are *not* a random group of Japanese prisoners of war. Most of us are, if you will, a section of the United Kingdom temporarily-in-exile.' He paused again and scanned the room. 'Try to keep that foremost in your mind if you are taunted or abused by our enemy. Try not to engage or react; do not give the Japanese the satisfaction of seeing your anger or any sign – heaven forbid – of feeling sorry for yourself.'

As he talked, Peggy did not remember his face to be as long as it appeared now. His dark green eyes roamed about the room. As he talked, he gave the impression – and she knew this was illogical – that he was engaging with them one individual at a time. He wore his black hair long, longer than the night of Natasha's party – the black locks partly covered his ears, falling over the collar of his white shirt. How could his shirt be so dazzling white in these circumstances? She spotted a thin pencil moustache above his lips – that was a feature she hadn't noticed when they'd first met. The dark line of hair gave his face a cavalier look. Taken together, Carter's physiognomy and his balanced physique indicated he might once have been a fighter – or at least a man who had fought – and seemed poised to fight again.

He continued to look around the assembly hall, making eye contact with as many as he could, before continuing. 'The British people in this room will know they are all heirs to the world's greatest heritage: *Great Britain!* And our Mission, if you will, is to demonstrate our Britishness every day until we exit this pit.' His eyes swept the room. 'And I'm sure the rest of you, whatever nationality you are, feel the same about *your* heritage and how you plan to demonstrate your superiority to our captors.' He spat out the last word.

A muffled cheer arose. Carter raised his hands, quelling a few voices breaking into, 'There'll always be an England.'

Natasha held her hand to her throat and winked at Peggy. 'If Marcus is here, all will be well,' she whispered. 'I know this man. He is good for us. You are pleased, yes, Peggy?' She nodded, as if Peggy's embarrassed glance had answered her question.

Carter went on to talk about volunteers needed for: the kitchens; a newspaper; engineering; camp police to keep order; and wood cutters for fuel.

Tom Trencher moved closer to Peggy. He took Tash's hand and pulled her into their huddle.

'You know that Marcus has Indian blood? I mean dot – with his index finger, he tapped his forehead - not feather – he moved his hand up at the back of his head - decoded, that means his background is Taj Mahal, not Redskin?' Tom paused, pleased with his little joke. 'I hear the pen pushers in Whitehall and Washington are trying to make all western consulates and embassies more of a mirror of their mixed citizenship. Carter's a bit of a guinea pig for the Brits.' Trencher winked conspiratorially. 'So the Indian bit gives him an edge on the promotional stakes. We Americans hear that the Whitehall bosses feel that people like Marcus have been pushed aside in the Foreign Service. It's time to stop that.'

'C'est vrai?' Natasha asked.

Tom narrowed his eyes, smiled knowingly. 'Is it true they've been pushed aside? On that, I shall maintain a diplomatic silence. Let me say that, as half-British, perhaps Marcus feels his patriotism more keenly than the rest of us more authentic types.' He turned to Natasha. 'I think that came through in his little speech, n'est ce pas?'

''But you're only half British, Tom.' Peggy couldn't resist the taunt.

He narrowed his eyes. 'Because I'm a white American whose father came from the UK?'

Peggy half-smiled, 'I'm not sure whiteness has anything to do with patriotism.'

They looked back at Marcus, who was still speaking: 'I suggest the last thing we want in this wretched place is any kind of vacuum. By that, I mean, we must organise ourselves as only we British know how.' Again, another small cheer arose.

'I shall be forming a temporary residents committee – and by the way – the title is deliberately chosen, for that is what we shall be, temporary residents – in this Fu-xing dump.'

'Jolly good!' shouted a voice.

'Precisely,' said Carter. 'There will be five of us on the Committee: me, as chairman; Mervyn Jones, whom some of you – but, I suspect, not enough of you – know as the Bishop of Shanghai. Doctor Albert Faure, representing our medical establishment; Myke – with a 'y' Amble – our man from Lancashire, who was a director of England's National Trust before he became personnel director of Blue Funnel – and Tom Trencher, head of foreign affairs at the American Consulate.' A beat. 'Not that there'll be time for any of those at Fu-xing.' Again, there was a burst of male laughter. Peggy saw Tom look at his shoes.

Marcus nodded towards their group, lifting his hand towards Tom before his eyes found Peggy and lingered. He smiled and gave a tiny nod. He didn't look at Natasha.

'I'm sorry to have to tell you that there is only cold water for washing, baths and showers.' The crowd groaned. 'Any hot water that we can generate must be used for washing cooking pots, plates and utensils. But heating? I have to tell you what my old Matron said when I told her I was cold, "Put on another jumper!" '

'Marcus, you mean there'll be no heating?' cried a voice. 'But how will we survive the cold?'

There was a ragged chorus of 'Put on another jumper!' followed by patches of laughter from the crowd.

Half-laughing himself, Marcus continued. '

'We shall ask any qualified medical men – and we have twenty-eight doctors here, which is wonderful – to report to our committee man, Doctor Faure. We need to set up medical protocols, infirmaries and, not least, establish the most germ-free ways of storing our food.'

He surveyed the room. When he spoke again, his voice had deepened.

'Ladies and gentlemen, girls and boys, please be aware that disease will be our greatest enemy – more than the hostility of our charming captors. Our experts – the biologists and chemists – will soon let you know what methods we can use to combat the greatest scourge – malaria. We'll have rosters produced by the end of the week that cover everything we can think of, from 'KP' – that's Kitchen Patrol for those of you who weren't in the army – to medical and educational needs for our young people.' He smiled at a cluster of children around the table. 'Yes, lads and lasses, sorry to say, school will continue.' There was a muted groan.

'Now, please settle in as best you can. Those of you, like me, who were at boarding school will know that nothing is as bad as the first night.' His eyes swept the room again.

'Oh, and if you want to telephone Mummy…' he paused, 'you can't.' There was a murmur of laughter as he got down from the table.

INSOMNIA
Fu-xing 1942

Two hours later, Peggy was trying to sleep; it was a challenge because she was disturbed by the body sounds of others and the smell of massed humans. A stream of sounds and smells slipped through the thin sheets that quartered her cramped domain. The river of night would trickle on until that moment when daylight eased into the room.

What did she loathe more: The night that stretched before her – or the first full day of her internment?

There was no way she could evade the present moment. But thank God Marcus was here and in charge. She mused that if 'cometh the hour, cometh the man' were true then – even allowing for her own feelings – there could be no better man than Marcus. She thought briefly what this internment might do to how they felt about each other. But did he feel the same?

'He must,' she decided. One thing she did know: she didn't want anything between them to be tainted by the extraordinary circumstances of *Fu-xing*. If they all survived, if Stan came back to her – as she was certain he would – then a future would become apparent.

Jonny wriggled against her. She put her arm around his little body, wanting to hug him but not wake him. Her son was clutching his beloved cloth monkey, Jacko, Stan's gift to him when he went 'shipside'.

Peggy was grateful that Jonny had no idea of their situation. For her little man, *Fu-xing* was simply another place, another bed. As long as his mama was close, Jonny was happy.

Perhaps two-year-old Jonny, she thought, had an attitude she could learn from: he lived moment to moment – at the age of two, he didn't dwell on the past or imagine a future; he lived in the perpetual now.

For a few moments, Peggy imagined Stan spooning against her, holding her as she now held Jonny. This was where her life had brought her, where she had been placed. For now, this moment, holding her child, was the only home she knew.

She felt herself sliding towards sleep but then her mind, 'the chattering monkey', as she'd once heard *Chao-xing* call it, delivered a flood of negative thoughts. An inner voice tried to deceive her into thinking that everything she was experiencing was a dream. 'None of this awful day has happened; Stanley did not leave you to face this horror without him.' And then the new thought: 'Thank God Marcus is here.'

Peggy's head rolled back and forth on the itchy mattress. Quiet sobs engulfed her. Her inner voice said, 'But Stan *did* leave you. This day *has* happened; you and Jonny *are* alone in a Japanese concentration camp. You used to think that marriage was like a bow and bowstring, and children, the arrows. The war, the Japanese, have stolen Stan, your bowstring; you are still the bow, but now your greatest task is to make safe that one arrow – your son.'

The metronome of negative thoughts continued to beat down on her. Someone a few beds away wailed in fright, 'a nightmare within this nightmare,' Peggy mused. Another voice murmured, 'it's fine, it's fine.'

Night resumed its fractured hum. The sound of clanging pots reached her from somewhere. Was that dinner being washed up, or breakfast being started? She wondered. She was floating in a half-world.

Peggy knew that all the men in the colonial service were the sons of well-to-do families; most of them had received a superior education. A few of them, like Tom, were Rhodes Scholars – their education funded by Cecil Rhodes's intention – as Stan had once explained – 'for the extension of British rule throughout the world.'

Every colonial officer had been trained to stay calm in a crisis; had been taught how to think, when to act. And certainly never, ever, to panic or retreat; Carter, she judged, was a fine example of that heroic type.

Her thoughts tumbled on: Peggy's parents had always voted for the country's elite, most of them from Eton and Oxford University, and most of them in the Tory Party Her mum and dad had instilled in their children the belief that 'the toffs know what's best for us.' Yet when she reflected on: The pointless savagery of the First World War and the stupidity of the high command – 'lions led by donkeys'; the sacrifice made by her father and the seventeen million others on all sides who had perished – Peggy knew she was right in thinking. as she always had done before she came to China, that she could depend only on herself.

Her mind opened up to Marcus again. She knew little about him, but she believed what Tom had told her: Carter was bright, someone they were now calling 'a high flier' but more his own man than Stan. Her husband seemed insecure compared with Carter; Stan liked to please people, especially his superiors – an aspect of him that troubled her. For example, Stan's eager acceptance of PP's patronage, the car and driver, the large house. And didn't she like it, too?

With Marcus, she felt his natural authority seemed fitted to keeping them safe. She was glad Marcus Carter was here and, as she considered the turn of events, she tried to see the man through a practical – not emotional – lens. Like her, he was someone who could cope. She would help him to get them out of this dreadful place. Or at least to survive this prison camp until they had defeated the Japanese.

A HORROR STORY
Fu-xing 1943

Marcus was pleased with the way his committee had responded to the challenge of setting up the camp. They would have a dependable heating system, Tony de Bruyn, the engineer, assured them. Myke Amble could guarantee that fresh produce – planted and supervised by teams of parents and children – would start to yield in the spring.

Marcus had now to turn his attention to the critical matter of medical resources. The burly Frenchman came to his quarters.

'Albie, I need your help with medical matters.'

The doctor nodded his head of thick white hair. *'Absolutement!'* He beamed at Marcus. 'As you English like to say, *"Pas de problem".'* They laughed together.

Faure became serious as he took his place on the bed. Marcus sat on the only available chair.

'Of course, I am happy to help the British,' he gave a wry smile. 'Even though the English are our ancient enemy. But I will not touch the Japanese.'

Marcus was puzzled. 'As a doctor, is it not your obligation – your duty, in fact – to treat the sick, no matter who they are?'

Faure pulled himself up so his back could rest against the wall. He closed his eyes then rubbed his head. Marcus realised the big man was agitated.

'Certainly, if they were human, I would treat them. But I would rather treat a stray dog before any of these cretins. Why do I say such a thing?' Faure rubbed his brow. 'Let me explain: One month ago, over one hundred Japanese soldiers broke into my medical quarters in the French concession. They were a rogue group, led by a thirty-year-old captain, Tatsuka Kobe – his name I will never forget. He told me he had orders to capture or execute any Allied prisoners being treated in my wards. He asked me if I was treating such men. Obviously, I said I was not.

'Kobe screams at me and searches until he finds fifty-one British and Canadian soldiers. Yes, it is true we have hidden them in a secret ward. Of course! We did not want the enemy to find them. The patients are lying in their beds. And three British and four Chinese nurses are taking care of them. I knew many of the men will die from their wounds but, but... we are trying to make them comfortable.

'The captain – putain, son of a whore – when he finds the men, he does not know what to do with them. Maybe he thinks they will slow down his march to the Bund.'

Faure had paused, closing his eyes, then spoke again. 'Kobe has me go to the room where he finds the soldiers. Again, he screams at me, accusing me of deceiving him. He says I am a liar! He says what happens next is all my fault because of my deception.

'Kobe brings ten of his soldiers into the ward. One of his men pushes me into a chair. He binds my hands behind my back and puts a filthy rag into my mouth. But of course, I can see and hear everything.' Again, Faure paused, his breath now coming quickly.

'The patients are moaning in their beds. Some of them are crying because they do not know what will happen. Kobe tells the men to be silent – *incroyable!* Then he shouts in Japanese to his armed guard. Of course, I do not understand. One of his soldiers – I remember this so clearly – he looks puzzled; he makes Kobe repeat the order. It is then I know it must be bad.'

Faure eased himself off the bed and started circling the small room. His breathing increased as he spoke. 'As I watch, I am yelling into the rag in my mouth, but no one can hear.' The doctor rubbed his hand in front of his mouth.

'Kobe's men start to bayonet the terrified men as they lie in their beds. Remember: the men they are killing are all soldiers, being killed by soldiers; they scream, they swear, they try to get up, but it is of no use. They are all stabbed to death.' Faure made wild stabbing motions, lashing out in all directions.

'The bedsheets have great crimson patches, soaked with the blood of these poor men. I could have closed my eyes, but what a terrible act of cowardice that would have been.' Faure dry-heaved with the memory. 'It takes a long time before our fifty-one soldiers, our patients, are silent. Dead.'

Marcus stood up and, sitting next to him on the bed, wrapped his arm around the Frenchman's shoulder. He had no words to offer.

'But it was not over.' Faure shrugged away Marcus's arm. 'Kobe leads the Japanese soldiers who have done the killing into another room. Other Japs push the seven nurses into the same room.' Marcus shook his head disbelievingly, got up, and stood facing Faure as he continued to describe the scene.

'The door is left open; I notice this. As I sit strapped to my chair, I hear the Japanese shout and laugh while they are raping the women!' Faure's eyes widen with horror. 'I hear their screams.'

'An hour later, perhaps less, the filthy captain – this turd of a man – comes out to face me. What does he say to me? He says that all of this happens because I have lied to him. He says to me, 'All your soldiers dead. All your nurses dead. We burn these people and mattresses. Then we march to the Bund. *Banzai!* He shouts the last word.'

His gaze firm, Faure studied Marcus. 'Now you know what I think of the enemy, why I do not wish to treat them. They are worse than the pigs they raise for their pork.'

Marcus was too shocked to speak. He knew that the doctor needed a moment to re-bury his memories.

Finally, the Frenchman spoke: 'But I've lived long enough to know that my energy will be wasted hating them. Instead, I will embrace my energy and use my twenty-eight doctors that Monsieur Trencher tell me we have – and my nurses – to build the best hospital in all of China, here in Fu-xing.' He smiled broadly and punched the air, 'Oui. En marche!'

Marcus commissioned Albert Faure as Chief Medical Officer, Fu-xing.

MOSQUITOES
Fu-xing 1943

The relentless, high-pitched whine of mosquitoes arrived at Peggy's ears every night. She shared the frustration of the other insomniacs around her as they slapped and swore at the blood-seeking insects.

Peggy had a concern greater than her own comfort: her son's health. 'Jonny must not get sick, Jonny must not get sick.' She repeated the sentence like a prayer. She was scared – no – terrified by the thought that her little boy might become a blood feast for their malarial bites.

Growing up in England's mild climate, Peggy knew nothing of tropical diseases. Shortly after she arrived (when it was too late to change her mind, she recalled), Stan had told her that in the Far East, 'wherever there are people, there will be mosquitoes and malaria.'

'The mosquitoes, particularly the females,' Stan had explained – my, how he loved to explain, she remembered – 'are drawn to carbon monoxide and other human emanations in the air. Mosquitoes need to draw blood from a human host; they infect the victim before passing the malaria parasite to the next person, using the protein that they've stolen to perpetuate their breeding cycle. It's wickedly clever,' he had said, she remembered, shaking his head in wonder. 'Most people think that man's enemies are animals that can tear us from limb to limb: lions and tigers. Yet any scientist would tell you that our apex predator is the mosquito; one day, it could wipe humanity off the face of the earth.'

Peggy said, 'Oh dear, Stan, not this week, I hope.'

Stan had chuntered on as if she hadn't spoken, remembering his own bouts of malaria, almost speaking to himself.

'I've been lucky,' he had continued. 'I've only had one bout of malaria, but I wouldn't wish it on my worst enemy. I was hallucinating. In my mind, I was climbing the walls. Meanwhile, sweat was pouring off me – the bedsheets had to be changed every few hours. My head felt like a tin can with a little man hammering inside it. I had fevers and chills – even in the hottest room! The malaria stayed with me for ten days. In the end, a mixture of quinine and God-knows-what-else brought me back from what seemed like a sort of hell.'

Electric fans were considered to be the best weapon against the mosquitoes. At home in the Settlement, Peggy remembered how Stan had insisted on having large electric fans spinning in every room. The air that the fans generated, he said, disturbed the insect's flight and thinned the carbon dioxide; this made it harder for the insects to locate their human prey. Marcus Carter was wrestling with the mosquito problem, too. His *Fu-xing* committee knew that the Japanese would laugh at any demand for one thousand electric fans. Instead, they asked for mosquito nets.

Weeks passed before the guards brought the nets. The Japanese dumped armfuls of the yellowing material at each sleeping area. When the internees opened them, the nets were pitted with holes. Everyone agreed the nets would be useless. Marcus was told to do something about it.

Over the past few months, Marcus had tried to become friendly with one of the senior guards, an older sergeant named *Ono Shozo*. Fluent in Japanese, Marcus took the guard to see the nets. Grimacing, Marcus stuck his thumb down, the universal sign for disapproval. 'These no good, Shozo-san. I must speak with the Commandant.'

While waiting for a response from the Commandant, Marcus had quizzed the guard about *Ushiguro*'s background; he had noticed that the Commandant's skin was darker than most other Japanese. *Ono* explained that *Ushiguro* came from *Okinawa*, a tropical island some thousand miles from Tokyo. There, he explained, people generally spent more time outdoors; this fact, he suggested, might explain their different complexion. He added, 'Okinawans live long time – some more than one hundred years. They eat special potato – only grow Okinawa. Make them strong – live long.'

'I see,' Marcus had said. 'Otherwise, they are the same as all Japanese; they hate Westerners?'

Ono gave a laugh that was more of a yelp. 'Hau! Japanese not hate Westerners – not when you all go home.'

'As soon as we can, Shozo-San.'

'But what I mean is... are Okinawans different from mainland Japanese?'

Ono considered the question, puffing on his hand-rolled cigarette, before shaking his head.

'They... soft? They have good kokoro.'

'What means kokoro?' Marcus had not come across the word before.

Ono made a circular motion, encompassing his whole upper body: 'Kokoro,' he repeated.

Afterwards, Marcus had thought about the word and *Ono*'s attempt at an explanation. He concluded that the guard had meant *kokoro* to indicate a whole aura for the whole person: heart, mind, spirit. Marcus thought such an attitude might make his negotiation less difficult.

Two days later, *Ono* said, 'Commandant see you now.'

Ono Shozo led him to a low-slung bungalow, perhaps a quarter of a mile from the building housing the internees. Marcus had heard that the bungalow had once been a small guest house when the acreage had been privately owned. He made a small bow as *Ono Shozo* muttered something to the guard at the door. Carter smelled incense.

The commandant was seated at his desk in the living room, his bullet head covered by a skein of loosely coiled black hair. He was studying paperwork. Marcus noticed a wisp of smoke from a joss stick burning on his desk.

Riku Ushiguro did not rise from his chair. Marcus felt insulted, which he knew was the Commandant's intention.

'Please, don't get up.' Marcus said with a small smile so that the man would know what was implied. 'We can talk in your native tongue if you prefer.'

The Commandant looked up from his papers. 'English, please, Carter-San, I like to practise. We last met when we agree on terms of you being here, yes? You are pleased with arrangements?'

Marcus was surprised to hear *Ushiguro* again address him with the respectful 'San'. Unsmiling, he replied, 'Pleased with the arrangements? Ushiguro-San, I think you told me your terms and I had to agree.'

The Japanese shrugged. 'True. But this is war, yes? You in camp. Me here.'

Marcus looked around the Commandant's drab office. He wrinkled his nose. 'You are happy with this?'

The insult was unmistakable; Marcus wondered for how much longer they would trade them. He went on: 'We British have an expression, and you may have heard it: one battle is not a war.'

Marcus continued talking, looking past *Ushiguro* to the window. 'I am surprised a military power such as yours, Commandant, with a history of so many wars, would begin to think it might conquer a territory as vast as China's.' He tipped his head almost deferentially before saying, 'Perhaps Mao is right when he says that China is like a gallon jug which Japan is trying to fill with half a pint of water and that…'

The Japanese cut him off, his face tightening with anger. 'Mao is traitor to his people to bring communism to this sacred region.'

'I would think that Mao would know what is best for his region; after all, he is Chinese, and this is his country. As you, no doubt Commandant, know what is best for Japan. Perhaps Mao believes that to live under communism is better than to live under fascism.' Marcus smiled before adding, 'Did not your ally, Herr Hitler, declare that communism is the blood enemy of fascism?'

The two men stared at each other. Marcus wondered whether the Japanese would debate military strategy with a foreigner – and a prisoner, at that. He doubted it.

Marcus tried to break the tension. 'As to your question: I would like to say we are pleased with arrangements…' he paused, 'but we are not.'

The commandant got up from his chair and turned his back to his visitor. He gazed at the brick wall some five metres away. 'Why you not pleased with Fu-xing?' he asked softly. Then he turned around, his voice rising: 'We try *not* make you pleased. You prisoners-of-war!'

'That's the point,' said Marcus, his face colouring, trying to control his anger. 'We are *not* prisoners-of-war or enemy combatants; we are civilian internees. We have rights that are different from prisoners-of-war.' Carter pressed on: 'The mosquito nets you've provided are useless. They are full of holes; a squadron of the little blighters could fly through just one of the holes without touching sides.'

The Japanese turned back and continued to address the brick wall on the other side of the window: 'If glorious sons of Nippon can fight and sleep without nets,' he said in a level voice. 'Then British internees can sleep without nets.'

Marcus was silent for a moment, willing the commandant to turn around again. When he did so, the Englishman said, 'Do you *want* a malaria epidemic at Fu-xing, commandant?'

'Malaria not contagious,' *Ushiguro* snapped. 'Malaria is problem everywhere in China and Japan. Yes, people die. In war, people die.' His face was a mask of indifference.

Marcus shook his head and spoke softly. 'Ushiguro-san: you and I are responsible for the lives of over one thousand internees, plus nearly three hundred children and what – one hundred and fifty of your soldiers? What if your men start to go down with malaria because basic precautions have not been taken?' Marcus chanced a grin. 'I imagine even mosquitoes drink Japanese blood.'

The commandant, ignoring the barb, looked thoughtful. His lizard stare held Carter's eyes.

He blinked. 'In the sixth century, when your country was in Dark Ages, Buddhism reaches our islands. We take some Buddhism for our Shinto religion; we call it Zen Buddhism.' He paused and looked towards the window before asking, 'You know Buddhist karma, Carter-San?'

'Of course.' He wondered where *Ushiguro* was taking the conversation.

'Good. We must let events unfold, like blanket, kotsu kotsu.'

'Kotsu, kotsu?'

'This means we allow matters to unfold one step at a time. You cannot pull open the petals of a flower to make it bloom.'

Marcus smiled. 'I do believe in karma, Commandant, but I also know that if we let present events unfold, as you call it, people will die. Your blanket will suffocate us. We must not attract karma through wrong thinking or wrong action. Accepting something you *can* change invites bad karma.'

Ushiguro cocked his head to one side. 'Shinto tells us that man lives – and hopes for best. Wabi-sabi – you know wabi-sabi?' Marcus nodded assent as *Ushiguro* continued. 'Wabi-sabi teaches us that all is imperfection and impermanence, but people are good in heart - this Shinto belief. Ushiguro believe most prisoners are good in heart.'

'But I must insist, Commandant, that you not persist in calling us your prisoners. We are internees, citizens of Her Majesty's government…'

'… and guests of our divine Emperor Hirohito.' *Ushiguro* finished for him.

The Japanese took a step forward and began to circle Carter. Marcus twisted around, trying to follow *Ushiguro*'s unblinking inspection as the Japanese continued to lecture him.

'I say that most prisoners are good – but some hate Japanese, Carter-San. Your Field Marshal Wavell say Japanese below human, yes? In Hong Kong, he says this on radio. Britishers think we not so good as you because we smaller… we foreign.'

Ushiguro snorted, looking incredulous at the idea. Again, he studied the ceiling for a moment and then turned to face the Englishman. 'This make you think you always win wars. But now? You. Are. Beaten.' He tipped his head to one side, 'Yes?

Marcus considered the man's words. "I am not here to philosophise with you Commandant.' Then he, too, tipped his head, his eyes questioning.

Ushiguro made a small smile. 'Ah, the mosquitoes, yes?' Marcus nodded.

The commandant said, 'I accept your point that wrong actions bring about unfortunate results.'

He returned to his desk and sat down again. He steepled his fingers as he studied Carter. Marcus got the feeling that the Japanese was enjoying the philosophical diversion. He was prepared to tolerate more talk if the discussion secured his goal.

'Now perhaps you ask: if Commandant Ushiguro thinks some of us are good, why he lock us up?' The Japanese tipped his head from side to side as if considering his own question. Softly, he said, 'We lock you up to protect you.'

Carter was puzzled. 'From what – or who – do you feel the need to protect us?'

'From us – the Japanese.' The Commandant shook his head as if wearied by the discussion. 'The rape of Nanjing will stain our nation for centuries.'

Carter looked away. 'The Japanese were animals. Worse.'

Ushiguro spoke slowly, as if to a child: 'Yes, but Nanjing happen for many reasons: poor coolies make poor soldiers. Many of our soldiers at Nanjing were old, bad men. Other soldiers torture them for disgrace they bring to warriors with great traditions – and this is *before* battle of Nanjing. Poor, bad men in army are many – more than warriors from military families. These men – what you say – rubbish?' He didn't wait for Marcus to answer. 'Then tortured men are sent to Nanjing? What you expect? They want Chinese to pay for their own misery. Bayonet! Kill! Rape! Girls, boys, everybody!'

Marcus said nothing. *Ushiguro* continued, 'But this not only cause of many executions and torture of civilians at Nanjing. Some Japanese in high command see Chinese as rats...' he stopped, struggling to find the word. '... vermin! All Chinese must be destroyed before they contaminate purity of Japan.'

Marcus couldn't help himself: 'I can see why your people have so much in common with your Nazi allies. Your belief that you are a master race; your inability to laugh at yourselves – just like the Germans.'

Ushiguro raised his hands in defence. 'To keep Japan pure – nothing wrong. But Carter-San,' - now he was whispering –'this is Japanese military plan: high command in nineteen-thirty-seven need every officer to know that we can sow terror through rape, torture, and death of every Chinese civilian in Nanjing. And foreigners see this, and you flee! We throw out western forces and bring Japanese order and modernity to East Asia.' He stood up, eyes glaring. '*That* is master plan.'

Looking flustered from the anger in his speech, the Commandant dropped his voice to a conversational level. 'You understand, Britisher? This is plan made by Japanese high command deployed in China. All lead to rape of Nanjing.'

Ushiguro took a deep breath and walked around his chair and sat down. He nodded at Carter, his eyes half shut. 'I call this state hate.' Opening his eyes, he looked up at Carter before adding, 'I not agree, and that is why such things not happen at Fu-xing. Do not fear us. No killings. No rape. No torture.'

'You will protect us from you?' Marcus said, eyebrows raised.

'You not believe me? Yes, we protect you from us.'

Marcus clenched his jaw. 'Then start by protecting us from the mosquitoes. Find a way to give us five hundred good nets so we can, at least, protect mothers and their children.'

Ushiguro nodded, and Marcus detected the beginning of a smile. 'Hai! We see.'

MALARIA
Fu-xing 1943

Two months after the nets were hung, Jonny – who until then had been a normal, busy little three-year-old, albeit growing up in abnormal circumstances – became unwell.

Like any child so young, Jonny's eustachian passage – that helped to equalise pressure on each side of his eardrums – was underdeveloped. Peggy's son was soon suffering from catarrh and chronic earache. A few days later, when Peggy touched his brow, she immediately knew he was ill.

'Tash, feel his brow.'

'My mother had a solution for that. Wait.' Five minutes later, Tash was back holding a small vial of olive oil, taken or borrowed from somewhere – she wasn't prepared to say. Natasha poured some of the oil into a teaspoon, warmed it with a match and, turning a protesting Jonny on his side, she poured some drops of warm oil into his aching ear. *'Una momento,'* she said, fingers to her lips. Peggy thought how grateful she was to have found Natasha.

Tash had been the first to spot the malaria symptoms in Jonny. 'He's become very grouchy.' Tash announced one morning. Then Peggy saw Jonny throw Jacko, his cloth monkey, on the floor. The boy burst into tears. Peggy handed the monkey back to him, but, again, Jonny threw it from the bed and, again, started to cry.

'I've never seen him do that before,' said Peggy, concerned.

'I think he is mad at his daddy. The monkey: he makes the link to his daddy. When he throws away the monkey–'

'He throws away his father?'

'Bien sur. This is what I am thinking.'

Peggy turned away, her eyes filling with tears. 'Skattie, liebchen.' My God, Peggy thought, this woman can even make German sound loving.

Natasha put her arm around Peggy and hugged her. 'What do I know?'

Peggy dabbed her eyes. 'No, you're right, Tash – it makes sense.'

An hour later the little boy was constantly swallowing, pointing to his throat and saying, 'Hurt, hurt.' Under protest, he opened his mouth; Peggy could see that his throat was inflamed and his breath, usually so sweet, smelled stale.

'Alors, le petit c'est beaucoup miserable,' said Natasha as she surveyed the hunched little figure on the mattress. 'Viens, nous chercherons le medicin.'

They soon found Albert Faure – already the French doctor had dubbed himself *'chef du medicin.'*

When Faure realised Natasha could speak French, he turned his attention to her.

The doctor had diagnosed that Jonny's sore throat and high temperature would likely be followed by chills and a high fever. He gave Natasha his diagnosis. *'C'est fievre ou paludisme.'*

Tash translated for Peggy. 'He says it's yellow fever or malaria. Poor Jonny has probably been bitten by an infected mosquito. The good thing is, if it's malaria, it's not contagious.'

'And if it's yellow fever?'

'Much more dangerous,' said Faure, who had overheard Peggy's question, *'Nous esperons* – we hope – it is only malaria.' Even so, he may have a type of malaria that comes and goes. Only the future can reveal if that is so.'

'So this may pass and then…?' Peggy's fingers were curled as she pressed her nails into her palms, hard.

Faure gave her that annoying French shrug – not mitigated, she thought – by his uncertain smile.

Faure and Natasha continued their conversation. The doctor's face gave away nothing, but Peggy could see that Natasha looked increasingly worried.

Natasha again turned to Peggy: 'He says Jonny has all the clues – symptoms – of malaria. He says that for children, les hallucinations…'

'Hallucinations?'

'Mais oui… hallucinations. Jonny will have many hallucinations, and the doctor says that for a child… these can be frightening. Why you will ask? Because our sweet boy has no – how to say it – reference, no ability to put what is happening to his body into something that has happened before. He does not know that he can survive.'

Peggy's hand flew to her mouth. 'Can survive? You say 'can'? He has never had anything like this before.' Then, 'Will he be all right?'

Natasha turned to the doctor. Peggy heard the words 'coma' and 'prognosis' and 'avenir'. The doctor said a few more words in French before Natasha again translated. 'He says this is not a mild condition, malaria is a serious disease – but still not as bad as yellow fever.' It came out as 'plague serieuse', which, to Peggy, sounded worse in French. 'Monsieur Albert says – and this is unlikely, but we should be prepared – Jonny may fall into a coma.'

Now Peggy went cold with fear. Jonny had been a healthy child since she brought him home. Her immediate thoughts, expressed to Natasha in a flood of words were: Is this doctor the right person to be looking after her boy? Should Jonny be taken to a hospital? Were there any functioning hospitals left in Shanghai?

Faure gave the Gallic shrug that, like all Frenchmen, would become his default way of communicating. 'Shanghai General is open.'

MARCUS VISITS
Fu-xing 1943

'Peggy' For a moment, the word hung between them. She didn't know why she felt unsettled by his presence. The camp was so large that, for months, she had managed to avoid meeting him without others present. They were not strangers. That was the problem.

Marcus now stood before her, wearing shorts with a grey shirt, sleeves rolled up. He looked strong, almost healthy – a miracle considering their situation. His long legs were covered with black hair but not too thick to be unattractive. Peggy wondered how he managed to look so fit and capable.

'Oh, hello, Marcus. I'm glad you're here, but it's a difficult time with Jonny. As you can see, he's not very well.' She was pressing a flannel to Jonny's brow. She was worried by the flush in his cheeks. She glanced down at her son and was amused to see, despite his discomfort, that he was looking at Marcus Carter with one eye open.

Peggy, Natasha, and the Trenchers had settled into an uneasy but essentially practical, domestic routine. None of them could pretend that it was a happy arrangement, but with compromises here and there, they made it work. Peggy helped with elocution lessons for the children, and that kept her busy during the day. She and some other mothers, mostly younger than her, had set up a creche for children as young as Jonny.

Marcus smiled at the boy on the bed. "Ah, I finally meet Jonny,' Marcus whispered as he put his hand to his lips and nodded his head towards the boy.

'Jonny Parker,' said her son, head peeping over his sheet

'Well, how do you do, Jonny Parker. I would like to shake your hand, but I've been feeding the pigs.'

'Piggies!'

'Yes,' Marcus continued, 'I have washed my hands, but I'm not sure they're clean enough for shaking your hand.'

'Why?'

'That's a good question, Jonny, but you see: piggies are very clean animals, but they live in a mess.'

'Why?'

Peggy was struggling not to laugh. This was the only piece of normality she'd encountered in the past twenty-four hours.

Marcus said, 'Jonny, your mummy will tell you all about piggies when I've gone.' He paused and winked at Peggy. 'Won't you, mummy?'

Peggy nodded, her eyes smiling at him.

'May I sit down – perhaps here?' Without waiting, he sat down on Natasha's bed. Tash had gone to fetch some congee and a slice of bread – their breakfast.

'Peggy,' He said her name again as he looked at her with his deep green eyes. She was concerned by his furrowed brow. 'It's so good to see you again – privately, well, almost privately,' he grinned at Jonny. 'It's awful that I have to be the bearer of bad news…'

Her stomach clenched. 'Have you heard something about my husband?' She glanced at Jonny then back at Marcus, giving him a look of warning.

'No, nothing, I'm afraid. Tom Trencher told me he's not with you in camp.' He wouldn't meet her eyes. 'Tom said nobody's sure' he paused as if summoning the name *'where* Stan is.' He looked up, his face clenched. 'Not even you.'

She tried to pass off his remarks with a smile. He looked at her closely before he added, 'Don't you find that odd – I mean, that nobody knows.'

'Not really. It wasn't part of Stan's job to tell everyone his movements, including me.' She succeeded in keeping a trace of sarcasm from her voice; she gave another smile. 'He's at sea, Marcus, and I'd be surprised if Tom Trencher knew his whereabouts before me.'

Nodding, Marcus said, 'Of course, of course: that makes sense.' He clapped his hands softly. 'Actually, I came here to talk about malaria.'

He scrunched his face: 'I regret to say that Commandant Ushiguro says he won't allow Jonny to be taken to hospital. Malaria, apparently is not contagious – any spreading of the disease is done by the insects. We have to believe him. Dr. Faure has confirmed that Jonny has the onset of malaria but says he's confident he can treat the boy here.'

Now Marcus nodded towards Jonny, who was sleeping – or pretending to – with one arm across his eyes.

'You have children here?' she asked.

'Not anywhere, as far as I'm aware.' His eyes crinkled. 'I'm unmarried. For the last few years, I've been busy civilising the world for the Foreign Office, or so they like to believe.'

'How are you coping?' she asked.

He gave her a small grin. 'Isn't that my question?'

'I mean, your committee.'

'Ah, the Fu-xing committee!' He rolled his eyes, and for the first time in a while, she found herself trying to suppress a smile.

'Peggy, without being complacent, I'm pleased with the progress. The men have grasped the challenge; Myke Amble, in particular – and you may have noticed this – has dragooned the children into digging and tending allotments. Fresh vegetables will start to come through very soon. There'll be more of them as the weather gets warmer. Aside from ensuring that we get a regular supply of edible food – which, with heating, is the most important task – we need to make sure that the children continue to get an education. He smiled at her, 'And I should offer belated thanks for all you're doing with the young ones.'

Now that she'd been able to look at him for longer than a moment, she noticed that his brow had permanent worry lines, certainly, he was no youth; probably mid-forties, she guessed. He had made himself responsible for all this, their welfare, if it could be called that. Was there any training for such a situation – plunged into a concentration camp and suddenly responsible for hundreds?

There was a silence between them. As they looked at each other, it seemed neither wanted to break the silence of their communication.

There were quick footsteps, and the sheet was pushed aside. Natasha walked in holding two bowls, slices of dark bread resting on top.

'Bonjour,' Tash said emphatically, in a tone that blended surprise with delight at the sight of Peggy and Marcus.

'Marcus! You are here, at last.' She looked around the small space. 'In our boudoir.' She pealed with laughter. 'We think you have been hiding from us. Has Peggy told you how happy we are that you are in charge of Fu-xing?' Natasha, never able to get the name right, always pronounced the word 'Fooking.'

Marcus, not in the least embarrassed, gave a huge grin. 'I'm sure she'll get around to it'

Tash was wearing one of the two pairs of slacks she had brought with her. The pants were russet-coloured and were matched by a grey sweater worn over a wrinkled, pale green blouse. She looked, Peggy thought, like a movie star playing a woman down on her luck.

'May I?' Carter got up and took the bowls from her and placed them on top of the cardboard box that served as a table.

Natasha, looking at Peggy, rolled her eyes theatrically, 'Are we in trouble? Have we been naughty?'

'Heavens, no,' said Carter, frowning. 'Why are people already thinking of me as some kind of headmaster?'

Peggy and Natasha laughed. 'Well, you are the man in charge,' said Peggy.

'Absolument,' agreed Natasha, her palms face up, conveying, 'it's obvious.'

He shrugged, 'Well, Peggy needs to know how grateful I am for her help with the children; her lessons and their help with the vegetable growing keeps them out of trouble.' He paused and gave her a direct look, 'And you, Mademoiselle Natasha?'

Natasha countered with her own Gallic shrug: 'I can dance, so I could teach a little ballet, perhaps.'

Carter beamed. 'Perfect! That would be wonderful.'

He turned, preparing to leave. 'Peggy, I would like to know a bit more about your husband, but I don't have the time now. Perhaps we can have lunch soon; maybe tomorrow?'

Natasha threw back her head to give a loud, disbelieving laugh. 'Will lunch be at the Cathay or the Palace? Or maybe you will slip away for brunch at Café Bonheur?'

Carter looked embarrassed. He continued to address Peggy, 'Why don't I meet you at the food line at thirteen thirty hours, and we'll find somewhere to chat?'

'Perfect,' said Peggy. He bowed to her then took Natasha's hand, 'Au revoir, Natasha. I can see that Fu-xing has not changed you, and I'm very glad to see it.' He lifted the sheet at the entrance and was gone.

'You embarrassed him,' said Peggy.

'Oh, darling *can we have lunch?*' You British are so funny with your politesse. Anyway, I've always liked him, and it is clear he's attracted to you. He wants to talk a bit more about your husband – isn't that de rigueur at the start of an affair?'

Peggy suppressed a smile as she said, 'I wouldn't know, Tash.'

'But of course,' she pouted and put on a whiney voice. 'Oh, he is so mean to me, he doesn't understand me.'

Peggy laughed, 'Well, ma cherie, none of that is true of Stan.'

Natasha held her by the shoulders. 'Liebchen, I am telling you: there is lightening between you and M'sieu Marcus. When you are together with that man… like now… I know I do not belong in the room.'

A FU-XING LUNCH
1943

For her lunch with Marcus – which Natasha teasingly told her would be Peggy's 'first Fooking date', she dressed in her only pair of slacks, navy blue, and a badly wrinkled pale blue blouse. Like most women in the camp, she had ceased to bother with a brassiere. After a few days, she wondered why she ever had.

She moved slowly through hundreds of internees packed around the food area. There was no dining area; people took the small bowls back to their tent, ate what they'd been given and, after washing and rinsing bowls in cold water at the ablution block, returned them to the distribution point.

She wondered if the crowd would thin as she pushed forward. In fact, as she grew closer to the food line, there were more and more people. People jostled each other to claim bowls of undefined muck that, in a normal world, they would never consider giving to their pets.

The Japanese had reduced the internees to living like starving peasants. The primitive conditions made it clear that their captors were unprepared for accommodating the hundreds in their charge. Any trace of dignity was being stripped away; social background had become meaningless in the fight for survival.

As she made her way forward, the smell of unwashed bodies made her close her eyes, as if blinding herself to the people pushing against her would neutralise their odour. She looked around for Marcus and spotted him at the head of the food line. He waved when he saw her, and she moved towards him. Others closed up so she couldn't squeeze in; she stood outside of the line, parallel with him as he was being served.

'Soup or soup?' he shouted at her. She nodded and smiled.

The next minute he was stretching over to hand her a bowl of soup with black bread on top, their mouldy crusts removed.

'Here we are: SOS, I'm afraid,' he said, breaking away from the queue, with a look of despair, as though it was somehow his fault that they were, yet again, eating the same old stew.

Peggy had been looking around for somewhere to sit, but the crush of people made it impossible to do anything but stand.

Marcus tossed his head to indicate they should move. 'Let's go to my quarters,' he said. 'This scrum will be here for at least another hour, or…'

'Or until they run out of food,' Peggy finished for him.

Peggy soon discovered that Marcus's 'quarters' was one room, Peggy saw that there were only two obvious places to sit: the bed or a chair. She chose the chair. Marcus settled on the iron bed.

As soon as Peggy sat down, she felt the tiny room become more intimate. Her heart spun in her chest – her legs went watery, her hands clammy. What was happening? In seconds, her mind seemed to empty then fill with the snatch of a new show tune: 'bewitched, bothered and bewildered' – was this what it felt like?

She dared not look at the man on the bed. Instead, they continued to chew quietly, each conscious of the other. A minute later, Marcus stopped eating. Peggy looked up; Marcus was staring at her, his eyes popping as if in horror at what was in his very full mouth. They both burst into laughter. Marcus held a hand to his mouth, trying not to spit out its contents.

'We should *not* do this more often,' said Peggy, her shoulders shaking with suppressed laughter, glad of the break in tension.

'Oh really?' said Marcus, holding up a piece of bread. 'I'm rather enjoying this fine example of the baker's craft.'

When they'd stopped giggling, he said, 'Look, Peggy, I think the only way we can deal with this appalling situation is to keep our chins up and our British sense of humour intact. What are the alternatives? The Japs won't believe that we can turn our colonial culture of organisational skills and discipline – the system they hate and want to depose – into a psychological weapon of resistance.'

He paused. 'But I didn't ask you to lunch with me – however amusing Natasha finds it – in order to hear a lecture on what I see as our mission here…'

Peggy held up her hand, 'No, no. Believe me, I feel exactly as you do,' she said. 'And please, pay no attention to Natasha – she's young.'

'We're together on this?'

'Of course. But a lot of what's happening is the result of a lack of awareness, *our* lack of awareness about the intentions of the Japanese. And a total underestimation of their military strength.' Peggy felt her colour rising as she said this; at the same time, she remembered she had voiced her fears at Natasha's party when she'd first met Marcus.

His green eyes grew dark, the lids half-closed to add unwavering focus. He looked into her eyes when he asked the next question.

'And your husband – Stan – was he aware of the Jap's "intentions", as you call them, and their military strength?'

She was shocked by his question; had he brought her here to interrogate her? She wondered how much she should tell him about Stan and the Japanese.

Peggy put aside her bowl. 'Stan was romantic about the sea but very little else – except me.' She smiled, she hoped with conviction. 'He thrived in China, more than he'd ever done in England.' She looked down at her hands for a moment, thinking how dry, red and wrinkled they seemed. 'Stan was – is – a pragmatist: he would support your beliefs if they had worked for him. What I'm saying is: your ideal of deploying – as you call it – our colonial culture as part of our survival skills? Well, he would have embraced those ideals but only if he'd seen them work in practice.'

How kind his eyes were, she thought, even when he asked, 'Is that why he worked for the Japanese? Why he accepted a high rank in their Navy?'

Before she could respond, he added, 'Tom told me.'

Since meeting Tom as they waited for transport on Bubbling Well Road, and remembering his questions about Stan, she had wondered if Tom was her friend. Now she knew.

'Tom has never been put in the sort of situations that he's so quick to judge. My husband, who was at the front – not behind a desk at some Consulate – forgive me!'

'It's all right, Peggy. I'm not offended.' He smiled. 'We also serve who sit at desks and file.'

She reached out and touched his arm. 'Sorry, I wasn't thinking.'

'Please go on.'

She paused, trying to remember what she was saying before her gaffe. 'Stan knew that unless he helped the enemy on terms he could control, somebody else would. He called it sleeping with them to smother them.' She shrugged. 'In that way, Stan *was* a pragmatist, as I've said; he did what needed to be done.' she raised her eyebrows. 'As I suspect you do, too.' She looked away, thoughtful, before continuing. 'Stan might not have put it in your terms as a way of exercising our colonial culture – in that way, he was not a deep thinker – he just got on with the next thing.'

Marcus frowned. 'But he accepted a rank in their navy. Surely…'

'…He was never serious about his appointment as a Captain in their Navy. He treated it as a joke, as a way of achieving his ends. His bosses at Blue Funnel and the Consulate, *as Tom knows full well*, thought the same. If Blue Funnel didn't show them the Customs protocols, their competitors would.'

Marcus got up and walked up and down in the small space, five steps in each direction. He turned to face her, and now his eyes were not as soft and caring as they had been a moment ago. 'Do you know where he is?'

Suddenly she was suspicious; why was it important for him to know? What was Tom planning; and had he made Marcus an ally in his quest to locate Stan?

'I've explained: my husband never told me his routes or his destinations. That was company policy. Why is it important now?'

Marcus shrugged. 'Well, if we could locate him, we could at least get word to him where you are and that you and Jonny are alive.'

'He knows that.'

'How could he?'

She gave a small smile, relieved that this man's concern was sincere and not the disguise for something sinister.

'He knows because he knows me; he knows I can cope – even better when he's not around.'

Marcus returned her smile. 'Even so, you must miss him.'

'Jonny does,' she said. 'But I know we shan't see him again until this show is over.'

PIGS
Fu-xing 1943

When she returned to Tent City, she found a jubilant Natasha. 'The fever has gone,' she announced.

'That's wonderful news. Thank you for sitting with him.'

'And so?'

'What?'

'The lunch, the affair?'

'Oh, Tashie, there is no affair. We had a perfectly pleasant lunch – aside from the food.' She held up her hand: 'Pah, pah, pah,' to forestall any more questions.

The malaria had given all three of them a week of sleepless nights. Every few hours, Peggy and Natasha had turned Jonny over in bed, wiped his brow, and flipped his hard pillow. He whined and muttered, but they stuck to the routine. She had given the boy her own bed and snuggled in with Natasha, both of them clinging to the sides to avoid falling off the thin frame; Tash's feet hung off the end of the bed.

Her son's face had been the colour of paper and beaded with a light sweat. Peggy knew that children as young as Jonny didn't sweat, they got damp. When gripped by the malaria, his legs would jerk as he moaned through each hallucination. Sometimes he tried to climb out of the bed, trying to evade the clamp of nightmares. Once, he had screamed 'Zhang!' in his sleep.

Peggy decided to wake him – there seemed no point to him suffering through a nightmare.

She picked him up and held him. 'Shush, shush, darling. Mummy's here. You were having a bad dream.'

'Bad dream, naughty dream!' he said and then, over ten minutes or so, haltingly, through a dozen sobs, he told her about his bad dream: 'Zhang in snow, huh, huh... want hug me... huh... huh... me hug Zhang but she go...

huh, huh… Zhang go…' he sobbed. Bewildered and frightened, her little boy clung to her, his burning body like a hot water bottle against her skin. She thought, 'he didn't say anything about the soldier or the gun,' but with that thought came the realisation that specifics didn't matter – whatever had happened was now buried deep in his subconscious to return, or not, some time in his future.

Peggy used her new friendship with Marcus to scrounge extra congee for her son. Marcus asked Dr. Faure to write a medical note; he used the slip of paper to justify the extra rations. Marcus told Peggy that 'only a child could recover that swiftly from such a terrifying experience – most adults take at least a month to recover. However, your little man needs protein, and that's in short supply. I'll see what I can do.'

The day after Jonny's fever broke, he started to walk around. Peggy knew that his young immune system, coupled with quinine and other drugs, had helped to conquer the malaria – for now.

A few months later, emerging from the building, planning to find Natasha and Jonny, they were both rushing towards her. 'Peggy, Peggy, you must come and see this. All the handsome young men are going to chop wood for us.' Natasha turned and ran back with Jonny the way they had come, calling over her shoulder, 'Vite, Peggy. Jonny loves this.'

When they reached the forecourt of the main building, she found a crowd of at least one hundred prisoners. They were standing in clumps beneath the trees in a field of bluebells. The men stood with axes hanging loosely at their sides, watching what appeared to be some sort of ceremony.

Looking closer, Peggy noticed twenty guards, rifles cocked and bayonets fixed, standing among the axe-carrying men. She spotted *Ushiguro*, standing silently at the edge of the group. Mervyn Jones, the Bishop, stood in front of the men, Marcus next to him. The clergyman raised his hands in what looked like a benediction. Natasha giggled 'You British, so funny.'

The bishop spoke or rather, seemed to declaim: 'This is great work you are doing, men. The Lord will look kindly on you and add power to your arms. You will be wielding the axes of the Empire, striking a blow for all of us here – and for free men and women everywhere. God be with you.'

There was a ragged cheer from the men and small crowd of internees.

The men turned and began to march away. Then they began to sing a song so predictable that Peggy burst into laughter, joining Natasha in the unexpected glee of the moment.

'Hey ho, hey ho, it's off to work we go,' the men sang in a variety of tones. Three-year-old Jonny waved and sang in his piping voice. Nobody knew the next lines, so everyone kept repeating the first line. In less than a minute, the men disappeared into the morning mist, their voices drifting back, thinning, ending.

'Piggies!' said Jonny. He pointed in the direction the men had gone. 'Go see piggies, mama.'

Peggy looked at Natasha, 'What's this about?'

They were in a crush of people waiting to get back into the building after the woodcutters had left. Natasha blushed as she whispered, 'I promised him he could see the pigs.'

'Oh, you mean the protein supply? I hear that's another thing that Carter has arranged with Ushiguro: that we should increase the herd so that we have a source of protein, instead of that awful buffalo muck.'

'If you say so,' said Tash. Then she gave a sly grin, 'Why do you call him Carter? Why not Marcus?'

Peggy blushed. Tash raised an eyebrow and pointed a finger at her, laughing silently at her friend's obvious discomfort.

'Piggies! Piggies!' Jonny was insistent. Peggy knelt down to talk to her son. 'Darling, we won't be able to get close to the pigs because they play on the other side of the creek, near to the fence. You remember that fence that Mister Ushiguro told us we should stay away from? Well, that's where the piggies live, near the fence.'

Fifteen minutes later, she and Jonny crouched in a grove of gingko trees. The creek was some ten metres below them and about twenty metres in the distance. On the far bank, she could see a herd of pigs, grunting and squealing in the mud. The animals had their backs to the creek, snuffling and snorting around some scraps of food. Any one of them, she calculated, might have weighed three hundred and fifty kilos. Beyond the pigs was the fence that was the camp's boundary. Two guards sat on their rucksacks facing the animals and the boundary fence. Smoking and chatting with each other, but closer to Peggy and Jonny, they also had their backs to the creek.

Talking to each other, not attending to their surroundings, were reasons why the guards couldn't see, minutes later, what Peggy and Jonny saw. Her little boy, with his perfect eyesight, tugged her sleeve and pointed.

Peggy and Johnny watched as a pig-tailed Chinese male, wearing the traditional black clothes of a coolie, appeared from the area of the fence about fifteen metres away from where the soldiers sat. The coolie slid into the waters of the creek. The man seemed to be breaking *into* the camp, which struck her as odd.

The coolie was wading away from the boundary fence and towards the spot where she and Jonny crouched in the reeds; Peggy knew the Chinese couldn't see them or the guards – who were positioned higher up on the bank. She looked at Jonny and put her fingers to her lips. Her son gave her a cheeky grin and, enjoying the conspiracy of silence, mirrored her action. Peggy watched as the Chinese grew nearer. She knew she would have to reveal her position at any moment, hoping to lure the intruder towards them and then – what?

The decision was taken from her in the next seconds.

Above them, there was a crash of sound. Half-a-dozen red kites, seeing the man enter the water and, sensing a change that might threaten them, took to the air with a chorus of high-pitched screams – 'Hell-o, Hell-o.' The guards turned at the sound. In a moment, Peggy ducked and took Jonny down with her, so they both were on their knees. The boy wriggled furiously to show his irritation, but he didn't make a sound.

The guards were peering at the Chinese as he moved through the water towards the opposite bank where she and Jonny were hiding. The guards took a moment to wonder why the man was heading towards the camp rather than away from it. Peggy was equally puzzled. Then both guards started chattering in Japanese. One of them ran to the bank and, bayoneted rifle at the ready, shouted to the coolie. But by then, the intruder had his back towards the guard. The Chinese ignored the guard's shouts. He tried to move faster through the murky water towards them. The guards continued to shout and scream.

After another half-minute, the other guard dropped to one knee and took aim at the coolie's back.

The crack of a rifle shot; Jonny gripped her hand, making a small, frightened sound. The Chinese man's arms flew up, and he fell forward into the creek. The water closed over him. For a moment, the silence was broken only by Jonny's whimper, a sound so tiny she could barely hear it herself.

The Chinese was still alive – they could see his legs, or an occasional foot, thrashing in the waters. The two guards – one throwing a length of rope around his shoulders – rushed into the muddy filth. Reaching their victim, both Japanese shouted *'Banzai! Banzai!'* as they plunged their bayonets repeatedly into the water. Peggy tried to cover Jonny's eyes. He struggled against her. She was terrified the guards might see them.

After a minute, the waters were still. The soldiers, panting, withdrew their rifles and, while one guard took the rifles to the edge of the creek, the other man uncoiled the length of rope that he carried. He bent down, water up to his elbows. He seemed to be doing something under the water with the rope. The second guard rejoined him, and then both men took an end of the rope and, with shouts and much giggling, they began to haul the body in the water back to the bank.

Meanwhile, the pigs – milling about on the riverbank – had become interested in the new activity. The animals – there might have been ten or twelve of the brutes in shades of dull pink and grey and black, mostly black – started to rush and push and jostle and bite each other; they squealed with excitement, a fury of curiosity. The Japanese started to shout at the pigs, but it had no effect. Peggy assumed that the animals could smell the bloodied corpse. They were hungry.

The Japanese hauled the body into the shallows but had moved it no more than six feet up the bank before the pigs began to fight for a position from where they could attack the body. As soon as the soldiers moved away, the pigs fell on the corpse. Their squeals reached a crescendo, an orgy of feeding as a black mass of shifting shapes blanketed the dead coolie.

Dizzy with the horror of what she was seeing, Peggy fell to her knees. The camp, the Japanese, alone with Jonny, Stan's absence, the permanent want and deprivation of her life crowded in on her – but mostly, rising above the sound of the fighting, hungry pigs – the sense of no ending.

She caught her breath and held Johnny's head against her hip. 'Sweetheart, we should get back to Tashie and try to forget what we saw.'

The boy looked puzzled. 'But I saw it, mummy,' he said.

ALENA ZOLTAN
Chongqing 1944

Stanley Parker was 1500 kilometres south-west of Shanghai. The day before, as part of Chiang's party, he had arrived at Chongqing. The city was deep inland, at the confluence of the Jailing and Yangtse rivers. The city was the wartime capital of the Kuomintang, the Chinese Nationalist Party. For four years, the Japanese had bombed the region without pause; it was said that more ordnance had been dropped on its buildings than on any other metropolis in the world. By making Chongqing the capital, Chiang was signalling to the Japanese that it would take more than bombs to destroy his people.

On the plane from *Changsha* to *Chongqing*, Alena had huddled with *Chiang* as they reviewed strategy for the meetings with *Mao*'s emissary, *Chou en-lai*.

Stan could hear the clipped tones of the Chinese leader's voice a few seats ahead, but his mind was filled with images of Peggy and Jonny being taken to a concentration camp. He had no idea how this was done: had they been rounded up like stray animals and placed in a transport? Trucks? Buses? Had they been marched from the Settlement to some other destination? What had happened to their home, their servants? Had there been killings? Had his wife and son – he was only two, for heaven's sake, he must have been terrified – been dragged out and interrogated? Most sickening thought of all: had either of them been hurt, Peggy assaulted?

And Peggy: How had she handled this invasion of her home? He knew she would not have made it easy for the Japanese to make her leave. Then, he hoped, considering the helplessness of their situation, her maternal instincts would have prevented her from taking any action that would put their young son at risk.

One thing he knew for sure – and guilt pierced him as he thought of it – she would have been furious for him not being there.

Alena came back to sit with him as the plane bumped through the last hundred miles of their flight. 'Chiang wanted me to be sure you were all right,' she said, lowering herself into the seat.

Thoughts of his family were pushed back by Alena's scent. As the plane banked, her body pressed against his. In an instant, he was aware of the comforting, yet arousing, effect on his senses. Did she feel it, too? Then he remembered having read that few women touched a man without forethought.

He looked straight ahead. 'No, I'm not all right, Alena.' Why did it comfort him simply to say her name? Why, even now – in the turmoil of his family crisis – did instincts he thought extinct, return?

Her hand sought his and squeezed. 'You can't be all right, Stan, of course you can't. I understand. But it will pass. There is nothing you can do. Nobody will be killed. The Japanese will respect the expats, I promise you. The Japanese will not want to provoke an international incident until they are ready.'

He turned to face her. 'Ready to kill their prisoners?'

She shook her head vigorously. 'No, Stan. Your wife – Peggy? – and your son will be placed in a camp with other expats, leaving the Japanese to fight the war against China.' She frowned, her green eyes suddenly moist.

'How can you be so sure?'

'Because as a Chinese, that's what I think, and Chiang thinks it, too. Believe me, I can tell you that nothing protects you as much as your British nationality.' He was sorry when she released his hand, but he still felt the comforting pressure of her shoulder next to him until they landed at *Chongquing*.

From the airport, they were driven in convoy to the *Kuomintang* compound at *Jinlong* Village.

Chiang had made his new headquarters at the village – the base camp of the Army's Mechanisation school. Stan could see why the internationally minded Chinese leader was drawn to the architectural style of the compound. In the dying light of the day, he could still discern the main building's faux European architecture – it reminded him of his own house in Bubbling Well Road. Like his home, it might have blended better in a Bavarian forest than in a Chinese village. The main house was built in an **E** shape, two wings with a centre missing. Apart from the Chinese terra cotta tiles on the roof – which struck him as reminiscent of Spain – the walls of each of the two wings were constructed of thick, red brick. It was as if, aside from simple huts, the Chinese were still struggling to find an architectural style that defined them. They were borrowing bits from Europe seen in picture books. The result was a hybrid visual effect that was stoic, ponderous – not unlike *Chiang* himself, he thought.

The part of the building where people worked was in one of the two wings. The other wing was where people lived. *Chiang* and his wife occupied the front of one wing with fine views of a forest. Stan and Alena had been allocated rooms in the back section between the two wings, which, as they were to find, gave them the privacy they needed.

***

Soon after they arrived in *Chongqing,* Stan realised that Alena Zoltan, fluent in Mandarin, Japanese, English and Polish, was well qualified to be *Chiang*'s chief of staff. Alena decided whom the Nationalist leader should see, when he should see them, and for how long, a true gatekeeper. In addition, she knew *Chiang* well enough that, when she spoke to outsiders, people knew that she reflected him accurately. Alena also made a point of getting on with everybody – she had no favourites. Sometimes, Stan thought the price was too high. Alena's other task, ordained by the uxorious *Chiang*, was to ensure that his wife's needs were met.

Madame *Chiang*, a diminutive woman whose size contrasted with her personality, also acted as her husband's official translator. *Chiang* insisted that Alena, with her language skills, be present whenever he and his wife met foreign dignitaries. Alena's role was to ensure that domineering 'Madame Chiang' did not insert her own views in place of her husband's.

PORK
Fu-xing 1944

Most people agreed that the 'engine' of the camp, as Carter called it, was running smoothly. Food was better in quality. The internees knew that their 'Fu-xing fruit and veggies', as Myke proudly dubbed their produce, was much better than the vegetables provided by the Japanese or the itinerant Chinese merchants.

Supplies – such as potatoes and turnips – that had been set aside for winter had proved the worth of Amble's ideas about proper husbandry. Earlier, when the men had been chopping trees for their heating needs, someone had suggested that they collect the crab apples and berries, all in plentiful supply. The fruit had been stored or made into jams.

Yet despite all of Myke's efforts – and those of the children who, as he had predicted, took up their tasks with enthusiasm – the diet was inadequate, especially for most of the adults, who willingly gave up their meagre rations to their children. Within a year, many men had lost nearly half the weight they'd had when entering camp. Albie Faure and his medical teams – who kept records of such things – reported that the average weight of the Fu-xing internees had dropped to thirty kilos.

'Most men are thinking about their loss of weight all the time,' the doctor told the committee. 'They enter scores every day. Every day they check if their calves are going soft, if their muscles are weaker. I am concerned that there will be an outbreak of beriberi because of malnutrition and not enough vitamin D. If we cannot increase food supplies – especially of protein, of which we have virtually none, *les gens vont mourir* – people will die.'

***

A day after hearing this news, Carter was relaying it to *Ushiguro*.
The commandant listened carefully before saying, 'I can get you more rice

but…'

'But it's protein we need,' Carter cut in. 'I know your soldiers eat beef, pork and chicken, but our people have practically *no* protein – except the bits of animal life and the odd gristle of buffalo we may find in the congee. Unless we can solve the problem, you are going to have to answer to your superiors for many deaths. This is not protecting us, Ushiguro-san; this is killing us by ignoring us.'

The Japanese pursed his lips and stared at his desk as if the answer might lie somewhere in the wood. Silence ticked by, a silence that Carter was about to interrupt when *Ushiguro* raised his hand to stop him speaking.

He looked up at his prisoner. 'As always, Carter-san, you exaggerate your situation. This is war, you are prisoners, things are difficult.'

'I understand that,' Marcus said. 'But as I've already told you, we are *not* prisoners! We deserve better treatment.'

The Japanese stood up, signifying the end of the discussion. 'I will arrange for more chickens to be brought into the camp. We cannot obtain cows.'

'And the pigs?'

'We will slaughter some of the pigs we have. You can have limited quantities of pork until I can arrange for more pigs and more breeding.'

***

As he walked back from the meeting with *Ushiguro*, feeling almost buoyant, Marcus bumped into Peggy. For reasons he couldn't explain, for the past few days, she seemed to have been ignoring him. He felt a surge of pleasure at the sight of her. She was wearing her grey top – once white, she had told him – with black and white striped pantaloons. But after his conversation with Ushiguro, he became aware that she was losing weight; she was becoming gaunt, her face was developing lines he hadn't noticed before. He, too, realised he'd been able to tighten his belt by two inches.

He knew better than to comment on her weight.

'How can you manage to look so chic among this scruffy mob, Peggy?'

'Oh, I wish that were true, Marcus. But thank you for the compliment,' she gestured at a bench. 'Can we sit for a moment? There's something I have to tell you.'

They sat, and she faced him, but her brown eyes avoided him. He looked at her as she fiddled with a sweater in her hands. Her head was down.

'What is it?'

'The Japs killed a man.'

Immediately, he was alert, 'An internee – one of ours? Who? Where?'

'No, no, he was Chinese – not that it makes a difference. He was trying to get into the camp, which seemed strange. He was wading across the creek, trying not to be seen. The Japs told him to halt, but he wouldn't – so they shot him.' She shook her head, 'I don't understand, Marcus, why was he trying to get *into* the camp?'

He shrugged, 'Who knows? Some Chinese servants feel lost without their masters, they can think of them as their real family, you know; he may have tried to get back to them. Or it could have been as simple as him returning from a tryst with his girlfriend.'

'A tryst? How sweet you are,' she smiled.

Marcus's eyes popped. 'And you were alone when you saw this drowning?'

'Jonny was with me.'

'And he saw the whole thing? My God, the poor wee lad.'

'I know. I feel terrible. We should have left, but I thought if we stayed, we might have helped the Chinese.'

He threw up his hands, 'Never try to help in that way, Pegs. They will shoot you, no question.'

Marcus reached for her hand. In an instant, her hand tightened in his. He felt aroused; years had passed since he had felt this close to a woman as beautiful and vital as Peggy, not even at her best. He knew he was attracted to her and, in that instant, she to him. As these thoughts raced through him, they were quickly followed by the knowledge she was vulnerable, without the missing, mysterious – and yes, he did seem mysterious – Stanley Parker.

He brought his thoughts back to the moment: 'And you're sure the Chinese drowned – you didn't leave before it was over?'

'Oh, he definitely drowned, Marcus. The guards shot and bayoneted him in the water and then left him to the pigs.'

He gave her a puzzled look. 'Left him to the pigs – meaning?'

Peggy was silent.

'Oh, Christ!' Marcus blurted; he dropped his head into his hands.

They sat in stunned silence; Marcus because he was thinking about how this might affect the deal he'd made with *Ushiguro* minutes ago; Peggy because she did not want to say anything more about the scene she'd witnessed.

After a minute, Peggy said, 'What shall we do, Marcus?'

He realised it was only the second time she had used his name in as many minutes. He didn't reply at once. He wanted to play her words over in his mind a few times.

Again, she said his name, this time tightening her grip: 'Marcus?'

'Hmm. I don't think we have to tell the Commandant.'

She pulled her hand away, 'Why ever not? His soldiers will tell him.'

He shook his head, 'Not necessarily. Yes, they have orders to shoot in those circumstances, but the man was Chinese – which means he is less than nothing in their eyes – and the pigs destroyed the evidence. There's no proof that any of this happened. The guards know they will be interrogated, maybe even tortured. I don't think they'll report it.' He nodded briefly before repeating, 'I mean, there's no evidence.'

He saw colour rising in her cheeks. He'd made her angry.

'That's ridiculous! I saw it, and Jonny saw it – well, at least the killing. We can't pretend it never happened – a man, even a Chinese – as if that mattered – can't be killed and eaten by pigs, and no one cares.' She was tossing her auburn curls in a fury. He thought how beautiful she still was – thinner, haggard even – but still a woman you would notice anywhere.

Again, he took her hand. She resisted his touch at first but then relented. He began to trace his finger in the hollow of her palm.

'I'm going to tell you something that, under no circumstances should you tell anyone else – not even your friend Natasha.' He paused, trying to assemble the words in a sequence that might make them seem logical.

'I've just reached an agreement with *Ushiguro* that he will let us have more protein because our diets are suffering without it. All of us are losing weight.' He waited for her denial, but she nodded. 'The Japanese are bringing in more chickens, and a few moments ago, he said they would slaughter some of the pigs, so we can add pork to our rations.'

They were silent. Then Peggy said, 'Oh.' She looked at him intensely 'That means…'

'I know. But if we don't get the added protein, some people will start to die. Doctor Faure assures me of it.'

She removed her hand, looked away, and started again to fiddle with the sweater. After a while, she said, 'I suppose this means we have a dirty little secret – you and me and Jonny.'

'Can Jonny keep a secret?'

'I think so. Children enjoy secrets – the more important, the better. Jonny's three. I don't think his innocent little mind could process the implications of the pigs eating a man – if he ever thought that – and then us eating the pigs.'

Marcus winced.

She gave a small snort that sounded close to derision. 'But that's what we must do, isn't it, Marcus?'

He nodded, staring at the floor.

They continued to sit in silence for a handful of minutes until he said, 'Peggy, this may not be the best time, but I wonder if you'll allow me to help you – in Stan's absence, I mean.'

Her eyebrows furrowed, but he saw a smile on her lips.

'That's so sweet of you, but, really, I am more than capable of taking care of myself and my son.' She gave a short laugh, 'It's something that really irritated Stan.'

He smiled back at her, 'Well, I'm not Stan, and I'm here. And if I'm totally honest, I'd like to spend more time with you and Jonny.'

'Oh,' she said again, not being able to think of anything that would cover her surprise and the surge of happiness it brought. When she was back in her room, she hugged the thought of what he'd said.

Until she met Marcus, she had never believed any man was good enough. She didn't have to believe that anymore.

'PIGGIES EAT MAN!'
Fu-xing 1944

With typical British irony, they had dubbed their group of nine who ate together – Peggy, Tash, the Trenchers, the Langs and the three children – 'the Ritz dining club', or simply 'the Ritz'.

They made up a roster of who would collect the food each day. An hour before 'the Ritz' met, the designated couple, armed with everyone's IDs, would head off to stand in the food queue.

A month after the killing of the Chinese intruder, the members of the 'the Ritz' sat eating in Trencher's tent.

'I say,' said John Lang. 'This food is a step up from the muck they usually serve.' He moved his head from side to side and wiggled his jaw. 'Hmm, I do believe it's pork. What do you say, Trencher?'

Trencher frowned, then put a small piece of meat in his mouth. He chewed. Peggy watched him, her breathing stilled.

'Dammit! I think you're right. It *is* pork.' He smiled, 'Carter said something about getting Ushiguro to give us more protein. Good man!'

'What's pork, Dad?' asked David Lang, looking across at his father. The boy was a year older than Jonny but, so far, had not inherited his father's good looks.

'It's the meat of pigs, son.'

'So now we're eating pigs?' said Sue Lang. 'It's come to that. I have to say I've never been partial to pork – and hunger makes a good sauce – but not *that* good.' She took the piece of meat off her plate and passed it to her husband.

'Well, sweetheart,' said Tom Trencher. 'Even a starving Jew might eat pig. And dear Sue, you're not even Jewish.' He chuckled at his own joke.

Jonny, who had been listening to this talk of pigs, piped up, 'Piggies eat man.'

Everyone except Peggy laughed. Trencher lifted up the boy and said, 'No Jonny, man eat piggies, not piggies eat man.' Tom, still laughing, tickled Jonny's tummy.

Jonny wriggled in Trencher's arms and yelled, 'Piggies eat man, piggies eat man. Tell, mummy, tell!' Tears appeared swiftly, as only a child can summon them, and his face became as red as a carrot. Tom put Jonny down.

Peggy was conscious of everyone looking at her, waiting.

She took a deep breath and reached over to take Jonny in her arms. By now his tears were in full spate, deep sobs wracking his little body. She was in a dilemma: did she keep her promise to Marcus? Or did she tell her son his eyes had been lying to him?

'Well,' she said. 'Jonny and I think we saw some pigs attack a man.'

She was aware that they were all staring at her. Her face was hot, and she knew it must be reddening, even as she stared back at their own startled faces.

'When was this?' asked Lang.

'And where did they *eat* this man?' asked Trencher.

'Pas des enfants,' said Peggy, shaking her head and staring at the children. 'I'll tell you when we've put them to bed. It's up to you whether you eat the pork, but I'm sure it's fine.'

They put aside their plates. They avoided each other's eyes.

***

'Hells bells!' said Marcus when she told him how the story had leaked out. 'What did they say?'

'Of course, they were appalled but agreed that it should be kept between us. I didn't tell them you knew. None of us will eat pork again – probably ever.'

'And Jonny?'

'I don't know. I've tried to impress upon him it's a secret. Again. The other two children like the idea of sharing a secret with the grown-ups.'

Marcus rubbed his chin. 'Well, no point in telling the Commandant, either. I just wish there had been some way of guaranteeing that only the Japs would eat the…' he searched for a word. '… the Chinese pork.'

They both pulled faces and hugged.

That night in bed, she re-lived their conversation more than a few times. How insane was this place – pigs had brought them closer.

She fell into an uneasy sleep: She was running from a giant black hog and then, out of a fog, came the figure of a man. He was slashing the air with a knife; the man was Stan.

JONNY'S CRISIS
Fu-xing 1944

The following evening as light was fading, Peggy was trying to write a quick letter to Miss Jeffrey at the salon. The sheet that was the door was whipped aside, and Natasha's face – crumpled, tear-streaked – peered in.

'Peggy, come quickly: something has happened to Jonny. I have told Marcus to fetch Doctor Albert.'

Twilight was sliding into night as Natasha led her out of the building.

'Tash, for God's sake, what's happened? Why did you let the children go on playing in such bad light?' asked Peggy, thinking to herself, 'people without kids just don't anticipate these things.'

Her friend didn't answer.

On most late afternoons, Natasha supervised an hour of exercises on the small lawn in front of the main building. The idea, she explained when she put it to Peggy and the other mothers, was to get rid of any excess energy before bedtime. She led the children through a game of piggyback that she called 'leaping lemurs'. They played hopscotch, 'French cricket', three-legged races – anything and everything that would make the children remember this weird childhood as 'fun'.

'Today, we play a new game.' Natasha told Peggy as they hurried to the front lawn. 'The children, they like it very much. Ito makes the rope go around and around and…'

'… The children jump over it.' Peggy finished for her. 'And the guard, Ito? He played, too? Good God, Tash.'

'Ito is very nice. The children love him. He misses his six children that he leaves behind in his country. He plays with the children every day.'

'I shouted at Ito to stop.' said Natasha, trying to explain what had happened, her hand over her mouth, tears streaking her face. 'I knew it was getting too dark for the children to see the rope. But the children were having such a good time. Jonny was shouting, 'Please, Tashie, please: just five more minutes.'

'I wouldn't try to blame Jonny if I were you.' Peggy was angry.

'No, no. It is true.' Her perfect features were distorted by regret and shame.

Peggy could hear Jonny's screams as she ran towards the children huddled in the dusk. The sound was new to her, unlike his other cries when hurt, distressed or frustrated. This noise was an animal howl of pain coming from the core of his little body.

As Peggy reached the children, Ito, the Japanese guard, was murmuring, 'Okay, okay, Jonny,' in a soothing voice. He held down Jonny's upper body by the shoulders while the boy's hips and legs writhed on the grass. Ito seemed to be making sure Jonny could not see what had happened to his left arm.

The young group stood gawping at Jonny, their faces a mixture of curiosity and excitement. Despite their protests, Natasha ushered them towards the buildings. 'But we want to *see*, Natasha! Will Jonny go to hospital? Can we play Jump the Rope tomorrow, too?'

Peggy bent down, saying, 'Sumimasen,' she edged the guard to one side.

Clearly upset, Ito said, 'Gomennasai, missy, gomennasai.' Ito's apology, even the tears running down his cheeks, meant nothing to Peggy. All she saw was the flash of white bone that had pushed through her son's freckled forearm. Peggy gagged.

Jonny sobbed, 'Mummy, Mummy,' his face a rictus of fear and tears and snot.

'Poor baby, oh my sweetheart,' she said as she lifted him carefully. Jonny, knowing his mother now held him, started again to scream, only pausing to inhale enough air to power another wail.

Standing up unsteadily, Johnny in her arms, she could see Marcus and Albie Faure running towards them.

As they rushed up, Marcus said, 'Please, Pegs, let Albie take over.'

'I am not leaving my son; bad things happen when I do.' She knew that Tash was in earshot, but she didn't care.

Marcus was insistent, 'You don't have to leave, but you must trust Albie; he's a good man and a good physician. Come, the three of us can take Jonny to the sanatorium.'

The next moment Ito arrived with a stretcher. The three men carried the crying boy towards the building – Albie and Marcus holding the stretcher – Ito and Peggy following. Had she turned around, Peggy would have seen Natasha standing alone in the field, quietly sobbing, as the night arrived.

Ten minutes later, Jonny's howling had ceased. Albie Faure had given the boy a painkiller that had calmed him. Peggy walked alongside the stretcher holding Jonny's good hand. 'She kept repeating, 'It's all right, darling. Doctor Albie will fix everything. What a brave soldier you are. Wait till I tell Daddy how brave you are.'

Her little boy looked up at her, lower lip trembling, and said, 'Want my daddy.' She closed her eyes, thinking she should not have mentioned Stan. 'I know, I know.'

Marcus's voice came from behind. 'When Daddy comes shoreside, you will be the number one person he sees. We will fix that.'

'Promise?'

Peggy turned around and smiled at Marcus. 'We promise.' she said.

After a three-minute walk from the field, they reached the set of small rooms that passed as a medical centre. As they were arriving, Albie explained that Jonny's arm had suffered a 'greenstick' fracture because the new bone – like a young twig – had bent before it broke. 'It's an easy fix,' he reassured Peggy. 'A first-year medical student could do it.'

'I want you to do it, Albie. I don't care how simple it is. I don't trust the Japanese to do it correctly.'

Minutes later, however, the Japanese medical superintendent – sleepy eyes set in a bland face – insisted that one of his own doctors perform the procedure.

'He just wants his doctor to practice on my son, I think.' Peggy whispered to Albie.

'It's possible,' Faure nodded. 'But in a situation like this, the Japanese are the bosses.'

Peggy's face scrunched up, 'But Marcus – you appointed Albie chief Medical Officer.'

'Yes, Peggy,' he replied, his brow wrinkled. 'But as a Japanese guard was present, they insist they fix the fracture.'

'But one thing has nothing to do with the other.'

Faure gave a Gallic shrug, 'I am sorry, Peggy, they are the bosses, and they make the rules.'

The Japanese surprised them when he said in English, 'Yes, I regret that, for you, I am *le chef*, the boss.' He put his hand out, 'Doctor Sora Saito, at your service. Let me assure you,' he paused, he looked at his clipboard. 'Missus Parker – no one will be experimenting on your son.' He turned to

Albie, 'Where is this woman's husband?'

Marcus cut in, 'Mrs. Parker's husband is not in the camp with her. Meanwhile,' he hesitated, and Peggy wondered what he was about to say, 'I am her protector.'

Peggy was too stunned to react. She heard the Japanese say. 'That is fine. We shall proceed. I will ask Doctor Tomohiko to do the operation immediately.'

There followed five minutes of negotiation with three-year-old Jonny as she assured him she would return in an hour to make sure he was all right and tuck him in for the night.

***

As Peggy walked back to their rooms, she said to Carter – without breaking stride or looking at him – 'Thank you, but I don't need a protector.'

Marcus halted her with a touch on her elbow. 'Of course, you don't. I know that, Peggy. But the Japanese are patriarchal. They will only deal man-to-man.'

Looking at him, Peggy raised her eyebrow, 'Is Marcus Carter the protector of all the women in the camp – the ones without husbands, I mean?'

'Not all of them. I've delegated some of the unprotected women to other men on my committee. They have lists.'

Despite her concerns about Jonny and what he might be going through, Peggy smiled.

'Tom is Natasha's protector, to give one example.'

'Does she know that?'

Marcus shrugged. 'She suggested it when I talked to her.'

'You never asked if I would mind if Marcus Carter was my protector.'

He snorted. 'That's because I knew darn well you'd hate the idea. Anyway, the word "protector" wouldn't have come up if it weren't for today – Jonny's accident, I mean.'

Peggy didn't want to end the discussion. She didn't want a protector, but if she had to have one, she only wanted Marcus to play the role.
After all, she thought, how bad could things be before she needed a 'protector'?

Twenty-four hours later, Peggy was standing over Jonny's bed in the poorly ventilated sanatorium. His left arm rested on a pillow next to him. He was groaning in pain. She knew at once that something was wrong. The plaster Paris had a sheen to it; she realised the cast had not dried.

She yelled, 'Doctor Saito!' Two nurses scuttled from the room in fright.

Minutes later, the superintendent entered the room, the nurses cowering behind him.

'Is there a problem?' The doctor's face had not lost its blank, disengaged look.

'This cast is still wet, as you can see. I want the plaster removed and replaced by Dr. Faure before gangrene sets in and my son loses his arm.'

The Japanese peered at the cast, 'Hmm. Should be dry by now.'

'I am not here to debate this…' she paused before adding contemptuously, '… *doctor.*'

The Japanese opened his mouth to speak.

'You have nothing to say to me. This is my son. You have put him at risk. I want a qualified doctor of my own race to see him. I want this stupid mistake corrected. I assure you that in a civilised society, you would not be permitted to practice.'

Saito strode from the room. Within minutes, Albie Faure joined her. Immediately he understood what had happened.

'This is so wrong, so needless and stupid,' he said, as soon as he saw Johnny's arm.

Peggy spoke to her son, 'Darling, Docor Albie is going to remove the cast.' The boy's eyes lit up.

'No, my love. He's going to put on a different cast, a better one, that will heal quicker.'

'No, Mummy! Please, Mummy, I don't want more operations.' The three-year-old was about to cry again, and she knew that would set her off into another slough of hopelessness. She shook it off.

'It won't be another operation. That's all finished. This is so your arm will get better quicker..' She paused, 'You must be brave like Daddy says.'

Later that day, after he had applied the new plaster cast, Dr. Faure told her that, because the original surgery had been bungled by the Japanese, the arm would always look slightly bent. The Frenchman said – without any enthusiasm – that the only way to correct the shape would be to break the arm again, perhaps when he was older, and re-set it. Peggy, round-eyed, looked at him, then shook her head violently and walked away, stifling her sobs.

A LETTER FROM STAN
Fu-xing 1944

The tedium of the camp affected everyone; they had been imprisoned for nearly two years. The routine; the sullen attitude of the guards; the foul food; the weight loss; the cramped quarters and consequent sleeplessness; the endless effort required to preserve a semblance of dignity and, most critically, the frustration of having no news about the war.

Peggy found refuge in supervising classes for the children in elocution; she also led play-reading evenings and helped to produce concerts – a two-act interpretation of 'Richard of Bordeaux' and Shaw's 'Joan of Arc'. Peggy cast Natasha as much-too-tall Joan, the Maid of Orleans, which gave her young friend the flexibility to mix her English with French.

The Japanese were bemused by the British efforts at amateur dramatics. The behaviour of the internees was all part of their bafflement about Europeans. As far as they knew – when they separated truth from propaganda – the Allies were losing the war while their captured citizens were play-acting. Standing at the back of the hall as he watched a performance of 'Saint Joan', *Ushiguro* shook his head and said to Carter, 'So funny you do this in middle of war. And you say *we* inscrutable!'

***

Sometime in that summer, Marcus arrived with a letter from Stan. As he handed the envelope to her, he said, 'I'm sorry, but Ushiguro's people read all letters before passing them on, that's why the seal is broken. This came via Geneva in a batch from the Red Cross,' he said. 'I notice the envelope is postmarked May 1943, but there's no explanation for the six-month delay. I'll leave you to read it.'

A letter from her husband should have excited her, but any news from Stan was nothing compared to the giddy desire she felt when Marcus was close. Somehow, they had managed not to become physically intimate.

They shared a magnetism, but Peggy was conscious of her status as a married Catholic woman. Marcus respected her principles, and, besides, for him, every day was filled with tasks that only he could administer; the last thing both wanted was to be caught in a cocoon of gossip.

Since the incident of Jonny's broken arm, the previous winter, she and Marcus had seen each other every day. All their encounters were innocent, and even though she might have wished it ('I don't!' she lied to herself), in the camp, it was impossible to be alone. That said, she knew that some married couples and younger people found private spaces, sometimes bartering goods with others to stand guard.

'But I'm a married woman,' she reminded herself as she opened the battered envelope.

The first thing she noticed was that Stan was in Egypt.

S.C. Parker, Chief Officer, Anglo Saxon Petroleum Co. Alexandria, Egypt, 14th May 1943.

'My dearest Peggy,

'I am writing to you again in the hope that you will eventually receive this letter. I have not heard anything from you since April last *('doesn't he know we can't write? That was my last letter before we were arrested,' she muttered to herself.)*

'It must be terrible for you being in that place and cut off from everything. I hope and pray every day that you are both safe and well. I wonder if you get sufficient to eat? *('no, we don't, and there's nothing you can do about it.')* And how is our little Jonny?

('Is that all you've got to say about your son?' she thought. Not 'how tall is he? Tell me some of the things he says. Does he have any chums? Is there a school in the camp?' No – none of that. Just 'I wonder if you get sufficient to eat and how is our little Johnny.' Tacked on to another sentence and without even a question mark.) Peggy closed her eyes, trying to suppress her disappointment at Stan's apparent indifference to his son's condition. Until that moment, she hadn't realised how much anger she had been suppressing. There was more...)

'Things with us are very quiet, and we are having an easy time. I have not been too well myself, mostly tummy trouble; this country is renowned for that sort of thing. *('You're having an easy time; just a bit of tummy trouble? Poor darling.' She rolled her eyes.)*

'I sent a cable to Pa on his birthday. He told me he had a bad fall, so his doctor is keeping him quiet for a while.

'I have not heard from your sister Connie for a while, but when last I heard, things were going all right.

'Well, my darling, I must draw my letter to a close now with the hope that this will be one letter nearer the time when we shall be together again.

'All my love to you both, darling, and a happy Christmas if it is possible. I'll be thinking of you.

'Always your loving Stan.'

Peggy read and re-read the letter, searching for some sign that they soon would be together again. But there was no hint. Of course, she realised, the censors would not have allowed it. In fact, the address in Egypt might be a ruse to mislead the Japanese. He could be anywhere.

She sat for a long moment, trying to diagnose her mood. As she faced her feelings and got past the guilt, she admitted to herself that her concern for Stan was fading.

She tore up the letter, knowing she was being unfaithful to him in her heart. And that being so, did it matter? She didn't know where he was, and she fought the new feeling that, increasingly, she cared less.

A TRYST
Chongqing 1944

Stan and Alena took breakfast together on their second day at the Kuomintang camp. It was a sunny but cold morning, the temperature nudging three degrees Celsius.

When she tapped on his door, he saw that Alena was wearing her long leather overcoat over her shoulders. 'My God, the heating has always been inadequate here. Of course, Chiang insists on that – to harden his soldiers. And as he's both stoic and ascetic, the freezing air – look' she puffed the air visibly – 'suits him very well.' She rolled her eyes. 'The rest of us?' Stan caught a glimpse of her black slacks and white shirt under a cream cardigan before she shrugged into the coat and cinched her belt.

'Come, let's have breakfast,' she said. 'I have organised a wonderful day.' They walked down the hallway.

***

Stan wasn't looking forward to another plate of congealing congee. Alena led him into a large room that must, he decided, be the cafeteria. About two dozen Chinese soldiers were noisily sucking up their breakfast congee. The men studied the Europeans when they walked in. Alena made for a sectioned-off area, and Stan followed.

'What's this?' said Stan, his eyes gleaming as he surveyed salvers of bacon, scrambled eggs, sausages, mushrooms, and tomatoes. A Chinese manservant came in and parked a plate of toast and a coffee urn.

Alena, grinning, turned to Stan: said, 'Don't tell me you can't recognise a full English anymore?'

'But, but…'

'But you'd rather have a plate of tepid congee?'

'This looks marvellous, Alena. How did you organise it?'

She nudged him with her shoulder. 'Don't you know? Chief of Staff includes chief of kitchen staff. I ordered it when we left Changsha.'

She took off her coat which, barely a minute before, she had put on. He wondered if she was nervous. He looked at her clothes. 'Are you going to be warm enough?' It was a simple question but, oddly, seemed more personal than he'd intended. He rushed to the next sentence. 'Really sweet of you to organise such a magnificent breakfast.'

'Well, they do say the way to a man's heart –' she stopped, and Stan realised she, too, had spoken without thinking; perhaps they were both nervous.

He laughed lightly, to allay her obvious embarrassment. 'Ah ha! Do they say that in Chinese, too?'

Stan filled his plate. The soldiers filed out and made a slight detour to pass their table. Stan looked up and smiled, but the men gave him only surly looks as they passed.

Alena explained that the day might be the only free one for some time. Stan knew that *Chou en-lai* and his delegation were due in two days. Everything had to be prepared for a series of meetings aligning the military strategies of *Mao*'s Red Army and *Chiang*'s Nationalist Army. Alena had told him that, while *Chiang* might have seemed urbane and relaxed in *Changsha*, he would not tolerate any mistakes being made in front of VIPs, and 'especially not those with links to Mao.'

'Why? Is he scared of Mao?'

'The man's a thug, as we all know – except Moscow,' she said, grimacing. 'They regard him as their golden boy.'

***

After they'd finished breakfast, Alena took Stan outside to where a Jeep was parked.

'Where's the driver?' Stan asked.

For an answer, Alena slid behind the wheel. 'That would be me,' she said.

'Where are we going?'

Three hours later, Stan was looking at a giant Buddha statue, its size magnified by other small Buddha heads placed around the huge reclining figure.

Stan read the small poster explaining the origins of the Dazu Buddhas. He looked at Alena, eyes wide with mock fright. 'You're not going to force me to see all ten thousand Buddhas, are you? I shall be dead by then.'

'Ten thousand? Heavens, no. Only nine thousand five hundred.' She laughed. 'These Dazu figures were carved from rock six hundred years after Christ was crucified.'

They were standing close to one another in the small viewing booth. Next to them were a young couple, clearly more interested in each other than in the Buddhas. From the corner of his eye, Stan watched as they nuzzled each other then kissed. It was an unerotic yet deeply touching moment. He imagined kissing Alena.

A wave of guilt washed over him. He thought, 'Why has she brought me here to waste a day? Has she forgotten that Peggy and Jonny are prisoners of the Japanese?'

Her next sentence made him wonder if his thoughts were visible. 'Don't feel bad about spending this day with me, Stan. For the moment, there's nothing you can do to free your family. Chiang is the only one who can help you.'

Stan bit his lip. 'It's highly unlikely that Tang will listen to him. Chiang and Mao are their top enemies.'

Alena pointed to the figure of the Buddha. 'Then we can only do what the Buddha recommends: enjoy the moment.'

And they did. It was too cold to sit on the hard benches; they walked among the collection of small lakes, each a shiny pellet of ice.

'I'll tell you my story if you'll tell me yours,' Alena said. They were hunched over small bowls of *dim sum* purchased from a street vendor. The man's stall was beside a blazing brazier, but after an explosive exchange of Chinese with Alena, the man had insisted that they take the food and move away. 'He says he doesn't want us hogging his heat. He says if he allowed that, everybody would be crowding around his stall, stealing his heat…'

'… and buying his excellent dim sum,' said Stan. 'Makes you wonder if Communism will ever catch on here. They do like their independence.'

'And Mao plans to knock it out of them. But let's not talk about that now, Stan – we'll be talking politics for the next two days. Let's tell each other how we landed here, helping Chiang Kai-shek to fight Communism.'

They shared stories: Alena, like Stan, was an only child, the daughter of a mixed-race Asian tea merchant, Hugo Wang. Wang, sixty-two, had plucked Eva Zoltan, a sixteen-year-old, red-haired Slovenian beauty, from Budva, a seaside village in Montenegro. At the turn of the century, Wang had brought Eva back, trophy-like, to Peking. Five years later, Alena Zoltan Wang was born. Eva Zoltan had insisted on keeping the name 'Zoltan' for her daughter as a tribute to her Slovenian homeland. After the young woman's education at Saint Paul's school for girls in London, Alena finished her upbringing at La Rosay in Switzerland. At eighteen, the young woman dispensed with her last name, Wang. Alena Zoltan was reborn.

'But you haven't told me how you've ended up working with Chiang.'

Alena nodded, smiling, and Stan thought guiltily, how lovely she looked. 'Chiang, who had known my father for years, came to pay his respects when he was dying. Hugo made him promise to take care of me.'

Stan, smiling, shook his head, 'Well, he's done more than that by making you his chief of staff.'

'He trusts me, Stan. We are family. And I'm up to the job – it's not nepotism.'

Stan said, 'A ha! Talking of which…' He gave Alena an account of his early time in China, meeting Peggy in Derby, and her influence on his career – an influence, he explained, that seemed to be waning.

He explained why he felt that the return to China – and his elevation to officer – had made him less reliant on Peggy. Even as he talked, though, he felt that sharing this insight about his marriage was an act of betrayal.

'Surely you feel more your own man, though?' She tipped her head as she asked the question, apparently guileless, her eyes filled with concern.

He nodded, 'I do, I do. But that independence hasn't brought us any closer.'

She was silent for a moment before adding, 'Do you miss her?'

He couldn't answer her question. He looked at his watch. 'Shouldn't we get on the road?'

***

A few hours later, back at the *Kuomintang* compound, Alena hurried off to meet with Madame *Chiang Kai-shek*. Stan ate supper in the cafeteria, asking the lone chef to make him a cheese omelette.

Back in his room, he reflected on his day with Alena Zoltan. Had there been any news about Peggy while they were away? Surely if there had been a change, news would have reached him? Alena would have heard, and she would have told him immediately. Unless Madame Chiang, with her incessant demands, had driven it from her mind.

As Stan was about to knock on Alena's door, he knew his motives were mixed. He wanted to know about Peggy but, after the intimacies they had shared that day, he wanted to see Alena again. He knocked.

THE THREAT OF MAO
Chongqing 1944

The following day, Stan wondered what Peggy would think if she could see her man sitting at a conference table with Generalissimo Chiang Kai-shek. Immediately, he hated himself for his arrogance; God knows what was happening to his wife and son. Also, when he considered how, in a few days, one person had changed his life, he knew his thoughts were a betrayal of two people who were still a precious part of him.

The part of the building where the meeting was taking place was in the 'working wing', as Alena called it. When he entered the conference room, he saw a dozen Chinese seated against the wall. Their heads swivelled as he entered, faces impassive. Aside from this quick movement, there was no acknowledgement of his arrival. The Chinese returned their attention to listening, some taking notes.

He didn't know where to sit. *Chiang* sat at one end of the table in conversation with another man. Stan recognised the hunched figure of *Chou en-lai*, who had come to *Chiang*'s headquarters as *Mao Tse-tung*'s envoy. Alena sat opposite *Chou*, taking notes, and making an occasional comment. When she heard Stan arrive – she had her back to the door – she turned and gestured for him to join the table.

He saw the Red General lean into *Chou*, presumably, Stan thought, to explain the Englishman's presence. Having Alena's permission to join the table, Stan wondered where he could sit that would draw the least attention to himself. He found an empty chair on the opposite side of the table, some distance from Alena, where his presence wouldn't distract. She smiled warmly at him, her pale green eyes softened as he took his seat.

Stan knew he had to be able to see his lover. Already he thought of her that way, caressing the word. Without seeing her, Alena's aura would, he feared, overcome him. Heat swarmed through his body. Seeing her again aroused him, made her human, not merely a presence that consumed him. For a moment, he thought he might faint, as ridiculous as it seemed.

His attraction to Alena – in fact, their attraction to each other, she later confessed – had been sudden and complete: a bolt of lightning, a true *'coup de foudre.'* He had never been in infatuation's terrain - even with Peggy - he had no idea of its geography, no idea why he had fallen – instantly and alarmingly – in love. The feelings possessing him were unlike the simple attraction he felt when he had first met Peggy.

He had admitted to himself – and to Alena last night – that from the moment when Alena had walked into his first meeting with *Chiang* in *Changsha,* she had invaded his hours. Yesterday among the Dazu Buddhas, Alena made each moment seem freshly minted, unique. He hoped that *Chiang*, his new boss, was unaware of the radiant heat binding him to this woman.

***

Awake in the early hours of the morning, Alena had told him that *Chou* was there on a specific mission: to persuade *Chiang* that Mao's Chinese Communist Party and its attack group the Red Army, should operate separately from Chiang's national army.

For some curious reason he found that when she talked politics in bed, he became aroused

Now he heard a conversation growing louder at the end of the table. *Chiang* was speaking in Mandarin, and Stan understood why *Chiang* was angry: Moscow wished him to contemplate giving autonomy to *Mao*; the exact Mandarin word that *Chou* used was *'chensi'* – contemplate. Stan was sure that *Chiang*, ever the realist, understood he would not be given much time to 'contemplate' the proposal. *'Chensi'* was the velvet glove around Stalin's fist.

Stan was aware of *Chiang*'s negative views about this new way of governance. In their talks in *Changsha*, the General had told him how, after visiting Moscow, he'd been disillusioned by what he'd seen of Communist society.

His reaction had upset the party elders. Stalin and his inner circle had hoped that *Chiang* – then young and left-leaning – might be a 'Trojan horse' candidate. Their plans were upended when, on his return to *Shanghai*, the General had made it clear that he did not support the idea of China as a Communist state. *Chiang*'s behaviour convinced Stalin that the ambitious young soldier would do nothing to help the cause of communism. The 'head of all the Russias' did not want *Chiang* anywhere near *Mao*'s Red Army.

***

That morning Stan could hear *Chiang* arguing with *Chou*: The General was saying that he could see no logic in the chain of command being split. In a strong voice, he asked *Chou*, 'Why yield control of our fighters to that opportunist, *Mao*? He is incapable of thinking through his strategies; he tears down everything, but he knows nothing about building something in the wilderness he's created.' Stan saw *Chiang* lean forward, his voice urgent: 'Do we not have a common enemy – the Japanese?'

Stan knew he could never be more than an observer in the room. But an observer for whom? *Chiang* had explained that Stan could report back to his government that he had been in the room when *Chou en-lai* had laid out Russia's intentions, 'If your country ever needed a reason to support us, I want you to tell them about my meeting with Chou. I know why he's come here: he's just a cog in Stalin's plan to use Mao to conquer China and make it a communist vassal.'

'But *you* can tell them that,' Stan had protested. He was unwilling to be drawn into political shenanigans; he had troubles enough of his own.

Chiang had smiled, and then, in a quiet voice, he had said, 'Of course I can, but you are English. I hear your father – the Commodore – is a respected man, and he has influence. Most of all, they trust him and you. So do I.'

Stan didn't ask *Chiang* how he knew so much about his background; he must have heard some of it when Pennington had decided to enlist him in spying on the Japanese. The Chinese military intelligence, weak though it was, would have done the rest of the investigation. Stan was, after all, an open book and preferred to live his life that way.

Then he remembered his night with Alena and wondered how much that had changed.

Weeks later, when he and Alena had time to talk about what they meant to each other, they concluded that their impulse to be together – in addition to a fierce physical attraction – was partly motivated by the loneliness of being two Europeans among millions of Asians. Lust certainly there was – but no calculated seduction by either of them; just a synchronicity of thought and action that sparked whenever they were in each other's company.

One of the facets of Alena's personality that Stan found so different from Peggy's was her emotional trust in him. In their love-making, she gave all. Stan had assumed that he was hyper-sexual because Peggy rejected him so often – it heightened his need and led him to believe he was unreasonable in his sexual demands. Part of this conclusion was supported by talking with other 'once-a-month' husbands.

With Alena, however, there was never a time when she was unresponsive. Stanley felt their love-making had moved him – from black-and-white with Peggy – to vivid colour with Alena. He realised that the colours might fade, but with Peggy, he felt it had never existed; he'd always felt that Peggy disliked being in bed with him; Alena relished it.

More important to Stan than their love-making, though, was Alena's unfailing warmth. When he reached for her as they crossed the madness of city traffic, she seemed to grip his hand gratefully – unlike Peggy, who flicked his hand away, perhaps because it might betray her chronic need for independence. Alena preferred to walk arm-in-arm, but Peggy often bustled ahead, seemingly oblivious of Stan's habit of taking a slower, more reflective speed. When working in his tiny office, Alena would often arrive with coffee. After ruffling his hair and kissing his cheek, she'd sometimes tiptoe away in an exaggerated fashion, pretending he was so important he really shouldn't be disturbed. These actions delighted him. Such small, tender gestures were enough for Stan to feel something deeper than infatuation. He felt truly loved.

***

After the meeting had concluded, a joint press statement was issued, and *Chou en-lai* departed. The three of them – *Chiang*, Alena and Stan – agreed that *Chiang* had to fall in with Moscow's edict to 'contemplate' such an arrangement. *Chiang* puffed his cheeks with disdain: 'Mao is a bad person, he creates class warfare, and if he doesn't find it, he creates it. Stalin has never forgiven me for breaking with the communists fifteen years ago. He has his revenge, for now.'

OHTA ARRIVES
Fu-xing 1944

At five o'clock that evening, Marcus appeared at their tent. He nodded at the 'Ritz group' as they ate an early meal – they had learned that the earlier they got their food, the more edible it was. People were spread out on beds and chairs.

'He's ready,' said Marcus. Peggy, who had been too nervous to eat, passed her plate to Tom.

'Here, finish this, please,' she said.

'Who's ready?' said Tom. Peggy didn't answer him and got up to follow Marcus.

A minute later, she and Marcus were walking arm-in-arm along icy paths towards the Commandant's quarters. 'Have you found out anything more – about the meeting, I mean? She couldn't keep the quaver out of her voice.

He searched for her hand and gripped it. At his touch, she felt the tension leave her body.

'No, nothing more. Really, Peggy, I have no idea why he's called this meeting. All I know is that Ushiguro wants to see you, and I have insisted,' he put on a pompous voice, 'that, as her Majesty's representative of British subjects at Fu-xing, I be allowed to attend.' He grinned at her, and his hand tightened on hers. 'It will be fine, I'm sure.'

There were two guards outside the Commandant's office. The Japanese soldiers inspected them before one of the guards turned and tapped on *Ushiguro*'s door. After a moment, the door opened.

Peggy walked into the room. When she recognised the man sitting at *Ushiguro*'s desk, her breathing shortened, then palpitated. Why did her head seem on fire? Why this storm of fear?

'How delightful to see you again, Missy Parker.' A figure rose from the desk and bowed. *Ohta Tang*'s dark eyes found hers.

Tang was dressed immaculately. The Admiral wore the winter uniform of a senior officer of the Imperial Japanese Navy. He projected the same power as he had three years ago on the '*Nanjing*.'

A throb started at the base of her skull. Her breathing became shallow, her mind a tumult of thoughts and fears. She felt Marcus's hand on her shoulder.

'Why are you here?' she asked, her hand at her throat.

'Please.' *Tang* gestured for her to sit at the single chair facing the desk. He resumed his own seat.

'Excuse me, sir, but I am Mrs Parker's representative.' Marcus stood behind her chair; she was glad they were together.

'I know who you are, Carter.' Given his relaxed position in the chair, it was obvious that *Tang* was not about to show respect to the Englishman. 'Ushiguro-San approves of your stewardship of our prisoners.'

'Not prisoners, Admiral, internees.'

Tang gave a thin smile. 'As you say, internees.'

***

From the corner, where he had taken a position behind a small table, *Ushiguro* said, 'Most honourable Admiral Tang has agreed to your presence, Carter-San, on the understanding that you will not participate in these discussions.' His eyes became slits with what passed for a smile. 'You are to be a silent witness.'

Carter said, 'Unless her rights are compromised, or her person threatened.' Peggy could hear the force in his words.

Tang raised his hands as if to end the budding confrontation. 'Gentlemen, please. I must be back on the 'Nanjing' by twenty-three hundred hours tomorrow. We should proceed.'

Tang looked at *Ushiguro*. The other man nodded. Peggy heard a door open behind her. The next minute, a guard was pouring tea for her, then for *Tang*. Again, came the constriction in her throat, the dry mouth, the reach for breath. She had no idea why *Tang* had come to *Fu-xing*, but she felt it important to show that she was not panicked by his presence.

She tried to ease the dryness in her throat as she lifted the teacup and drank the hot, clear liquid. As she put the cup down, she noticed a single ceramic eye staring up at her – it was part of the pattern at the base of the cup. She had four similar Japanese teacups at home – Stan had brought them from *Kyoto*. The eye only appeared when the cup was filled with liquid. Stan had explained: 'When you drink from it, the eye is supposed to remind you of your conscience: Is it as clear as the tea?'

Tang inclined his head towards her as he raised his cup, 'Missy Parker, as I said before, I am delighted to see you again – although, if I may comment on such a lovely lady's appearance – I fear you have lost much weight.'

'Fu-xing cuisine…' began Carter, but *Tang* glowered and put his fingers to his lips. 'Sh, sh, sh.'

The Admiral's marble-black eyes found her again. He leaned forward in his chair. 'Missy Parker, I imagine the first piece of news you wish to hear is about your son.'

Of course, they had Jonny, she thought; they had all of them.

Peggy's stomach lurched, 'Is Jonny all right?'

Tang, unsmiling, nodded.

She needed more: 'You've seen him?'

Tang made a thin smile, 'No, I have not seen Jonny myself, but I sent an aide, and he assured me your son is in good hands. Here, my officer took a picture.'

Peggy almost grabbed the photograph from him. The under-exposed picture showed her little boy seated in a wicker chair by a window. There was a pretty Chinese nurse on either side of him. To her relief, Jonny did look well, if thinner than before. When she tried to return the photo, *Tang* waved it away, making it clear it was hers to keep.

Tang's voice brought her back to the room. 'There seems to be no reason why your son shouldn't be returned to his mother. Although, I must say that the food – even hospital food – is better than…' his eyes flicked to Carter, 'cuisine Fu-xing.' He peered at Peggy, 'Of course, his return can be arranged.' He made an expansive gesture, 'Everything…' he stressed the word, 'Missy Parker, can be arranged.'

She heard Marcus speak behind her, 'I am sure Mrs. Parker would like her son back, sir.'

'Carter!' *Ushiguro* snapped from across the room.

Tang's eyelids fluttered, she assumed with suppressed anger. Peggy was rigid. She said nothing; she didn't want to postpone *Tang*'s explanation of the reason for his visit.

The Admiral leaned back and steepled his fingers. His eyes bored into her, 'Missy Parker, it has taken us too long to locate your husband, but now that we have done so, we wish to speak with him.'

'Where is he?' she blurted out the question. 'And why are you here, Admiral? If it's my husband with whom you wish to speak, then why have you driven from the Bund to Fu-xing to speak to me? I, too, would like to speak to my husband.' She paused, then: 'How did you come by this information – finding out where he is?'

Tang smiled at her, 'So many questions, Missy Parker!' He looked down at the desk, averting his eyes. 'We have friends in Fu-xing camp.' And we Japanese also have excellent technology,' he added.

Peggy's thoughts leaped: Tom, Natasha, *Chao-xing*, John Lang: who else did she know in Fu-xing? One name kept returning: Tom Trencher.

At the moment, though, she thought that identifying the informant was less important than knowing where he was and what they wanted from Stan.

'I asked you where he was, Admiral.'

Tang shook his head, 'We shall talk again tomorrow.'

'Then at least tell me how you think he can help you.'

Tang moved his head from side to side. To Peggy, it seemed as if he was searching how to answer.

'You will remember, Missy Parker, that two years ago, your husband assisted Captain Masataka in Shanghai. He gave my officers an excellent understanding of local customs and excise protocols.' She noticed how perfectly he pronounced the word. 'I had hoped my association with your husband would be a *nagai tsukiai*.'

Peggy interrupted him: 'a long and trusting relationship.'

Tang beamed, 'Exactly! You have not forgotten, Missy Parker. Then perhaps you can tell me why your husband seems to have forgotten our agreement.'

The man was unbelievable, she thought.

'You really believed Stanley Parker would betray his country?' She shook her head as she raised her voice. 'There was no agreement, as you call it, Admiral. You were the occupying force.' Her voice strengthened, 'My husband knew that if his firm didn't help you, his competitors would; that's all there was to it.' She heard Marcus shuffle his feet behind her before she felt his hand on her shoulder.

Tang's eyes flicked between them as if trying to establish the connection.

Peggy continued, "Admiral, surely you understand that my husband was being practical when you people conquered Shanghai?' She saw *Tang's* head move back a fraction at her phrasing, but she went on: 'As I say, both my husband and his firm, Blue Funnel, knew that they would have to help – or see the Japanese destroy their business.'

The Admiral got up and started to pace the area behind the desk. 'But, Missy Parker, your husband may have been practical, but he was also honourable; he helped me and my officers; he respected the principle of *on* and *giri*.' He pointed at her, his finger scolding. 'He helped us. Now it will be my honour to help him.'

He paused, smiled, 'And that is why we would like Parker-san to see his wife and child, to reunite your family, Missy Parker. And I am sure is *your* greatest wish. This is how we thank him for his service to the Imperial Japanese Navy.'

Peggy *was* baffled. First, *Tang* seemed angry at Stan's disappearance, and yet now he was talking of helping him? She remembered Stan telling her that business with the Japanese always involved the scratch-my-back exchange of favours, the *on* and *giri* of commerce. Stan had helped *Tang* with what was known as *on*. Now – bizarrely and late – *Tang* was prepared to return with *giri*.

Tang swung on his heel and confirmed exactly what she was thinking: 'We would like to continue the practice of *on* and *giri*.'

'I don't understand,' she said.

'Missy Parker, you probably are not aware that we have received intelligence that your husband is now a confidante of our supreme enemy in China, Chiang Kai-shek.'

He paused to let the statement hang in the air while his eyes, again, bored into her. He went on: 'Since you last heard from him, your husband joined Chiang Kai-shek's inner circle. Parker-san now knows everything about the current and planned future movements and battle plans of the Chinese Nationalist Army.'

He smiled broadly and added, 'In pursuit of a new round of *on* and *giri*, we would like to have that information.'

'Ha!' she heard Marcus's explosive sound behind her. *Tang* raised a warning finger at him.

Peggy's mind was spinning. She found it hard to believe that her Stanley was so highly placed in the exiled Chinese government. And a close ally of *Chiang Kai-shek?*

She knew that her ideas about Stan had changed over the past few years: since coming back to China, Stan's reputation and abilities had resulted in some small fame and a promotion. Perhaps it was possible that Generalissimo *Chiang* had asked for him; or that the Merchant Marine had seconded him to the Chinese Command. Yet it all seemed far-fetched.

She became aware that *Tang* was standing in front of her.

'Let me be sure I understand,' she said, looking into his dark eyes. 'My husband helped you by teaching your officers the rudiments of marine surveying, and now you wish to repay that service by permitting him to see me and my son.' She couldn't resist it – *Tang* was so cocksure – 'Oh, and along the way to granting him *giri*, you want him to start another cycle of the process by asking my husband to betray his country.'

Raising an eyebrow, *Tang* said nothing. Peggy took it as confirmation of her last sentence. The silence grew.

She held *Tang*'s basilisk stare. She could hear Marcus breathing behind her, but he, too, stayed silent. Finally, Peggy said, 'And how do you propose to get this information?'

He smiled at her and closed his eyes, 'You are going to get it for us, Missy Parker.'

After a moment's pause, Peggy said, 'I need the bathroom.'

Tang nodded, grimaced. 'Of course. The guard will attend you.'

Like Marcus, Peggy had hoped to steal a moment talking to Marcus about *Tang*'s ridiculous idea, but it was not to be; *Tang* held up a restraining hand when Marcus attempted to follow her.

Peggy went into one of the washrooms and sat down in a stall. She felt tense, her thoughts jumbled: even if *Tang*'s information were true, would Stan betray the Chinese and its ally, his own country? But now, presented with the alternative – which might be never to see his family again – did he have a choice?

Her speculation continued: maybe *Tang*'s motives were more personal; maybe the Admiral resented the fact that Stan had, as it were, walked out on him. Did *Tang* see this as an insult, a huge loss of face – that most terrible of Japanese offences?

Five minutes later, she was asking the same question of *Tang*: 'Why would my husband do such a thing? Why would he trust you, Admiral?'

She heard Carter stir behind her. 'Admiral, sir, with respect, Mrs. Parker and I must discuss this before she decides.'

Tang put his hand up, his palm facing Marcus Carter. 'Carter, there is nothing for Missy Parker to decide. The decision lies with her husband.'

Peggy whipped around to face Marcus. 'What is he trying to say?' Of course, she grasped the implication of *Tang*'s plan, but she needed to have it confirmed by someone she trusted – now, maybe even loved.

Marcus looked past her at Tang. 'I'm not doing your dirty work for you, Admiral,' he said. She could see angry patches on his face.

Tang seemed unaffected by Marcus's outburst. He tipped his head to one side, his gaze ranging from Marcus to Peggy. She wondered whether the Japanese was trying to establish their relationship.

'A simple plan, Missy Parker: my gift – my *giri*, if you will – is to free you and your son. In return, Parker must take the decision to tell us about his work with Chiang Kai-shek.'

Peggy paused to think through the consequences of *Tang*'s idea. 'Will you take me to my husband, or bring him here?'

Tang shook his head. 'We cannot risk the enemy engaging in some foolhardy plan to thwart us. Initially, we shall arrange for your husband to speak to you by telephone. We shall offer the reason that both you and your child are dangerously sick and that you need to see him, urgently.'

'You think he will accept the lie that we are *both* mortally ill and must give him some dying message?' Again, she was incredulous.

Tang shrugged, 'We need to get his attention, Missy Parker.'

'And then what?'

'During the conversation – which will be short and which we shall monitor – you must lay out the plan I have described.'

'I see: be a traitor to save your wife and child.'

'That is a very blunt assessment.'

'Accurate, though. And you think he will agree to this crazy notion? You think the Chinese will not monitor the conversation and act?'

Tang shrugged. 'What can they do? We have the man's wife and child. We speculate that he will not dare authorise any pre-emptive strike.'

Tang rubbed his hands in a methodical way, as if he were washing them slowly. When he spoke, his tone was mild. 'Because if he does not help us,

I fear we shall have to take – I believe the Americans call it – 'Extreme measures.'

The Japanese walked back to the desk and, as if to terminate further discussion, drew the curtains against the night.

'We shall send for you when your husband is ready to talk. You are free to go.'

INTERLUDE
Fu-xing 1944

'I have no fear of death,' she said to Marcus as they stepped outside and began to walk back to their quarters. The cold wind had eased as they hurried through the early darkness.

'What did Tang mean by saying he might have to take extreme measures?'

'One of two things, I would say: finding a way of disposing of you and Jonny.' Peggy's hand flew to her throat as Marcus quickly added, 'which I doubt very much he would do. It's clear to me that Tang likes and admires you.'

'Or?'

'Seeking out Stan and executing him. About that, he would have no qualms.'

Shozo Ono, Marcus's guard, was walking twenty paces behind them.

Peggy said, 'I overcame my fear of death when I decided to follow Stan to China. But I shall kill myself if anything happens to Jonny.' She stopped and turned to Marcus. Somehow, she managed a short laugh: 'How ridiculous that sounds!'

He put his arm round her and moved them forward again. 'It will never come to that, Peggy. Stan will find a way of misleading them; manufacturing information, laying false trails – whatever it takes to keep you and Jonny safe.'

She turned to him. 'I don't think I can face the others tonight – especially Tom, who probably betrayed Stan's whereabouts.' She looked up at the starless sky. 'Yes, Tom would be happy to bring Stan down.'

Marcus reached out and touched her hair as he drew her close. 'We have no proof of that, Peggy. And anyway, how would Tom know where Stan is?'

She knew he was right. Wanting Tom to be a traitor didn't make him one.

Marcus squeezed her arm. 'I want you to stay with me tonight.'

She opened her mouth to speak, but no words came. She knew she didn't want to be alone.

Behind them, *Shozo Ono* coughed. 'Hai, ikuzo!' he said. When they turned around, he was pointing at the path ahead, motioning them to move on.

***

They undressed in the dark. Peggy was first to settle in the narrow bed. The hour was early for bed – only a few minutes after eight – but they knew it would take an hour to get warm enough for sleep. She heard Marcus rubbing his teeth. Through the gloom, she saw him take a gulp of something. Moments later, when he kissed her, he tasted sweetly of alcohol. 'Sorry, darling, just a swig of brandy. Medicinal use only. Shozo gets it for me. I like to think it keeps the germs away… well… that's what I think.'

She nudged him under the blanket. 'Lots of medical evidence for that, is there?'

'Heaps,' he said, with an answering nudge.

She felt the hairy, naked length of his leg against hers. She knew her own legs were less than smooth, such indulgences were long gone. She knew Marcus wouldn't care about the state of her legs. She leaned over to touch his lips with her fingers. 'I want to be with you, Marcus, but so much is unclear now. Is it all right if we just hold each other through the night?'

He stroked her hair. 'Of course, of course.'

Hours later, she drifted awake. He was spooning her, his arm heavy against her shoulder.

'You awake?'

'On and off,' she said.

'Tom: why are you so sure he's the one who betrayed Stan? I think there could be a simpler explanation.'

'Such as?'

'Tang knew Stan's ship would be visiting the Treaty ports. I'd be surprised if his people weren't monitoring every stop he made. If Stan was seen leaving the ship at one of those ports, word would have got back to the Admiral. Tang knew that Chang Kai-shek had bases at Changsha and Chongqing, and, despite it being in Chinese territory, he probably had

Kempeitai spies there, too. I'd put my money on that as the way in which he found out about Stan's defection.'

She turned in the bed so she was looking at the ceiling, knowing that if she faced him, her resolve would evaporate. Even so, his arm – now resting across her covered breasts – gave her a feeling of closeness that she'd forgotten.

'It's possible. But Trencher has always been envious of Stan; he resents the way he's risen so swiftly among the Shanghainese. Tom would like to believe Stan's been favoured.'

'Favoured: how?'

'Because Stan's father is a Commodore. But I know that Stan has done it all by himself.'

She felt his arm tighten against her, 'Oh, and Peggy Parker has had nothing to do with that?'

She smiled into the darkness. 'Maybe at the beginning, before we were married. But since I arrived in Shanghai, I've seen that Stanley doesn't need me any more in that way.'

'And how does that make *you* feel?'

'Relieved but disappointed,' she paused. 'But now I have Jonny. He's my investment. I don't want him to be another of those confused children coming out of the war with nothing but a lost childhood.'

She felt his head shaking next to her; still, as much as she wanted to, she wouldn't turn to him.

He said: 'Hmm, but that's still an odd way to talk about your son – an investment.'

'Marcus, I can't see a future beyond Fu-xing, but if there is to be one, then I have to be sure that Jonny and I are ready for it.'

Marcus reached for her with his hand, rubbing their clasped hands along his thigh. 'We should try to catch another few hours of sleep,' he said. He turned to the wall and edged away. 'Nothing personal,' he said. 'But it's a lot easier for me if I can't feel you.' Five minutes later, she heard his breathing.

Peggy lay awake. Like *Chao-xing*, Peggy had started to call her mind 'the chattering monkey'. Now it was chattering away in her head: Why did ambition blind so many men? Why did so many of them always want to win? Even her father used to say, 'Happiness is seeing your neighbour fall off his roof.'

She continued to speculate: Did Trencher think that Stan's complicity – as he saw it – with the Japanese, deserved punishment? Did Tom resent Stan's success so much to wish him death? Or was Marcus's less complex explanation the right one?

Even accounting for Stan's new aura of competence: how credible was it that he would become a confidante of *Chiang Kai-shek*?

Peggy thought it most likely that Tom had told *Tang* that Stan was helping the Chinese. But that would make Tom a Japanese agent in the American Embassy; it was a shocking idea, but if she was right and Marcus wrong – then what?

Yet until the moment this evening – when *Tang* told them it had taken too long to find him – Stan's location had been a mystery. It was as if he had fallen off the face of the earth.

Where was he?

OHTA'S OFFER
Cairo, Egypt 1943

Stan was in Egypt. The flight manifest for the twenty-hour flight from Chongquing to Cairo listed him as 'Special Adviser to Chiang Kai-shek'. Chiang had asked him to join Alena as part of his entourage attending the Cairo Conference. Chiang's team would join Roosevelt, Churchill, and Stalin. The venue for the meeting of Allied leaders would be the American Embassy.

Two days before the conference, a shocked aide had told Stan that a Japanese was on the line asking for 'Chief Officer Parker'. Puzzled, Stan walked briskly through to the Embassy library and picked up the phone. He identified himself before a voice said, 'This is the Civilian Assembly Centre at Fu-xing. Admiral Ohta Tang of the Imperial Nipponese Navy will call you tomorrow at noon – Cairo time. That will be six p.m. here in Fu-xing. Please make yourself available.'

***

The following afternoon, readying himself for the call from *Tang*, Stan drew the library curtains to block the bright November sunlight. As he did so, through the crystal air, he caught a glimpse of the Giza pyramids, some twenty kilometres to the south-west. On the previous evening, he and Alena had visited the site. They'd both been astonished by the size of the pyramids, the sandstone still stark against the glowing Egyptian sky.

'Good news!' Alena had said the previous evening. 'Stalin's not coming. He's said he'd prefer to meet FDR and Winston in Tehran – without *Chiang* or his wife.' Stan knew that Stalin's dislike of the Generalissimo was exceeded only by his loathing of the volatile, voluble Madame *Chiang Kai-shek*.

'And our chaps are all right with that?'

'Absolutely. My source at the White House tells me that Roosevelt is keen to forge a personal relationship with Stalin, to lock him in securely as an ally. He'll find that easier to do with the two of them in Persia, without the *Chiangs* hogging the limelight.'

'And Churchill?'

Alena shrugged. 'Roosevelt's been briefed to not give dear Winston any impression that he's less than favoured nation when it comes to Friends of FDR, so to speak.'

'God, what children!'

'No, Stan – men.' She kissed him lightly on the nose.

***

The following day, as Stan sat down at his desk at the Embassy, the phone rang promptly at noon.

'Stanley?'

'Peggy, dear, I can't believe the Japanese are letting us talk.' Twenty-two months had passed since he'd left *Shanghai*.

'Stanley.' Peggy repeated, her voice cold. The line could not have been clearer – 'the superiority of Japanese technology' thought Stan; the same system, he assumed, that had located him.

'Are you surrounded by Japanese?' As soon as he asked, he realised the stupidity of the question.

Her voice was still flat, loveless. 'Stan, I'm in a concentration camp, remember?'

'Of course, of course. But I really meant: Does that mean everyone can hear this conversation?'

(Ping)

Stan had been warned the day before that there would be an electronic sound every twenty seconds – presumably to let the parties know that the line stayed active. He was certain both the Japanese and the Americans at the Embassy were recording every word – the line would have been far from secure.

'Yes. And it's being recorded. Where are you, Stan?' Now her voice sounded defeated.

A beat. The Japs know where I am, he thought; why hold back?

'I'm in Egypt, Cairo.'

There was a pause of half a minute.

(Ping)

He realised that Peggy would be shocked to hear that he was so far from *Shanghai*. To break the silence, he said, 'I'm sorry that this must be a shock to you, Pegs, but I'm following orders. You know I can't explain *why* I'm in Cairo.'

'Huh. Yes, that's always been convenient.' Her voice lacked any hint of warmth.

He ploughed on, thinking there was no point in spending time on a domestic tiff. 'Is it true what Tang – says – and I know you're listening, Admiral – is it true that the Japanese are prepared to release you and Jonny?'

'There are conditions, Stan. The call was their idea, not mine. I didn't know where you were, of course – other than that letter you sent me from Alexandria…'

'…But I sent that months ago.' He remembered he wrote the letter when he and Alena travelled together to Cairo to begin early preparations for the conference.

(Ping)

'Are you stationed in Cairo now? Your letter was the first I've had from you since we arrived at Fu-xing last year.'

There was another silence that lasted for under twenty seconds.

(Ping)

Why had the letter taken so long to reach her? He was about to ask about the letter when she said, 'Jonny is unwell.'

He kicked himself: why hadn't he asked about his son? Before he could hate himself more, Peggy spoke again.

'Your little boy has had many, many illnesses. He's broken his arm. Now he's in hospital, recovering from malaria of the most persistent kind; it's a type that may come and go for years.'

'How is he, otherwise?' Again, another dumb question. He bit the inside of his mouth. He was nervous and racked with guilt. What did the Japanese want? The back of his neck always began to ache dully under stress; it was aching now.

(Ping)

'Otherwise, Stan? Otherwise, he's alive. Tang-san gave me a photo of him. He's lost weight. I know he'd rather be with me.'

'My God, what a disaster this has been. How did we ever lose each other?'

'You were away – remember? You said we'd be safe.'

Stan imagined *Tang* next to her, enjoying the domestic *frisson*.

'And you, Pegs, how are you?'

'I'm not well. That's why they want you to see me.'

'You're ill? In what way?'

'None of the medical staff here has the knowledge or the machines for an accurate diagnosis. They say I have to be taken to Tokyo. They want you to go with me.'

(Ping)

For the first time, the line developed a storm of static. When the static stopped, and the ping resumed, Stan's voice broke through.

'You know I can't do that, Pegs.'

There was another long pause.

(Ping)

She would have been shocked by the speed of his refusal.

Peggy again: 'If you won't help them, Tang-san says they will then have to resort to what he calls extreme measures. You probably know what that means.'

Tang broke into their conversation.

'Parker-San, this is Ohta Tang.'

'Ohta.'

'Parker-San: there is a condition attached to our most exceptional offer to release your wife and child.'

'The condition?'

Another pause.

(Ping)

'We want to get you to Tokyo with Peggy and your son.'

'Tang-San, there must be more to this: Why would we have to meet on enemy territory if all you want is for me to be reunited with my family? It's absurd. The idea only makes sense if you wish to interrogate me – then possibly execute me – for something you think I may have been doing. '

'Hai! Did you not know we Japanese are savages? Often, we kill people for no reason.' The irony was unmissable. Tang continued. 'Certainly, we have a number of questions related to your work for the Chinese, especially Chiang Kai-shek.'

(Ping)

'Chiang Kai-shek? How do you connect me with the Generalissimo?'

'Don't play us for fools, Parker. The Kempeitai has information that places you in Cairo with our greatest enemy. You are there now. That is why we are talking to you.

'Tang, I know Chiang Kai-shek. He is an ally.'

'You deny working for him?' Stan heard *Tang*'s voice drift away, but he caught him saying, 'Missy Parker, would you mind?' There was a shuffling of papers.

'Parker, are you still there?' they had both dropped the pantomime of respect implied by the single word 'San'. Stan remembered one of Tom Trencher's sayings when a conversation hardened: 'Let's get down to the rat-killing'' *Tang* was at that moment.

(Ping)

'You have never met Chiang. Is that true, Parker?'

Now Stan tensed. His sphincter reminded him of its exact location. He needed to tread very carefully. 'That is not what I said,' Stan paused. 'I said that I know Chiang Kai-shek – like millions of others.'

Stan heard papers being shuffled.

(Ping)

'Ah, but you are different. You know him so well that you are now with him in Cairo to attend a conference, the details of which are still unclear. We hear that since meeting him, you have joined Chiang's inner circle. We hear you help him with background research on the people he meets. Are you not now in Cairo with Chiang and Madame Chiang Kai-shek for that purpose? To be at the Cairo conference, perhaps with the Allies?'

'All very fanciful, Tang, but if you think you know so much, why interrogate me?' Stan knew he was blustering, and *Tang* probably recognised it.

He heard *Tang*'s chuckle, remembering the sound from the dinner on the '*Nanking*'.

(Ping)

'Oh, Parker, the information we have is but a small example of how much more we know about your dealings with the Chinese high command. Obviously, Parker, you are close to our enemies.'

'Your enemy is my ally, Admiral.'

Stan heard more shuffling – he presumed of files.

'Is that all you have?' Stan's voice sounded challenging, 'The Kempeitai's preposterous story that I am Chiang's confidante?'

'Tut, tut, Parker. You sound – what would you say – upset? No, Parker, one-time Captain in the glorious Nipponese Navy, we have more information about your... your relationships.' The deliberate use of the word gave Stan pause; *Tang* sounded very sure of himself.

Stan heard *Tang* say, 'Missy Parker, you may wish to excuse yourself from what I am about to say; you might find my questions embarrassing. No? As you wish.'

(Ping)

'Parker: since joining Chiang, you have made the acquaintance of a foreign woman named Alena Zoltan.'

Stan realised that the Kempeitai seemed not to have connected him with *Changsha*, or his subsequent months at Chinese HQ in *Chongqing*. But if they knew about Alena, that was enough.

'I may have.'

(Ping)

(Ping)

'Parker?'

He worried what effect the admission would have on Peggy. A throb of guilt hit his stomach.

Tang again: 'Come, come, Parker.' This time *Tang* guffawed; it was a derisory sound.

'I made the acquaintance of a Miss Zoltan, yes,' Stan said in a flat tone. 'She is a colleague.'

'In what way?' *Tang* was relentless.

Stan felt he needed to move the conversation on to thicker ice. 'Seems to me that you don't know very much, Tang. You're throwing darts in a dark room, hoping one will hit something.' Stan clapped his hands. 'All right, Ohta,' he said. 'Let's conclude this silly conversation: Seriously, you don't expect me to surrender to the Kampeitie and have them haul me to Tokyo.'

(Ping)

'Our military police are *not* interested in you, Parker. I am the one who is interested in Chiang's plans. And only *you* – who I thought was my friend in a long and trusting relationship – you, sir, are the one who can tell me.'

'I've told you: I don't have any such information.'

'Think carefully, Captain. You are condemning your wife and child to death.'

'You, Ohta Tang, are the one who will be executed if you persist in this plan.'

Tang snorted, 'Let me educate you, Captain Parker: victors do not become war criminals; only the conquered do.'

(Ping)

Stan matched *Tang*'s tone: 'And now let me educate *you*, Admiral Tang: It is only a matter of time, a short time before the Americans conquer Japan,' he paused. '… Your threats of death and victory are empty. You will not harm my family. Justice will be terrible.' Stan, shaking, put down the phone.

Tang had been right, he was upset, even rattled. For a minute, Stan tried to steady his hands. Fear seemed to act like acid in his stomach. The enemy knew about his work, and they had his wife and son. It might end badly, but if he had estimated *Tang*'s character correctly on the '*Nanking*', the Admiral was unlikely to kill Peggy and Jonny. In that sense, he had gauged that *Tang* was an old-style warrior: the man respected the vulnerable. He had to believe he had called the man's bluff correctly.

There was a tap at the door. 'All done?' Despite the lightness of her tone, Alena's face was full of concern. He motioned her in. She flicked the door shut. He told her about the phone call.

Alena was shaking her head as if in pain. 'Stanley, you are betting the lives of your family on the goodwill of a Japanese.'

'… Who I know very well.'

'Dearest, are you sure about this? You're risking what you hold most dear.' She came close. He drew her in to him.

'I'm holding what I hold most dear, Alena. I know Tang. He won't do harm to my family.'

'But Peggy…'

'… Peggy will cope,' he shrugged. 'Huh. She can be magnificent in these situations. She once told me she liked being alone in certain circumstances and that she never really needed anyone. I remember her exact words: "Stan, I don't need you – like many women need their husbands. I can make my own way in life."' He looked down. 'She enjoys coping, Alena. Part of her likes marriage, but I know part of her hates the implied dependency. I've told you about that side of her. You?'

She shrugged, her green eyes ranging over his face. He knew how haggard he must look.

'Of course, I need you, Stan. I hope I always will. But I don't want to add pressure to your situation with your wife and son. Despite what you say, I can't believe they need you less than I do.' There was a pause while she stroked his hair. 'But I don't understand why you can be so confident of Tang's mercy.'

'Alena, I don't know how I can describe this to you: you speak Japanese. You're familiar with their customs?'

She nodded, but he could see she was puzzled.

Stan continued. 'For example, you know about *on* and *giri*?'

'The exchange of favours? Yes.'

'You may remember I told you about the work I did for Tang in Shanghai?'

'When you helped them with customs, etcetera?'

Stan nodded, 'Well, the idea was I'd help the Japanese with that and, one day, they would return the favour.'

She shook her head, frowning. 'And you think he'll return the favour by not executing your family?' He heard her breathe out deeply. 'It's still an enormous risk, Stan.'

'I think I know Tang well enough to take that risk.'

'I love you, my dearest Stan. But not enough for you to leave your family. I don't want to spend my life with a guilt-ridden man.' She stroked his face.

'No guilt. Peggy is indomitable – stronger than me in so many ways.' He nodded, agreeing with himself. 'We should go.'

As they opened the door, they heard Madame *Chiang Kai-shek* clapping for attention. This was her habit, regardless of who she needed: Alena, Stan, or 'Coolie Number Fourteen', assigned to her by the American Ambassador; all were clapped for, their names shouted until they appeared.

'Alenaaaaa!'

'Better run along,' said Stan.

Alena shook her head and hurried away.

After the call with Stan had ended, *Tang* began to pace the room; the air seemed to pulse with his outrage. He held up his hand, a signal that no one should speak. After a minute walking back and forth, then gazing from the window, he barked one word: '*Mizu!*'

'*Sugu nit!*' said one of the guards. He shuffled forward and, with a deep bow, placed a jug of water and a glass on the desk.

Tang filled the glass. With deliberation, he drank two glasses of water. He raised his right hand, his index and middle fingers pointing up and said, 'You Britishers, you pretend to be noble, you pretend to be better than the rest – but have no idea of honour.' He came forward, narrowing his eyes as he looked at her. Then, to her surprise, his face seemed to soften.

'Your husband says he does not work for Chiang and this Zoltan woman, and yet he is willing to gamble your life and your son's – as proof of his innocence. Ha!' He shook his head. Peggy thought he looked perplexed and frustrated. Filled with similar feelings, she looked away, her eyes filled with tears.

Tang looked past her at Marcus. Half a minute passed before he spoke again, his voice soft. 'Carter, do you know what we say to our kamikaze pilots – the young men that volunteer to fly their planes into the American battleships?'

Marcus shook his head.

'We say that it is better to die than to live as a coward.' He gestured towards Peggy, 'Parker dishonours his wife, and he betrays his heir.' He continued to talk to Marcus but pointed at Peggy. 'Missy Parker? She is worth one hundred of him.'

Peggy found her voice, 'Then why kill us?' She stared at *Tang*; she would not blink, she would not plead.

Tang started to pace again; all eyes were on him when he stopped and faced them.

'You will hear my decision in an hour. But I can assure you that – what is your English expression – "until hell freezes over" – we shall pursue your husband, and when we find him, we shall kill him. Not for running away, not for any secrets he might or might not have hatched with Chiang Kai-shek – but because he placed a higher value on *his* life than on the lives of his wife and child.' He drew up his body with a huge breath. 'That is a *great* dishonour!' The words seethed from him, freighted with anger and disdain.

Tang beckoned to *Ushiguro*, bowed to Peggy, and nodded at Marcus. The two Japanese, accompanied by the guards, left the room.

Marcus crossed the room to her. As she hugged him, Peggy said, 'Oh, god, Marcus, this never ends.' She felt incapable of words. Stan had betrayed his family.

'It's over, Peggy. *Tang* will never go through with an execution.' He pulled her closer. As he did so, she realised that she had never wanted as much as to be hugged by this man.

***

Later, *Ushiguro* told them that there would be no execution. He said that *Tang*'s anger was directed at her husband, not his wife and child. The Admiral would continue to think about the matter, but his goal now was to make sure Japan won the war.

PARTINGS
Fu-xing 1945

At Fu-xing, on a day in early October 1945, American Mustang fighter planes dipped and belly-rolled over the camp. A jubilant Peggy, standing by a first-floor window, held hands with her excited five-year-old as they watched the victory rolls.

'Ito! Ito!' Jonny jumped up and down, shouting to the Japanese guard who had been with him when he broke his arm. The soldier looked up. He was marching with his comrades, all retreating through the front gate. When he spotted Jonny, a smile brightened his pale face. He adjusted his rucksack and waved. Five seconds later, he was gone, blending into the khaki mass of men exiting *Fu-xing*.

An hour later, American jeeps sped into the camp. Everywhere they looked, huge men – who turned out to be GI's – were taking charge of operations. Peggy wondered what the American soldiers must have thought when they saw Jonny. Her little boy looked gaunt; his distended rice belly and bent arm made him appear less than healthy. Peggy knew, though, that his spirit was intact. They had survived.

***

There was no Rolls Royce to take *Ushiguro* away. The car, by then a dusty wreck stripped of its parts, had been abandoned. Hours before the liberating troops arrived, the Commandant had driven away in the little green van that had brought his dogs to the camp. They never saw the Commandant again. Of his Great Danes, there was no sign. Later, Peggy learned that the Commandant had shot both animals months before, feeling unable to feed their massive appetites while so many people went hungry.

Natasha Pavlovich chose to remain in Shanghai. She and Peggy were standing together, talking quietly as they waited for transport from the camp into the city. Around them was a confusion of trucks and jeeps; Chinese, Americans, and freed internees. Jonny, wide-eyed at the melee bustling around them, stood clutching Peggy's hand.

'Why wouldn't I stay in Shanghai? This city still excites me. There will be so much to draw. I believe that the people who return to Shanghai will only be the type who love the city as much as I do.' Natasha's eyes glittered. 'Vagabonds and adventurers and men who are stupid and rich and are prepared to be undone by women.' Her laughter pealed with just enough enthusiasm to sound sincere.

The young Russian swept Jonny into her arms. 'Mein liebchen, I shall miss you so much. When you are even bigger, I will find you – wherever you are – and marry you.' Jonny shook his head vigorously, eyes filled with horror. 'No, no, no – I'm marrying my mummy!' he yelled. 'Put me down, put me down.' Laughing, the two women exchanged glances.

After Natasha had left, Marcus arrived with Peggy's trunk. He took the time to explain that Tom and *Chao-xing*, frozen in their marriage, would be transferred to Washington D.C. Tom would join the Central Intelligence Agency where his on-the-ground experience could be employed as an analyst on what was called 'the China Desk'.

Peggy knew she had unresolved feelings about Tom: had he helped Tang to locate Stan? She would never know. What she did know was that the man and his wife had been kind to her in *Fu-xing*. In the final analysis, she felt there was insufficient sincerity in the friendship for her to seek them out for anything but a hypocritical farewell. She let it pass.

'And you?' Peggy asked Marcus as they walked to the truck that had finally come to take her and Jonny to the harbour.

'London has confirmed me as Head of Mission,' he chuckled. 'I've been told I'm to be awarded some kind of gong – heaven knows why – for my work in Fu-xing.'

'Why, that's wonderful, Marcus. And richly deserved.' She resisted the urge to stand up on tiptoes to kiss him.

'Well, that's as may be.' He smiled ruefully. 'I have to stay and mop up. And then we shall see.'

He tousled Jonny's hair. He hugged the boy and looked across the boy's head at Peggy. They were silent until Marcus said, 'And you, dear, sweet Peggy. You must find Stan.'

'Of course.' She turned away, not moving. She didn't trust herself to kiss him, or even look at him for more than a moment.

Jonny looked from Peggy to Marcus and back again. He grinned with all the charm of a five-year-old. They knew her son wasn't going to move until they climbed on the truck.

Without warning, Marcus wrapped his arms around Peggy, her face close enough to kiss. Jonny was looking at them, seemingly sensitive to every nuance between them. Marcus lifted Peggy and placed her, standing, in the truck. Then he bent down, lifting Jonny to stand beside her. Peggy, overcome, placed her head in her hands.

Marcus turned away as the truck edged forward, and Peggy felt Jonny search for her hand. 'We'll see Marcus again, won't we Mummy?'

She didn't answer.

EVERYTHING GOES
Shanghai 1945

Peggy, Jonny and the first group of five hundred internees from the Fu-xing camp were repatriated aboard a hospital ship bound for Liverpool.

The day before sailing, Marcus had arranged for her to spend some time at the house on Bubbling Well Road. He understood why she wanted to be alone.

Peggy took a rickshaw through the shattered streets. But if she was expecting an eerie silence, she was disappointed. While the streets had yet to generate their loud noise and bustle, it was clear that the Chinese were ready to return their city to working order. Shop doorways were being swept, shattered glass removed. Tables and chairs were pulled into the streets to allow owners to work inside. Peggy marvelled at their industriousness, at the absence of any visible despair. It was if the mood had become 'the Occupation is over. The Japanese have gone. Time to get busy.' Some even called to her as she passed in the rickshaw 'Come shop, missy. This way, missy. War over. We want to say thank you for good price!'

The rickshaw scrunched up the driveway. The Parker house seemed as it did when she first saw it: white, imperial, almost virginal in its lack of apparent damage. She asked the rickshaw wallah to wait. Looking at the large house and imagining a good tip to match it, the man beamed and nodded.

She couldn't bring herself to enter the front door. Instead, she took a path along the side of the house and into the garden.

Hungrily, it seemed, nature had invaded: the lawn, the gates, the paths, the perimeter wall, all were disappearing under a tangle of rioting vines and creepers. The pond at the southern border had surrendered to an invasion of choking green. Peggy doubted that the solitary heron she had watched roost there, would ever return. The grove of sycamores had gone, chopped down and, she suspected, used for firewood as the Japanese struggled to avoid defeat in the closing days of the war.

A door slammed, Peggy swung around, alarmed. But it was only the door of the back porch, swinging wildly. The open door drew her in. Newspapers, in untidy heaps, chased each other. She spotted a soldier's kepi with its single Japanese star. She kicked it across the room, cried 'shit!' then laughed with the release of a tension that, until that moment, she hadn't been aware of.

The furniture had gone, making the rooms seem even larger. How could she lament the loss of a few sticks of furniture that Natasha had judged 'rental drab.'?

She felt a chill in the silence of the big house. Memories slept. She looked around the bare living room and resisted the thought of going upstairs. As she turned to leave, she remembered Colonel Tomoyuki's words, 'Everything goes.'

***

The ship had stopped briefly at the northern end of the Suez Canal to bring on supplies, and to receive packets of mail couriered by the Red Cross through the friendly Mediterranean seas to Port Said, 'Peggy Parker?' Like Father Christmas, the young Able Seaman pulled yet another package of mail from a large canvas bag at his side. He gave Peggy a small bundle of letters, plus a large manila envelope. She noticed that the return addresses showed the letters from people who, she knew, had died while she'd been away: her mother and father, and her frail brother, Richard. She decided it would be too heart-breaking to read them. Maybe she would do so later. After the war, after what she and Jonny had endured, she wanted to bury everything that seemed part of her past.

As the ship pulled out of Port Said, she stayed alone in the cabin she shared with her son. Jonny, ever curious, would be up on deck as the ship cast off. She opened the large manila envelope, addressed to her in Stan's handwriting.

She pulled out the papers. She was puzzled by the first slip of paper; it was a lawyer's receipt for fifty-five dollars ('one hundred twenty-five dollars still owing' stated the receipt). The large envelope was postmarked 'Reno, Nevada' and was covered with a rash of American stamps. She stood as she read the larger set of papers. The documents looked legal. As she studied them, dropping each completed page to the floor, she realised that the document represented the 'undefended divorce' of Stanley Parker from Winifred Parker, 'aka Peggy' it read.

When she'd finished reading, puzzled only because she couldn't process what the words meant, she picked up the pages from the floor, and laid them out in order on the bed. Then she sat on the bed and, silently, read the bald legalese again. Stanley had divorced her; according to the document, she had not objected – it was 'undefended'.

Her breath went away, came back, went away. 'Stan has divorced me?' she said to the empty cabin. She shook her head. She clutched her hair, and pulled it hard. A long, aching noise rose in her throat. She swept the papers from the bed.

She was alone. Stan had abandoned her and their child. Then relief, unexpected, flooded her. She was free of worrying about Stan – where he was, what he was doing, when he would be back, what he wanted from her – which often, now that the threat had been removed – seemed like everything.

She slid off the bed and lay on the floor, papers were strewn about her. Face wet with tears, her emotions undefined, nonetheless Peggy slept.

FINDING HOME
London 1945

Peggy and Jonny stayed in England only briefly. Though Britain was one of the victors, the war had broken the nation. She had to explain to her five-year-old son that the curved yellow fruit had to be peeled, that it was safe to eat, and that the object was called a banana.

Peggy became angry and frustrated by the poor livelihood she and her son had to endure. Was this endless rationing of food and clothing their reward for surviving *Fu-xing*?

She had spent two months in correspondence with Peregrine Pennington at Blue Funnel, trying to get some satisfaction about her financial standing. He was sympathetic but couldn't help her: 'I'm sorry, Peggy, but Stan is moving to America with his new wife. In a month or so, his contract with Blue Funnel will end.' He had added, with the pomposity she'd learned to expect, 'We do not live if we do not suffer.'

Stan had wired a few dollars from New York to his son. A few weeks later, another letter arrived, criticising Jonny for taking too long to reply. Stan had written to the six-year-old: 'Does your mother not instruct you in your filial duties?' She kept the letter to show Jonny when he was older; he needed to understand the Victorian upbringing she had helped him to escape.

Eventually, worn down by lack of funds and the unattractive prospect of a future in her own country, Peggy had had to explain to her puzzled sisters the appeal of again living abroad ('what's wrong with Derby, Win?'). Peggy knew, after living in Shanghai, that she could never have a life in England again: there was too much history; too much greyness.

Easing into the harbour on a hot November day, the ship was soon tethered to the dock. In recent months, ships had brought large numbers of refugees from the wars in Europe and the Far East. The Afrikaner nationalist government was happy to welcome all white immigrants.

At the age of forty-two, Peggy was no longer the vibrant, attractive woman who had landed in Shanghai in 1937. The stresses of physical life in *Fu-xing* had stolen more than ten years from her face and body; her thick, auburn hair had thinned and was laced with grey; her eyes – once a sparkling hazel – were drawn and shadowy. She walked with her head down. The confident, bustling stride had yet to re-appear. She was tragically thin, to the point of being ashamed to look at herself in the bathroom mirror. 'Marcus wouldn't look twice at me now,' she mused.

From England, she had written to tell Marcus of Stan's decision to make a new life with a new woman. He had written back sympathetically, wondering if, perhaps, a divorce was a positive outcome for her.

'I, for one, am happy for you, Pegs, although my motives for writing that may be questionable. You must know I still care deeply for you. I believe in my heart that our story has not ended.'

***

As the ship tied up in Cape Town, Peggy remembered the moment when, a decade before, she and Natasha had steamed into Shanghai Harbour on the *Tantalus*, their young hearts beating with excitement at the thought of life in a new, exotic world.

In Cape Town, there were no Chinese running, like ants, to receive their luggage. Instead, groups of African stevedores loitered on the jetty, awaiting the disembarkation.

'Look, Mummy, it really is flat like a table. Can I climb it?' Jonny tugged at her hand, pointing at Table Mountain – cloud-ringed, epic, displaying its mass to the world.

People smiled at her son. She wondered if they thought he was being fed properly. She would have to explain that England's post-war diet had done little to add weight to her restless boy.

'Mummy, can I? Can I climb the mountain?' She looked down at her lad's freckles and his odd, stick-out ears. A thought flashed past: 'What a funny little chap!' Stan might have said.

Stan wrote only one letter to her in Cape Town; he addressed their relationship directly: 'As to your living alone and writing to say you loved it, you made me aware of that for many years, way back in Shanghai. Have you ever thought it ironic, Peggy, that the distance you put between us in our marriage is the very thing that allowed me to know love when Alena came into my life? Finally, it gave me no reason to return to you. But it is my ardent wish that, one day, I shall meet my son and be able to explain.'

***

Three weeks before her first Christmas in Africa, Peggy looked out from her kitchen window. Jonny was due from the pick-up game of cricket he played with his pals on the Common.

'Here's my little man,' she said to herself as she saw him walking up the sunlit path. But she drew in her breath when she saw the figure behind him. They were at the door before she could be sure who he was.

Next came Jonny's excited voice, 'Look, Mama, look who's here.'

Marcus Carter stood in the doorway, 'Hello, Peggy.'

EPILOGUE

Brooklyn, NY
1987

Alena Zoltan hugged Jonny until he had to say, 'Ma'am, I can't breathe!'

She held him at arm's length, studying him with her pale green eyes set in a face that still held the palimpsest of beauty. The hands holding his were slender but marked by liver spots. He thought, 'she's older than she looks.' For some reason, the idea pleased him.

She said, 'The way you look – so like my Stanley! Come inside, please.' As she led him into the apartment, she asked over her shoulder, 'How did you find me? How did you know?'

He wasn't ready to answer her question. Instead, he scanned the half dozen black-and-white pictures hung from rails around the tiny living room.

'Is that…?'

'Yes, they are all pictures of Stanley – with me, with friends. He always liked to have lots of pictures of our life together.'

'And who is this man?' Jonny asked. There was a picture of his father with a Chinese military man; Jonny thought his uniform over-decorated with medals. Alena smiled, 'That is the Red General, Chiang Kai-shek; your father and I served him.'

'My father worked for the Chinese?'

'In secret, yes. Against the Japanese. Your mother never told you?' She pointed to the only easy chair. 'Please.'

He sat down. He began to realise that the room was a shrine to his father.

'No, I had no idea what he did in the war – except leave my mother and me,' he shrugged. "Perhaps my mother wasn't permitted to tell me.'

The Zoltan woman pulled over a dining room chair and sat opposite. She gave him a weak smile; Jonny wondered if she felt embarrassed to have him there.

She smiled, 'I am happy if you call me Mrs. Zoltan – if it saddens you to call me Mrs. Parker.'

He didn't answer. 'Well, it was a fluke I found you – a complete chance: I was sitting in my hotel this morning, reading a magazine, and found an article about Hicks Street. My father's letters came from one-six-seven, Hicks Street. As I say, a fluke.'

She nodded. 'We came here after the war. We were naturalised as Americans. We never lived anywhere else.'

They both fell silent. Jonny continued to look around the poorly-furnished room. Alena Zoltan stared at him.

'Did your mother speak of us?' she asked after a minute's silence. 'You would not have come here if you were satisfied with what your mother told you. Nothing is chance. You were meant to come here.' She raised her eyebrows. 'I am surprised Peggy – yes? – that she did not tell you of the risks he took to help the Chinese.'

Jonny frowned. '*He* took risks?'

She smiled, her eyes creasing, 'Oh, you think your risks were greater? That may be so. But he could not have come back for you in Shanghai without being killed. By staying with the Chinese, and you with the Japanese, there was always a chance you could all survive, and you did.'

'Playing Russian roulette with the lives of others takes a certain kind of arrogance.' Jonny looked around the room, not wanting to catch her eye. Alena didn't respond.

To fill the silence, Jonny said, 'My mother was Catholic; she didn't believe in divorce. She remarried only when my father died, what, thirty years ago?'

Alena nodded. 'I understand. Catholics can be very strict about these things. I am Buddhist.' He heard her breathe deeply. "We are more... relaxed.' Again, she smiled. He sensed, unlike him, that she was becoming more at ease.

He was still wondering what to call her; he couldn't call the person sitting opposite him 'stepmother' – he knew his mother would not have approved. Peggy always referred to Alena Zoltan as 'the Asian'. He dismissed the concern.

Now the Asian with the pale eyes asked, 'Your mother never spoke of me? She didn't think I am – that I existed?'

'No, she knew you; about you – but she told me that you and my father only met through an accident.'

'Accident? We met in China in the last years of the war. On the day we met, your father got information that his family had been captured. Perhaps that's why your mother thought it was an accident. And then it was too late.'

'For what?'

'For him to go back to Shanghai. I have told you why.' She pushed her slippers around with her feet. She got up and began to move around the room, touching things. Jonny was getting the impression that his questions were again making her feel uncomfortable. He wondered if she was beginning to regret that he had found her.

'But you got him to divorce my mother.' He watched for her reaction.

'No, no.' The woman shook her head furiously, her face flushed. 'Your father told me that since he first met your mother, she never made him feel that she has, she was…' she searched for a word

'In love with him?' Jonny offered.

'Exactly. That she was in love.' Again, she stopped, avoiding his eyes. 'He believed she made him her, her…'

'She wanted him to be successful?'

'Sure.' She paused, looking at him. 'You are a nice young man, you speak nicely.' She arched her eyebrows. 'Maybe your mother wanted to make you the same way as your father?'

He ignored the remark. 'Then why did he divorce her? All my mother ever said was: it was the war.'

She smiled at him, 'Do you want something, Jonny: tea, coffee, water, a beer?'

He shook his head, 'Uh huh, no thanks. I'm fine.'

She stood in a corner of the small room, arms folded, looking at him. Jonny hoped she didn't think he was going to stay.

She said, 'Stanley told me there was an argument in a telephone call with the Japanese. He could not do what they wanted.'

'And what was that?'

'To betray his country – in return for seeing his family again. There was an argument about it, and it meant he could never go back to Shanghai. Better to be divorced.'

Jonny's head was spinning with the new information. If it were true, his mother had never mentioned it. Did it matter – now – whether it was true or not?

He went back to the matter of the divorce. 'Reno is where he divorced my mother and married you?'

'True.'

'My mother told me that the marriage means nothing because it was in Reno. She told me my father would return to us; she made me pray for that.'

'Pray?'

'Yes.' He wrinkled his nose at the memory of how innocent he'd been, every night mumbling, 'And please God, send Daddy back to us.'

Alena Zoltan shrugged, puckered her mouth. 'We are here now. All that is past.'

For a moment or two, they said nothing.

'Did you have children, Mrs. Zoltan?' There, he'd said it.

'We tried many times, but no, I could not keep the babies. I did have a son – from a previous…' Again, Jonny saw her struggling to find the word.

'Encounter?'

His insult fell flat. 'I was married before. My husband was killed in the desert. My son died in the Korean war. He was only twenty-two.'

In another room, a clock struck three.

Jonny stood, began to walk around the room.

She said. 'Your left arm – I see it is a little bent.' Again, her eyes creased as she smiled. 'Your father told me you had broken it in camp, and the Japanese set it badly.'

He put his left hand in his pocket. 'That's true.'

He stopped pacing and stood in front of her. He was about to tell her he had to leave when she said, 'Tell me, Jonny: Do you think your life would have been better with your father?'

The question was unexpected. 'Who knows? My father didn't think we were worth coming back for.'

Suddenly, she became agitated. 'After the war, he suggested that you come here, to us in America. Didn't your mother tell you?'

'Ha! He thought after all that, getting me through the camp – she would give me up – leave her with nothing? What an insult – even to ask.'

Jonny stopped, turned, took a breath, and pointed to a black and white picture of a ship.

'What's this?'

He knew he had to change the subject, or he would get nasty and, for no reason he could think of, he didn't want this woman to see a worse version of himself.

'This ship – what's so special?'

She said, 'That was your father's first command, the "Shenkin". That ship meant a lot to him. He died aboard a ship.'

'At fifty-five, his weak heart finally gave in – my mother told me.'

'He was sitting in a deckchair. I was told he died looking at the sea.'

'Where is he buried?'

She nodded, almost to herself. 'He lies in the China Sea. It's what he would have wanted.'

'Huh.'

Alena Zoltan frowned at him, but he saw affection there. 'Jonny, you are too young to be so cynical.'

He tipped his head. 'Maybe so. I will say that my father lived his life on his terms.'

'And your mother? She is dead, too, yes?'

He nodded. 'But she was very happy with her second husband – an excellent, dependable man.'

Alena took a deep breath. 'Don't judge your father badly, Jonny. Your father, too, was dependable. But he never felt your mother needed him.'

'If you say so. I really don't know. My wife and I – our children? We all need each other.'

'Is there anything I can do for you?' He tried not to make it sound perfunctory, but he'd got all he needed from the meeting.

'Oh, please, no. Your father left a little money for me – and I have some savings.' She paused. 'I have enough. But thank you.' She stepped forward to hug him. 'I am so glad you took the trouble to find me.'

He couldn't look at her, but as he turned away, he said, 'I'm glad you told me as much as you could, Mrs. Zoltan. Thank you.'

She nodded and smiled. 'I'm pleased we met. Your father spoke so much about you.' As he went through the door, he heard her say, 'I don't suppose we shall meet again.'

He waved his hand in the air but could not bring himself to turn around.

Jonny Parker ran down the stairs and into the hot afternoon.

ENDS.

BIBLIOGRAPHY

I found it enormously helpful to read books by authors more knowledgeable than me in the ways of the East. I thank them all and strongly recommend these books for further information:

1. 'The internment of Western Civilians under the Japanese, 1941-1945' by Bernice Archer.
2. 'The Forgotten Ones – women and children under Nippon' by Shirley Fenton Huie.
3. 'The distant land of my father' by Bo Caldwell.
4. 'The Rape of Nanking' by Iris Chang.
5. 'Shanghai 1937' by Peter Harmsen.
6. 'What is Japan?' by Taichi Katsumoto.
7. 'How to do business with the Japanese' by Herbert Jung.
8. 'Made in Japan' by Akio Morita and Sony.
9. 'When tigers fight' by Dick Wilson.
10. 'The way of Zen' by Alan Watts.
11. 'No ordinary time' by Doris Kearns Goodwin.
12. 'MAO, the unheard story' by Jung Chang & Jon Halliday.

Author's Note

I hope my readers have worked out that the real author of this story is the boy, 'Jonny'.

The story has been inside me for decades, but it was only when, quite by chance, I had bumped into my father's second wife in 1987 and visited Shanghai in 2019 that the story insisted it be told. The tale is 'historical fiction' for – aside from the painful memory of breaking my arm and the American planes liberating us – I remember nothing of those years.

This is a novel, something 'new' or, as I like to call it, a 'novoir'– memories re-cast, where all the characters, except historical figures, are inventions, figments of imagination, as indeed are most scenes and incidents.

It's been said that 'truth is stranger than fiction', but sometimes fiction is truer.

Brian Clewly Johnson
London, 2022